MW01172120

# FIGHTING FOR Eve

*An Eve Sumptor Novel*

by

## JOURDYN KELLY

# THE EVOLUTION OF
## Lainey Sumptor

# JADED
## ANGELS

# Also by Jourdyn Kelly

# One

*L*ainey Sumptor looked up from her book as her wife stumbled into the bedroom and fell face-first onto the bed. The muffled groan was quite comical, but Lainey kept her slight chuckle silent. Even the sight of an exhausted Eve Sumptor made Lainey's pulse quicken. That was the love she felt. The pure, unadulterated passion that she hoped would never go away. Right now, however, Lainey knew she had to play the dutiful, concerned wife. So, she closed her book, lowered her glasses to the end of her nose, and looked over the rim.

"Are you okay, honey?"

Eve flipped over, dramatically throwing her arm over her eyes in a woe-is-me fashion. "I run a multibillion-dollar business and have successful galleries worldwide. People have *literally* tried to kill me. And the one thing that brings me down is... fourth grade math."

Lainey laughed, choosing to gloss over the multi *billion*-dollar admission. She had never heard Eve talk about her wealth, especially so flippantly. Of course, Lainey's name was now on all the accounts, but she had never bothered to count the zeros. At no time in their relationship did Lainey ever care about Eve's net worth. She would not start now just because an amount was attached to it.

Eve tweaked Lainey's toes. "You're laughing at me?"

"No, my love. I was just envisioning you helping Darren with his math, and the vision I have is of you asking him more questions than he asked you."

Eve narrowed her eyes. She would neither confirm nor deny that actually happened. "I would tickle you, but I don't want to get up. I'm filing that away for an IOU."

"I told you I would do it." Amusement filled Lainey's body. This was how her life was now. Full of love, fun, and affection. Completely different from her last marriage. Sometimes Lainey had to pinch herself to make sure she wasn't dreaming.

The two women were consistent with sharing the homework load Darren brought home. And they were doing a damn good job of faking their way through Kevin's assignments while reading or drawing with Bella. They each had their strengths and weaknesses. New math, however, caused them both headaches. The humorous solution was usually an intense game of rock, paper, scissors as the deciding factor. A game Lainey frequently lost. She could swear Eve could read her mind. The entire exchange was yet another difference from her former life. It used to be Lainey's "duty" as a mother and wife to care for her family. With Eve, it was a partnership.

Eve groaned as she turned back onto her tummy to look up at her wife—who looked like an incredibly sexy teacher at the moment. "You've been doing it for the past couple of weeks. It was my turn." She took a moment just to absorb the beauty of her wife. "I love you like this."

The words confused Lainey as much as they filled her heart with bliss. "Like what?"

Eve rested her chin on the palms of her hands. "Hair up in a bun, nightshirt on, lying in bed reading your book. You never let anyone but me see you with your glasses. It makes it more intimate and private. I love it. I love you."

*Well, damn.* There wasn't another soul on this earth who could set Lainey's body on fire the way Eve could. The words were simple, but the meaning behind them was significant. Her pulse picked up its pace even more with how Eve looked at her. Her skin flushed with heat. Still, Lainey couldn't help herself. Teasing Eve was one of her favorite pastimes.

"You want a massage, don't you?"

Eve savored the feel of laughter bubbling up. Her life—their life—had been filled with sorrow and turmoil. Having these sweet, peaceful moments touched Eve's heart more than anything else.

"That wasn't what my end game was, but I wouldn't say no." Eve's eyes roamed the length of Lainey's bare legs as her wife crawled towards her. This would be a very short massage if Eve's body had anything to say about it. Her stomach clenched when Lainey straddled her backside. The warmth of Lainey's sex was enough of a sign for Eve that she wasn't the only one affected.

Lainey feathered her hands up Eve's t-shirt-covered back, massaging tense shoulders with the amount of pressure she knew Eve loved. Even after nearly two years of marriage—and an even longer friendship—the newlywed feeling was still there. When they weren't doting on the kids, they cherished each other. It had been a long, arduous road to get to the point they were at now. Neither wanted to take for granted the bliss they felt being together.

Lainey bent down to nibble Eve's ear, knowing it drove Eve insane. On one of her many explorations of her wife's body, Lainey discovered that certain areas on Eve reaped more benefits. That sensitive area right behind her ear was one of those spots. Lainey felt Eve shiver beneath her.

Eve allowed Lainey to linger a moment longer before turning her head, inviting a more intimate kiss. Just as their lips touched, Eve's phone rang. *Fuck it,* Eve thought. Nothing was more important to her now than the woman straddling her ass.

Lainey immediately felt the change in Eve's body. The tension was back but for a completely different reason this time. And as much as she wanted to continue this bit of foreplay, Lainey kissed Eve's temple and moved away. She, of course, knew whose ringtone that was.

"You should get it, honey."

The groan Eve let out was born out of frustration. She didn't want to be answering the damn phone. She wanted to be ripping her wife's clothes off and making mad, passionate love to her.

"I have specific ringtones to ignore some calls, baby."

"I know. But it could be important. Or, at the least, an explanation for not phoning earlier."

Eve blew out a breath. For her, there was no explanation. It was a fuck up. Nothing more, nothing less. There wasn't an urgent need for Eve to be on the phone listening to excuses. Nonetheless, Eve obliged and pulled her phone from her back pocket.

"Hello, Adam."

"It's about time." Adam's voice dripped with sarcasm and anger.

"I was... busy. What can I do for you?"

Adam knew precisely what Eve meant by "busy." There was a time when she was busy with him. Now that that time was over, Adam felt a pang of resentment. His hand tightened around his phone as he tried to hide his annoyance.

"It's my time to talk to Bella."

"It was your time," Eve checked her watch—a gift from Lainey on their first anniversary. "Five hours ago."

"Yes, well, something came up. I'm calling now." Adam attempted to make it sound like an innuendo, as Eve had. He wanted to hear the jealousy in Eve's voice. He longed to hear the anger she'd had when she thought he had been cheating on her. He scoffed. *He* wasn't the one who was cheating. No, Adam had merely *pretended* to have other interests to get a reaction out of Eve.

"And now Bella is sleeping," Eve said evenly. She would not fall for his childish tricks. This wasn't the first time Adam acted like an ass. It wouldn't be the last. "You'll have to wait and call her at an earlier time."

"Or you could wake her up. She loves talking to her daddy."

"I'm not waking her up, Adam."

"Why is she asleep so early anyway? Can't your libido wait? Being a mother should be your priority."

Though she felt the anger rise, Eve kept her composure. This was a tactic she had seen before with Lainey's ex-husband. It had worked on Lainey, and Eve always quickly reminded Lainey that it was all a mind game. Now she reminded herself. She held her hand out to her wife. When Lainey immediately took hold, Eve felt grounded.

"It's past nine, Adam." She deliberately ignored the libido jab.

"Which isn't late. Bella should be able to stay up." It irked Adam that he hadn't piqued Eve's irritation. Her calm demeanor drove home the fact that she was completely over him.

"She's four. She has a bedtime. Otherwise, she'll be cranky all day."

"Was that Lainey's idea?" There was a bitter taste in Adam's mouth when he said Lainey's name. He had trusted her. He trusted her even after he found out she had slept with his wife. That was his mistake. Adam should've known that any woman who would cheat on her husband wasn't honorable. He hadn't blamed Eve. He and Eve hadn't been married. Until Paris. Lainey had seduced Eve on the "business trip," and it was all downhill for Adam afterward.

"Excuse me?"

"You weren't strict before, Eve. There were times Bella would stay up way longer just to see you when you got home from the gallery. Or wherever you were."

Lainey felt Eve squeeze her hand and stroked her thumb over Eve's soft skin. Whatever Adam was saying to her was upsetting her. Lainey now regretted insisting Eve take his call. She would have to do a *lot* of apologizing in *many* different positions.

"It was *our* decision as a family." Eve's voice held none of the animosity she felt. She attributed that to Lainey's calming touch. She allowed the gentle circles Lainey was drawing on her hand to level out her blood pressure. "None of which changes the fact that Bella is sleeping, and you can't talk to her right now."

"She's *my* daughter, Eve. You may try to forget that, but *we* made her."

The strain in Adam's voice gave Eve a touch of satisfaction. "Maybe you'll make more effort next time, Adam." Eve glanced over at Lainey and thought of a recent conversation they'd had. "Though, while I have you on the phone..."

Adam felt a jolt of anticipation. Their past conversations lasted only as long as it took to put Bella on the phone. If she wanted to extend this exchange, there was hope for him.

"I knew you'd regret your decision," he said with bravado. "You finally realize *she* can't give you what I can, right?"

*More games*, Eve thought with disgust. Again, she used Lainey's touch to keep herself from falling into Adam's trap. There was a reason

Eve kept their communication short and about Bella. Whenever Adam had an opportunity, he would start this shit. If it wasn't arrogance, it was a pathetic attempt at being sorrowful about the end of their marriage. Tonight sounded as though it was going to be delusions of grandeur.

*Lainey gives me so much more.* "I have regrets, Adam. But marrying Lainey most definitely isn't one of them. In fact, I wanted to talk to you about consenting to Lainey adopting Bella."

Lainey's thumb stopped its mindless movement as surprise filled her senses. She hadn't expected Eve to bring up the adoption. Certainly not during such an antagonistic phone call. She and Eve had discussed the adoption of all three kids. Eve had already started the process for Darren and Kevin. But they had put off asking Adam for the time being and filed for Lainey to be Bella's legal guardian. It was a "workaround"—as Reghan called it—until they could proceed with the adoption. Should Bella need medical attention or—God forbid—something happened to Eve, Lainey would be able to take care of Bella legally. It wasn't as satisfying as adoption, but it was a step.

In the meantime, they were hoping the more time that passed, Adam would get over the divorce. At least, that was Eve's hope. Lainey knew from experience that Eve was impossible to get over. As much as it irritated her, she understood Adam's hostility and resentment. It was especially evident whenever Lainey answered Eve's phone when he called. Listening to this conversation, Lainey couldn't help but wonder why Eve thought this was the right time.

"Are you fucking kidding me? She takes my *wife,* and now she wants to take my kid?"

Eve held the phone away from her ear as Adam shouted at her. She gave Lainey an apologetic look when Adam started yelling foul things she knew Lainey could hear. *I'm sorry,* she mouthed. It wasn't just an apology for Adam's behavior. It was also for the abrupt attempt to discuss this with Adam without talking to Lainey about it first. Eve would have to do a *lot* of making up after this.

"Lainey didn't take me away from you, Adam," Eve said when he finally took a breath. "I did. I deserve to be happy. Lainey makes me deliriously happy." Eve wouldn't apologize to Adam again. She'd done enough of that. And, frankly, she had finally made the right decision—a decision for *her*. Eve's entire life had centered on pleasing others. When she ultimately chose Lainey, Eve did so without hesitation or regret. It was Eve's turn to get what she truly wanted in life. Happiness with the person she loved with her entire soul.

"I want Lainey to adopt Bella because we're a family," Eve continued. "Bella loves Lainey. Adam, you call every other week. Sometimes it's every other *two* weeks. When you *do* call, you try to get Bella to talk about me or what Lainey and I do. You've visited once since we moved here. Hell, you don't even know who Bella's pediatrician is!"

"Whose fault is that, Eve?"

"Yours. You chose money and your business over your daughter. Now I'm asking you to make it official. Let Lainey adopt Bella. Consent."

"And give up my rights as her parent?" *She's the only link I have with you.* "You're fucking insane."

"How much will it take, Adam?"

"You think you can buy me out?"

"I did before. How much?"

"Not even the great Eve Sumptor has that much money. I will never consent to that woman getting my daughter."

"It will happen. Think about it, Adam. Think about how you can get out of the debt you've put yourself and your company in. You could get something you want in return, or you could get nothing. Make your choice."

"You don't know fuck about me or my business," Adam snarled. He was fucking pissed that Eve was right. But he'd be damned if he'd give Lainey the satisfaction of taking everything from him.

"Don't I? As I said, think about it. Bella deserves a parent who is consistently present and loves her unconditionally. Not someone who keeps sporadic contact for selfish reasons. I will fight for this, Adam. I'll give you a week before I go to Reghan to begin the process."

With that ominous warning, Eve ended the call. She hadn't meant to threaten him. Apparently, he brought out the worst in her these days. Nonetheless, everything she had said was true. Adam used Bella as his connection to Eve. She was tired of seeing a disheartened little girl when her daddy didn't call. And it was always Lainey who made Bella forget the heartache and feel special.

"That didn't sound like it went well."

Eve looked up at Lainey, who had slipped her glasses up to the top of her head. With her hair pulled back from her face, Lainey looked younger than her forty-three years. Eve studied Lainey's face, bare of any cosmetics. The smooth skin—soft under Eve's fingertips—held only faint lines around the eyes and mouth. Laugh lines that had only recently begun to show. And Eve loved every one of them. They told the story of the love and laughter they finally had in their lives. She wasn't about to let another mistake from her past change that.

Eve sighed. "I know I hurt him when I chose to be with you. But it's times like this I wonder why I ever . . ."

Lainey caught Eve's hesitation. "Loved him?" Eve lowered her eyes, and Lainey reached over to lift Eve's chin. "Honey, you don't have to censor yourself with me. I know you loved him. Hell, I even advocated for the two of you at one point."

Eve took Lainey's hand and kissed her palm. "Why did you do that when you felt the way you did about me?"

"I *still* feel that way about you," Lainey corrected. "And I wanted to see you happy. You deserved—deserve—to love and be loved. At the time, I didn't believe I could truly be the one to give you that. Not with all the obstacles we faced."

"So you wanted me to have the second-best thing?" Eve grinned. It wasn't a joking matter, she knew. At least, it hadn't been. But she'd be a mess if she couldn't look back at her past without some emotional distance.

"I wanted to see you happy," Lainey repeated with more authority. "Even if it wasn't with me."

Eve pulled Lainey to her, giving her a searing kiss that would've brought them both to their knees had they not been sitting down.

"This is why I love you," Eve murmured against Lainey's slightly swollen lips. "There's not a selfish bone in your body." *And you love me —despite my flaws—for all the right reasons.* She didn't know why she didn't say that aloud to Lainey, but she believed Lainey felt it in every touch.

Lainey did feel more behind Eve's words. She always had. It was a bond she would cherish for the rest of her life. Eve had suppressed her emotions for so long. Lainey knew it was still a work in progress, getting Eve to say everything she needed to say. Until then, Lainey would listen with her heart. However, there was one thing Eve said that wasn't entirely true. She nudged Eve onto her back and straddled her.

"Oh, I have many selfish bones when you are involved, my love."

Eve—urprised by the move—grinned wickedly at her wife. "Oh yeah? Would you like to share one of those *bones* with me?"

Lainey lowered her head and kissed Eve passionately. Toys were no stranger to Lainey and Eve's sex life. And after hearing Eve talk so openly to Adam about how Lainey made her feel, it was like fireworks had been set off in Lainey's heart. It was Lainey's turn to make a choice. And her choice was to give in to each and every desire she felt right now.

"I'll share more than one with you," Lainey promised with another kiss. "I'll go get ready. You find the cuffs."

Eve's eyes widened. "You're taking prisoners tonight, aren't you?"

Lainey shrugged and booped her wife on the nose. "The last time we did this, you ended up taking over, and I'm still wondering how you pulled that off. This time, I'm going to be prepared. *And* I'm going to finish what *I* start."

---

LAINEY STEPPED BACK into the bedroom and stopped dead in her tracks. Eve Sumptor—in all her naked glory—was sitting on the bed, seductively twirling fur-lined cuffs around her finger.

"It should be illegal being that sexy." Lainey sauntered over to her wife and plucked the cuffs from her. She deposited her own contribution to tonight's festivities on the nightstand and motioned for Eve to lie back.

"Hmm. I don't think we have another pair of handcuffs." Eve looked longingly at Lainey. The nightshirt she wore was white and skimmed the top of her thighs. Eve had to admit it was one of her favorite looks on her wife. Lainey Sumptor made white look *good*. "Maybe I should be the one using them on you."

Lainey straddled Eve once again as Eve's head hit the pillow. "Don't even try it. Arms up."

Eve immediately obeyed. She couldn't help it. Bold Lainey brought Eve to her knees with desire. Their headboard wasn't exactly "cuff-friendly." But that didn't keep Eve from honoring Lainey's silent request to keep her arms up until released.

"Are they too tight?" Lainey asked softly.

Eve smiled up at her loving partner. "Baby, I can slip my hands out of them. You can make them tighter."

"I never want to hurt you."

It took considerable will for Eve to keep her hands where they were. She didn't want to ruin the mood they were going for.

"I always tell you, Lainey, the only way you could hurt me is if you didn't love me anymore."

"Then we have absolutely nothing to worry about." Lainey gingerly tightened the cuffs, gasping lightly when Eve took a cloth-covered nipple in her mouth. "Sneaky."

Once that was done, she leaned down and kissed Eve's lips. She allowed herself only a morsel of what she truly wanted. If she lingered too long on those enticing full lips, Lainey was afraid she wouldn't be able to stop and take in all that was Eve. She sat up and raised to her knees, grabbing the hem of her nightshirt to pull it over her head. The look of pure hunger in Eve's eyes sent shock waves to Lainey's demanding libido.

"I never felt beautiful or desirable until you looked at me that way." Lainey reached over and grabbed the vibrator from the nightstand. "I never felt bold or adventurous until you gave yourself to me."

"My body is yours, Lainey." Eve's blood flowed directly towards her heated, saturated center, and she fought the urge to take over. Having Lainey on top of her, in control, was too delicious to interrupt. "Take it."

Eve's consenting submission was one of the most exquisite gifts she could give to Lainey. Once again, Lainey leaned down. This time, however, she took Eve's taut nipple in her mouth. She sucked it gently before taking it between her teeth. A quick nip had Eve's hips bucking.

"I love your body," Lainey whispered. "I love feeling your skin on mine. You're so soft." She shifted her attention to Eve's other nipple, giving it the same sensual treatment. "You taste incredible."

"Lainey," Eve managed between heavy breaths. "Baby, please."

Lainey moved up until she was looking into Eve's gray eyes. She kept the contact as she lowered the vibrator to where she knew Eve needed it. She turned it on to the lowest setting. Something that always drove Eve crazy.

*"No one needs this setting. It's such a fucking tease."* Eve would say with frustration.

That was precisely why Lainey was using it now. That little bit of teasing led to intense orgasms. Lainey should know. Eve had taught her the trick one extraordinarily impassioned night. *What goes around comes around,* Lainey thought as she circled the tip of the vibrator on Eve's clit. The smooth movement of the toy told Lainey all she needed to know. Eve was wet and ready for anything Lainey offered.

She clicked the second setting, upping the pulsating against Eve, eliciting a sharp intake of breath from her lover.

"I love watching you," Lainey murmured. She finally turned on the highest setting, savoring the low moan that came from deep inside Eve. "I love the way your body moves when you're close. And the way your eyes darken and your cheeks flush right before you cum."

That was all it took for Eve. The intense pressure on her clit was one thing. But hearing Lainey talk brazenly to her? That's what always sent Eve over the edge. Pair that with the way Lainey was grinding herself on Eve's thigh, and there was no stopping the rush of ecstasy. Eve arched off the bed as the intense orgasm ripped through her body.

Lainey was right there with Eve. Even if she hadn't been riding Eve's silky thigh, the sound and feel of Eve climaxing beneath her would have set Lainey off.

She switched the vibrator off, knowing all too well how it felt on such a sensitive clit. After tossing it to the side, she reached up and uncuffed Eve's hands.

Released from her restraints, Eve promptly buried her hands in Lainey's hair, pulling her into a scorching kiss. Eve flipped their position, bringing Lainey's arms up above her head and holding them there. She intertwined their fingers while their tongues danced their sensual dance. "*My turn,*" she whispered fervently. This was how it was with Lainey. Her body was constantly on fire with need. The more Eve had Lainey, the more she needed. And Eve would spend the rest of the night —the rest of her life—showing Lainey just how vital she was to Eve's life.

# Two

The sizzle and scent of bacon and sausage filled the air as Lainey stood at the stove and listened to her boys argue playfully.

"Yeah, well, you used to think Spider-Man was the best," Kevin teased. They'd had many of these squabbles before. Every six months or so, Darren changed his mind about who his favorite superhero was. Right now, it was a tie between Wonder Woman and Scarlet Witch—much to his moms' satisfaction. Kevin knew it was because Darren had respect for strong women. And maybe a little crush.

"So! I can change my mind. Mom, tell Kevin I can change my mind," Darren whined. He had seen his mom's smirk and decided to play along with Kevin's teasing. Besides, it was nice to be open and honest about these things finally. His father would never have approved of Darren liking "girl" superheroes. It was too "sissy." Darren always made himself feel better by drawing "girl" superheroes taking down villains that looked suspiciously like his father.

"Kevin, Darren can change his mind," Lainey said with mirth.

"Mom, tell Darren he should stop drawing Jack getting his butt beat by women in capes."

"Darren, you need to . . . wait." Lainey looked up from the scrambled eggs. "What?"

Darren rolled his eyes. "None of them wear capes."

"You draw your father?"

"Noooo. I draw villains being brought to justice. It's not my fault they resemble real-life people."

Kevin snickered. "You *literally* draw them."

"Draw what?" Eve stole a sausage from Darren's plate.

"Hey! That was my sausage!" Darren swatted at Eve's hand.

"Well, excuse me!" Eve widened her eyes and made a face at her youngest son. "I remember a time when you were happy to share your *shosheges* with me." She ruffled Darren's hair and winked at a laughing Kevin before making her way to Lainey.

Lainey sighed happily—forgetting about Darren's drawings for now —as Eve wrapped her arms around Lainey. "Good morning, my love." She offered her lips for a kiss.

Eve readily accepted, loitering a little longer than was probably suitable for the eggs.

"Uh, hello, kids in the room." Kevin pretended to shield Darren's eyes.

Eve stuck her tongue out at their oldest and went back to kissing Lainey. "Good morning, baby." She nuzzled Lainey's neck. "*Thank you for last night,*" she whispered close to Lainey's ear.

Lainey glanced over at Darren and Kevin, who were no longer paying attention to them. They'd seen them canoodling so many times before that it didn't faze them unless they wanted to tease their moms.

"*My pleasure.*" Lainey hooked her free hand around Eve's neck and pulled her back for one more kiss. Her body still hummed from their lovemaking the night before. Eve certainly gave as good as she got, and they only got a few hours of sleep. *Totally worth it.*

"And mine," Eve winked. She took a piece of bacon, feeding half to Lainey, who had her hands full making—Eve looked over Lainey's shoulder—bunny pancakes? "Bunnies?"

"They're Bella's favorite. Could you pass me the chocolate chips, please?"

"Ah, *that's* why they're her favorite. You put chocolate in them." Eve smacked Lainey's firm ass, receiving a raised eyebrow in return. "And because they're cute," Eve added with a chuckle. Lainey was a wonderful artist. But that didn't always extend to art via pancake batter. Lainey, however, never let that stop her from doing something to make Bella happy. And for that, Eve was incredibly grateful. "Where is our little girl anyway?"

Lainey's heart swelled each time Eve referred to Bella as theirs. She knew they had a fight on their hands with Adam. The way Adam felt about Lainey—and the fact that he was still in love with Eve—almost guaranteed he wouldn't consent to Lainey adopting Bella. But Lainey knew Eve better than anyone else. Once Eve had an idea in her head, she would do whatever it took to make it a reality.

"Bella is in the playroom," Lainey answered.

Eve's brows furrowed. "Is she okay?"

"Yeah, she is, honey. She was drawing and wanted to finish that before she came out here."

"I see." Eve glanced toward the downstairs playroom. Eve's daughter was a lot like her. When it came to emotions that were too difficult to deal with, she liked to express them with art. Eve worried that Adam's nonchalance about calling Bella regularly was wearing on the young girl.

"She's fine, honey." Lainey patted Eve lovingly on the arm. "You know that when she finishes drawing, she'll tell you all about it enthusiastically, thus letting her feelings out."

"You're right." Eve sighed. "It just pisses me off. I never thought he would do this."

*He*—Adam—was a great father in the beginning. As Bella grew and showed her bond with Eve, his attention changed. Lainey noticed it but never said a word. She never thought it was her place. Now . . .

"Adam is jealous, Eve. He has been for a long time now."

Eve frowned. "My relationship with you should have no bearing on his with Bella."

Lainey shook her head. Eve was astonishingly intelligent in almost everything else. But with feelings, Eve was still learning. "Not of me, love. Of Bella."

"Why on earth would he be jealous of his daughter?"

"Because she gets your attention and unconditional love." Lainey lifted an indifferent shoulder, but inside she fumed. Jack had been the same way when the boys were born. His love only extended as far as what he could get out of it. She never expected Adam to be that way. Lainey was usually a great judge of character. How could she have been so wrong about him? Unless what *turned* him was Lainey stealing the love of his life. But she preferred not to think about that. Perhaps it was selfish. *She* was selfish. It didn't matter anymore because Lainey was *finally* with the love of *her* life.

"That is f—"

"Baby."

Lainey hadn't needed to say anymore. The glance at the boys and her warning tone said it all. Eve's brain immediately rerouted to a more G-rated version of what she wanted to say.

"Ridiculous." Eve rolled her eyes. That certainly wasn't as satisfying as all the curse words she could have used to describe Adam's behavior. What kind of father was jealous of their own kid? Eve's entire body shivered at the answer that popped up in her mind. *Tony.*

She refused, however, to believe Adam was anything like Tony. There was no way she had been *that* wrong about him. And Eve wouldn't entertain the idea that her leaving him and marrying Lainey would have pushed him that far.

"I think it's true, though." Kevin scratched his cheek, proud of the stubble that was forming there. "Jack was jealous a lot."

Lainey cringed every time Kevin called his father by his first name. Not that she blamed him, of course. It was Jack's decision not to be in his sons' lives any longer. That was perfectly fine with Lainey. But it still felt odd hearing the boys speak so indifferently about their father. On the other hand, Lainey rarely thought of Jack these days. That was what happiness did for you.

"Kevin is right. Jack wanted kids right away. *Boys* to carry on the Stanton name."

"Thank God I'm a Sumptor now," Kevin muttered as he shook his head. He did not want to carry on that bigot's "legacy."

Lainey grinned at her son. She kept her own thanks silent, trying hard not to vocalize her disapproval of Jack. She didn't think it was good for the boys to hear her speak ill of the man who fathered them. So, if she ever had complaints, she kept them for Eve's ears only. Current conversation excluded, apparently. Lainey gave herself a pass since Kevin started it.

"My point is," Lainey began again, "once the boys were born, Jack resented the attention they received. It took me away from my 'wifely duties.'"

"No offense, baby, but Jack is a Neanderthal asshole, and I'd rather not hear about your 'wifely duties' with him."

Lainey chuckled at Eve's obvious jealousy. "I meant cooking and cleaning, honey. And, yes, he was quite . . ."

"Neanderthalish?" Eve supplied with a signature wink.

Lainey blew a frustrated breath out of her nose and narrowed her eyes at her wife. "Just trust me when I tell you that Adam behaves this way with Bella because he's jealous."

Before Eve could answer, they heard a pitter-patter of feet and a thud. Eve and Lainey eyed each other for a split second before running towards the sound. A few feet from the playroom, Bella was sitting on the floor, holding her knee. Her bottom lip trembled, and tears filled her eyes, but they never fell. Nor did Bella make a sound. As calmly as they could, Eve and Lainey walked briskly to her, assessing the situation as they got closer. Nothing seemed to be bleeding, protruding, or broken, much to their relief.

Eve sat down next to her daughter. "Hey, Baby Girl. Did you fall?" Bella nodded, lip still quivering. "Are you hurt?"

"N-no, Momma." Bella swiped at her eyes with the back of her free hand.

"Can I see your knee?" Eve asked softly.

Bella shook her head.

Lainey kneeled beside the little girl. "Come on, Sweetie. How will we know which Band-Aid to get you if we can't see the owie?"

Bella looked up at Lainey, one tear finally spilling over onto her cheek. "Owie, Mommy."

Eve's heart broke at her daughter's small voice. She also wondered why Bella had refused to allow Eve to see how hurt she was.

"Oh boy. That scrape is at *least* two Grogu Band-Aids," Lainey announced as she examined the minor scrape. It was barely bleeding and way too small for two Band-Aids, but that didn't matter.

Bella squinted at her knee, studying it. "Fwee ban-aids, Mommy."

"Three!" Lainey gave Bella a skeptical look but inspected the scrape again. She tapped a fingertip on her chin. "Hmm. You may be right. Three it is." Lainey stood again, receiving a silent plea from her wife. With a slight nod, Lainey returned to the kitchen to grab some bandages.

"Hey, Bug, can I talk to you?" Eve asked as Bella got up to follow Lainey.

"'Kay, Momma."

*Why does she sound so scared?* For the moment, Eve shook off that dreadful feeling and pulled Bella close. "Are you listening, baby girl?"

Bella took Eve's face in her hands, staring into her eyes. This was her way of letting Eve know she had her full attention. Bella often did this when Eve needed to have a serious conversation with her.

"Leaving, Momma?"

Eve was taken aback by the question. She hadn't left town without her family since she and Lainey had married. "No, Bug, Momma's not going anywhere. I wanted to talk to you about your daddy. He called after you went to sleep last night, and I told him I wouldn't wake you up." Eve paused. She realized she was about to give her four-year-old a lot of power but felt she owed Bella the truth. "If he calls late again, do you want me to wake you up to talk to him?"

Bella's lips pursed, and she tapped her little fingers on Eve's cheeks as she thought about it. A slight hum came from her, causing Eve to suppress a smile. She had always thought Bella was an old soul in a toddler body.

"No, Momma."

Eve's eyebrows quirked. "No?" Bella shook her head. "Are you sure?" A nod. "Okay, Bug. If you change your mind, all you have to do is tell me, okay?"

"'Kay."

"Now, why didn't you want to tell Momma you hurt yourself?"

Bella's bottom lip trembled again. "I a good girl, Momma."

"Yes, you are." Eve tapped Bella's lip with her fingertip. "Tell me what's going on, Baby Girl. You know you don't have to act tough around me."

"I don't wanna live wif Daddy," Bella blurted, her voice full of emotion. More emotion than should be possible for such a little girl.

Eve frowned. "What?"

"If I good, I stay wif you and mommy. I din't mean to run in the house."

"Oh, my sweet girl." Eve gathered Bella into her arms and squeezed her tight. She had a good idea of where these fears came from. It was time to monitor Bella's phone calls with her dad. "You aren't going anywhere. You will always be here with Mommy and me. And when we get old and frail, you'll be there to take care of us."

Bella giggled—the desired effect Eve had been going for. "Momma, you silly! You alweady owd!"

"What?!" Eve feigned a heart attack, falling back to the tiled floor in a dramatic "death." She let out an audible "oomph" when Bella attacked her. "Oh, *now* you want to play? After you called me old." Eve tickled Bella relentlessly, savoring her small daughter's squealing laughter. In the back of her mind, she vowed to make Adam sorry he ever tried to use their daughter as a pawn in a stupid game he'd never win.

"Unkie!" Bella laughed.

"So you give up?"

"Yes, Momma!" Bella swatted at her momma's hands as the "tickle monsters" crept toward her. "Stop, Momma!" She was panting from the tickle session.

"Okay, fine. You did say 'unkie.'" Eve pushed a lock of blonde hair out of Bella's eyes. "No more fear, yeah, Bug? I want you to be able to tell me anything. You don't have to hide anything from me, Bella. I love you so much."

"Love you, Momma."

"Good," Eve smiled warmly. She sniffed the air. "Do you smell that?"

Bella inhaled energetically. "Pancakes!"

"Mmhmm. But what *kind* of pancakes?"

Bella sniffed again as though the aroma alone would tell her exactly what the pancakes would look like. "Bunny!"

Eve's eyebrows shot up. Did bunny pancakes really smell different?

Then she remembered the chocolate. "That's right. Mommy made your favorite. Are you ready to go eat and get those *three* Band-Aids?"

Bella nodded, then looked at her knee again. "Two?"

Eve got so close to Bella's knee that her nose practically touched it. "Nope. I'm pretty sure you were right the first time. You're going to need all three." Bella beamed with pride. Apparently, the more bandages meant, the more badass the wound was. Eve could appreciate that.

"Comin', Momma?"

"Yes, ma'am. I'll be right behind you. Save me some pancakes, please."

"'Kay!"

Bella's assurance was distant as the little girl did an enthusiastic run/walk to the kitchen where the pancakes and Band-Aids were.

"Somehow, I don't think I'll get any bunny pancakes," Eve muttered as she pulled out her phone. She scrolled to the contact she was looking for and initiated the call.

"Hello?"

"I need you to draw up papers today."

"Good morning to you, too, Eve."

Eve grinned at the feigned irritation in her lawyer's tone. "Good morning, Reghan. I need you to draw up papers today."

As Eve Sumptor's attorney, Reghan Brannigan was used to calls like this. With what Eve was paying her, Reghan was at Eve's beck and call. Even on what was supposed to be a lazy Saturday morning.

"Whose world are you taking over today?"

This wasn't business for Eve. Luckily for her, Reghan wasn't your typical run-of-the-mill business attorney. Eve never did anything *typical*. When it came to people she trusted with the most sensitive interests of her life, Eve played it close to the vest. Reghan being proficient in different areas of the law, suited Eve. That's why she paid Reghan a premium retainer.

"This is personal. I want Adam served today with papers for termination of parental rights."

Reghan was silent for a moment, which was quite the feat for the usually outspoken lawyer.

"Has something happened?"

Reghan's question had nothing to do with the need to be nosy, and Eve knew that. Reghan's business was to know everything about a situation before diving headfirst into it.

"I want Lainey to adopt Bella," Eve responded simply. She knew her answer wouldn't satisfy Reghan's inquiry. But the truth was that Eve had been impulsive when she called, letting her emotions drive her. Something she never did before Lainey. It was a change she would have to keep a rein on, especially when it came to business.

Never one to beat around the bush, Reghan gave her best advice as an attorney *and* a friend. Eve had an amicable relationship with her ex-husband as far as she knew. Of course, he was salty about Eve's marriage to Lainey, but clearly, something had changed if Eve was requesting this now.

"Eve, I think even *you* will have trouble convincing a judge that Adam is a deadbeat dad."

"I'm not so sure you're right, Reghan. I've kept track of how many times he has called Bella. He's been here to visit *once* and spent most of that time berating my wife instead of bonding with Bella. And now, I have my suspicions that it's about me when he talks to Bella. Or scaring her into being afraid of me."

"Suspicions aren't proof, Eve."

"Perhaps not, but I'll be monitoring their calls now."

They were getting into sketchy territory here. "You cannot legally record the conversation between Adam and Bella without Adam's consent, Eve. However, per your custody agreement, you have the right to sit in on the phone calls. Adam did not petition for private visitations with Bella, so with sole parental responsibility, you must make the best decision for the minor."

*Spoken like a lawyer*, Eve thought. But Reghan was correct. The custody agreement left Eve with the ability to make every decision for Bella without Adam's involvement. She fought—and paid—for that right because of Adam's animosity towards Lainey. Eve hadn't wanted a long battle between them. Not only would it have affected Bella, but Eve was certain it would have taken a toll on her new marriage.

"My best decision for Bella is to stop letting Adam play with her emotions. So, how fast can you have the papers couriered to him?"

"Well, um . . ." Damn. She should have been more prepared for this. Reghan had sensed from the beginning of the divorce proceedings that things could go awry. Though Adam seemed to love his daughter, Reghan should have listened to her gut feeling about the price of that love. Now she was scrambling for alternative—i.e., less contentious— ways of satisfying Eve's request.

"Um is not covered under your retainer, Reghan."

Reghan blew out a breath. "Give me an hour, Eve. I'm still getting used to the laws here in California. *Maybe* there could be an easier path to get to where you want to be. Having sole custody could work in your and Lainey's favor. It would be ideal to have Adam's consent, but it may not be necessary."

Eve's mood perked up a bit at that news. She had anticipated another fight and payout. While she would give up her entire fortune for her family, Eve didn't particularly want to give Adam more money.

"You have an hour. My requests are for Lainey to adopt Bella and for Bella's last name to be the same as mine. We already call her a Sumptor, and I want it legal."

"Very well. You're the boss."

Eve's eyebrow quirked. There was a cursory glance towards where she knew Lainey was with the kids. Eve Sumptor was many things. But in this house, boss seemed a little out of place.

"You don't agree with what I'm doing?"

"You know I do. I should have advised you to do it sooner. Anyway, I'll get you everything you need. Expect my call."

Reghan didn't bother to say goodbye, and Eve didn't need it. She knew very well that Reghan was on a mission now. There wouldn't be any wasted time on pleasantries. Eve slipped her phone back into her pocket.

"I thought we were giving Adam a week."

Eve winced at the sound of Lainey's voice behind her. How ironic that the one person who scared her the most was the one who carried her heart.

"That was the plan," Eve agreed as she turned to her wife. "But I know you saw the fear in Bella's eyes before. I won't have Bella afraid of me, Lainey. She will *not* grow up in constant fear the way I did."

Lainey closed the short distance between them and took Eve into her arms. "That wasn't a complaint, my love. I want that little girl to be mine just as much as you do." Lainey stepped back, still holding onto Eve's waist. "I'm just worried about what he might do if he gets agitated enough."

Eve nodded in understanding. "I don't think there's much he *can* do at this point, baby. We'll know more once we get documentation from Reghan." She caressed Lainey's cheek with her fingertips. This woman owned every part of Eve. And there was no one else on earth she wanted to share Bella with. Especially if . . . "Again, I should have discussed this with you. I'm sorry. But it's the one part of our lives that I feel isn't complete yet. If anything were to happen to me . . ."

"No."

"Lainey . . ."

"No, Eve. I just got you. I'm not going to stand here and talk about losing you. I swear to God I will be so pissed off if . . ." Lainey couldn't even finish the sentence. Thinking about losing Eve made Lainey's entire world feel like it would collapse. "Listen, I want to be Bella's mommy legally. I want her to have our last name. *That* is enough of a reason to be doing this. Don't take us down a dark path. Please."

"Okay, baby."

Eve brought her lips to Lainey's, kissing her gently. She knew Lainey hated talking about anything that included not being together. When Eve and Lainey got married, Eve wasted no time putting Lainey's name on everything Eve owned. Galleries, Sumptor, Inc., bank accounts, Eve's living will. The words "what's mine is yours" meant something to Eve regarding Lainey. It had been a revelation for her. Never once did Eve have the desire to share everything with Adam when they married.

"Hey, I thought you were patching up Bella's boo-boo."

A smile played on Lainey's full lips. Hearing Eve Sumptor say things like boo-boo would never not tickle her. "Well, I *was*. Then the boys got involved. They started oohing and ahhing about how a scar would look cool. Our Bella was strutting around the kitchen when I walked out, showing off her battle wound."

"She's a tough cookie," Eve chuckled. She could see Bella doing just that. The girl was a character, for sure.

"Like her momma." Lainey's eyebrows furrowed at Eve's pensive look. "What's wrong?"

Eve shook her head. "Nothing is wrong. It's just . . . I hope Bella knows she can be a kid. I want her to cry. I want her to show her emotions. I want her to have temper tantrums." Eve paused. "Okay, maybe not so many temper tantrums. But I still want her to know that she can do all those things and still be okay."

Lainey caressed Eve's cheek. "I'm so proud of you."

Eve felt the blush creeping up and cleared her throat. She and Lainey weren't shy about anything with each other. Yet, those five words made Eve feel . . . bashful.

"Proud?"

"Yes." Lainey cupped Eve's face in her palms. She found Eve's humility charming. "You've come so far in the past few years. Seeing how you are with Bella, wanting her to express herself fully, makes me incredibly happy."

Eve lowered her eyes. She had no response to that. There was a time when Eve hoped she would be half the mother *her* mom was. After spending the past couple of years with Lainey, Eve aimed for *that* level of perfection. With two fantastic role models, Eve had learned a few things.

"Bella deserves to be a kid," Eve shrugged. "Isn't that what every mother wants?"

Lainey could practically feel the unease radiating from Eve. There were still some areas in Eve's life that were harder to navigate than others, and praise was one of them. So, Lainey would back off the compliments and move on to the normalcy of life.

"Are you ready to eat?"

She couldn't help it. Eve's brain involuntarily went straight to mischief. The result of which induced a sultry grin.

Lainey rolled her eyes playfully. "Is that all you ever think about?" Truth be told, being with Eve—in every way—was constantly on Lainey's mind, too. Unfortunately, there were times when the past crept into Lainey's thoughts. Eve had never made it a secret that sex was essential to her and Adam's lives. It shouldn't bother Lainey that they both had a past. But it did.

"Hey." *Like an open book*. "I need you to know that what I have with you—the passion, the desire, the need, the want—is *vastly* different from anything I ever experienced with Adam."

"Sometimes, I wish you couldn't read me so well."

"Why? That's what makes us . . . us."

"Yes, but I don't like feeling jealous, and I'd rather you didn't pick up on it when I do." Lainey smiled softly to ease the blow of her words.

"You have nothing to be jealous about, however endearing I find it. Just remember one thing, baby. *You* are my first, my only, and my last. The first and only woman," Eve explained when Lainey tilted her head in question. "First and only love of my life. *Last* marriage."

Lainey's eyes filled with unshed tears. "Back at ya," she muttered, trying to keep her emotions in check. "Now, let's go get some food before the kids eat it all."

"Do I get bunny pancakes?"

Lainey laughed. "You, my love, can have anything you want."

# Three

*E*ve padded across the expanse of the room to her little cove she had designated as her painting area. She smiled to herself as she sipped her piping hot coffee. Mondays were notoriously hated by most people. Eve loved Mondays, especially after such a relaxing and beautiful weekend with her family. Yes, today was a fresh start to a productive week. Beginning with a painting she'd had on her mind since Saturday night.

*"Do you ever wonder what life would have been like had things been different for you?"*

*Lainey's head rested against Eve's shoulder as she trailed her fingertips across Eve's soft skin. She had been thinking about the past lately. Everything that had happened had led them to this point. Lainey couldn't regret that. But she could wonder if she and Eve would have found each other in different circumstances.* Better *circumstances. Especially for Eve.*

*"I haven't really thought about it,"* Eve admitted. *Her entire body was relaxed from their recent lovemaking. Lainey's fingertips lazily making tracks over her skin only served to unwind Eve even more. She allowed her eyes to close and relied on her other senses to take over.*

*"I have. If I hadn't married Jack, I probably would have traveled more. Or made better use of my Masters in art."*

Eve squeezed Lainey a little tighter. "You're doing that now. The only difference is, you have the boys and Bella."

"And you." Lainey took a deep, contented breath. "I don't think I would change anything if given a chance. It all led me right here to your arms."

Eve smiled. She certainly wouldn't change anything either. If her rough road was the only one that guided her to Lainey, she would walk it every single time. Of course, there were things she would have preferred not to experience. Her mother's murder. The brutality of the men who crossed her path. But in the end, her reward far outweighed the sacrifices. She had a beautiful family, a house full of love, and happiness.

"Your mother would be proud of who you've become," Lainey murmured softly.

Taken aback by the words, Eve opened her eyes. How was it that Lainey always seemed to know what was on Eve's mind?

"What made you say that?" she asked curiously.

Lainey's sleepy movements stopped as she looked up at Eve. "I don't know. It was just a feeling I got. I wish I could have known her."

Lainey didn't know what possessed her to bring up Eve's mother. It wasn't a subject Eve talked about often. If ever. But now that she had, Lainey wanted to know more. There were no photos—that Lainey knew of —no stories that weren't riddled with tragedy. That always made Lainey sad. She always wondered if Eve's talent came from her mom because she couldn't imagine it came from Tony.

"She would have loved you," Eve said softly.

"Would she have approved of us?"

Eve smiled. "Oh, yeah. I don't think it would have mattered to her that you're a woman. You make me happy, and that's all that Momma would have cared about."

Momma. Lainey's heart swelled at the endearing term. Now it was Eve's turn to carry that affectionate name with Bella.

"Do you look like her?"

Eve's chest rose as she drew in a deep breath. For once, she didn't feel the weight of sorrow when speaking of her mother. Eve could attribute that to it being Lainey asking the questions. Lainey was navigating the conversation in a positive, personal direction. Something she was very skilled at. And just one of the many reasons Eve loved Lainey.

"Yes. Her hair was slightly darker, and her eyes were more blue than gray. But our features are the same." Eve glanced down at her wife adoringly. "When she was happy, her eyes lit up so bright. But when she wasn't, they would cloud over like a sky readying for a thunderstorm. Momma never had to say a word for me to know what kind of mood she was in."

Lainey thought about Eve the same way. When Eve was angry, her eyes turned an ice-cold gray. When she was passionate, they brightened to a fascinating translucent silver.

"Was she an artist?"

Eve's brows furrowed. "I—I don't remember."

It was rare for Lainey to ever see Eve as anything but a confident woman. The voice that just came from her wife was anything but confident, and Lainey regretted asking the question.

"I'm sorry, my love . . ."

Eve bent her head and kissed Lainey gently. "Please don't be. You can ask me anything." She tried to relax again, but her mind searched for information she couldn't find. "I don't know why I can't remember. I must have gotten it from somewhere, right? Lord knows Tony didn't have a talented bone in his body."

"It could be just something you were born with," Lainey suggested carefully.

"Maybe." Eve practiced the pranayama breathing Lainey had learned from Ellie. It was a great technique that helped her calm her mind. She smiled when Lainey began doing it with her. That's how Lainey was. Instead of grilling Eve about what was bothering her, Lainey allowed Eve to work through it first. Eve found it easier to open up on her own timeline, and her wife understood that like no other. "I love you."

Lainey snuggled even closer. "I love you, too. Are you ready to go to sleep?"

Though Eve's brain was still trying to recall the things she had forgotten about her mother, sleep sounded good. Especially with Lainey beside her.

"Yeah, baby, I am. Tomorrow is a new day, right? Not everything has to be solved tonight."

*Lainey sat up, pulling Eve with her. She arranged their pillows and scooted down to get settled. Eve got comfy beside her, and they assumed their usual position. Lainey's head rested on Eve's shoulder as Eve's arm wrapped around her. They would stay like this for a long while before moving slightly apart and drifting asleep.*

*"Lights off," Lainey requested, and the automated lights immediately turned off. The technology wasn't new, but Sumptor, Inc. was working on improvements. Lainey enjoyed the benefits of testing the prototypes.*

*"You really like that, don't you?" Eve chuckled.*

*Lainey patted Eve's chest where her hand lay. "Yes, I do. Now go to sleep."*

"SHOULDN'T YOU BE GETTING READY?" Lainey emerged from the bathroom, putting her earring in as she walked. Eve was currently sitting behind her easel, coffee in hand, hair up in a messy bun—God, Lainey loved that look—and wearing a t-shirt stained with different paint colors. She looked incredibly relaxed—and undeniably sexy. Lainey considered forgetting about everything she needed to do today to just stay here in this room watching Eve paint. Unfortunately, today was an important day for Eve. So why wasn't she dressed?

Eve looked up, confused. "I, um . . ."

"You forgot, didn't you?"

"I did not forget that . . . I . . ." Eve's deliberate pauses cried out for Lainey to fill in the blanks.

"That you have interns starting today," Lainey assisted.

"Exactly. And I definitely need to be there instead of my capable managers because . . ."

Lainey bit her cheek to keep from laughing. "Because these young ladies work very hard to win a spot at Sumptor, Inc., and it would be nice for them to meet the woman that inspires them."

Eve scoffed playfully. "If they want an inspirational woman, they should meet *you*."

"Stop." Lainey sidled up to Eve, fitting herself between Eve's bare legs. That was another thing that made Lainey contemplate forgetting everything today. In her studio or here in the bedroom, Eve's painting attire usually consisted of . . . very little. Lainey glanced over at the blank canvas to get her mind off her more lascivious thoughts. "If you want to stay here and paint, my love, I can call Dorothea, and we can reschedule your meet . . ."

"No, no." Eve wrapped her arms around Lainey's waist. "You're right. These girls work hard to gain a spot at Sumptor, Inc., and I should be there to welcome them to the program."

Lainey twirled a stray strand of Eve's hair around her finger. "I still remember the first time I saw you walk in on my first day."

Eve grinned. "When you thought Herman was E. Sumptor?"

"Guilty," Lainey chuckled. "But in my defense, you were not as visible back then as you are now. Or, more accurately, I hadn't done enough research. I just knew Sumptor Gallery was the most prestigious gallery in the city, and I wanted to work there. Who was Herman, anyway?"

"Executive management of custodial services."

Lainey laughed heartily. "He was a janitor?"

"No, he is *head* of the janitorial division of Sumptor, Inc.," Eve said with feigned indignation.

"Well, excuse me. *Anyway*, once I knew who you were, I was in awe of you. And perhaps a little attracted."

"Just a little?"

Lainey rolled her eyes. "You know, on second thought, maybe your capable managers can take care of the interns."

Eve squeezed Lainey to her, wrapping her legs around Lainey for good measure. "You're not jealous, are you?"

"No, of course not. I'm merely thinking of you and your need to paint."

"Ah. Naturally." Eve lifted her head and gave Lainey a scorching kiss. She knew Lainey was teasing her. After everything they'd been through, Eve wouldn't—couldn't—look at another human being the way she looked at Lainey. She'd found the love of her life. There wasn't a thing Eve would do to jeopardize her life with her family. "Hey. Why are you dressed?"

It took a moment for Lainey's brain to start functioning again after that kiss. "I," she took a breath and started again. "I have a few things to take care of at the gallery. The shipment from Italy is coming in, remember? I thought I'd go in and take care of it while you inspire future women entrepreneurs."

"Want to switch?" Eve asked with a smile. She had forgotten about the shipment, which wasn't typical for Eve Sumptor. Before, Eve would be the first at the gallery, opening the shipment and going through everything with a critical eye. However, after a forced "staycation" during the pandemic, Eve found she enjoyed being home with her family more than anything. She could attribute it to being burned out. Eve had dealt with problems—big and small—all her life. Being happy, healthy, and in love had spoiled her. And Eve was unapologetic about that.

"I'll call Dorothea," Lainey offered again. The boys were doing their virtual classes, Bella was doing her preschool thing with Lexie, and Lainey would be out of the house for a few hours. This would be the perfect time for Eve to paint. Besides, Lainey knew Eve preferred being home more often than not these days. Lainey couldn't fault her for that. Their home was beautiful. Not just aesthetically, but it just felt . . . right. Who wouldn't want to bunker down where they felt safe and loved?

"It's okay, baby. This is my program. I'll go greet the new interns. Then I'll come home, do some painting, cook us dinner, then make love to my wife."

"Well, that certainly sounds like a good plan to me." Lainey kissed Eve's forehead. "You're sure?"

"Yes, ma'am." Eve untangled herself from Lainey and stood up. "I'll go get dressed. Want to ride together? I can drop you off at the gallery since I'll probably be done before you."

"I'd love that."

"Good." Eve tugged Lainey's left ear. "You're missing an earring, by the way."

Lainey's hand flew to her ear. "Damn it. You're a distraction!"

"Oh, sure. Blame me!" Eve swatted Lainey's ass as she walked by her, then began running when Lainey came after her.

LAINEY FILLED a travel cup with coffee, preparing it precisely how Eve liked it. She then filled another travel cup with green tea for herself. After checking her watch, she typed out a quick text to Lauren to let her know she'd be late this morning.

"Mommy!"

Lainey set her phone down and turned to an excited Bella. "Hey, Sweetie! Aren't you supposed to be in school?"

"Yeah. I drawed you dis!"

Bella held out a piece of paper with a colorful drawing of the entire family. With one glaring omission. Adam.

"How beautiful! You know where this goes, right?"

"Fidge!"

"Exactly!"

"What are we so excited about?"

Lainey looked up at Eve's amused voice and her breath caught in her throat. Gone were the loose t-shirt and short shorts, and in their place was an immaculate white pantsuit. The perfectly tailored jacket hung open over a crisp white vest and tight slacks. Eve's tanned cleavage was a stark contrast that caused Lainey's mouth to water and inappropriate thoughts to swirl around in her head.

"Momma, wook!" Bella took her drawing out of a stunned Lainey's hands and ran to her momma. She held out her artwork proudly, a huge grin gracing her cute little face.

Eve winked saucily at Lainey before turning her attention to her daughter. She kneeled beside Bella as she took the drawing and studied it as she would any artist in her gallery.

"Hmm. The colors are bright. Eye-catching. The use of grass on the roof gives this piece a whimsical feeling. And the smiles on the subjects are an intense demonstration of the happiness surrounding them. Simply put, this piece is exquisite, and I wholeheartedly agree that it is definitely 'fidge' worthy."

Bella giggled incessantly at her momma. "I put it up?"

"Yes, please." Eve stood, wrapping her arm around Lainey as she stepped up beside her. "Did you notice anything?" Eve asked quietly, watching Bella find the perfect spot for her artwork.

"That your power suits could render anyone and everyone speechless?"

Eve glanced over at Lainey with a grin. "*You* bought this for me."

"Yeah, I didn't think that one through. Or I should have put this in the 'you can only wear this for me' pile." Lainey blew out a breath and muttered something about Eve not playing nice. "But to answer the real question, yes. I noticed what—or rather *who*—was missing."

"I did it!" Bella did a little happy dance, laughing hysterically when her moms joined in.

"Oh! I'm missing the dance party."

Eve cleared her throat and straightened her jacket. "We'll have to, ahem, make sure we invite you to the next one, Lexie."

Bella's nanny/teacher smiled. After more than three years of working with Eve Sumptor, Lexie finally got acclimated to the powerful woman's presence. Especially seeing the more "human" side of Eve. She credited Lainey for bringing out Eve's more relaxed disposition. Lexie had never seen Eve this happy or carefree with Adam.

"Well, I'd be happy to join. But *this* little girl should be at her desk writing some numbers." Lexie looked down at Bella with a playfully stern look. "When I said it was time to stretch your legs, I didn't quite mean dancing around the kitchen."

"Sowwy, Wexie. But I wanned to show Mommy and Momma my pichur."

"I understand completely. It is a *wonderful* picture!"

Eve adored the rapport between Bella and Lexie. Lexie had been a godsend during the divorce and move from New York to LA. When Lexie had agreed to make the move with them, Eve knew it would help Bella adjust to all the occurring changes. The young woman had become a part of the family. Having Lexie—and her psychology experience— here was beneficial when Eve and Lainey had to leave the house.

"You two look nice. Are you going to the office?" Lexie watched Bella's reaction with interest. Bella had gotten used to having her moms at home now. On the rare occasions they went out to work, Bella tended to act out her disapproval. Bella never liked when Eve had to go away, but this fear of being away from Eve and Lainey, even for a few hours, was a fairly recent development. Getting past this phase was a work in progress. Eve, Lainey, and Lexie decided the best way to deal with Bella was to be firm and forthright.

"You go out?" Bella asked with narrowed eyes.

Lainey beckoned Bella to her and took her face in her hands. She bent and kissed Bella on the forehead. "Yes, ma'am. Momma and I have to go into the office for a bit."

"That's right, Bug." Eve brushed a hand over Bella's soft blonde hair. "We'll be out for a few hours."

"Why, Momma?"

"Because it's our job. I know it has been confusing for you, but as things get back to normal, that means more time at the office or gallery, Baby Girl. We've talked about this."

Bella scrunched up her face as she thought about what her momma said. "You come home?" she asked finally.

"Of course. You know we would discuss it with you first if we had to go away for longer than one sleep, right?"

Again, Bella took a moment to think, then nodded her head once. "I 'member, Momma. 'Kay, love you." Bella gave Eve a quick hug, then did the same for Lainey. "Love you, Mommy. Come on, Wexie, I gotta go work!" Bella grabbed Lexie's hand and pulled her away.

Eve chuckled. "I wonder where she gets her bossiness from?" Both Eve and Lainey looked at each other as the culprit, then laughed. "By the way, Lexie is right. You look beautiful."

"She said nice." Lainey looked down at her wine-colored pencil skirt and amethyst silk blouse. "A far cry from the drab gray thing I was wearing the first time we met, isn't it?"

Eve wound her arms around Lainey and pulled her close. "All I remember is what you said you had on underneath," Eve murmured close to Lainey's ear.

"You never play fair, my love." Lainey kissed Eve's soft lips before patting her on the butt. "We're going to be late."

"How tempted are you?"

Lainey allowed the sultry question to linger in the air for a moment. How incredible it was to be this in love. She had waited for this feeling her entire life without even knowing it. God, she hoped it never went away.

"*Very.*" Lainey kissed Eve again, then nudged her away. She grabbed Eve's hand and pulled her along. "Come on, Eve. I gotta go work!"

# Four

"*L*auren? Do you have the invoices for the Italy shipment?"

With clean white gloves, Lainey began carefully unwrapping one painting that had just been delivered. Italy was a source of incredible art for Sumptor Galleries. It was also a wonderful source of memories for Lainey. She felt free when she traveled there with Eve. Their first time going there, they were both still married. Yet, when the wind whipped through her hair and the aroma of olive trees surrounded them as they drove down narrow streets, Lainey could let her heart wish. Now she allows her body to fulfill those wishes.

"They're on your desk. Would you like me to get them?"

Lainey had been lost in her thoughts and was startled that Lauren was now next to her. She glanced down at the artwork on the table, then over at her colleague. Something about this painting she was examining reminded her of Lauren. The woman in the painting was faceless, but the hair and stature were similar. Lainey shrugged it off, chalking it up to an overactive imagination.

"No, thank you. I'll look over them when I'm done here."

"Yes, ma'am." Lauren grinned when Lainey gave her a look. "Entschuldigung. I know I'm only supposed to call the *other* Mrs. Sumptor that to get on her nerves."

A smile tugged at the corners of Lainey's mouth. "If you tell her that, I will deny I had anything to do with it."

Lauren "crossed" her heart with her forefinger. "Our secret." She caught a glimpse of the next painting Lainey unwrapped and frowned. A familiar feeling tickled the back of her brain. The sensation wasn't a pleasant one, so Lauren shook it off. "Where is Mrs. Sumptor? She's usually here on shipment day."

"Mmhmm, she is. But she had another engagement today, so I'm filling in."

Lainey used every technique that Eve taught her when analyzing a painting. She felt the texture with her fingertips, following the strokes of the paintbrush carefully. She brought out her loupe and inspected the signature. Lainey bent, sniffing the paint. She'd always thought that was odd when a majority of the paintings at Sumptor Gallery weren't old. But Eve had taught Lainey how to tell the difference between old and new. As well as ink vs. paint. While the gallery sold reproductions, it was the real deal that patrons wanted to see.

"What do you look for when you do these examinations?" Lauren asked with interest. She took her job as a curator seriously, seeing Lainey as a mentor. The more she could learn here, the higher the possibility of perhaps heading a gallery in her home country of Germany.

"Authenticity," Lainey answered as she checked the layering of the painting. This was new art, and paints had come a long way since the days of da Vinci. Still, forgeries were considerably uncomplicated if you knew what you were looking for. "I'll show you what to look for on the next one. Then we'll go older so you can see the differences."

"They don't teach this in art history where I come from."

Lainey chuckled. "No, they don't here either. Apparently, it's a completely distinct set of skills that includes forensics and chemistry." She shook her head. "I don't think I'd be great at either."

Lauren frowned. "But you know this?" She picked up Lainey's loupe that was engraved with her initials. "You even have your own *lupe.*"

"A gift from Eve. Both the loupe and the knowledge of how to do this."

Lainey took the loupe, rubbing her thumb over the inscription on the backside of the small magnifying glass. *Forever yours.* She remembered the night Eve gave it to her. They were here at the gallery alone, not long after their move from New York. Their lives together had just begun, and Lainey felt vulnerable and scared of the future. Oh, she knew she loved Eve with all her heart. And Lainey had the impression that the emotions were mutual. But with all the changes going on in her life, Lainey's confidence was on shaky ground. How long would Eve love her once they lived together and Eve found out how boring Lainey was?

It was a silly fear, Lainey knew. But when years were spent with someone who criticized your every move, the fear was natural. At least that's what Eve told Lainey while holding her close. Of course, Eve had known something was wrong. She could always read Lainey's moods. It was one of the biggest reasons Lainey was continuously honest with Eve. About everything. Even her insecurities. So, when Eve handed her the loupe, already inscribed with *Forever yours,* Lainey knew it wasn't a reaction to those fears but a genuine sentiment.

"Experience teaches you more than textbooks, Lauren. Watching Eve do this, learning hands on, has given me all the confidence I need to determine whether what we're showing or selling is worth a penny or priceless."

"I'm sure the hands-on part made it worth it," Lauren joked, then immediately apologized. "That was unprofessional."

Lainey couldn't help but laugh. It's not like Lauren was wrong. Having Eve's hands on her made *everything* worth it. "Yes, well, you won't be getting *that* kind of experience. But I will teach you everything Eve has taught me about art."

"Thank you, Lainey. I appreciate you and Eve giving me this opportunity." Lauren pulled out her own pair of white gloves and slipped them on. She'd work on getting her own magnifying glass at some point. For now, she was happy to watch and learn.

"There are thousands of galleries and museums in Germany. What made you come here?" Lainey asked as she handed Lauren the box cutter. She pointed out the safe areas to cut, then stood back to give Lauren room.

"Sumptor Galleries are the best," Lauren answered simply. "When I heard you were opening a new gallery, I didn't hesitate to . . . throw my hat in the ring, as I've heard people say. It didn't matter where it was. I wanted to be there." She shrugged. "Perhaps one day you will open one in Berlin."

"Is that the end goal? To move back?" Lainey gestured to the table, instructing Lauren to lay the painting flat.

Lauren's automatic answer should have been yes. It had been since she decided to come here. Since then, however, she had made friends. Good friends. Friends that made her forget how lonely her life had become.

"I don't know." Lauren repeated the sentiment in her native tongue as she accepted the loupe from Lainey and turned her mind to her training.

---

"Good morning, Mrs. Sumptor."

"Good morning, Dorothea." Eve took her messages from her assistant, flipping through them with a modicum of interest. "Are the new recruits in the conference room?"

Dorothea grinned. "They sure are. I have to say, they look like a good bunch this year."

Eve laughed. "We take forever to choose them. They're a good bunch every year."

"True. Though, I think you might have to put a little elbow grease into getting one of these young ladies ready for the business world."

Eve looked up from the messages and quirked an eyebrow. "Oh? We have a difficult one?"

"She has . . . spirit. Nothing you can't handle, I'm sure."

"Because I'm tougher than she is or because I used to be like her?"

Dorothea guffawed. "I didn't say it! All I'll say is there's a reason I bake cookies for Lainey all the time."

Eve threw her hands up in exasperation, then leaned on the desk to look Dorothea in the eye. "Tell me the truth. Is *that* why everyone calls her Lainey and me ma'am or Mrs. Sumptor? Because she's so nice and has whipped me into shape?"

"I don't have a clue what you're talking about."

There wasn't a single crack in Dorothea's demeanor. The only thing that told Eve she was being teased was the sparkle in the older woman's eye.

"Right. I'll get to the bottom of this conspiracy. Mark my words." Eve turned towards her office just as she heard a softly muttered "*Good luck with that*" from her assistant. She ignored it with a secret smile. Lainey had definitely softened Eve, and Eve wouldn't have it any other way. However, when she stood in front of these girls looking to be the next "Eve Sumptor," that demeanor would change.

The business world wasn't kind. Especially not to young women. And though Eve would never be cruel to those she would mentor, she needed them to be aware of the world they wanted in on. Eve scratched, clawed, and fought her way to the top. Her goal with these internships was to give these young women a better—slightly easier—chance at success. They'll have to work hard and smart, but the path will be paved.

Eve tossed her messages on her desk and sat for a moment to gather herself. Leaning forward, she picked up the family photo that sat beautifully framed on her desk. The picture was from Eve and Lainey's wedding day. God, Lainey looked exquisite that day. Not that she didn't look beautiful *every* day, but there had been a glow surrounding Lainey on their wedding day that nearly brought Eve to her knees. Even though it felt impossible, she fell even deeper in love with Lainey as she watched the woman who owned her heart walk down the aisle.

"Mrs. Sumptor? Should I tell the interns that you will be with them soon?"

Dorothea's mechanical voice filled the air through the intercom, slicing through Eve's sweet memories. *Oh, right. I'm here for a reason,* Eve thought with mirth.

"Yes. I'll be there in five minutes," Eve responded as she ran a fingertip across the photo. Eve contemplated calling Lainey simply to hear her voice. Her introvert tendencies had amplified in the past year. Lainey calmed the anxiety within. Anxiety that only Eve's wife knew about. Eve Sumptor would not—could not—show weakness. She pulled out her phone just as it dinged with an incoming message.

**Good luck today, my love. Show them why they've worked so hard.**

Eve smiled. Leave it to Lainey to know what Eve needed and when she needed it.

**Thank you, baby. Perfect timing since I'm about to jump into the deep end. Forever yours. <3**

With her confidence restored, Eve squared her shoulders and made her way to the back entrance of the conference room. This allowed Eve to observe the chosen few without being noticed. These young women had been intensely vetted by herself, Lainey, and Rebecca Cuinn—a close friend and business consultant of Eve's. However, the impromptu first impressions gave Eve the information she truly needed. She learned the hard way that the faces people show you are not the same as when you're not looking. After being betrayed by those she trusted enough to hire, Eve made sure she could always see what she was up against. So she stood in the back of the room, arms folded, and listened.

"I bet she's a real hard-ass to work for. You have to be when you're a woman in the business world. And she's, like, richer than that Tesla dude, so . . ."

*This must be the* spirited *one,* Eve thought as she continued to keep an ear on each conversation. Little Miss Spirit sported a French accent. Eve wondered if this one was from the girls' home she sponsored in Paris.

That one girls' home—with Lainey's help—turned into five homes in some of the most desolate areas. It was becoming a tradition that at least one girl from each home was chosen for the internship. It helped keep the group diverse, something Eve insisted on. Every culture, every walk of life had something to offer. These girls didn't have wealthy parents to pay their way through life. In fact, most of these girls grew up in foster care or in single-parent homes. They were the ones most businesses would overlook because of their social status. Eve, having clawed her way up from the streets of Paris, knew all too well how disparaging that could be. Creativity and skill weren't prejudiced. All they needed to succeed was opportunity. That's what Sumptor, Inc. provided.

"I just can't believe she's a lesbian. That's like the *only* reason I'm here."

"Like you have a chance with her. Have you *seen* her wife?"

"I didn't mean I want to *do* her. Though who wouldn't? But, like, she's an inspiration for the LGBTQIA community, you know?"

"Good thing you clarified. I'm pretty sure Sumptor could make you disappear."

*Spirited may be too nice of a word . . .*

"Do not start rumors."

This came from a young lady who had been quiet the whole time. She, too, had been listening and watching. Eve tilted her head and oversaw the exchange with interest, wondering if the two knew each other. They both had French accents, though there was a subtle difference in the dialect.

"Oh great. A kiss ass." LMS, as Eve had now dubbed her, snarled at the girl who made the remark. "You can turn it off now. I'm sure Sumptor will see right through your charade. Besides, it won't help you. Only the elite will make it through, and that's me."

"You think this is a competition between you and them?" Eve pushed away from the wall and walked toward the group. They all stood completely still as prey being stalked by a predator would. The color drained completely from LMS's face, making her nearly as white as Eve's suit. To Eve's amusement, the girl recovered quickly, and her stance turned defiant.

"Well, yeah. That's what we're here for. To fight for a permanent position at Sumptor, Inc."

Eve shook her head. "You're here to learn many skills. One of them is how to grow and learn from those around you, and it seems you are poised to fail in that area." A perfect eyebrow arched as she studied the girl. "What is your name?"

"Emilie. Emilie Rousseau."

Emilie had a chip on her shoulder. And after the initial shock of seeing Eve in the room, the girl had no fear. Or respect. There was no courtesy handshake, unnecessary gratitude, or even feigned placations.

"Emilie," Eve repeated with a perfect French accent. The name meant rival or eager and certainly suited the young woman. LMS seemed content to be both. "*Approprié.* Have a seat, all of you."

Eve took her place at the head of the conference table but did not sit.

Instead, she unbuttoned her jacket and put her hands on her hips. Lainey would call this Eve's power posture.

"Contrary to how Emilie described this internship, you are not competing against each other. We chose each of you for your individuality and skill set. What determines how long you stay is how you work together and whether your skill set can be broadened. The business world is a cold, hard place. Especially for women. In order to keep climbing, we have to offer our hand to help those around us."

Emilie scoffed. "Is that how you got ahead? I heard you were ruthless."

This caused the young woman Emilie was arguing with before to roll her eyes. "Can't you shut up for one minute?"

"No. I have . . ."

"Enough," Eve barked. "What is your name?" she asked Emilie's sparring partner.

"Giselle Cadieux, ma'am."

"Why are you here?" Eve knew exactly why each of them was here. She knew their strengths, their weaknesses. Each name came with information that flickered through Eve's brain as those names were paired with faces. However, words on a report weren't firsthand impressions. Especially when those impressions were enhanced by the experiences of life.

"*Euh.*" Giselle looked around the room. Every eye was on her, and she felt the heat of embarrassment rising up her neck. "I was asked?"

Eve softened her gaze and smiled. "*Oui*, you were. Do you know why?"

"Because I excel in research and development?"

"Are you asking me or telling me?"

"*Pouah!* You are right. This is no competition. *I* am here because I'm a computer genius, and I can out hack anyone in half the time."

"Sumptor, Inc. has no use for a hacker, Emilie. What we can use is someone to develop programs and apps that provide a service." Eve turned back to Giselle. "You have been involved in more than a dozen innovative products that contributed to the betterment of society. *That* is why you're here. And precisely why you will team up with Emilie." Eve held up a hand before either girl could argue. "My name is on this building. That means I make the rules. If this is what you call being a 'hard-ass,' so be it. You are not obligated to complete this internship."

Eve addressed the entire room then. "If *any* of you have a problem with how I do things, you are free to leave. However, I will not be questioned. I do things for a reason, and my decisions are final. Find a way to work together." She eyed Emilie briefly. "The only competition you're in is with yourself. You may think I'm a hardass, a bitch, or ruthless. Honestly, I can be. The world is not one-dimensional. We can't be either. Which means we all have those qualities but must also possess the other side. I've read all your essays describing why you wanted to be an intern at Sumptor, Inc. If you want a life like mine, you must understand—and embrace—that it's not just your future in your hands. You also hold the future of everyone that comes after you."

---

"HELLO, MY LOVE." Lainey accepted her wife's quick, sweet kiss before continuing her task. Once the sculpture was arranged precisely how she wanted it, she took her gloves off and turned to Eve. "You're earlier than I expected."

"Am I?" Eve looked at her watch. Here she was, thinking she'd spent a reasonable amount of time with her interns. She even managed to get a few things done at the office before she couldn't take it anymore. The need to be back with her family became overwhelming. Too much socializing was draining for Eve these days. *I wonder if I should ask Dr. Woodrow about that.* She shrugged as she followed Lainey towards the back of the gallery.

Lainey punched in a code to unlock a cabinet. After depositing her gloves and loupe, she locked it back up. "How did it go?"

Eve opened her arms, and Lainey automatically walked into them. "It was interesting."

"Oh boy. Don't tell me we picked a bad bunch."

"No, not bad. Though, Dorothea called one of the girls spirited."

"So, an attitude?" Lainey absently rubbed circles on Eve's back as they held each other in a loose hug. She took in a deep breath, appreciating the wonderful scent that was uniquely Eve.

"She's ambitious," Eve corrected. "Something we'll have to watch. I paired her with the other young lady from France since they were butting heads from the get-go." She kissed Lainey's forehead. "Emilie is her name. And she thinks I'm a ruthless hard-ass."

Lainey snorted. "She said this to your face, or were you observing?"

"Observing. Though when I announced my presence, it didn't take her long to cover her surprise with spite."

"What does her file say?" Lainey wasn't worried about Eve's ability to handle someone like Emilie. If any concern was needed, it was for Emilie's capacity to deal with someone like Eve.

"Foster kid. She's most likely used to fighting her way out of situations. I paired her with Giselle not only because of their obvious aversion towards each other, but because they seem to be polar opposites."

"Your hope is Emilie will push Giselle, and Giselle will ground Emilie."

It was a confident statement and spot on. Eve gave up on wondering how Lainey knew her so well. It had been like that from the beginning. There was an unbreakable bond between them that defied any logic. Eve bent her head and kissed Lainey on the lips.

"You got it, baby. As for the others, I think we have a very well-rounded group. They're intelligent, talented, and focused. I believe we're in for an interesting year."

Lainey beamed. "Perfect. Now, I'm ready to go home and see the kiddos. Are you?"

"Absolutely."

# Five

*E*ve covered her mouth with the back of her hand as she yawned. The week had been long and tedious, and she was giving herself ten more minutes to work. Then she was out of here. Sumptor Gallery would soon hold its first showing in months, and Eve volunteered to stay late and finish a few last minute details while Lainey went home to be with the kids. Of course, Lainey only agreed if Eve promised not to be much longer. *Ten more minutes*, Eve thought again as she put in her ear pods. Once they connected, she ordered Siri to call Lainey. *Doesn't hurt to talk while I work.*

"Hello, my love. Are you on your way home?"

Lainey's soft voice always brought a smile to Eve's face. "Almost, baby. Just a couple more things to do, then I'm out. How did I do this before? I'm exhausted." The lilt of laughter touched Eve's ear, causing her to shiver.

"I think we've all gotten used to being a little more . . . relaxed."

"Relaxed," Eve repeated. "Is that the word you use for lazy?"

Lainey tsked. "We are not lazy. I seem to remember you having a *lot* of stamina last night. And this morning."

"Mmm. With you, everything inside my body comes alive."

"Ahem. Maybe we should continue this conversation when you get home. By the way, Princess Bella has waited up for you."

Eve chuckled. "Oh, she has? I best wrap things up here, then. Did she get a call?"

"No," Lainey sighed. "I have a feeling she has stopped waiting, and I don't know whether or not to talk to her about it."

Eve shook her head. *Goddamn it, Adam.* "I believe you're right. As for talking to her about it, let's discuss that later tonight. She's already told me not to wake her up if he calls late, and I imagine after tonight, she'll have more opinions about it."

"She's four, Eve. Bella shouldn't have to worry about things like this. Her biggest worry should be whether to play with her dolls or her cars."

"I know, baby. Things would be so much easier if Adam would just consent to terminate his parental rights."

"He won't, my love. I have no doubt he loves Bella, but even so, he wouldn't consent out of spite for me. Nor will he allow Bella to be a Sumptor."

"There's a way, baby. There's always a way."

Lainey chuckled. "I learned a long time ago not to doubt your abilities. Now, why don't you pack it in for the night? I miss you, and I'd like to feel you put some of those abilities to use."

Eve drew in a sharp breath. "I'm on my way. I love you."

"I love you, too. Be careful, okay?"

"Always." Eve ended the call and checked the entrance to ensure it was locked. She remembered a time when she could find things to do that would keep her at the gallery until the wee hours of the morning. Now she was hurrying through the building, making sure lights were off, picking up her stuff, and heading out the back door with a smile.

"Eve."

"Shit!" Eve gripped her keys defensively as she spun around. "What the hell are you doing here, Adam?"

Adam stepped out of the shadows into the dim yellow light that barely lit the back alleyway. "We need to talk."

"Then you come to my house like a normal person. You don't skulk in a dark alley and jump out at someone." Eve relaxed marginally but kept her keys at the ready. She wasn't afraid of Adam, really. However, she wasn't altogether trusting either. He had changed in so many ways since their divorce. Even before, if she was being honest with herself.

"I wasn't skulking." Adam let his eyes roam over his ex-wife. The faded jeans clung to her tightly like a needy lover. And the white V-neck t-shirt dipped low enough to make his pulse jump. That only pissed him off. "Besides, isn't *she* there?"

"My wife? Or my daughter?"

Eve could tell she hit a nerve when Adam's nostril flared. She didn't care, though. This was the first time she'd heard from her ex-husband since Reghan sent him papers outlining Eve's intent to allow Lainey to adopt Bella and the name change. Adam had even missed three scheduled calls. Even at four, Bella had hit her limit. She was no longer sad when the call didn't come. In fact, after being sad about the first missed call, the next missed ones, Bella went on with her night as though nothing was wrong.

"Bella is *our* daughter, not Lainey's."

"You're wrong. Lainey is the one who is taking care of her right now. She's the one who dries Bella's tears when you don't call. She's the one who fixes her boo-boos when she gets hurt."

"Because she *stole* you from me!" Adam yelled.

Eve shook her head. "We were talking about Bella, not me. That's your problem, Adam. You can't take me out of the equation when it comes to your daughter. Not when you talk to her and apparently not when you're talking *about* her."

Adam scrubbed his face with his hands. He hadn't shaved in a few days, giving him the beginnings of a full beard. This wasn't going how he imagined it. When he decided to talk to Eve face to face, he convinced himself that Eve would remember how they were together and come back to him. There was an inkling of hope, though, since Eve was alone at the gallery.

"Look, I came here to talk to you one on one to see how you really feel. Is this what you want, Eve? To kick me out of your life completely?" Adam took a step closer. "We were good together. You know, I can still remember the night you told me you were in love with me."

"Adam, don't."

Another step. "You remember it, too, don't you? The night you were shot because of her, you said, 'I'm so in love with you.' Tell me you remember."

"You don't want to have this conversation with me, Adam. Believe me." Eve watched as Adam took another step. She tightened her grip on her keys again, pressing the unlock button simultaneously.

"Why not? Are you afraid it'll make you remember how you feel about me?"

Eve sighed. "When did you become so delusional? Do you really want the truth, Adam?"

"Tell me, beautiful."

Eve's skin crawled at the old "pet" name. It was a term she used to enjoy hearing him say, and now it just sounded like desperation.

"I wasn't saying that to you," Eve confessed. "Lainey had just gone back to her husband, and frankly, I didn't want to be alone anymore. But it was *Lainey* I wanted to be saying those words to, Adam. You just happened to be there."

"That's bullshit! I saw it in your eyes! You even told that Billy guy I was the love of your life."

*Tread carefully, Eve,* she told herself. Then nearly laughed because she had already made an enormous splash, and there was no coming back from that, so she'd have to ride the waves she just created.

"I've apologized enough, Adam. But I admit, I shouldn't have married you. It was selfish. And there's Bella, so I can't regret it. I do regret hurting you, though." Eve saw the flicker of optimism in Adam's eyes. *Time to put this to rest for good.* "I loved you, Adam. But I wasn't *in* love with you. I told Billy that to keep him off balance. But I've been in love with Lainey from the moment I met her. Ideally, I would like us to be cordial, for Bella's sake. However, you must know that there's no future for you and me, Adam. Lainey is the true love of my life."

Adam saw red. Fucking Lainey. Fucking Eve! They had both ruined his life. He took another step—this one full of menace—towards Eve. "Why should you get everything you want while I lose everything?"

"Back away from me. First, I deserve something good in life. I've lived through hell. Second, we came to a very lucrative deal for you in our divorce. You can't blame me for how you've mishandled your business or finances. You can't be bothered with calling your daughter, so I can't imagine that's a sore spot for you." Eve took a moment to compose herself. She should've been on her way home, not having a contentious conversation with an ex who shouldn't even be here. "Give me an amount, Adam, and let's get this over with. I need to get home to my family."

Before Eve knew what happened, Adam had her pressed against the car, his hand wrapped around her throat. Despite her predicament, fear wasn't the first emotion she felt. It was rage. Eve's knee connected with Adam in a swift, sharp movement in his most sensitive area. When he released her and bent to catch his breath, Eve pushed him away from her with a force she didn't know she possessed, sending Adam to his ass. She kneeled next to him as he wheezed.

"Wrong move. That's the last time you'll ever touch me. You thought you had lost everything before? Now you'll know what that really means."

***

"Hey..."

"Lainey, Adam is in town." Eve wished she didn't have to burst her wife's good mood, but she needed to warn Lainey.

"What? Why? Where?"

A weary sigh escaped Eve. "He was in the alley waiting for me when I walked out of the gallery."

"Why is he creeping around? What does he want?"

"We'll talk about it when I get home, baby. But if he somehow shows up at the house before I get there, don't let him in. He's agitated and delusional."

"He thought you'd take him back, didn't he?" Anger rose in Lainey. Fucking Adam. Why the hell couldn't he just accept the fact that Eve didn't love him anymore? Why wouldn't he just leave them alone?

"I'll tell you about it when I get home, okay?" Eve repeated. She knew Lainey would be pissed when Eve told her what happened, so Eve wanted to collect her thoughts and calm herself before getting into it.

"Eve."

"I promise, baby. I'll tell you everything. I'm twenty minutes out, okay? I don't want Bella to know he's here. Not with how he's acting."

"Fine. Just hurry. But be careful. I love you, Eve."

Eve smiled. "I love you, too, Lainey. See you soon."

---

EVE PULLED into her driveway and looked around before stepping out. Adam's outburst had unnerved her. If he could show up unexpectedly with delusions, what else was he capable of? She had sole custody of Bella, but would Adam go back on their agreement? The agreement she paid millions for? If she had to pay more, she would. If she had to take Adam to court and forcefully terminate his parental rights, she would. Especially after what he did to her tonight. Eve could no longer trust Adam with Bella.

Lainey wrenched open the front door as soon as Eve hit the first step of the porch. With the next step, Lainey was in Eve's arms.

"Are you okay?"

Eve held on tight to Lainey, basking in the softness of her body. She inhaled deeply, taking in Lainey's scent that always calmed her.

"I'm fine, baby. Come on, let's get inside." Eve closed and locked the door behind them. "Is Bella still awake?"

"Yes, of course. She wanted to wait up for Momma. We'll get her ready for bed, read her a story, tuck her in, and then you're going to tell me everything that happened."

Eve smiled down at Lainey and gave her a quick kiss. "Sounds like a plan."

"Momma!"

Eve kneeled to catch a running Bella. "Hey, my sweet girl. Did you miss me?"

"Yeah! Mommy gave me ous cweam and pwayed go fish wif me!"

"Ice cream, huh?" Eve looked up at Lainey with a sly grin.

Lainey put her hands on her hips and looked at Bella with feigned betrayal. "I thought that was our little secret, missy!"

"Oopsie," Bella giggled. "I din't tell momma dat we ate it all!"

Eve laughed. "I'll pretend I didn't hear that." She tickled Bella, making her giggle even louder. "Did you at least share with your brothers?"

"Nope! Dey goed to dere rooms, so me and mommy ate it alllll!"

"Well, that will teach them, won't it? And it'll teach me to stay at work so late, huh?"

"Yep!"

Eve shook her head at her daughter's silliness. *This* is how Bella's life needs to be all the time. Full of happiness and sneaky ice cream dates with Lainey. Eve would be damned if she let Adam ruin that for her.

"Okay, my *extra* sweet girl, are you ready for mommy and me to tuck you in?"

"Story?"

"Of course. Whose turn is it? Mine or mommy's?"

Bella tilted her head and tapped her chin. She looked up at Lainey, then back at Eve, and tapped again. "Hmm." She pointed at Lainey. "Mommy's!"

Eve knew all too well it was her turn to read Bella a bedtime story. However, she also knew that Lainey didn't just *read* the stories. Oh no, she changed voices and acted out some of the parts. Eve couldn't compete with that. She tried to do the voices, but she would never measure up to Mommy's caliber.

"I see how it is. Pick the one who gave you the ice cream." Eve's eyebrows shot up when Bella gave her a cocky grin. *Oh boy. I'm in so much trouble with this one.* "You better get your little booty in gear. Go brush your teeth. We'll be right behind you."

"'Kay!" Bella took off in a half-run/half-walk, her little "booty" sashaying away with all the self-satisfied attitude a four-year-old could conjure up.

"Do you fear the day she becomes a teenager as much as I do?" Lainey asked as she stared at the retreating girl.

"More."

"TALK." Lainey closed their bedroom door and leaned against it, crossing her arms. She didn't know what the whole story was yet, but she already felt the urge to do harm to Adam.

Eve could see the ire building in Lainey already. *At least it's not directed at me.*

"Can we at least get into bed first?"

"Eve."

*Oh, that's a tone I don't want to mess with.* Eve sighed and sank down on the bed, beckoning Lainey to her. After a millisecond of hesitation, Lainey acquiesced. Eve pulled her close when Lainey was within arm's reach, holding her around the waist. Then she told Lainey everything, tightening her grip when Lainey became furious.

"He put his fucking hands on you?"

Eve's eyebrow jumped. Lainey rarely said that word. When she did, Eve knew it was because Lainey was beyond pissed.

"Something he'll never do again, baby," Eve soothed.

"You're damn right he won't. If he does, I'll kill him."

Despite the threat that tumbled out of Lainey's mouth, Eve grinned. "I appreciate you protecting me, but I'd rather have you here than in prison for murder."

Lainey rolled her eyes. "Figure of speech. But I wouldn't mind throat punching him. Or maybe giving him another knee in the crotch." Lainey blew out a frustrated breath and sat down next to Eve. "You know what sucks?"

"This whole situation?"

"Yes. But also the fact that I know how he feels. I've been where he is, Eve." Lainey closed her eyes, gathering her thoughts. When she opened them up again, they were shining with unshed tears. "My heart shattered every time you said you loved him. I would smile at you and encourage you while I was dying inside. Then you asked me to be your matron of honor. At first, I thought you were punishing me. I was sure you knew how I felt about you, yet you still asked me. God, it killed me standing beside you, listening to you say 'I do' to someone else."

"Lainey . . ."

"Let me finish, please? I don't know if I'll ever have the courage to say this again." Lainey entwined her fingers with Eve's purely for the connection. "Then you got pregnant." She hesitated, drawing in a deep breath. Eve had already been through so much. Was it wise to be saying all of this? Lainey looked Eve in the eye and saw nothing but love shining back. Marriage was all about the good and the bad, right? Once this was all said, it never needed to be repeated. "I knew that baby would never be ours, and I died a little inside each time I saw Adam touch your stomach the way I wanted to." She scoffed. "Plus all the other implications I didn't want to think about. He was with you when you went into labor while I was in the waiting room. I never regretted my decision to stay with Jack as much as I did right then. So, yeah. It sucks that I know how Adam feels. He and I are so much alike when it comes to you."

Eve's heart broke with Lainey's confession, but she was quick with her disagreement.

"You're nothing like Adam, baby. You never once threatened me or put your hands around my neck, even feeling all those things. I wish you and I hadn't wasted so much time apart. I have so many regrets. Letting you go is the one that hurts my soul the most. Bella helps, but like you, I wanted her to be ours. And she will be. But please do not think you're anything like him. *He's* not even the man I thought he was. I don't know him anymore. I *do* know you. And I know you would never do what Adam did."

"That's not true, though, is it?" Lainey said miserably. "I've hit you."

Eve frowned. "When . . .?" As soon as the question was out, Eve remembered. When she closed her eyes, Eve could see that day so vividly. God, how she hated herself for what she said to Lainey.

"I deserved that," Eve said softly.

"Bullshit. I had no right . . . ."

"After the awful things I said to you, Lainey, you had every right. But if you want to know the truth, that isn't what hurt me the most that day. What hurt me was the pain in your eyes. What devastated me was the truth behind the emotion when you said you hated me."

"I didn't mean that." Lainey turned to Eve, tucking her foot under her leg as it hung off the bed. "I hated what you said. But I could never hate you."

Eve cupped Lainey's cheek in her palm. "Can we forgive each other and ourselves for that night?"

"I thought we had," Lainey answered tearfully.

"I think we've done a good job of forgiving each other. Maybe we're on the road to forgiving ourselves?"

Lainey inhaled through her nose, held it for a moment as she counted to ten, then let it out slowly through her mouth. It was a technique Ellie taught Lainey to center herself.

"What are we going to do, Eve? Is he going to take Bella from us?"

Eve shook her head. "He fucked up the moment he laid his hands on me. I've already texted Reghan, and she's going to file first thing in the morning. It's no longer about Adam's consent." She crawled up on the bed and leaned back on the headboard, holding her arms open. "Come here, baby."

Lainey didn't hesitate to take her favorite place in the world. In Eve's arms. As she snuggled close, she listened to Eve's heartbeat. Adam could have taken that away from her tonight. Was he more of a threat than just taking Bella away from them?

"I wasn't scared," Eve said suddenly. "Even with his hand around my throat, I wasn't scared. Do you know why?"

Too choked up to respond, Lainey shook her head.

"Because I know that you'd be there for Bella if anything ever happened to me. That gives me more peace than you'll ever know. Plus," Eve bowed her head to kiss the top of Lainey's, "I was too angry to be scared."

Lainey closed her eyes and imagined the scene. In her head, she fast-forwarded to the part where Eve kneed Adam in the balls. She drifted into a calmness. A small smile formed on her lips, playing that part on a loop to fuel her dreams.

"Are you smiling?"

"Maybe," Lainey yawned.

"You're thinking about me kneeing him, aren't you?"

"Maybe," Lainey repeated with a silent chuckle. "It's better than thinking about the alternative. And if I keep that in my head, maybe I won't have nightmares."

Eve squeezed Lainey closer to her. "I'll keep the nightmares at bay." She kissed the top of Lainey's head. "Want to take a bath?"

Lainey exhaled, ridding herself of all the negative energy she held as Eve told her what had happened. "How about a quick shower? Then I really want you to just hold me all night. Is that okay?"

"That sounds perfect, baby." Eve knew her wife better than anyone. Once agitated, it took a while for her to calm her mind completely. The one thing that always helped was a quiet evening simply being in each other's presence.

Six

"Good morning, baby. I made coffee." Eve smiled at Lainey, accepting a sweet kiss.

"I smelled it from the bedroom. It's like heaven." Lainey took a mug from the cabinet and filled it with the aromatic liquid. "Mmm, extra bold. Perfect."

"You're perfect," Eve winked.

Eve could still make Lainey blush as easily as she did when they first met. "Where are the kids?"

"Classes," Eve answered with a smirk. Lainey always changed the subject when she was flustered. "They were finishing up breakfast when I came in."

"Early," Lainey muttered. "Is it weird that I'm looking forward to the weekend? I enjoy making breakfast for them and spending time together."

"Not weird at all. They're different animals when it's a school day. Darren has enough time for a high-five, Kevin mutters a 'mornin'." Eve slanted a look at her wife. Like mother, like son, she thought with amusement. "And Bella…" she shook her head. "That girl has energy to spare. I would blame the ice cream from last night if she wasn't like that every morning."

Lainey chuckled. "I'm guessing she quickly gave you a kiss before grabbing Lexie and telling her everything they would do today in class?"

"Ding ding." Eve touched the tip of her nose. "Get this woman a prize."

Lainey set her coffee down on the counter and wrapped her arms around Eve's waist. "I'll take you as my prize."

Eve's eyebrows raised as she touched her forehead to Lainey's. "Oh yeah? Well, who am I to deny you?" She dipped her head and pressed her lips to Lainey's. "Wanna play hooky?"

"If it means staying here at the house until we know Adam has gone back to New York, absolutely."

"Are you that worried about him, baby?"

"Aren't you?" Lainey laid her head on Eve's shoulder. Despite being in the safe cocoon of Eve's arms the night before, Lainey's brain couldn't rid itself of the images of Adam hurting Eve. He *knew* everything Eve had been through, and he still did that to her.

"I worry about you worrying about him."

Lainey rolled her eyes, giving Eve a playful slap on the arm. "You don't have to act tough with me, Eve. You were tense last night. What he did affected you more than you want to admit."

Eve drew in a breath, letting it out as she nodded. "You're right. You always see more than I care to show." She sighed. "He's changed so much, baby. I don't like how unpredictable he's become." Eve checked her watch. "Reghan should call soon. I think when everything with Bella and the adoption is in motion, I'll feel better."

Before Lainey could respond, the doorbell sounded throughout the house. Eve picked up a remote and turned on a monitor on the opposite wall of the kitchen. She frowned when she saw two uniformed police officers flanking two other men in jeans and suit jackets.

"If Adam pressed charges on you for kneeing him, I swear..."

Eve pressed a finger to Lainey's lips. "No swearing anything illegal, baby. Let's go see what this is about, shall we?"

Lainey followed Eve to the front door. A sinking feeling in her stomach had her feeling nauseous. She couldn't say why she suddenly felt a sense of dread she hadn't felt since Tony showed up at Eve's gallery, but it scared her. Illegal or not, if Adam did something to get Eve in trouble, he would get an ear full from Lainey.

Eve rubbed Lainey's arm before opening the door. "Yes?"

"Eve Sumptor?" The taller of the two men asked gruffly.

"That's me."

The man stepped back, allowing the uniformed officers to get by. "You're under arrest."

"What?" Lainey attempted to get between the officers and Eve, but Eve gently pushed her back. She knew Eve was protecting her, but damn it, Lainey was trying to protect Eve! Fucking Adam! "She didn't do anything! Whatever he said she did, he's lying!"

The man briefly glanced at Lainey before nodding to the officers. The woman officer politely asked Eve to turn around and put her hands behind her back.

"What is the charge?" Eve asked, refusing to budge until she knew what this was about.

The man's partner spoke up. "You're under arrest for the murder of Adam Riley. You have the right to remain silent..."

Eve couldn't hear the Miranda Warning over the ringing in her ears. *Murder?*

"Murder?" Lainey's breath caught in her throat. Adam was... dead? This wasn't happening. "You're making a mistake. Eve didn't... she was here with me." Lainey continued to plead with the officers, but those pleas fell on deaf ears. She looked at Eve, who was in a state of shock. That was Lainey's only explanation for Eve's silence and the far-off look in Eve's eyes. "Eve?"

"Bella." Eve's voice cracked when she said her daughter's name.

"I have her, my love." Lainey knew what Eve needed from her. Eve needed to know Lainey would take care of Bella and break this news to her gently if Eve couldn't do it herself. But Lainey told herself this was all a misunderstanding, and Eve would be home in no time.

"Call Reghan."

"I will. Everything will be okay, honey." Please let everything be okay. There wasn't a single doubt in Lainey's heart or head that Eve was innocent. The authorities would see that soon enough. "I'll be right behind you!" she called out as the cops hauled Eve to their cruiser.

"No! Please, Lainey, stay with Bella. Please."

Lainey had only heard Eve sound desperate once before—when Tony had a gun to Lainey's head. As fiercely as Lainey wanted to be there with Eve, she agreed Bella was the priority right now.

"Mom?"

Lainey whirled around to see Kevin standing there, looking as confused as she felt. "Kevin, you should be in class."

"What's happening?"

"A terrible mistake, that's all. Nothing to worry about." Lainey pulled out her phone. Her hands shook violently as she tried to remember what the hell she was doing. She felt warm hands around hers and looked up at her oldest son. The compassion in his eyes nearly broke her. "I—I have to call Reghan."

"Okay." Kevin gently took the phone from his mom's hands. He was scared. Kevin had never seen his mom like this before. Whatever the hell was going on, it was huge. He scrolled down to Reghan's number and hesitated before making the call. Normally, Kevin could rely on his mom for guidance. But he didn't think he'd get much of that right now. *Well, time to man up. Maybe when I get Ms. Brannigan on the phone, mom will snap out of it.*

"Reghan Brannigan."

"Um, Ms. Brannigan? This is Kevin Sumptor. Um, Eve and Lainey Sumptor's son."

"Yes, of course. What can I do for you?"

"Um, I'm not sure." Kevin looked at his mom, but she was still looking at the door where Eve had disappeared. "They took Eve."

"Who took Eve?"

"The, uh, cops." *Crap. Now what?* Kevin just happened to walk in at the very end of whatever that was. "I don't know..."

Lainey snatched the phone away from Kevin yet held onto him as though she needed support to stay standing. "They arrested Eve, Reghan."

Reghan was immediately alert from the fear in Lainey's voice. "On what charges?"

"M—murder."

"What!" Kevin's eyes widened in dismay. He knew they teased Eve about being a mobster, but he didn't believe Eve could be capable of killing anyone.

"Excuse me?" Reghan was out of her seat and gathering her things as she spoke. "Who did she allegedly murder?"

Lainey's entire body felt numb. All she could see was Eve being taken away in handcuffs. All she could hear was, "you're under arrest for the murder of Adam Riley." If she didn't pull herself together, Lainey wouldn't be able to do the one thing Eve needed her to do. Take care of Bella.

"Adam." An audible gasp came from the phone and from Kevin beside her.

Reghan's mind was reeling. She had received a text from Eve the night before telling her to expedite the paperwork for parental termination after Eve's encounter with Adam. Of course, Eve had given what Reghan thought of as the condensed version of what happened, but she couldn't see that situation turning into murder. And it wasn't like Eve to lie.

"Do you know what precinct?"

"Oh, God. I don't! Reghan, she wouldn't let me follow her. Eve made me promise to stay here for Bella."

"Lainey, it's okay. I'll find her, and we'll get this sorted. You take care of that little girl, and I'll call you when I know something."

Lainey looked at her phone. "She hung up," she said absently.

"Mom? Hey, look at me." Kevin waited until Lainey's eyes met his. "What can I do?"

"I—I don't know."

"Do you want me to call Ellie? Or Rebecca?"

Lainey shook her head. "No, no. I don't think Eve would want them to know about this. At least, not yet. There's no need to worry them about something that's obviously a mistake." *Please let the police be mistaken about Adam being dead.* Lainey wasn't a fan of Adam's, but she would never wish for his death. She loved Bella—and Eve—too much for that.

"Okay, so?" Kevin looked around, feeling a little lost. Suddenly, their beautiful home seemed a little colder. "Tell me how to help, mom. Should we keep this from Darren? Maybe, um, wait for Eve to get back before telling Bella? I mean, they can't keep her, right? She didn't do it."

Lainey leaned on Kevin, thankful for his strength. She was going to need it until she got Eve back. Lainey just hoped she could keep it together for the next couple of hours. She had to believe Eve would be released by then. Otherwise, Lainey didn't know how she would cope.

"We'll wait until we have more information," Lainey said finally. "You need to get back to your classes."

"Mom..."

"Kevin, please. Eve wouldn't want this to interrupt your studies. I'm going to wait for Eve... or Reghan to call me with what to do, okay? Things will be difficult when we have to tell Bella about—Adam. Let's give her a few more hours of normalcy."

"Yeah, okay." Kevin blew out a breath and scrubbed his head with frustration. "This blows. I mean, why the hell..."

"Language."

The teen rolled his eyes, his lips twitching even at this crucial moment. He was nearly eighteen, and his mom was still censoring his mild cursing.

"Sorry. But I don't understand any of this. Eve would never hurt anyone."

"I know, honey. Reghan will sort it out. For now, try to concentrate on school. I may have to leave for a bit, so I need you to make sure you're here for Bella, okay? I know I'm asking a lot of you..."

"Mom, that's what I'm here for. Eve and Bella are my family. I have Bella and Darren covered. You just focus on bringing Momma Eve home."

Lainey's smile trembled. *Momma Eve.* She wished she could promise Kevin that she would. But the sinking feeling in her stomach felt heavier every minute that passed.

"I'll do my best. I'll text you when I find out what's happening, but don't miss classes. Got it?"

"Got it. But Mom, if you need me, that's more important than class. Got it?"

Lainey sniffed and hugged her son. "Got it."

She watched Kevin walk away, turning back to look at her once before disappearing into the study. There was only a slight hesitation before Lainey lifted her phone and made another call.

"It's Lainey Sumptor. I think we need you."

---

"I'M DETECTIVE RUIZ, and this is my partner, Detective Ashford. Do you understand why you're here?"

Nothing.

"What was the nature of your relationship with Mr. Riley? Was it amicable? Contentious?" Detective Ashford tried, tapping a folder that lay in front of him.

Nothing.

"Ms. Sumptor, you're not doing yourself any favors by not talking to us."

Eve merely looked at the detective. It was on the tip of her tongue to correct his prefix but wouldn't give him the satisfaction. She knew these tactics. She has used these tactics.

"Look, we can't help you unless you tell us your side. Things happen, right? We've been in the business long enough to know that. So, what happened? Things got intense, and he came at you? Are we looking at self-defense?" Nothing. Detective Ruiz sighed. "Tell us why you asked your ex-husband to come here, Ms. Sumptor."

Eve's eyebrow twitched at that, yet she remained silent. She could ask for her lawyer, and this "interview" would be over. But Eve was curious about what they knew. They arrested her mere hours after her confrontation with Adam. That told Eve they were sure they had the right person. But why? Any surveillance they had would show Eve walked away and Adam was very much alive. This was the perfect situation where the less you talked, the more blanks others filled in for you. So, she kept her mouth shut and let the detectives keep revealing tidbits.

"You have a daughter with the deceased, correct?" When Eve didn't answer, Detective Ashford continued. "Was he trying to take custody from you? Or was he threatening to tell your current partner about the affair?"

Another "tidbit," Eve thought grimly. They're grasping at straws if they thought she was having an affair with Adam. They were also trying to rile her up by calling Lainey her "current partner" instead of her wife. Unfortunately for them, Eve was an expert at schooling her emotions.

"Ms. Sumptor..."

"My client will not be saying anything else." Reghan burst through the door with confidence and purpose.

"Your client hasn't said anything yet," Ruiz argued. "Maybe you could get her to understand that cooperating will only help her."

"Cooperate?" Reghan looked down at Eve's hands that were hand-cuffed to the table. "You have her cuffed to the table like a violent criminal, and you want her to cooperate? Are those necessary?"

There was hesitation on the part of the detectives. Eve imagined that was a scare tactic used for two-bit criminals who didn't know their ass from their rights. It would have been laughable had Eve not been offended. First, she wasn't a criminal, especially not a stupid one. Second, Eve most certainly knew her rights. And third, these detectives were teddy bears compared to the people she had come across in her life. Whatever they were looking for, they wouldn't get it from her. With that realization, they finally uncuffed her.

"Thank you." Reghan put up a hand to stall any questions from the detectives. "I need to speak with my client alone, please."

Ruiz sighed as he got up, gesturing to his partner. "Fine. But if we don't get answers soon, we're taking her to arraignment."

Once the detectives were out of the room, Reghan pulled a chair next to Eve and sat down. "What the hell happened?"

Eve rubbed the red welts around her wrists. "That's a good question. Did you talk to Lainey? Is that why you're here? How is she? How's Bella?"

"Eve, we need to focus on your life right now."

"They *are* my life, Reghan."

Reghan sighed. "Kevin called me."

Eve's brows shot up. "Kevin? How... why?"

"I don't know, Eve. I received a very nervous call from your son saying they took you. Then Lainey got on the phone. If I'm honest, she sounded confused and scared."

Eve closed her eyes. Once again, she was bringing turmoil into

Lainey's life. Only this time, Eve had no idea what was happening. For someone as meticulous as Eve, being in the dark was dangerous.

"Is he really... dead?" Eve asked finally.

Reghan nodded. "Yes, unfortunately. My assistants had confirmed it by the time I got here. I need to know what happened last night, Eve."

"I told you what happened, Reghan. Adam showed up, I said things he didn't want to hear, he put his hands on me, and I kneed and pushed him, and he fell. He was very much alive when I left."

"Is that what you told the detectives?"

"I invoked my right to stay silent."

"Good. That's best. Are you sure Adam was okay? Maybe he hit his head when he fell, and you didn't notice?"

Eve leaned forward, looking Reghan in the eye. "He fell on his ass, Reghan. He was *alive* and well when I left," she repeated. "He was pissed off and cursing me as I drove away. Adam is Bella's father. If he had been hurt, I would have called an ambulance."

Reghan had been an attorney for a long time. She liked to pride herself on being able to tell when someone was lying to her. Eve, however, was hard to read. Reghan's gut told her there was more going on here that neither she nor Eve knew about. Starting with what the authorities had on Eve that caused them to arrest her so quickly.

"Okay, we definitely need more information here. Let's get you to arraignment where we can get you out on bail, and I can discover what evidence they allegedly have on you."

"How long will that take?"

Reghan looked at her watch. It was still reasonably early. Though experience has taught her that if the detectives wanted to be spiteful, they could technically hold Eve for forty-eight hours before taking her to be arraigned. Since Eve didn't cooperate, Reghan imagined this would be the perfect opportunity for the detectives to make things difficult for Eve.

"I'll see what I can find out. In the meantime, they'll take you to booking..."

"Booking," Eve interrupted. "Meaning I'll have a mugshot and my fingerprints taken?"

"Correct."

"Reghan, I can't have that on my record. The art world will never work with me again. My reputation will be ruined."

It wasn't the first time her reputation had been in the crosshairs of someone wanting to destroy her. But Eve thought that part of her life was dead and buried. Literally. Who the hell was doing this to her now? And why?

"Eve, I will do everything I can to get you out of this. Once I do, we'll work on getting the arrest expunged."

"Don't just get me 'out of this,' Reghan. Find out what the hell is going on and stop it from getting worse. This *arrest* happened extremely fast, and I want to know why."

A slight shiver ran through Reghan. She wasn't easily intimidated, not even by Eve Sumptor. But this Eve was different. A hardened, calculating woman replaced the generous, patient wife and mother of three that Eve was to her core. Reghan almost felt sorry for whoever put Eve in this situation. And if Reghan didn't get Eve out of it—well, she didn't want to think about that.

"I will. Eve, the next few hours are going to be tough. You'll be in lock-up until they transport you to arraignment. That's where we'll find out what the official charges are and request bail."

"If they deny bail?"

"Let's take this one step at a time, okay? Is there anything you need?"

"Lainey."

Reghan felt the sorrow, need, hope, and love wrapped up in that one whispered name.

"I'll make sure she's at the arraignment."

# Seven

The click of Lainey's heels reverberated through the nearly empty corridor of the courthouse as she paced. Her heart hadn't stopped pounding since she received the call from Reghan to meet here for Eve's arraignment. She scoffed silently. It hadn't stopped pounding since the authorities took Eve from her. That was four hours and thirty-six minutes ago.

"Lainey?"

Lainey spun around at Reghan's voice. She desperately searched for her wife, to no avail. "Where is Eve?"

Reghan took Lainey's arm and guided her towards a bench. "The LAPD is transporting her here. She's fine, Lainey."

"Fine? She's been arrested for the murder of her daughter's father. There's no way she is fine, Reghan."

Reghan sighed as she checked her email on her phone. She was waiting for word that the prosecution had sent over their discovery. "Eve will need you to be strong for her, Lainey," she said distractedly.

Lainey snatched the phone from Reghan's hands. "I don't need you to tell me to be strong for my wife. I have that covered. What I need you to do is *focus* on how you're going to get Eve out of this mess."

Startled by Lainey's rare show of aggression, Reghan was speechless for a moment. That was something that never happened. "I am *completely* focused on Eve, Lainey, believe me." She held her hand out for her phone. "I'm waiting on confirmation that prosecution has sent over evidence."

Lainey lowered her eyes as she handed Reghan the phone. She hadn't meant to lash out like that. Fear had that effect on people. "I'm sorry..."

"Don't be. I prefer you kicking my ass than the alternative."

Lainey appreciated Reghan's straight talk. Eve made the right choice by hiring Reghan to be her in-house counsel. They needed someone who wouldn't coddle but who would fight tooth and nail for them. Reghan fit that bill. "Did they send the evidence? I want to know what it is."

Reghan rechecked her email and frowned. "No, they didn't."

"Is that a good or bad thing for Eve today?"

"I'm hesitant to tell you it's positive. This all happened so fast that I'm unsure what the D.A. sent to the judge. I detest feeling unprepared, and I can't help but think that's exactly what they planned."

"To catch Eve, and ultimately those around her, off guard?"

"Precisely." Reghan checked her watch. "Come on. Arraignment starts in ten minutes. They should bring Eve in soon." She stopped Lainey before they entered the courtroom. "I asked her if she needed anything. She said you. I know you don't need me to tell you *anything* concerning Eve and your love for her. But I thought you should know how vulnerable she is right now."

Lainey nodded and followed Reghan in. She sat on the bench right behind the defendant's table and took a breath. It was futile to try to relax, but Lainey wouldn't outwardly show her fear. Eve would see it, but the rest of the court would see a woman who believed in her wife. It was the truth. Lainey knew deep in her soul that Eve was innocent. The problem was, Lainey knew the lengths enemies would go to bring Eve down. *But who?*

*Vulnerable.* Lainey had seen Eve vulnerable before. In many ways. Today, Lainey was positive she would see a confident woman walk into this courtroom. Eve would make eye contact with everyone, even those who set out to put her behind bars. She would show them they don't intimidate her. Eve would stand tall and proud. She would speak clearly and respectfully when spoken to. And when Eve looked at Lainey, Lainey would see the pain, the fear, the confusion no one else saw. The realization that Eve showed even a little of that to Reghan meant the prosecution's tactics were working. Eve was off balance. Lainey hoped her presence helped center Eve.

The air changed around Lainey, and she looked up in time to see a side door open and two armed men bringing Eve in. Their hands were wrapped tightly around Eve's elbows, causing Lainey to flinch. Even with all the therapy Eve had been through, this could still trigger terrible memories. Lainey waited for Eve's eyes to reach her, then tried to convey all her love in one look. When Eve smiled—albeit a small smile— Lainey's pounding heart calmed.

"Are you okay?" Lainey whispered once Eve was seated in front of her.

Eve glanced at Reghan and received a quick nod before turning to Lainey. "I'm... glad you're here. Bella?"

Lainey blew out a breath. "She doesn't know anything yet. I wanted to wait until..."

Eve nodded. She was grateful Lainey chose to wait. In the best-case scenario—if there was one in this situation—Eve would be home, charges would be dropped, and she could hold Bella as Eve told her about Adam. Worst case? Well, Lainey could break the bad news to Bella all at once. That had to be better than . . .

"All rise for the Honorable Judge Craig Patrick."

Everyone in the courtroom stood as the judge walked in. He was a white-haired man in his fifties if Eve judged correctly.

"Be seated," Judge Patrick ordered. He picked up the docket in front of him. "The Court calls the State of California versus Eve Sumptor, case number 405. This matter is scheduled for arraignment and bail recommendations hearing today. State your appearance for the record, please."

"District Attorney Peter Howell and Assistant District Attorney Sloan Cross appearing for the State of California."

Reghan carefully schooled her emotions. "Eve Sumptor appears personally and by her attorney Reghan Brannigan, your Honor."

Judge Patrick looked at Eve as though he were trying to get a read on her before continuing. "Very well. It has come to my attention that State has filed only partial Information for this case?"

"Correct, your Honor. Due to the promptness of this arraignment, we haven't had time to get all Information filed. But the Court has most of it."

"Your Honor," Reghan began. "I haven't received any Information."

"It should be on its way, your Honor," D.A. Howell responded.

"Very well. The law is, then, that if the Information is not filed within thirty days of the bind over, the matter is dismissed without prejudice. Objections?"

"No objections, your Honor," Reghan said politely.

"No, your Honor," Howell agreed.

"Eve Sumptor, please stand."

Eve stood along with Reghan.

"You are accused of one count of murder in the first degree and one count of conspiracy to commit murder. How do you plead?"

"Not guilty," Eve answered immediately.

"The court accepts the plea of not guilty. Before proceeding to bail motion, I want to set a deadline by which pretrial motions should be filed, if any. Ms. Brannigan, how much time do you anticipate needing for such filing?"

"Your Honor, there is potential for many motions in this case. However, since Mr. Howell has yet to provide us with discovery, we'll need to determine those motions a few days after discovery is provided. As Mrs. Sumptor and myself do not wish to prolong these proceedings, I require no more than two weeks after I get Information to know what motions need to be filed."

"Information is en route to Ms. Brannigan's office, your Honor. We have no objection to that timeline."

"Very well. We will schedule a status conference in two weeks. At this time, we will move to the matter of bail. Mr. Howell?"

"Your Honor, in this case, we ask that the defendant be remanded into custody."

"This is outrageous, your Honor!" Reghan interjected. "The authorities *arrested* my client mere hours after the alleged crime. Was there even an investigation, or did they come after Mrs. Sumptor because of who she is? I have no Discovery, no reason to believe there's any correlation between my client and the death of Mr. Riley. Furthermore, my client is a philanthropist with deep ties here. To suggest remand is preposterous."

"This is an arraignment hearing, Ms. Brannigan. There's no need for grandstanding."

Reghan nearly threw up her hands in frustration but remained poised.

"Mr. Howell, please tell the Court why you suggest remand."

"Yes, your Honor. The defendant is a recent transplant to this city. She does not have the ties the defendant's counsel is suggesting. The defendant also has the means—disposable income and a private jet—to flee at any time."

"Mrs. Sumptor is not guilty, your Honor. She isn't a flight risk when she wants nothing more than to resolve this and clear her name."

"Judge, Mrs. Sumptor has fled from authorities before, eluding the FBI for three years."

"Are you kidding? Your Honor, my client was fourteen and not a suspect. She fled because she was scared her father would kill her."

"Speaking of, your Honor. The defendant has gotten away with murder before. We will bring evidence suggesting the defendant bought her way out of a murder charge five years ago."

Lainey gasped softly. She wanted to object. She wanted to tell them how wrong they were but couldn't. She wouldn't jeopardize Eve's case with an outburst. Though, from Eve's rigid posture, Lainey knew Eve's temper was near the boiling point.

Reghan was floored by this accusation. She had read and reread every transcript of Eve's father's death. It was a clear open and shut, self-defense case. Why in the hell would they bring it up here?

"What are you doing?" Reghan asked Howell directly. "My client was shot while defending her wife and herself that night. She did not *murder* anyone."

"Like I said, Counselor, we'll present evidence. You should have that in discovery when you get to your office." Howell addressed the judge again. "We strongly suggested remand, your Honor, for all the reasons we stated. Eve Sumptor is a flight risk. She left New York after shooting her father. Who knows where she will go now, given a chance?"

Judge Patrick held up his hand, cutting off Reghan's rebuttal. To be honest, she had gotten away with a few disrespectful interjections without the judge holding her in contempt. So, she kept her mouth shut as he deliberated. Surely he could see this was all a ridiculous mistake.

"You both have touched on the factors the Court should consider in setting bail. Taking into account the gravity of the charges—and the Court is making no determination on guilt or innocence, mind you—I rule that the defendant be remanded into custody until trial. Officers will take Mrs. Sumptor into custody immediately. Court is adjourned."

"*Oh my God.*" Lainey couldn't breathe. This couldn't be happening.

Eve sat there until she felt hands on her, pulling her from her seat. This was happening. They were really taking her from her family. Anger was beginning to push through the confusion. Then the sorrow came. When they turned her around to cuff her, she saw Lainey staring at her. The look in Lainey's eyes broke Eve's heart. What if this was too much for Lainey? What if Eve lost everything? After conquering those who tried to tear her down in the past, she was losing to someone she couldn't see. How could you fight an invisible foe?

"*I love you,*" Eve mouthed to Lainey. Fear nearly crushed her hope that Lainey would return the sentiment.

"*I love you,*" Lainey responded with tears threatening to fall. As Eve disappeared behind the door, Lainey's heart went with her. There's no one more determined than a woman in love. She would find a way to bring Eve back to her no matter what it took. Lainey stood when Reghan came up to her. "Where are they taking her? I want to see her."

"I'm sorry, Lainey. By the time they transport her, visiting hours will be over. However," Reghan continued before Lainey could argue. "I will get you in to see her first thing in the morning. You need to remember that Eve has not been found guilty of any crime. She is not a prisoner."

"Not a prisoner," Lainey scoffed. "They *took* her from her family, Reghan. For God knows how long. I'm assuming they're not trans-porting her to some swanky hotel. And why in the hell did they bring up what happened with Tony as though Eve..." Lainey couldn't even finish the absurd notion.

"I don't know yet. As soon as I get back to the office, I will go through everything the prosecution has sent. I'll have a better idea of what we're dealing with once I see the evidence."

"*We* see the evidence," Lainey corrected. "I want you to bring it over to the house so we can go over it together."

"Lainey, there are some things only Eve's lawyer can see. Any witnesses that may be mentioned have the right to anonymity until the trial."

"Redact what you must, but I want to see everything else."

"Lainey..."

"That wasn't a request, Reghan." Lainey shot one last look at the prosecuting attorney before leaving. She was perilously close to losing every ounce of calm she had managed to squeak out during the arraignment. She could have her breakdown later. Right now, Lainey's most important goal was fighting for Eve.

---

"SLOAN!"

Sloan Cross's footsteps slowed as she turned back to face Reghan. Thankfully, Howell was already gone, rushing out to make phone calls.

"Hello, Reghan." Sloan cringed inwardly at the casualness of her voice after what her boss had just done. She knew that little stunt would ruffle feathers. And Reghan's were certainly ruffled.

"What the fuck was that?"

Sloan shook her head. "I tried to get Howell to not go forward with that, but he's determined to win this case."

"Why? What is the District Attorney's problem with my client? And why the fuck didn't you warn me about this? You *know* Eve is my client."

Sloan shushed Reghan as she dragged her to a secluded corner. "You know damn well I can't disclose that kind of information, especially to the counsel of the person we're indicting. Reghan, the case was supposed to be mine, but Howell decided to take it himself. Eve

Sumptor is a high profile defendant, and it's an election year." She looked around again. "He's going to offer a plea deal. I suggest you get your client to take it."

"My client will not agree to a plea when she's innocent." Reghan squinted at the woman in front of her. "Was Discovery really sent to my office? You can at least tell me that, can't you?"

Sloan sighed. "Yes, it was. But... delayed." She checked her watch. "It's Friday afternoon, Reghan. That gives you the weekend to review the evidence and convince your client to accept a plea. It may not be a win for you, but it's what's best for your client."

With that, Reghan watched as the woman she had been seeing for the past month walked away.

"Shit."

# Eight

Kevin rushed to the front door when he heard the locks disengage. His mom walked in, large sunglasses hiding most of her face despite the dwindling daylight.

"Mom? Where's Eve?" he asked when she quickly shut the door behind her.

Lainey slid her sunglasses atop her head, revealing red-rimmed eyes. "How long have they been out there?" she asked rather than answering Kevin. She hadn't been expecting the press when she arrived home. Lainey had never been so grateful for having a gated driveway as she was today. They didn't always have it closed at Lainey's insistence. She felt it was too intimidating for their friends, who were always welcome. But, thankfully, Lainey listened to the little voice in her head that told her to close it when she left for the courthouse. The vultures couldn't get to the house to hound her children as long as it was shut. How in the hell had the news traveled so fast?

Kevin looked past Lainey, eyebrows furrowing. "Who?"

"Never mind." Lainey pinched the bridge of her nose. The headache had started the moment she drove away from court. The further she got from Eve, the worse the pain became. "Where are Bella and Darren?"

Kevin jerked his thumb behind him. "Lexie is fixing snacks for them. Mom, she knows. Apparently, it's been all over the news."

"Bella?" Lainey's stomach dropped so fast she thought she'd be sick. She hadn't wanted Bella to learn about this from anyone but her.

"No, Lexie."

*Shit.* Lainey's brain took a minute to get up to speed. There was so much to do, so much to think about, so many people to worry about. Was this how Eve felt when the weight of responsibility sat heavily on her heart?

"I'll need to speak with her," Lainey said finally, then frowned. "Wait, did she say something to you?"

"Nah, I just happened to be checking on Bella when I saw her reacting to something on her phone. I asked her if it was about Momma Eve, and she said yeah. We didn't say much else because Bella listens more than we think."

Suddenly, Kevin was in his mom's arms, being squeezed so tight he could barely breathe. It didn't matter, though. He hugged Lainey back, letting her take all the strength she needed from him.

"They're not letting her come home, are they?" Kevin asked softly. His mom's answer came in the form of a quiet sob. Tears formed in Kevin's eyes as he tried his best to comfort Lainey. But how did you console the inconsolable? His mom needed Eve. They all did. And Kevin knew Eve needed them, too.

"I'm sorry." Lainey wiped tears from her cheeks as she stepped back.

"I already told you, Mom, this is what I'm here for." Kevin knew how angry, confused, and sad he felt right now. He could only imagine Lainey felt all those things but one thousand times worse. It didn't fall on his shoulders to tell Bella her father was dead. It wasn't his burden to tell a four-year-old that her momma won't be coming home for who knows how long. However, it was his duty to be there for his mom. And for Darren and Bella when Lainey couldn't be. As much as he liked Lexie, this was *his* family. He wouldn't abandon them like Jack did.

"I—I need to take a walk and clear my head." Lainey battled with her need to be alone and her obligations to her family. But she knew if she didn't get herself in a better frame of mind, she would be no good to anyone. Particularly Bella and Darren.

"Yeah, go ahead. Lexie said she would stay as long as you needed her, and I'm here. Mom, you're not alone in this, okay?"

Then why did she feel so alone? Lainey touched Kevin's cheek and gave him what she hoped was a convincing smile. "I won't be long."

Kevin's chest tightened as he watched his mom walk away. Even with everything Jack did to Lainey, Kevin had never seen her this shattered. The only thing that stopped him from going after her to make sure she would be okay was the look in her eyes. Being broken didn't mean his mom would give up. Not when it came to Eve. Lainey would take a minute, then she would pick up the pieces and fight. That's who Lainey Sumptor was when it concerned her family. Still, that didn't mean she wouldn't need an army standing beside her.

THE WIND WHIPPED Lainey's hair around her face as she stared out into the dark. The moonless night swallowed the ocean, leaving only the sound of the waves kissing the shore before retreating once again. She looked up. The stars were hiding behind the gloom of the black sky. The nothingness of the night matched how she felt inside.

"I won't let you take her away from me again!" she yelled into the void. Lainey didn't know whom she was blaming. Perhaps it was everyone and everything. She laid accountability at the feet of every person who wouldn't let them live and love in peace. "Haven't we been through enough? Hasn't *Eve* been through enough? *Leave us alone.*" The whispered plea was carried from Lainey's lips into the wind.

"Lainey?"

Lainey felt the hand on her shoulder and spun around. "Eve?"

She was met by kind, compassionate eyes. Hazel eyes that were *not* Eve's. The heartache buckled Lainey's knees. She welcomed Ellie's warm embrace, holding back the tears this time.

"You know."

Though it wasn't a question, Ellie nodded. "Kevin called. He thought you could use reinforcements. Don't even think about refusing our help. We're all here, Lainey. Just like you and Eve were for us when we needed you. You and the kids are not alone in this."

There was a slight shift in Lainey. Being in the midst of unwavering friends was akin to being surrounded by armor. Every person in the group she and Eve thought of as family was singularly formidable. Get them together, and they were unstoppable. Hope began to peek through the bitter darkness inside Lainey.

"Wait," Lainey glanced up at her house. "When you say, 'we're all here,'..."

Ellie smiled. "I mean most of us are all here. Blaise brought wine and Ezra, Hunter and I brought food, and Rebecca and Cass brought Aunt Wills. Oh, and Patty brought comic relief, aka Mo."

For the first time since the world collapsed around her, Lainey chuckled. "I didn't realize how much I needed all those things until you," she paused. "Until you showed up." Her phone buzzed in her pocket, and she apologized to Ellie for the interruption before checking it. "It's Reghan. She's on her way with the evidence against Eve."

"Should we go?"

Lainey raised a brow. "That wasn't a real question, was it?"

Ellie smiled. "No. Just being polite. You're not getting rid of us now." She hooked her arm with Lainey's, and they made their way back up to the house. "We'll have to figure out what to do with the press."

Lainey took a long, deep breath. The air smelled of salt and sand mixed with Ellie's sweet scent that reminded Lainey of the pies Ellie expertly created. "It's hard to believe that Eve and I were laughing and looking forward to the weekend just this morning." She stopped before reaching the deck. "We didn't make love last night. I'm sorry, I know that's too much information."

"No, not at all," Ellie soothed. She wanted Lainey to be comfortable saying whatever she needed to say.

"Adam showed up, and though Eve denied it, I know he got under her skin. I didn't want him on either of our minds when we were together, so I convinced Eve to just hold me." *If I'd known what was going to happen...* "Ellie, I'm so scared."

"I know, sweets."

"What hurts the most is knowing Eve is alone, locked up in a small cell. She escaped a life like that many years ago, and she has been running ever since. God, I thought it was over. I thought she could relax now that her past was dead and buried—literally." Lainey brought her weary eyes to Ellie. "What if I'm not strong enough for Eve? If our roles were reversed, Eve would know exactly what to do. She would turn this world inside out for me. I'm not Eve."

"No, you're not." Ellie took Lainey's hands in hers. "You're Lainey. And you're exactly who Eve needs in her corner right now. *No one* will fight harder for her than you. I have no doubt that once this shock wears off, you will know what you need to do. Plus, you have us to lean on. What's that saying? It takes a village?"

Lainey gave Ellie's arm a grateful squeeze. "I think that only covers raising children."

Ellie shook her head. "Not when the village is us." She leaned closer and lowered her voice. "If all else fails, we'll sic Mistress on them."

Lainey snorted. "She can start with that damned District Attorney." She sighed wearily. "I have to tell Bella. I wish I could wait and give her one more peaceful night."

"Why can't you?"

"She and Eve have this pact. Eve never leaves overnight without discussing it with Bella first. She tells Bella how many 'sleeps' she'll be away, which soothes Bella's fears. I don't know how many 'sleeps' Eve will be away for, so what do I say to Bella?"

Ellie closed her eyes. Her heart hurt for her friends. When she opened her eyes, Lainey was staring off into the distance. "Bella doesn't know about Adam yet, does she?"

Lainey shook her head. "I'm a horrible person. With everything going on with Eve, I momentarily forget that Bella's father is gone and that I've kept it from her."

"That doesn't make you horrible. It makes you human. It makes you a mother that is trying to protect her child. Lainey, I'm on the sidelines, and it's overwhelming for me."

"Hmm." Lainey wasn't convinced, but how she felt about herself was way down on the list as far as her problems went. That list was getting very long, and time was dwindling quickly. She started for the door.

"Hey," Ellie said softly before Lainey opened the door. "We won't stay long. We needed to see if you were okay and let you know we're right here with you and Eve. But we don't want to get in the way."

Lainey nodded. "You're never in the way, and I appreciate you believing in Eve. But I do need to be alone with Bella and the boys tonight."

They walked into the house to see Bella playing with Ezra. Her squeal of laughter pierced Lainey's soul. She was going to break this little girl's heart, and there was nothing she could do to prevent that. Tears that seemed to be at the ready threatened to fall.

Blaise walked over and gave Lainey a hug. "We're here, Lainey." She pulled away but held onto Lainey's shoulders. "Greyson has offered Drake and Associates' services if you need them. We'll figure this out."

"Damn right we will." Rebecca nudged Blaise aside. "What idiot thought Eve is capable of this?" She kept her voice low for the children's sake, but inside she was raging. Rebecca had subjected Cassidy to a string of obscenities after she saw the news.

Lainey waited until they were all standing around her before giving a rundown on what had happened since that morning. How could a few hours feel like weeks?

"This is bullshit," Mo muttered grumpily. "They're treating Eve like she's a real mobster."

"Careful with the language," Patty admonished lightly. She couldn't blame Mo, though. Something wasn't sitting right with her since she found out what had happened.

Lainey glanced in Bella's direction. Thankfully, she was fully engaged in what looked like a game of who could giggle the loudest to be aware of anything else.

"Nothing makes sense to me," Lainey said suddenly. "First, Adam just shows up out of the blue. They argue, and he attacks Eve." She shook her head. "That's not who Adam is."

"People do stupid things when they're desperate," Hunter suggested.

"No, I agree with Lainey." Aunt Wills had been quietly observing until this point. "The attack was far removed from Adam's character. Then there's the matter of the arrest, which I believe was going to be Lainey's second point."

"Yes. The arrest, the arraignment, the remand. To me, this day feels as though it has lasted a lifetime. But in reality..."

"It was all too easy for the cops," Cass finished when Lainey paused.

82

"I'm sorry for bringing this up," Hunter said hesitantly. "But has anyone seen the body?"

Lainey frowned. "Neither of us have, no." She raked her hands through her hair with frustration. "The time between when Eve left Adam in the alley and when she was arrested . . ." Lainey calculated in her head. "Twelve hours. What happened in that time that made the authorities so sure they got the right person?"

"What about surveillance?" Blaise asked. "We all have cameras back there. No one came to my shop asking for footage."

"That's right," Ellie chimed in as she pulled her phone out. "I can bring up the app on my phone and find the footage." She opened the app and brought up the archived footage from the night before. "What time did you say?"

"Eve was home just a couple of minutes after eight. I remember because when she called to tell me she was on her way, I checked my watch to see if I had time to give Bella a bath. It takes about twenty minutes to get here from the gallery, so check footage from 7:30."

Ellie did a time search and frowned. "Blaise, can you check yours? I don't see anything from that time on until 8:00."

Blaise immediately took out her phone and checked. She even went back a little further just in case Lainey's timeline was off. "Nothing at that time."

"That's impossible," Lainey said. "Eve was there." She got her own phone and checked the footage from the gallery. The footage from inside showed Eve. She was smiling and talking. Lainey recalled that conversation and how lighthearted Eve had been. Lainey wiped a tear from her cheek as she watched Eve shut off the lights inside the gallery and walk towards the backdoor. "This is when she left, but there's nothing from our camera in the alley either."

"Are they down?" Hunter asked. "Those cameras would all be on the same grid, right?"

"Yes. But there's footage of Eve walking into the gallery earlier, and the motion sensors picked up a stray cat not too long after she left."

"There's some fuckery going on here," Blaise said as she texted Greyson. "I will have Greyson go out there and look at the cameras.

Maybe Adam tampered with them because I don't have any footage of him being there."

"Me either," Ellie offered.

"Fuckery is right," Lainey said absently. "I have to tell Reghan about this." The buzzer of the gate sounded just then, and Lainey switched over to a different camera. "Speaking of," she muttered as she granted Reghan access. Thankfully, Reghan waited by the gate until it was closed again to ensure none of the press slipped through.

"Momma home?" Bella ran up and threw her arms around Lainey's leg. "Hi, Mommy."

Lainey kneeled and brought the little girl in for a hug. "Hey, my sweet girl." The lump in her throat caused her voice to crack. *Just give her a little more time.* "Momma is, um, still out. Ms. Reghan is here."

"Oh. 'Kay. I go pway wif Ezwa. Love you!"

Another tear. "I don't know how to tell her," Lainey confessed to her friends.

"Would you like me to be there with you, Lainey?" Aunt Wills asked, her voice full of compassion.

Lainey shook her head. "Thank you, but I have to do this myself. I promised Eve." She scanned the room and found Kevin. With a slight gesture of her head, Kevin got up and whispered something in Lexie's ear. The two of them rounded up the younger kids and headed to the kitchen. Though Lainey couldn't think about eating right now, she was thankful that Ellie and Hunter brought food. "Excuse me."

Lainey made it to the door before Reghan could ring the doorbell. Pulling it open, she ushered Reghan inside and straight to the living room without a single word.

"I wasn't expecting others to be here." Reghan nodded to Lainey's guests. "In the interest of privacy, I can't allow anyone but you and experts to see this evidence."

"Why don't we go in the kitchen and have some food," Ellie suggested. "Knowing kids, they'll go for the pie first." She rubbed Lainey's arm in support as she and Hunter walked by.

Cass grabbed Rebecca's hand as Rebecca narrowed her eyes at Reghan. Aunt Wills flanked Rebecca's other side. After a swift nod in Lainey's direction, they joined the others.

"We'll be right here, child." Patty gave Lainey a quick hug and set off with the others, towing Mo behind her.

"They don't like me much, do they?"

"You're Eve's lawyer. Get her out of this, and they'll love you forever," Lainey responded.

"About that. Lainey, I will need you to convince Eve to do something neither of you is going to like."

Lainey frowned. "What is that?"

"To plead guilty and take the plea bargain the District Attorney is offering."

# Nine

"What did you say?"

"Lainey . . ."

"Are you fucking kidding me, Reghan? Why would I convince Eve to plead guilty to something she didn't do?" Already frayed nerves were now lit on fire inside Lainey. Her hands curled into fists, and she willed herself not to strike out. "It is your job to stand by your client!"

"It's my job to make sure Eve doesn't spend the rest of her life behind bars." Reghan exhaled heavily. "Lainey, I've seen the evidence. The D.A. is offering voluntary manslaughter. Eleven years served, and she gets out in time to see Bella graduate from high school. If she doesn't accept this offer, they *will* charge Eve with first-degree murder. They'll argue that Eve lured Adam here to kill him so you could adopt Bella. If the jury finds her guilty, Eve is facing life in prison."

It killed Reghan to say these things, but the lawyer in her spelled out the facts as though she wasn't talking about someone she genuinely cared about.

Lainey nodded slowly. She knew Reghan was doing her job, but Eve *wasn't* just a job. Reghan had been with Eve for more than three years now. Both Eve and Lainey considered Reghan a friend. That's why Lainey didn't understand why Reghan was so quick to give in.

"I want to see the evidence."

"I don't advise that, Lainey."

Lainey's brow raised. "Let's get something straight, Reghan. You work for the Sumptors. *I* am a Sumptor. That means when I say something, I'm not giving you an opening for a debate. I expect you to do as you're told. Show me the evidence that has you doubting my wife's innocence."

Reghan heard a harshness in Lainey's voice she'd never heard before. As much as she wanted to protect Lainey's perception of the woman she clearly adored, Lainey was right. Reghan worked for her as much as Eve.

"Yes, ma'am." Reghan set her briefcase on the coffee table and dug out her iPad. She would start with the text messages and move up from there. "This is a transcript of text messages between Eve and Adam."

Lainey took the tablet when Reghan handed it over, frowning as she swiped through a couple of pages of provocative messages.

*I miss your strong body on top of mine.*
*I can't wait to feel you inside me again.*

She felt dirty reading them. But there wasn't a single moment when she believed Eve would do this to her. And the texts themselves were all wrong. It wasn't Eve's style. She always told Lainey that if she had something sexy to say, she would do just that. *Say* it. Eve felt texting took the intimacy out of it.

"I don't know who this is, but it's not Eve."

"That's her phone number, is it not?"

"Yes, but even I know phone numbers can be spoofed, Reghan."

The texts never rang true for Reghan either. "We would have to prove that, Lainey, because they will use these texts as evidence that Eve lured Adam here with hopes of a reunion."

Lainey dismissed the idea with a mirthless laugh. "All anyone needs to do is see how Eve looks at me to see the truth."

"Unfortunately, however true that is, adoring looks don't equate to proof in a court of law. However, they have something that I'm afraid is irrefutable." She swiped to the next file while Lainey still held the iPad. "I warn you, Lainey, this will be hard to watch."

Lainey watched in silence as a video showed Eve stepping into the alley and locking the backdoor of the gallery. She jumped slightly when something caught her attention as she walked to her car. Though the quality of the video was clear, the dialogue was soft and hard to hear. Lainey saw Adam standing in front of Eve, and she turned up the volume.

"... I need to get home to my family."

Lainey's nostrils flared, and her grip on the tablet tightened as she watched Adam rush Eve and put his hands around her throat. Then there was a moment of pride when Lainey saw Eve knee Adam and push him away. She nearly applauded when Adam fell on his backside. So far, everything that Eve said happened was all right here in full color. How was this the prosecution's smoking gun? Then it happened. Eve—who left after telling Adam he would now know what it really meant to lose everything—came back from her car. She raised her arm, and Lainey caught a glint from something in Eve's hand. Lainey physically jumped, and her heart stopped when the loud pop of the gun sounded. That one sound echoed loudly in Lainey's head as confusion clouded her brain.

"This isn't right," she murmured.

"Lainey, this footage is from the gallery's surveillance camera."

"This isn't right," Lainey repeated. "This isn't what happened. Eve doesn't own a gun! I saw them search her car. Did they find it? And how did they get this video without asking us for it?" She pulled out her phone with shaking hands. Her mind churned out question after question, but all that did was make Lainey painfully aware that she had no answers. "I checked, Reghan. This footage is *not* here." Lainey turned her phone so Reghan could see that the timestamp on the video Reghan showed her did not appear on Lainey's security app.

"The alley is a public area, Lainey. It wouldn't be hard for them to get a warrant. And your CCTV feed is stored on the Cloud. I suspect they deleted it once they got a copy."

Lainey shook her head. "No. Reghan, something is going on here. Did you know that Eve's mother died when Eve was fourteen?" Lainey said suddenly. She desperately needed to get Reghan back on track here. She didn't have the time or extra energy to spend looking for another lawyer as brilliant as Reghan.

The change in subject rendered Reghan speechless for a quick second. "I know Eve's mom passed away, but I didn't know Eve's age."

"Fourteen," Lainey reiterated. "She was killed by Eve's father." She shoved the tablet at Reghan as she turned to face her. "Eve knows what that does to a child's mind and heart. Now, I know you know how much Eve loves Bella. Do you *really* think Eve would cause that much pain and devastation for Bella?"

Reghan lowered her eyes. "Of course, I don't want to think she would do that."

"Don't want to," Lainey repeated softly. "But you do."

The truth was, Reghan found it incredibly hard to believe someone like Eve would do something so heinous. It simply didn't fit with what Reghan knew of the woman. But it was her job to deal in facts, not beliefs. If a jury got the chance to see the evidence the prosecutor had, they would convict Eve. The video left no room for reasonable doubt. Reghan was trying to prevent that scenario for Eve's sake. And for Lainey's. "Explain what we just watched, Lainey."

Lainey backed away and began to pace. Reghan was right. The footage was incriminating. But whoever it was on that video, it wasn't Eve. She rubbed the back of her neck. What would Eve do? How would she think? This wasn't the first time someone tried to frame Eve. Evidence piled up against her, implicating her in horrible things. Fake evidence. Fake.

"It's a fake," Lainey said finally.

"A fake?"

"Yes. You've heard of *deepfakes*, right? That has to be what this is."

Though Reghan wanted to follow Lainey's line of thinking, there were too many missing pieces. "Okay, let's say you're right. Who is doing this? What's their motive?"

"I don't know!" Lainey inhaled sharply. Even pranayama breathing wouldn't help her right now. "A woman as successful as Eve is bound to have enemies, Reghan."

Reghan shook her head. "This is far too personal for business rivalries."

Lainey remembered Hunter's question about Adam's body. "Who identified Adam's body?" She didn't want to think Adam would do this. He could sometimes be an asshole, but Lainey knew he loved Bella. He wouldn't hurt her like this. Would he?

Reghan checked her notes on the iPad. "It looks like his sister claimed the body early this morning."

"Jill." It made sense that his sister would be the one to identify Adam. Their parents were older. A trip across the country, while already devastated, wasn't the best idea.

Reghan glanced up at Lainey. "Yes." She paused to read a little more. "It looks like she arrived here in LA this morning, claimed the body, and was allowed to transport Adam back to New York."

"No autopsy?" Lainey asked.

Reghan shook her head. "It doesn't look like it. By the time Jill Riley got here, they already had Eve in custody."

"And the video, I presume." If Jill was here, that meant Adam really was dead. It also meant he wasn't the one doing this to Eve and Bella. That narrowed down the list to... zero. She was missing something. *Someone.*

Reghan closed the case of her iPad and drummed her fingers on the surface. If something was amiss, they didn't have long to prove it. "Okay, Lainey. Let's say you're right, and someone is framing Eve. We have two weeks before court convenes for pretrial. That means we have two weeks to prove this video is fake and find out who that someone is."

Two weeks. If Reghan thought Lainey could survive without Eve for two weeks, she was sorely mistaken. If Lainey needed to learn how to turn the world inside out, she would. "I will prove it. Is there anything else I need to see?"

"I've shown you all I'm legally allowed to show." Reghan hesitated. "Bringing up Tony at arraignment was just the tip of the iceberg, Lainey. There will be others that they intend on holding Eve accountable for."

Others, Lainey thought. "Dead or alive?"

"Just... others," Reghan answered vaguely. "That's all I can say right now."

Lainey nodded. They really were intent on digging up Eve's past for everyone to judge. It was up to Lainey to make sure Eve never goes to trial. "Very well. I need time with my kids now. I expect to be visiting Eve as soon as visiting hours allow it."

"Of course." Reghan started for the door.

"Reghan?" Lainey waited until Reghan looked back. "Eve trusts you. However, my faith in you has taken a serious hit."

"Because you think my loyalty to you and Eve has wavered?" Lainey nodded. "You're wrong. Nothing about this case fits with the woman I know. Even if Adam said something to her that threatened you and the kids, *this* is not how she would deal with it. Eve hired me because of my integrity, Lainey, and I will do everything *legal* to get her out of this mess. But I must also prepare for the worst. Not because I don't believe in her or you, but because I don't always have faith in others."

Lainey joined Reghan at the door. "I would do anything for my wife, Reghan. *Anything*. I will prove her innocence."

"I believe you will. But, Lainey, it has to be legal, or it will only hurt Eve. You know better than anyone that no matter how close to the line Eve gets, she never crosses it. She wouldn't want you to, either. I'll be here early tomorrow to take you to see Eve. Try to get some rest, Lainey."

Tears welled in Lainey's eyes as she watched Reghan drive away. She saw the flashes of cameras in the distance when Reghan made it to the gate. *Vultures*, Lainey thought bitterly. Everyone had a job to do. She knew that. But her family was going through enough without the added stress of the media.

"They won't get close to you."

Lainey gasped. "You scared the hell out of me, James."

The man Eve trusted when her family needed security stepped out of the shadows. "My apologies, Mrs. Sumptor." He nodded toward the reporters. "I can set up a bigger perimeter for when you enter and leave the premises."

Lainey smiled sadly. When the threats from Eve's past disappeared, so did James. Though she liked James, Lainey had hoped they would never need him in this capacity again.

"Thank you, I would appreciate that. I don't want them anywhere near the kids." She glanced over at the towering man. "She didn't kill Adam."

"No, ma'am, she didn't."

He said it so matter-of-factly that Lainey thought maybe he knew something. But when she turned her sharp gaze to him, he shook his head.

"I don't have any information. I just know Eve."

She stood on her tiptoes and peered over James's shoulder. "Is he here?"

"Yes, but..." James scratched his nose. "I'm afraid Harris has been called in by the prosecution. If they catch him working for you, it may cause problems."

"Shit. They're going to try to get him to say Eve paid him off." Lainey groaned in frustration. "Who is doing this, James? Could it be someone from her past? Maybe someone close to Tony?"

"I don't know. After Tony's death, Eve refused to go after anyone else in his crew." He peered down at Lainey. "She didn't want you in danger anymore, so she let it go. But I'll keep my ear to the ground. Unfortunately, unless someone is trying to gain clout by breaking the peace, I don't see this being any of them."

Lainey felt a light breeze touch her face and closed her eyes for a moment to savor it. She felt as though she had been transported back four years and wondered if Eve would ever be completely free of her past.

"James? I want you to tell me something. And know that no matter what the answer is, it doesn't matter to me. I love Eve and nothing will change that. But I need to know the answer. Was Eve ever a mobster?"

She heard a low chuckle beside her and looked over to see James cover his mouth. He scratched the five o'clock shadow that held more gray hair than Lainey remembered.

"No, ma'am." He gestured to the chairs that decorated the porch and waited until Lainey was seated before joining her. "I'd known Tony since high school. For as long as I can remember, he wanted to be a big shot, you know. The tough crowds, lying, cheating, stealing, alcohol, drugs, sex. That's what he surrounded himself with. I thought he'd change after he met Marie." Another shake of his head. "Marie never wanted that life for Eve. And when Eve was old enough, *she* refused that life. That's a big reason Tony hated Eve. That woman is brilliant. She took what her mother left her and turned it into," he spread his arms, gesturing towards the house and Lainey. "This. She didn't have to lie, cheat, and steal for it, even if Tony thought she stole it from him."

This was a story Lainey hadn't heard before. She was allowing Eve to open up about her mother in her own time. But she couldn't help her curiosity.

"Where did Eve's mom get the money?" Lainey asked hesitantly. She hoped Eve wouldn't consider this a betrayal. Eve always said there were no secrets between them, so Lainey allowed herself to meddle.

James smirked. "*She* stole it from Tony. Eve got her intelligence—and her talent—from Marie." He cleared his throat. "Mare was hired to take care of Tony's finances. That's how they met. He took a liking to Marie and turned on the charm. His talent was being persuasive, and she fell for him. It was good at first. But he wasn't going to stay away from the game for too long. He had plans. After a couple of months of marriage, he returned to being his old self. The more he partied, drank, and slept around, the more money she skimmed off the top."

"Mare?" The nickname suggested an intimacy between James and Eve's mother. "Were you two... please don't tell me you're Eve's father. That would be an upgrade, but I don't think she can handle much more."

James snorted with suppressed laughter. "I was fond of Mare, but we never had an affair. I was too deep in that life with Tony, which meant I wasn't good for her. I promised I'd help her get out, then she had Eve. Mare's plans changed. She was still leaving, but she needed more money. She was building Eve a nest egg."

"Did Tony find out? Is that why he killed her?"

"No, I helped her hide that. Tony's entire game was taking from one person to pay the next for his debts."

"Rob Peter to pay Paul," Lainey muttered.

"Exactly. Tony had a loud bark, using people like me to intimidate rivals or make him appear like his bite matched that bark. We'd steal inventory—drugs, weapons, alcohol, whatever we could get our hands on—then he'd turn around and sell it for double the price. I'd take a portion of that and give Mare a number for the books." James shrugged. "Someone like me belongs in jail, not Eve. I did things I wasn't proud of and excused it by saying I was helping Mare and her kid get out of the life I was stuck in. But our closeness caught Tony's attention. He killed her because he thought the same thing you did. But he wasn't jealous. He was scared she would turn me against him."

"Why—how did you keep working for him after that?"

James looked over at Lainey. "It was the only way I could keep an eye on him. When Eve ran away, Tony was pissed. He was sitting in prison, and he blamed her. I had to stick around in case he found her. For Eve's sake."

Lainey turned to him full-on. Her pulse spiked, and anger rose from deep inside her. Instead of holding it back, she lashed out. "He did find her, James. And if you allowed what happened to her in Paris, if you had *anything* to do with it, you had better leave right now. I will not have you around her or my family if . . ."

"I didn't know," James interrupted, his voice gruff with emotion. "I swear, Lainey, I would have killed those men with my bare hands if I had known. Me sticking around didn't mean Tony trusted me. I was out of the loop for a long time, trying to prove my loyalty for Eve's sake. I didn't know he'd found her until she turned herself in and started getting an allowance from her inheritance. That son of a bitch paid his way out of prison to get to her. I should have killed him right then."

"Are you a murderer, James?" Lainey's heartbeat slowed considerably, knowing James wasn't part of Eve's nightmare.

He looked Lainey in the eye. "I've never killed anyone in my life. But I should have made an exception with him." James rested his elbows on his knees and hung his head. "Mare talked me out of it once after I found out Tony was abusing her and had paid off his debts with her body, too. But she begged me to leave it alone."

"Why?"

He looked up again. "Mare said she would do anything to ensure a better life for Eve. She would endure that abuse until she had enough money to get Eve out of Tony's reach. I think she knew Tony well enough to know that a target would have been put on her back if he died. And Eve's." James stared out into the darkness. "I owed it to Marie to watch over Eve after she was gone. I owe Eve for not protecting her mother the way I should have. My loyalty is to her and you. Anything you need to find out who's doing this, I'm here."

"Thank you. I—I'm sorry about before."

"Don't be sorry for protecting the ones you love, Lainey."

Lainey smiled. "I'm glad you're calling me Lainey now."

James stood abruptly and cleared his throat. "Yeah, um. I'm going to do a perimeter check. You should consider locking down for the night."

"Sounds like a good idea. Hey, James? Was Marie an artist?" Lainey asked.

James grinned as he took his wallet out and opened it. With surprising gentleness, James took out a folded piece of paper and handed it over to Lainey.

The paper was discolored and fragile from years of being in whatever elements James's wallet had been through. Lainey carefully unfolded the paper and gasped. The drawing depicted a woman smiling adoringly at a young girl of about five or six years old. The little girl's eyes sparkled with love. Eyes that Lainey knew so well.

"Is this?"

"Marie and Eve. Mare drew it one night while we were discussing her plans. Sometimes, she would get this far-off look in her eyes and just pick up whatever was near that she could draw on and come up with something like that. It was incredible."

"Eve does that," Lainey whispered. She looked up at James. "Why have you never shown this to Eve?" It was an assumption Lainey somehow knew was true. Surely this was something Eve would have shared with her had she known about it.

James looked away. "I didn't know how. Eve was a hardened woman before you came along, Lainey. Walking in and finding Marie like that," he shook his head. "I can't imagine the damage that did. Then everything else. I just... I never wanted to reopen that wound." He pushed the drawing back to Lainey when she tried handing it to him.

"It's yours now. Something like that coming from you will be much less of a blow to Eve. Give it to her when the time is right, please?"

With tears in her eyes, Lainey promised she would. She was so engrossed in looking at the artwork again that she didn't notice James walking away.

# Ten

"Where Momma?" Bella yawned widely as she pulled her blanket up to her chin.

This was the moment Lainey had been dreading since this morning. She had followed James's advice earlier, saying a grateful goodbye to her friends and locking up. Blaise took a copy of the damning video with her. She declared that the security firm her husband co-owned, Drake & Associates, had the perfect person to dissect the "pile of crap." Lainey wasn't used to having friends other than Eve. Definitely not ones who had your back no matter what you were facing. Now she was surrounded by women who still had no doubts about Eve's innocence, even after watching the footage. Even Lexie was all in, never wavering in her loyalty to the family.

Believing that Eve's future was in good hands with Blaise at the moment, Lainey turned her attention to her children. She took Darren aside, hoping he was old enough to comprehend what was happening. Of course, Lainey watered down the specifics of everything, but she was as honest as she could've been with him. They cried together, and Darren asked Lainey the one question she didn't have an answer to. Why? As she tucked him in bed, she vowed to do everything in her power to bring Eve home. It was a vow she intended to keep.

Then it was Bella's turn. Oh, Lainey did all she could to avoid this moment. A long bath, a long story time. A ton of cuddles. But Lainey couldn't hide the truth from Bella any longer. She laid down next to Bella, bringing the little girl to rest in her arms.

"I have to tell you something, Bug, and it's not easy." Lainey used Eve's nickname for Bella in hopes it would help bring Bella a little peace.

"Momma 'kay?"

A tear slipped from the corner of Lainey's eye. "Momma is fine, sweet girl. There was," she paused, trying to find the words. "There was an... accident with your daddy, Bug, and Momma is helping the police find out what happened."

"Daddy? Owie?"

It felt like a spear going through Lainey's heart as she looked into Bella's confused eyes.

"Yes, Bug. A big one."

"I gib him one my ban-aids?"

Lainey gulped down the lump in her throat. She sat up, bringing Bella with her. "Bella, I—I'm so sorry, my sweet girl. I'm afraid a Band-Aid isn't going to work. Your daddy..." This was harder than she imagined. And what she was imagining gave her stomach pains. She flinched a bit when she felt little hands on her cheeks.

"Mommy?"

Tears were forming in Bella's blue eyes. This little girl was intelligent, like her momma. She knew something was terribly wrong.

"I'm sorry, Bug. Your daddy is... gone." *Pathetic*, Lainey thought, chastising herself for being so vague with this beautiful little girl. Her cowardice made Lainey question if she was skirting around the truth for Bella's sake or her own. Bella's experience with death was limited, and Lainey struggled with how much to say—and what to say. She recalled a time when Eve had a conversation with Bella once about Eve's mom— or Grandmomma—and how she was in heaven. Maybe that was the way to go right now. It was the easy route to take, but that could be discussed down the road when Bella was older. For now, Lainey needed a young child to understand that her daddy was never coming back. "Sweetie, your daddy is in heaven with Grandmomma now."

Bella frowned. "Why?"

Lainey took Bella's hands in hers and kissed her forehead. "Sometimes unfair things happen, Bug. Your daddy was hurt, and it wasn't something anyone could fix."

Bella's bottom lip quivered. "Momma fix it?" she cried.

"No, Bug. Momma can't fix it," Lainey said. She didn't bother hiding the tears. She wanted Bella to understand that being sad was natural.

"I want Momma!"

"I know, sweet girl. So do I. But she has to stay away for a little while."

"Why, Mommy?" Bella sniffled, wiping her eyes and nose with the back of her hand in one fell swoop.

Prison was one thing Lainey didn't want Bella to understand. Especially relating to her momma. If she had to be more creative with this answer, she hoped Eve and Bella would understand.

"Because, Bug, she's working on finding out why your daddy had the accident." Partial truth, Lainey thought.

Bella frowned and sniffled again. When Lainey handed her a tissue, she used it once before throwing it on her bed.

"How many sweeps?"

*Dammit.* Lainey knew Bella well enough to notice the signs of an impending tantrum. To Bella, Eve broke her pact. She couldn't possibly know that Eve had no choice. "I don't know, Bug. She wanted to tell you herself, but everything happened so fast." Lainey fought to console Bella by keeping the contact between them constant. It seemed that telling Bella that Eve wished she could have honored their pact appeased Bella. Slightly. "I'll promise you something, okay?" Bella nodded sadly. "I'll be right here with you every night. We'll wait for Momma to get home together. Deal?"

Bella's little blonde brow quirked. "You can't sweep here, Mommy." She crawled out of bed and picked up her favorite stuffy and blankie, then held her hand out to Lainey. When Lainey took it, Bella pulled her along as she marched to Eve and Lainey's bedroom. "We sweep here and wait for Momma," Bella announced as she hoisted herself onto the bed and plopped herself in Eve's spot.

A tremulous smile formed on Lainey's lips. She had been dreading coming to bed by herself, smelling Eve's scent all around her, and being so incredibly alone. Maybe somewhere deep down, Bella knew Lainey needed her as much as Bella needed Lainey.

"Mommy?"

"Yes, Bug?" Lainey responded as she slid into the big bed and snuggled with her daughter.

"Daddy love me?"

*Damn you, Adam.* "Yes, sweet girl. Who wouldn't love you? You're the sweetest little girl in the entire galaxy."

"I mad at him," Bella replied as fresh tears began to flow.

Lainey saw the truth of that in Bella's recent artwork. And when Bella decided she didn't want Eve to wake her if Adam called late. But Lainey didn't want Bella to regret this portion of her life when she was older.

"Can we try to forgive him, Bug, and think about the happy times you had?"

Bella thought for a moment like she did with all her most important answers. "'Kay," she said finally as sleep began to set in. "Mommy?"

"Yes, sweetie?"

"You tell Momma come home."

"Okay, Bug. I'll tell her."

Lainey dimmed the lights and listened to Bella's breathing for a long while. Sniffles would periodically break the silence, but eventually, the sweet girl fell asleep. Lainey hoped Bella dreamt of unicorns and ice cream, something that took away some of the pain in her heart, if only for the night. As for herself, there would be no dreams. Lainey knew, as she stared up at the ceiling worrying about how Eve was holding up, that she wouldn't sleep until Eve was home.

---

"Eve Sumptor!"

Eve pushed away from the wall she'd been leaning on for the past hour. After that shit show of an arraignment, the authorities dumped her in a holding cell until it was time to be transported to a local jail. A place that would be her hell for at least the next two weeks. She was angry, tired, and the thought of not being with her family tore her up inside. What hurt even worse was knowing she was breaking her pact with Bella, and there wasn't a damn thing she could do about it. *Helpless.*

While Eve tried to stay focused on determining who was doing this to her, her heart had other plans. When Bella wasn't the center of her worries, it was Kevin and Darren. What would they think of her now? Would they still want to call Eve *mom*? God, would they want Eve in their lives? In their mother's life? *Tainted.*

And then there was Lainey. They've had almost two years of wedded bliss, but even that was marred by Adam's constant shit. Now there was a chance that Eve would miss their anniversary. Hell, there was a chance Eve would miss everything if she couldn't find a way out of this mess. Even if she did get out of it, could Eve blame Lainey if she wanted a divorce? How could Eve possibly believe Lainey would want to stay with someone who kept throwing their lives into turmoil? *Broken.*

"Hands," the officer barked.

Eve put her hands in front of her and was cuffed for the fifth time that day. It certainly wasn't a pleasurable experience if Lainey wasn't the one with the key.

"Where are we going?"

"A nice, cozy little place up the road," the officer sniggered.

His partner rolled her eyes. "We're taking you to Lynwood."

Eve remembered her from this morning—had it really only been a few hours? The woman had been respectful despite the situation. Eve glanced down at her nametag.

"Thank you, Officer Hanover."

The woman nodded. "Once there, it'll take about two hours to be processed. Lynwood is at capacity now, which means they won't be able to separate you from the inmates."

*Perfect.*

"Eh, she'll have to get used to it anyway," Officer Hanover's partner cut in as he opened the backdoor of the patrol car. Before he could put his hands on Eve, Hanover stepped in.

"Watch your head," she murmured as she guided Eve into the car.

"What the hell? You got a crush on the prisoner, Hanover?"

This offhand comment had Eve calling Hanover's partner *Officer*

*Tiny Dick* to keep herself entertained. Of course, she kept it in her mind only, but how satisfying would it be to be vocal once this was all over? *If it ends.*

"She's not a prisoner, Dukes, so try to be a little less of an asshole. Now shut up and get in the car. I'm driving." Hanover glanced at Eve in the rearview mirror as she threw the car into gear and began their journey to the jail. "Do you have any questions?"

Eve's eyes found Hanover's in the mirror. "No." All Eve wanted was to be home with her family. While in the holding cell, she had tried to mourn Adam's death. It was a shock, and a part of her would always feel sad about Bella's loss. What Eve found curious was her lack of profound sadness. She had been married to the man. Had a child with him. She couldn't understand why the grief wasn't more intense. Was it because of the situation she was in now? Would the shock wear off when Eve least expected it? Whatever was holding Eve's emotions at check was welcomed at the moment. She needed to keep her bearings where she was going.

"Name?"

"Eve Sumptor."

Eve sat straight in the cold metal chair, knowing that none of the emotions she felt inside were reflected on her face. She had been a prisoner before. Locked in a tiny room, used and abused for the entertainment of others. If anyone thought they could break her again, they were wrong. As long as Lainey believed in her, Eve could conquer any situation. *Please believe in me, Lainey.* Admittedly, it was getting harder to keep her composure the longer Eve went without talking to Lainey.

"Birthdate?"

"October 17, 1988."

"Emergency contact?"

"My wife, Lainey Sumptor." Eve's heart constricted just saying Lainey's name out loud. Hours felt like months when you were forced to be separated from the love of your life.

"Do you have any medical concerns we need to know about? Prescriptions, allergies?"

"No."

"How about psychological concerns? Are you in need of a doctor while you're being detained?"

*What I wouldn't give to talk to Dr. Woodrow and her notebook right now*, Eve thought sardonically. "No."

After a few more personal questions, the intake officer began listing what to expect while at the jail.

"Due to overcrowding, you'll be bunking with another inmate until your court date. If possible, we will move you to a separate pod until your court date. As you're not a prisoner, you may keep the clothes you're wearing and have a loved one bring you a change of clothes when they visit. You do have the option of changing into a jumpsuit provided by the state. Since you will be housed with the inmates, I recommend this. Your loved one can also put money into your commissary account, where you may buy hygiene items and snacks. You will wake up at six a.m. for roll call. This is mandatory. Breakfast is immediately following roll call. It is not mandatory that you eat, but highly encouraged. As you are not classified as a prisoner, you are not obligated to work. You may use your time between breakfast and lunch to visit the library or take any number of classes we offer. After lunch, there will be another roll call. Do not miss it. You may then spend time in your cell or the common room before dinner. After dinner, you will be expected to shower before the last roll call of the evening. Then it's lights out."

Eve sat quietly as she listened to the officer. How did she get here? Yesterday, she was an influential businesswoman readying one of her prestigious galleries for another showing. These openings attracted people from all walks of life, from politicians and celebrities to people who walk in off the street, guided by incredible art. That's what Eve loved the most about art. It wasn't discriminatory. It allowed everyone a chance to decipher it in a way that made sense to them. But now she was here in this cold, drab building that smelled of stale piss and despair, and she couldn't understand why.

"Do you have any questions?"

Eve looked up at the officer. "No."

"Fine. We'll bring you a tray from the cafeteria since you'll miss dinner. Once you're processed, you can make a call. Keep your fellow inmates in mind while on calls. They have loved ones they wish to speak with as well. Tonight, your call time will be shortened as lights out is soon. This will be your first roll call. Your CO will make sure you make it."

*Fellow inmates*, Eve thought sourly. She had no issue with the other women in this jail. She didn't know them. But Eve *did* know that she didn't deserve to be here. The only scenario where Eve would have killed Adam was if her family was directly threatened. What they were accusing her of—this cold-blooded murder of a man she once loved, the father of her daughter—was far-fetched at best. Who hated her enough to kill someone and lay the blame at her feet?

MORE THAN TWO HOURS LATER, Eve had finally been processed. After her mugshot and fingerprints were taken, she was searched for anything that could be considered contraband. Throughout it all, Eve stood tall and seemingly unaffected. Then they took her wedding ring. That calm façade nearly shattered. The only thing that kept Eve standing was Lainey's voice in her head telling her she loved her. The ring was an important symbol of their love, but Eve could feel Lainey with her even without it.

"This is CO Dunne. He'll escort you to the phones, then to your cell."

Eve nodded, absently scratching her side where the blue polyester shirt rubbed against her skin. Dunne grinned at her, and Eve's skin crawled for a different reason.

"We don't get many inmates that look like you," Dunne said as he led Eve down a cold, concrete corridor. "You don't talk much, do you? That's good." He glanced down at her. "We can get to know each other better without words."

"If you plan on trying to rape me," Eve began coldly. "You'll have to kill me first."

Dunne grinned. "So you do talk. Don't worry. You'll learn the rules soon enough."

"You may want to wait to see if I'm convicted first. It would be awful if you showed me your bad side right before I'm released and able to tell the story." Eve was playing with fire, she knew. But it would be a cold day in hell before she was brutalized by anyone else.

Dunne stopped and turned to Eve. "Be careful threatening someone who could be your only line of defense in this place. And your only connection to the outside world. I have the power to make your phone and visitor privileges go away."

Obviously, he believed that, but there was no way he could keep Eve away from her lawyer. Especially since she hasn't been convicted. She still had rights no matter what this power-hungry asshole thought. If he tried keeping her away from Lainey, Eve would make sure this CO's abhorrent behavior was exposed in the most public way.

"I'm not a prisoner, Officer Dunne. I'm entitled to my phone call."

Dunne seemed momentarily confused by Eve's defiance. Perhaps he wasn't used to the women in this facility standing up to him. But he wasn't Eve's problem. Yet. If Dunne became a problem, she would deal with him like she did everything else. *Such confidence for someone who doesn't know shit about what's happening.* Eve ignored her inner voice, raising a brow at the tall man in front of her.

"Fine. Enjoy your privileges while you can, Inmate." He leaned down slightly, stopping just short of being in Eve's personal space. "You better hope you're not convicted." Dunne marched off, clearly expecting Eve to keep up with him.

She did with ease. When Dunne stopped, Eve walked past him, straight to the phones.

"Dial 0," Dunne growled.

---

LAINEY'S VISION blurred as tears filled her eyes. Bella was snoring softly beside her, and Lainey was grateful that the little girl was able to sleep. But Lainey's mind was wide awake. What were they doing to Eve? Had she eaten? Was she being treated well? Lainey couldn't focus on anything but Eve. If she could just talk to her to make sure she was okay, maybe Lainey would feel a little less sick to her stomach.

Lainey's cell phone buzzed on the night table, and Lainey looked at the time before answering. **9:23**. Maybe Greyson had news. Then she flipped over her phone and saw the number. Lainey fumbled with her cellphone as she hurriedly tried to answer.

"H-hello?"

*"You have a collect call from an inmate at The Century Regional Detention Center. Do you accept the charges?"*

"Yes! Eve?"

There was a moment of static, and Lainey thought the line had gone dead.

"Lainey? Baby, can you hear me?"

"Eve!" Lainey winced when Bella stirred. She eased out of bed and rushed outside by the pool. "Are you there, my love?"

"I'm here, baby. Are you okay? How are the kids?"

Lainey held in a sob. Eve was the one being accused of murder, and she's still asking about others. "We're... okay. How are you?"

"As well as can be expected. I miss you, Lainey."

"Oh, honey, I miss you," Lainey cried. "So much. I'll be there in the morning with Reghan."

Eve sighed. "I wish you didn't have to see me this way."

"Eve, please don't ask me not to visit you."

"I wouldn't do that to you. I just... I want to know why this is happening."

"I do, too. I'm working on it, love."

"I know you are. Baby, I can't talk long, but I needed to hear you before I..." Eve felt the pricking of tears and cleared her throat. She had to wait until she was alone before she could show emotion. It definitely wouldn't be good to show weakness in front of Dunne. "I can't wait to see you tomorrow."

Lainey cried for Eve. "I'll be there as early as possible, my love." She exhaled softly. "I love you, Eve. Dream of me."

"I love you, Lainey. The only way I will make it through this is by keeping you and the kids in my heart."

"Wrap it up, Sumptor!" Dunne bellowed.

"I have to go, baby. Lights out is soon."

Lainey frowned. "Are you with the inmates?"

"Yes. We'll discuss this more tomorrow, okay? I love you."

"I love you. Goodnight, my love."

"Goodni…"

# Eleven

6 *:00 A.M.*
Lainey stood in front of the bathroom mirror and shook her head. There were bags under her red-rimmed eyes from lack of sleep and crying. Now she had to figure out how she would hide them from Eve when they saw each other. She glanced behind her, concern filling her eyes. Bella woke up multiple times throughout the night crying out for Eve. Lainey felt her pain deep in her soul. All Lainey could offer Bella was a modicum of comfort by letting her snuggle close and cry on her shoulder.

When Bella did sleep, Lainey used her insomnia to research the facility where they were holding Eve. That turned out to be a terrible idea. While she found helpful information regarding visitations, Lainey also came across horror stories from women who had been detained there. If anything happened to Eve...

Lainey picked up her phone and sent out a few texts. She hoped she'd be forgiven for the early interruption, but Eve needed to be exonerated sooner rather than later. And if Lainey had to put pressure on their friends to do that, so be it. Once that was done, Lainey slapped on a bit of powder in an attempt to hide the dark circles and a little blush to give her pale face some life. She checked her appearance once more. She wore jeans and a simple t-shirt—nothing revealing per the facility's rules—and swept her hair up in a loose bun. With a deep breath, she left a sleeping Bella and walked out of the room that held Eve's scent. Lainey stopped when she saw a large makeshift tent of blankets in the living room.

"Hello?"

Kevin poked his head out and smiled sadly at his mom. "Hey." He put a finger to his lips to hush things, then scrambled out of the blankets.

"What's going on here?" Lainey whispered.

Kevin followed her to the kitchen before explaining. "Darren couldn't sleep. He doesn't understand why this is happening to Eve. I don't think any of us do. He showed up in my room, crying—don't tell him I told you that. I thought about waking you up, but you... look like you haven't slept."

"Thanks," Lainey said dryly. "The blankets?"

"Oh." Kevin shrugged. "I thought it would help him sleep if we built a blanket fort like we used to and hung out together. We talked for a bit, but he was down for the count pretty soon after."

Lainey looked up, blinking her eyes rapidly to keep the tears from falling. "I keep saying this to you but thank you. I should have been there for him."

"Nah, Mom. He understands that Bella needs you more." He rubbed Lainey's upper arm before scooting past her. "Let me make you some coffee and cereal."

"Make it tea and hold the cereal." Lainey placed a hand on her stomach. "I don't know if I can keep anything down."

Kevin looked back at his mom. "You should really eat something, Mom. And sleep. You're not going to last long if you keep this up." When Lainey shook her head, looking miserable, he sighed. "At least take a protein bar and an orange with you. Just in case. I'm sure Ms. Brannigan doesn't want you passing out in her car."

"Are you going to pack them in a paper bag for me?" Lainey teased lightly. She couldn't get used to her son being old enough to take care of her.

"If I have to, yes. Or maybe I'll find Darren's Wonder Woman lunchbox." Kevin stuck his tongue out at his mom. He was trying to pretend everything would be okay. Deep down, he was more scared than he'd ever been. What would happen to his mom if Eve lost? The sound of Lainey's cell phone pinging brought him out of his glum thoughts. "Is Ms. Brannigan on her way?"

Lainey frowned. "Hmm? Oh, she'll be here in about thirty minutes.

Um, I have to check something in the office before I go. Bella is still asleep, and I want to let her sleep for as long as she needs to. But if you wouldn't mind just hanging with her and Darren today, I would appreciate it. Lexie will be here, but I think they need their big brother."

Kevin nodded, hiding a small, proud smile. "Yeah, sure. Maybe I could set up their easels in the living room, and they can paint out their frustrations."

There were those damn tears again. Lainey imagined Eve could use an easel right now. It was how Eve had survived Paris, and Lainey could only hope there would be an area and supplies somewhere in the hellhole. She hugged Kevin, thanking him again for thinking of everything for his siblings.

"Keep an eye out for Reghan, please? I'll be in the office."

"Hey! Your tea!" Kevin poured hot water from the kettle into Eve's favorite mug and handed it to Lainey. He lifted a shoulder when Lainey gave him a questioning look. "I thought maybe it would help you feel closer to her."

"I honestly don't know what I'd do without you." Lainey kissed him on the cheek and walked away quickly before she broke down. She closed herself in her office, taking a few deep breaths to center herself. When her mind was a little more settled, she sat in her chair and powered on her computer.

---

EVE SAT on the lower bunk, ready for roll call to begin. She hadn't slept the entire night and knew if there was a mirror in her cell, she'd see a woman she hadn't seen in years. Eve stood and went to the tiny sink, splashing water on her face.

"You should try sleepin' while you can," her cellmate said sleepily. "You wanna be alert around here, or it could get bad."

"Thanks, I'll keep that in mind."

Eve blew out a breath as she studied her surroundings. Last night, she had learned not to breathe in too deeply, or the smell could overwhelm her. Even the dingy cinderblock and the heavy metal door couldn't keep the stench out while they held you in. The small toilet, dirty from years of use and not much cleaning, sat close to the door. A small white desk was bolted to the wall on the other end of the six-by-eight cell. And bunk beds hung off another wall. It was as depressing as the tiny room she was held in in Paris. This "white" did nothing to bring Eve the peace it usually did.

"Roll call is in ten minutes, then breakfast." Eve's cellmate sat up on the top bunk and stretched out the kinks. "You're welcome to sit with me if you want."

Eve offered the older woman a pleasant smile. They hadn't been properly introduced yet, and Eve was hesitant to do so now, despite the woman's graciousness.

"I appreciate the offer, but I'm not hungry."

The older woman clicked her tongue. "A pretty girl like you needs to keep her strength up in here. You don't want the vultures in here to see weakness." She squinted her eyes at Eve. "You don't look like you belong here."

The *weakness* in Eve had been beaten out of Eve years ago. Lack of sleep and food wouldn't change that. "Would you believe me if I said I don't? That I'm innocent?"

The woman pursed her lips. "Everyone says that, but *you*, I believe. What did they get you on?"

Eve tilted her head and studied the old woman. She had to be in her late sixties, if not older. Wrinkles fought for dominance on a kind yet battle-scarred face. A face that had seen and been through a lifetime of pain and bad luck.

"Murder," Eve said finally.

The woman scoffed. "Clean-cut gal like you? Nah, I don't believe it." She lifted her chin at Eve. "Convicted?"

"No, awaiting my trial."

"That's probably why they put you in here with me. You got someone on the outside fightin' for you?"

Eve's heart and mind went to Lainey, and she smiled. "Yes."

"Good, good. That'll keep you going in here."

"Why are you being so nice to me?"

The old woman's laugh sounded more like a wheeze, and Eve

noticed the missing teeth when she smiled. How long had she been in here without proper dental care?

"Why not? Look, youngin', I've been a staple here for so long I've figured out the game. You learn to keep your head down and not make trouble," she shrugged. "The other women leave me alone, and the COs bring the newbies like you to me. I'm like the welcome wagon around here."

"How long have you been in here?" Eve asked carefully, hoping she wasn't overstepping.

"Oh, I was transferred here when they opened in 2006. I've been incarcerated since . . ." she squinted her eyes as if she were silently recalling the past. "1977."

Eve's eyebrows shot up. "That's . . ." The woman had been locked up for longer than Eve had been alive.

"A long time. Yep."

"May I ask what you're in for?"

"Seems only fair since I asked you," the woman grinned. "Same as you, I suppose. I killed my old man. Nobody cared that he'd been beatin' me for years before I snapped." She began to make her way down off the top bunk. Eve moved to help. "No, I got it. I've been putting off taking the bottom bunk for a while now. This'll be my bunk as long as I can still get up and down from here."

She finally made it down and took a moment to catch her breath. The show of strength and stamina from someone who looked incredibly frail on the outside impressed Eve.

"Not bad for a seventy-two-year-old woman, eh?" she chuckled. "Anyway, long story short, since we don't got much time, I poisoned the son of a bitch. He demanded I have food on the table for him every night at a certain time. So I did. With a little extra added."

"Didn't your lawyer claim self-defense for you?"

The woman scoffed. "I don't know what it's like out there today, but a man had a right to discipline his wife back then. My *public defender* didn't do much of anything. There wasn't anyone out there fightin' for me then and there ain't nobody now. But I don't mind anymore. I get three square meals, a roof over my head, and no one is smacking me around."

It wasn't pity Eve felt for the woman. It was a mixture of sadness and awe. After close to forty-five years of being imprisoned—for something she should have gotten leniency for—this woman was the goddamn welcome wagon. While most would probably be jaded, this woman tried to help the women who crossed her path. Eve held her hand out. "I'm Eve."

"Milly." Milly shook Eve's hand with a firm grip. "Not Mildred. You call me Mildred, and I'll throw you to the vultures."

Eve crossed her heart. "Milly it is."

She looked at her wrist, forgetting for a moment that all of her possessions had been taken from her. Including the watch Lainey had given her.

"We got about a minute 'til roll call. I'm guessin' you're waiting for visitation? Your old man comin' to visit you?"

Eve looked down at the woman, who was about an inch shorter. "Wife."

Milly cackled. "Don't announce that if you don't wan' a bunch of ladies lined up to get a go!"

Eve drew in a breath, immediately regretting it. "Lainey is the only one who 'gets a go' at me. I'll be happy to help anyone understand that."

Milly's gray, overgrown eyebrows raised. "You been through it, haven't you?"

Eve looked at Milly. "I have. And I won't go through it again."

---

*8:00 A.M.*

Lainey handed over her phone to the guard before walking through the metal detector. The only other thing she brought with her was her ID. She didn't want anything keeping her from Eve any longer than necessary.

"I need at least ten minutes alone with her, Reghan," Lainey said as the lawyer joined her.

"It's advisable to have Eve's attorney . . ."

"Reghan. Ten minutes."

Reghan nodded. "Yes, ma'am." She knew Lainey and Eve needed

this time together. Being Eve's lawyer, Reghan had more leeway with visitations. She also knew that Lainey wanted to be involved with as much of Eve's case as she could be. So, Reghan would cram in what she could when they spoke to Eve together.

"Lainey Sumptor?" A guard in a khaki uniform called out.

"Yes?" Suddenly Lainey's hands began to shake, and her heart raced.

"Follow me."

Lainey nodded to Reghan before disappearing through a heavy steel door. She jumped when the door shut behind her. Just being a visitor here was scary. Lainey couldn't imagine what it was like for Eve being here all night.

"First cubicle," the guard directed.

Lainey quickly wiped away a tear when she saw that a partition would separate Eve from her. They would have to talk using a phone receiver on each side of the thick plastic. They wouldn't even be able to touch. She sat on the edge of the metal chair and waited. Lainey had been staring at the door for so long that she had to blink when she saw Eve walk in dressed in blue scrubs. Her face was scrubbed clean of any enhancements, making Eve look so young. But it was the absence of Eve's wedding ring that caused another tear to fall.

Eve saw the tear, and her heart broke. She saw the dark circles, the sad eyes, the concerned frown. And Eve couldn't help but feel the weight of responsibility. She sat down, placing a hand on the window in front of her. Relief flowed through her when Lainey didn't hesitate to mimic the action. Eve felt Lainey's loving warmth even with four inches of plastic between them.

Eve picked up the receiver on her side, waiting for Lainey to do the same. "Hi, baby."

"Hi, my love. How are you?"

Sensing Lainey needed it, Eve gave her a small smile. "I'm . . . I want desperately to be home with you and the kids."

"We want that, too. How are they treating you?"

Eve rocked back and forth slightly as she thought about the guard. She wished to hell they could talk about anything but this. "I spent most of my day in a holding cell. When I got here, it took a couple of hours for the processing. By the time I was done, I had enough time to call you before being escorted to my cell. I haven't had much interaction with anyone besides a guard with delusions of grandeur and a seventy-two-year-old cellmate who is quite nice."

"Do I have to worry about this guard?" Lainey already knew the answer by Eve's body language. To someone who knew Eve the way Lainey did, the signs of being triggered by past trauma were beginning to show.

Eve decided against playing off the guard's ominous advances. Lainey knew Eve better than anyone, and Eve didn't want to add to Lainey's stress by lying.

She glanced behind her to make sure the guards watching them weren't close enough to hear their conversation. "Let's just say I should get out of here sooner rather than later. How is Bella? Does she know?"

Lainey readily accepted the change in topic. "She knows, love. She's mad."

Eve lowered her head. "I knew she'd be upset about me breaking our pact . . ."

"Not at you, Eve. She's mad at Adam."

"Adam?" Eve frowned. It drove her mad that she couldn't be there for her daughter. Instead, she was stuck in this fucking hellhole. "Did she say why?"

"I—I guess I really didn't give her a chance. Maybe I should have." Lainey sighed heavily. "I asked her if we could forgive him. Should I have let her have her feelings?"

"Have you talked to Lexie?" Eve closed her eyes and blew out a breath. "Is Lexie still there?" Undoubtedly, the astute woman knew something terrible was going on.

"Yes, honey, Lexie is still there. She believes you're innocent." Lainey hesitated. "All of our friends do."

"Y—you told them?"

That was surprising. Eve didn't think Lainey would talk about their personal business. At least not without discussing it with Eve first. But maybe Lainey needed the support that Eve couldn't give her right now.

"No, my love. I would never do that without talking to you about it first. It's . . . it's on the news, Eve."

Eve gasped. *The news.* "I'm ruined."

"You're not. No one believes it, Eve."

Eve scoffed. "Our friends may be biased for now, baby, but... How many employees have called to quit?"

Lainey tilted her head and studied Eve. She wished she could climb through the partition and hold her wife until the fear went away for both of them.

"Mikey called." Eve slouched even further in her chair. "Eve, honey, he's ready to come here to be a character witness. He said, and I quote, 'Anyone who thinks Eve could do this is fucked up in the head.'"

Eve's posture straightened some at that. "He said that word?"

Lainey nodded. "I don't think he even cared if his mom heard him. Also, Lauren called from the gallery. She went in early this morning and found a line down the block. The press was there, too, and she made sure to tout your innocence whenever they shouted questions at her. The people who know you, my love, believe in you."

"The press. Baby, I want you to call James. I know you don't like being..."

"He's here. I called him soon after they took you away."

Eve smiled and nodded. "You never cease to amaze me. Is Charlie here, too?" Charlie Harris, former NYPD Captain, retired not long after being promoted. Or, more accurately, he was forced out for crossing the 'blue line' and going against his partner. A man with that kind of integrity and talent for investigating couldn't just sit on a beach sipping Mai Tais. With Eve's recommendation, James hired him to work security.

"Yes."

"But?" Eve asked, sensing Lainey's reluctance to say more.

"He's being investigated," Lainey said simply. If she allowed it, Lainey would be buried under the pile of bullshit evidence that magically fell into place. But she had been in Eve's life long enough to be skeptical of such *magic*.

Eve frowned. "This is what they were talking about in court?"

Lainey nodded. "Listen, my love, Reghan will be here soon to go over everything with you, but I want you to promise me something."

"Anything," Eve responded immediately.

"Whatever you hear or see, promise me that you will *not* agree to a plea deal."

The frown turned into surprise. "Reghan thinks I'm guilty?"

"No, she doesn't. She's looking at the evidence and doing what she thinks is best for you." *If I can't figure out what's going on, she may be right.*

"What is the evidence, Lainey?"

Lainey looked at her watch. The ten minutes she asked Reghan for were almost up. "There are some... seductive texts between you and Adam with you luring him here with promises. And an incriminating surveillance video from the alley."

Confusion filled Eve's youthful features. "I don't understand. I would never..."

"I know, honey. I don't understand why this is happening either. To me, everything I saw was so blatantly... wrong." She held a hand up before Eve could ask questions. "Eve, please listen. Reghan will tell you what she knows, but I need to tell you what *I* know."

Eve nodded.

"I was so confused with everything I saw last night. I've been confused since the police came knocking at our door. I knew something was wrong. It felt wrong and not just because I love you. Then I received a notification today. Eve, the bank accounts have been closed."

"What? Why would they freeze our accounts if I'm in here?"

"No, honey, they didn't freeze them. Someone withdrew everything."

Eve's knee-jerk reaction was to stand up and pace, but she was literally tethered to this spot in order to talk to Lainey. "All of them?" She saw Lainey's eyes quickly flick towards the security camera pointed at them, then nod. *Not the offshore,* Eve concluded silently. "Do you know by who?"

"By me. At least that's what I was told when I called this morning."

Eve's grip on the phone receiver tightened. This *was* about ruining her. But whoever was doing this was trying to take down Lainey, too. There wasn't a chance in hell that Eve would consider the possibility that Lainey would take the money and abandon her. But what would the D.A. think? Would he try to get Lainey on conspiracy? "Greedy," she seethed.

She wholeheartedly agreed, but Lainey didn't want to say too much here. While the person—or people—doing this to them made the mistake of being greedy, they were obviously savvy enough with technology to frame Eve.

"I will find a way to prove you aren't guilty and get you out of here, my love."

"I believe in *you*, baby," Eve said softly. She leaned closer, tapping on the partition when Lainey lowered her eyes. "Do you believe in yourself?"

Lainey exhaled sharply. "I—if this was the other way around and I was in here instead of you, you would..."

"Go insane," Eve finished for her. "Baby, you are the stronger of the two of us. I would be ramming down the walls to get you out and screwing everything up if you were in here. You?" Eve smiled. "You're going to make the walls crumble just by finding the truth."

"What if I can't?"

Eve spied Reghan coming in and knew her private time with Lainey was up for today. "I trust you with my life," she whispered before glancing behind Lainey. "Baby, listen. I don't want anyone but you or Reghan visiting me, okay? I don't want them to see me like this. Promise me you'll tell them to stay away."

"I promise." Knowing how private Eve was, she didn't hesitate to comply with Eve's wishes. She just hoped their friends would understand.

"*Thank you,*" Eve mouthed, then looked up. "Good morning, Reghan."

# Twelve

$\mathcal{E}$ve sat alone at a cold, metal table in the back of the common room. Two hours had gone by since Lainey's and Reghan's visit, and the gears in Eve's mind hadn't stopped turning. Thoughts of Bella and the boys occupied the first hour. Before she left, Lainey managed to tell Eve about how much Kevin was helping with the younger kids. She was grateful beyond words that Kevin was there for Lainey. The young man had a bright future ahead of him. And Eve would do everything she could to return the favor he's showing the family now.

This last hour, Eve had been focused on the case and everything she learned from Lainey and Reghan. The video, the texts, the bank accounts. It reeked of a personal vendetta. The evidence was so well done that the cops were convinced they had the right suspect. Eve's car had been impounded, but there was no mention of a gun in the D.A.'s discovery. *Obviously,* Eve groused silently. And, according to Lainey, no one had been by to search the house or take the clothes Eve wore that night. It was clear to Eve that the prosecutor's entire case rested on this video. A video that couldn't possibly exist.

Lainey assured Eve that she had people working on authenticating —or discrediting—everything the State listed as evidence against Eve. Eve suspected she knew exactly who those "people" were, but names were never spoken. If they were being monitored—by the State or whoever was behind this—neither Lainey nor Eve wanted to show all their cards.

Reghan informed Eve that the D.A. was also pursuing the allegations of Eve bribing her way out of murder convictions in New York—Tony's *and* Jackie's. That included investigations into many of Eve's acquaintances. If she ever needed another favor after this, Eve was afraid her contact list would be significantly depleted. No matter how much Lainey assumed people believed in Eve, this bad publicity would be challenging to come back from. Even if she were exonerated in a court of law, Eve Sumptor would still be scrutinized in the court of public opinion.

"Well, well, look what we have here, girls. That is one fine piece of ass, delivered right to me."

Eve's eye twitched with irritation at the interruption. "I'm minding my own business. I suggest you do the same." Her voice was cold and steady, unflinching in the face of this new challenge.

The inmate laughed, and her little entourage joined in. "Oh, you *suggest*? Did you hear that, girls? She *suggests*!"

The group's cackles grated on Eve's nerves. She never understood why people couldn't leave others alone. But this was prison. She supposed that this show of domination was familiar here. That didn't mean, however, that Eve had to play.

"Do you think you can ignore me, bitch?"

"I think I would like to be left alone," Eve answered. "If you could spread the word about that, that would be great, thanks." Again, she was playing with fire. This wasn't a world she was used to. Eve Sumptor wasn't the boss in here. But the moment they sensed her fear, they would be relentless until Eve was released. And she had to believe she'd be released. If she was convicted, Eve would be outnumbered and out of luck. There simply wasn't a scenario where Eve wins with threats from inmates coming from one side and CO Dunne on the other.

"The only thing that's going to be spreading is your legs. Unless I have you down on your knees submitting to me."

Flashes of Paris came back with a vengeance, angering Eve. She had spent too damn long in therapy to revert back to square one because of this... nuisance. Eve stood and stepped up to the woman, gauging her chances if this turned violent. The inmate was covered in tattoos. Some were duplicated on the other women surrounding them. A gang? Eve assumed the one who spoke—threatened—was the leader, but not for being the strongest. In fact, she was shorter and plumper than the others. Perhaps she held the brain of this organization underneath her short, cropped haircut. So that's who she addressed.

Eve stood toe to toe with her. "The only one I submit to is my wife. I'm not a scared little girl. This place? A palace compared to where I've been locked up before. And you aren't even close to the scariest person who has threatened me. Do us both a favor and leave this alone. Go on with your time here as though I don't even exist. Because for you, I don't."

The woman's nostrils flared, and her jaws clenched as she ground her teeth. Then she smiled, showing off stained teeth. "Big talk. But I know women like you..."

"You've never known a woman like me," Eve interrupted. "Walk away."

The inmate stepped closer, causing her group to do the same. Eve was about to be surrounded. Her opponent was right. It was big talk. Eve could hold her own, but not if she was up against all six of these hardened women.

"*Déjala en paz,* Cig."

A much more intimidating woman showed up out of nowhere and stepped between Eve and... Cig? The woman Eve thought to be the leader backed down immediately.

"I—I didn't know she was yours, *Jefa.*"

*Boss,* Eve translated silently. She wasn't clear about what was going on, but even the "boss" didn't get dibs to Eve's body.

"Now you do. And if I see one tiny scratch on her, I'm comin' after you, Cig. I don't care if you did it or not. Got me?"

"Got you. C'mon, girls."

There was fear in Cig's voice but also a bit of defiance. It showed in the strut as she walked away and the glare she shot back at Eve. Eve didn't trust her to just leave well enough alone. Even with the threat.

Which meant Eve had to sleep with one eye open. That was something she was used to in her old life. Not now.

"I appreciate the help," Eve said to Jefa without looking at her. "But I don't belong to you, either."

Surprisingly, she heard a chuckle beside her.

"You're welcome. Don't worry, that was all a... what do they call it? *Treta*?"

"Ruse," Eve supplied.

"You speak Spanish?"

"I do. Explain the ruse, *Jefa*."

Jefa grinned. "It's too bad you belong to only one woman, *hermosa*."

Eve's skin crawled at the endearment. "Don't call me that. What do you know about me?"

"I know you got someone on the outside that loves you enough to pay *mucho dinero* for your protection." Jefa glanced at Eve. "And the way you stand up for yourself against the *putas* in here tells me you been fucked up before. That why your ol' lady droppin' the cash for you?"

"My wife doesn't know anyone in here," Eve said, refusing to answer the invasive question.

"Maybe she got friends in low places?" Jefa laughed and sauntered off, singing a very off-key version of the Garth Brooks song.

Eve shook her head. She didn't know how long any of these women had been here, but if she didn't get out of here soon, Eve was sure she would go just as crazy. She was also very curious as to how Lainey found Jefa.

---

"GOOD MORNING. How may I help you?"

Lainey smiled politely at the young assistant. "I'm here to see Greyson Steele."

"Do you have an appointment?"

"No, I'm sorry, I don't. If you could just tell him that Lainey Sumptor is here . . ."

"Oh!" The woman stood up abruptly. "Of course, Mrs. Sumptor.

Right this way." She scooted around the desk, smiling nervously at Lainey.

Bemused by the change in the atmosphere, Lainey had no choice but to follow wherever she was being led to. She was used to Eve getting that kind of reaction, but never herself. If she were honest, it was unsettling.

"Right in here, Mrs. Sumptor." The assistant held open a heavy door.

Inside the dark room was a multitude of monitors and computer equipment. Keyboards, trackballs, and other buttons Lainey had no idea what they did filled the desk area almost completely. Another young woman sat in an ergonomic chair, fingers flying on the keyboard. Each stroke made the monitors react differently. All Lainey saw was... gibberish.

"Good morning, Lainey."

"Jesus!" Lainey's hand flew to her chest, covering her pounding heart. "You can't just sneak up on people like that, Greyson."

Greyson Steele's deep chuckle filled the air. "My bad." He kissed Lainey on the cheek. "How are you doing?"

"Give my heart a minute to get back to normal, and I'll let you know." Lainey drew in a deep breath. It smelled much nicer here than at the prison, even with the aroma of electronics wafting through the air. "Any progress?"

Greyson glanced over at the girl in front of the monitors. "Maybe. Jules doesn't give updates unless she has something concrete."

"I know it's only been a few hours, but we *need* to get Eve out of there, Greyson. If we can't prove any of this..."

"We will." This came from the girl who never turned around or stopped typing.

Greyson ushered Lainey further into the room. "Lainey, this is Jules. She's our master hacker."

"Only hacker," Jules muttered while still pounding away at the keyboard.

"Right. Jules, this is Lainey Sumptor."

The clacking on the keyboard stopped, and Jules stood slowly, turning to Lainey. It was as if she was coming out of a hazy fog. "I—I'm sorry, I..." She cleared her throat and wiped her hands on her jeans before thrusting one out to Lainey. "I'm Jules."

Lainey smiled and shook the nervous girl's hand. Another emotion Lainey wasn't used to when people encountered her. "Lainey," she reiterated.

"I know." Jules wrinkled her nose, tapping her fingers on her thighs. "So, um, I've been going through the video frame by frame." She gestured for Lainey to follow her. "I found some glitches, but nothing that will prove it's a fake to those who don't know what they're looking at. The person who did this is good." Jules looked up at Lainey. "I'm better. You were right about this. It's not real."

Lainey's stomach dipped. That was one step closer to getting Eve out of jail. "If you can prove that there are glitches, shouldn't that be enough?"

Jules shook her head. "It has to be irrefutable. Surveillance footage is notoriously glitchy anyway. If that's all we have, they're not going to do dick about it. What I need to do is get into the guts of the video and find that freakin' string to pull."

"How long will that take?"

Jules shrugged. "Depends on the skills and experience of the person who did this. If they're a noob, I might find something quick. But, like, if they're a veteran at this, they can be, like, a ghost, you know."

*No, I don't know, but I have to trust you.* "Whatever you have to do, please do it as quickly as possible." Lainey studied the girl for a moment. She looked to be in her early to mid-twenties with intelligent brown eyes. It was unnerving to be putting her future—Eve's future—in the hands of someone so young, but if Greyson believed in Jules enough to recruit her, that was all Lainey needed. "You said you're a hacker, right?"

Jules nodded.

Lainey glanced at Greyson before continuing. "Our bank accounts were drained."

"What?" Greyson, who had been leaning on the edge of the desk, stood up. "When?"

"Sometime during the night. I got the notification early this morning that the accounts had been closed."

"Closed, not frozen?" Greyson asked. Just then, Greyson's business partner Cade walked in.

"What's up?" Cade kissed Lainey on the cheek. "How is Eve holding up?"

"She's..." *Trying not to crumble.* "Holding on. We all are. I was just telling Greyson and Jules that our accounts had been drained." She looked back at Greyson. "The money was withdrawn, and the accounts closed."

"By whom?"

Jules butted in. "Excuse me. Is either of you capable of giving Mrs. Sumptor answers? I didn't think so. Step back, please. Mrs. Sumptor?"

"Lainey, please." Lainey gave Greyson and Cade a look, then took a seat next to Jules.

"Okay, Lainey. Withdrawals, especially if closing the account, have to be made by an account holder, right? So either yours or the other Mrs. Sumptor..."

"Eve."

"Right. Either yours or Eve's credentials must have been used. Passwords, account numbers, security questions, etc. Do you know whose?"

"Mine."

Jules's fingers started flying over the keys. "Amateurs," Jules muttered.

Lainey leaned closer to the enormous monitor but still didn't understand a damn thing she was reading. "What do you mean by that?"

"I mean, if you're gonna frame someone for a murder, why take money before the trial even begins? Doesn't that, like, cast a doubt?"

"Not if they're throwing Lainey into that frame," Cade suggested. "They wouldn't be able to charge you with anything, but the prosecution could use it against Eve."

Jules twirled her chair around. "You mean, like, use it as proof that Eve would run if released?"

Lainey frowned. "Reghan texted me last night. She said she was going to go to the judge to request that Eve be placed on house arrest. It would certainly be denied if they think I did this."

Jules twirled back around and began typing again. "This is your info?"

Lainey looked at the monitor. This time she understood exactly what she was seeing. "Yes. How did . . .?"

"I used the basics. Your name, who you're married to, address. There was a bit more security surrounding you, but any experienced hacker could jump through those hoops." Jules looked over at Lainey. "If you want me to help you really secure your info, let me know. But for now, I'm going to dive into this and see if I can find a calling card or something."

"Calling card?"

"Every hacker has a signature. Could be a name, could be the way they write code. We're all egomaniacs. If we do something freakin' awesome, we're gonna wanna take credit even if you laypeople can't understand it."

Lainey chewed her bottom lip as she watched Jules type a little more. "Okay, I'll leave you to that. Thank you." She stood, straightening the skirt she changed into after visiting Eve. "I have to go to Sumptor, Inc. and see if I can salvage our intern program. Then there are the girls' homes... Anyway, about the accounts, you don't have to worry. I can still pay..."

"The hell you can," Cade interrupted.

"The oaf is right," Greyson said. He slipped Lainey's arm through his and escorted her out to the lobby. "You're not paying for this. We're doing it because you and Eve are one of us. And if I took money from you, Blaise would cut my... well, it wouldn't be pleasant."

Lainey laughed softly. "I appreciate everything you're doing. You'll have to forgive me because I'll frequently show up unannounced. I need to feel like I'm doing *something*."

"You're welcome here anytime. No appointment necessary. Just be sure to take care of yourself during all this. Eve and your kids need you to stay healthy, yeah?"

Lainey briefly closed her tired, scratchy eyes. "Yeah."

"I THOUGHT I'd find you in here." Dorothea placed a cup of coffee in front of Lainey and patted her on the shoulder. When she didn't find Lainey in her own office, Dorothea found her in Eve's, staring at the wedding photo Eve kept on her desk. "I thought you'd be home with the kids. Dare I ask how you are?"

Lainey finally took her eyes off the photo and picked up the mug, deeply inhaling the aroma. "It feels like I'm teetering on the edge of a bridge. If I fall one way, I drown. If I fall the other, I get hit by a bus. My only choice is to balance on this thin rail and hope to hell I can make it to the other side."

"If anyone can, my dear, it's you." Dorothea rested a hip on Eve's desk. "If you need anything, you know I'm here."

Even with the invisible threat, Lainey felt the *only* thing she had a handle on was who she could trust in her inner circle. Of course, there was the core of Eve and Lainey's friendships, the ones that helped their decision to move to LA. And then there were the employees. Lainey had fully expected Dorothea to decline Lainey's request to come into the office today. Not only was it the weekend, but the news of Eve's arrest surely weighed on everyone's minds. Yet, she found Dorothea sitting in her usual spot, fielding calls from media to clients.

"I should be home with the kids, but with everything that's going on, I have to make sure Eve has something to come back to when she gets out." Lainey sighed a long, weary sigh. Her eyes burned, and Lainey was afraid she would collapse if she thought about how fatigued she was. "Thank you for coming in on a Saturday. Are the interns here?"

"Yes, they're here. But you really need to go home and get some sleep. They're not going anywhere."

"Are you sure about that? Dorothea, I need to soothe the waters. Put out the fires. Or whatever idiom you want to use. I cannot let Eve lose. I refuse to let the person doing this to her—to us—win."

"Then I'll help you. I'll talk to the interns."

Lainey stood, bringing Dorothea with her. She hugged the older woman tightly. "You're helping by not believing the shit they're saying about Eve."

Dorothea's lips spread into a half-grin. "I don't think I've ever heard you curse before."

"Stick around. If this goes on much longer, I'll give sailors a run for their money." Lainey made her way to Eve's private bathroom. Thoughts about where Eve now had to shower or use the restroom flooded her mind, and Lainey had to shake them off. She wouldn't get anything done if she went down that rabbit hole. "Gather the interns in the conference room, please, Dorothea. I'll be there in a few minutes."

"Yes, ma'am."

Lainey checked her appearance in the mirror. God, is this how she looked when Eve saw her? Concealer would be Lainey's new best friend for a while, she thought as she turned on the hot water and dipped her hands in the even flow. *I could use a bubble bath.* Those pesky tears threatened again. *I should have taken that bath with Eve.* Lainey could kick herself for all the things she should have done. Moments like this made Lainey wonder if she had taken her wonderful, comfortable life with Eve for granted. *Not anymore.*

She wiped the smudges from under her eyes and pinched her cheeks to bring some color to her pale, tired face. A quick comb through her hair with her fingers made her feel less disheveled. Lainey's black skirt and slightly wrinkled silk top weren't the power suit she wished it was. But Eve would tell her it's what's underneath that matters the most. It wasn't the lingerie this time but Lainey's determination.

# Thirteen

"*H*ave a seat." Lainey eyed the young lady who sat confidently in Eve's seat. She strode up to her, tilted her head, and raised a brow. "Not that seat."

"Why? It's not like Eve will be here," the girl joked.

It took every ounce of willpower in Lainey not to slap the arrogant smirk off the girl's face. "You must be Emilie."

"My reputation precedes me."

"Being known for your attitude is not always a good thing. Now get up." When the girl didn't budge, Lainey put one hand on the back of the chair and a fist on the table. "Perhaps I should introduce myself. I'm Lainey Sumptor. It is *my* name on the building and *my* wife you're disrespecting. This is *my* seat when Eve—Mrs. Sumptor to you—isn't here. The last couple of days have been *really* shitty, and that fucking smirk on your face is not helping. Get out of my chair and sit your ass as far away from me as possible. *Now.*"

Emilie ducked under Lainey's arm and slinked away. The smirk was gone. In its place was pure dread. She went to the far end of the conference table and sat quietly with her head bowed.

"If anyone else thinks they have free rein because of what's going on, speak up," Lainey announced as she took the seat that Emilie previously occupied. She felt Eve's presence there. Lainey had been in this conference room many times, watching Eve hold court over employees or clients. Eve emitting such grace, confidence, and power was a sight to behold. And now, it was a memory Lainey could feed off of. "No one? Good. Let's get started."

Gisele raised her hand. "Mrs. Sumptor? The news, it can't be right."

Lainey's attention went to Gisele. *The other French girl.* "It's not. That's all I can say on the matter. I'm here because I know this could alter how you feel about this company and its owner. You've all worked hard to get here, but I want to know now if you are having second thoughts." She looked at Emilie. "I will not tolerate arrogance or gossip. If you stay, you will do the work you were sent here to do, and you will treat this experience like the rare opportunity it is. No talking about the case or speculating. If you go to the press, you're out. If you don't take this seriously, you're out. If you sit in this chair, you're out. If anyone disrespects Eve, you're out. I brought you here. I won't hesitate to cut you from this program if my rules are not heeded. Do I make myself clear?"

The interns—including Emilie—nodded. What Lainey saw in their eyes was another emotion Lainey wasn't used to getting. Petrified reverence.

<hr>

"SUMPTOR! YOU HAVE A VISITOR!"

Eve looked up, her eyes taking a moment to adjust to her surroundings. She was on edge, and there was absolutely nothing she could do to rid herself of that dreadful feeling. She needed Lainey. She needed her family.

"Who is it?"

"Do I look like your fucking secretary, Princess? Get up. Let's go."

If Eve really was a mobster, Dunne would definitely be on her hitlist. But in here, Dunne held the power. As much as that crushed her soul, Eve couldn't keep making waves. She had to bide her time while Lainey and Reghan found a way to get her out. If *they can.*

Eve followed Dunne through the visitor's door and stopped abruptly. It was on the tip of her tongue to have him take her back, but curiosity got the best of her. With effort, Eve straightened her shoulders and sat in the small cubicle. She stared at her visitor for a long moment before picking up the receiver.

"Katherine."

Katherine Bushnell's eyes widened slightly. "Hi, Eve." She shook her head. "It's weird seeing you like this."

"Did you come to gloat?"

"No!" Katherine glanced behind her as though she was being followed or watched. "I don't even know if I'm supposed to be here, but you saved my life, Eve. I owe you."

Eve leaned her elbows on the table. "Is someone after you?" She didn't know why she asked. What the fuck was she supposed to do about it if there was? That powerless feeling sat low in Eve's belly, making it ache.

"Not in the way you think." Katherine bent forward, dropping her voice conspiratorially. "I was served papers to testify against you. I don't even know how they found me or what they want from me, but I need you to know I'm not going to say anything."

They really were trying to bury Eve. The hope inside her was getting dimmer. "What do they think you have to say? I didn't do anything."

"Oh, I know, but Mr. Howell says he has questions about what happened between you and Meredith. And your relationship with Jackie."

"Jackie?"

"Yeah." Katherine leaned in again. "Look, like I said, I owe you. I'm not going to tell them about how you kidnapped me. And I don't really know anything about Jackie. Meredith handled all that stuff."

Eve sat back in her chair and bit the inside of her cheek. Her free hand curled into a fist, nails biting into her palms. The pain kept her from lashing out. "So, you came all the way here to tell me you owe me for saving your life while trying to trap me into saying something incriminating."

"What? I'm not..."

"You never were great at lying, Katherine. But since you're so interested in that night I met you at the warehouse, I'll tell you this. Tony's men were following you. *You* were a liability to him, just as Meredith was. I couldn't help her. But I *was* able to get to you before Tony did. I wasn't kidnapping you, Katherine. I was helping you get out. And you've lived a comfortable life since, haven't you?"

Katherine's eyebrows drew in, forming a deep crease. "I was being followed?"

Eve nodded. Her body relaxed its rigid hold on her enough to extract her nails out of her palms. She watched carefully as Katherine reached up and yanked off the necklace she was wearing. Katherine wrapped her fingers around it and stuffed it in her pocket.

"I'm sorry. They told me if I didn't help them, they would charge me with embezzlement. What was I supposed to do?"

"I don't know, Katherine. I would tell you to stop being selfish and maybe do some good for others, but I'm starting to see it's not always worth it." Eve stood. "Don't come back here." She hung up the receiver and turned to walk away. Her body ached from the unyielding stress of the past twenty-four hours. But it was her heart that hurt the most. What had she done in her life to deserve this? Hadn't she been through enough?

"Looks like the state of California has it out for you, Princess," Dunne smirked. "I think we'll be good friends soon enough."

Eve swallowed down the bile. Thankfully, Dunne left as soon as they got to the common room. At this time of day, it was full of activity. Inmates were chatting, playing card games, or watching the small television nestled up in the corner of the room. The chaos of it all caused Eve's heart to beat faster. She tried pulling in a breath, but her chest was too tight. She needed to get out of there. She needed fresh air.

By the time Eve made it to her cell, her entire body was shaking. She felt nauseous and lightheaded as she stumbled to her bunk. If Eve could be thankful for anything right now, it was that she was alone. Obviously, her cellmate had better things to do than watch Eve have a breakdown. Eve laid down and fought to regain control as she began to hyperventilate. If she couldn't last twenty-four hours in this place, what would happen to her if she was convicted? Could she survive being locked up again? Would she want to?

"*Lainey*," Eve whispered, her voice raw with emotion. "*Help me.*"

"*EVE.*" Lainey breathed deeply through her nose and held it for ten seconds before slowly blowing it out. She stood at her own front door, afraid to go inside. While progress had been made concerning the *evidence* against Eve, Lainey had still failed. Eve wasn't with her. And now she had to go into the house she shared with the love of her life... alone. Lainey blinked rapidly to keep the onslaught of tears from flowing, wiping away the ones that escaped. She took one more deep breath and then went inside.

"Mommy!" Bella ran to Lainey, arms wide.

Lainey kneeled and caught Bella in a fierce embrace that she was sure they both needed. "Hey, Bug."

Bella perked up at the nickname and looked behind Lainey. "Momma here?"

Lainey swallowed past the lump in her throat. "No, sweetie, not yet."

Bella pouted, her bottom lip trembling. "Why, Mommy?"

The knife in Lainey's heart twisted painfully. What was she supposed to say? *I failed you both.* "I —"

"Hey, Bells!" Kevin cut in, winking at his mom. "We're going to order some pizza. You want anchovies?"

And just like that, Bella's attention was pulled away. Lainey knew it wouldn't last long, but she was grateful for the brief reprieve.

"Eww, no! Olibs!"

"You say no to anchovies but want olives?" Kevin shook his head. "Want pineapple, too?"

"Kevin, you siwwy. Olibs no go wif pineapple! Olibs and shoshage. No p'roni, eitha!"

"We're just going to get you your own pizza, olive girl. Mom? Want some pizza?"

Lainey smiled. "No, thank you. Get what you guys want."

"Well, you can eat some of Bella's when you get hungry." Kevin helped Lainey up. "Everything okay?"

Lainey sighed. Bella was watching her intently. "It will be. Where's your brother?"

Kevin nodded towards the blanket fort that was still standing. "He's reading. He hasn't come out much today."

"Okay, I'll talk to him. Thank you, sweetie."

"Mommy?" Bella tugged on Lainey's skirt.

"Yes, Bug?"

"We sweep here 'night?" Bella pointed at the blanket fort.

"Is that what you want?" Bella nodded. "Okay, then. We'll sleep there. Why don't you go and make sure your big brother isn't ordering a hundred pizzas with anchovies and pepperoni?"

"'Kay!" Before Bella ran off, she looked at the fort and then at the front door. She nodded. "We see when Momma come home."

With that, Bella left Lainey broken. Lainey would give anything if Eve could walk through that door right now. Lainey had already pulled out her phone dozens of times today to call or text Eve, only to remember she couldn't. Still, it hadn't stopped Lainey from texting *I love you*, hoping Eve would read those texts soon.

Right now, Lainey had to focus on what was in front of her. Including a ten-year-old who was taking this harder than she had imagined. Of course, Darren had always been her sensitive one. Lainey attributed that to his artistic side. That was probably true in some capacity, but she could also blame the way Jack had constantly berated everything Darren loved.

"Hey."

Lainey jumped at the sound of Lexie's voice. "Holy mother of . . ."

"Sorry, I didn't mean to scare you."

"It's not your fault. I'm... jumpy. How were things today?"

Lexie glanced at the fort and then motioned for Lainey to follow her. "Darren stayed in there most of the day, and he didn't talk much. He did say he wasn't going to school on Monday, but that's about the most I got out of him. Bella has been quiet as well."

"Did the painting not help?"

Lexie shook her head. "Neither of them wanted to paint. Darren wanted to read alone, and Bella sat with Ju Ju. She would cry for a bit, then talk to her dolly, but she wouldn't say anything if I asked her what was wrong."

The regret was like a vice around Lainey's heavy heart. "I should have been here. After I visited Eve, I should have come home to the kids."

Lexie laid a hand on Lainey's shoulder. "Lainey, you *are* here for them. But you're also taking on everything Eve needs. I can't imagine the stress you're under. Please remember that I'm here for you. Your friends are here for you. Kevin is here, and he has been instrumental in helping me with the younger kids."

"He's a teenager, Lexie. He shouldn't have to carry that burden."

"I don't think Kevin sees it as a burden, Lainey. I think he's proud that he can help." Lexie smiled. "Please forgive me for saying this, but you look so tired."

Lainey sniffed. "It's only been thirty-something hours. How will I ever survive if…"

"We're going to stay positive," Lexie interrupted. "We're putting out in the universe that Eve will be home very soon. Which means you need to rest up."

"She's right, Mom." Kevin came into the living room with Bella riding piggyback. "The pizza isn't going to be here for another thirty minutes or so. Why don't you take a nap?"

"I should really see how Darren is doing," Lainey said. She reached up and booped Bella on the nose, receiving a faint giggle in return. It was so different from the boisterous laugh Bella usually had.

"Mom, I got this. Please rest for a bit."

Lainey sighed. "Fine, I'll lay down for ten minutes."

"Thirty," Kevin countered.

"Fifteen," Lainey negotiated.

"Twenty and go to bed early tonight," Kevin demanded.

Bella pointed at her mommy and shouted, "Nap, mommy or no ows cweam!"

Lexie and Kevin chuckled as Lainey stared at her daughter in utter disbelief. How dare Bella hold ice cream over her head after the day Lainey had. "Fine. Twenty minutes, a bowl of ice cream, and the fluffiest pillow in the fort at bedtime."

Kevin looked back at Bella. "What do you think, Bells?"

Bella tapped her chin as she did when thinking hard. She leaned in and whispered something in Kevin's ear.

"Counteroffer," Kevin announced. "Twenty minutes, a bowl of ice cream, and half of the pillow. The other half goes to Princess Bells here."

Lainey thought about it, then stuck her hand out to Bella. "Deal."

Bella shook Lainey's hand. "You take a nap in dere, Mommy?" she asked, pointing to the fort.

"No, baby girl, I think I'm going to go to my room for a little bit. Is that okay?"

One little eyebrow fell, then raised. Bella looked so much like her momma just then that Lainey had to force herself not to cry and look away.

"'Kay. Bedtime we go in dere?"

"Yes, ma'am."

"Did anyone ask me?"

Lainey turned her head towards an angry Darren. "Hey, sweetie . . ."

"This is *my* fort! Maybe I don't want anyone in here!" Darren ran to the sliding door leading out to the beach, opened it, and ran out.

"I'll go," Kevin said, gently setting Bella on her feet.

"No," Lainey stopped him with a hand on his arm. "I'll go. *You* need to take some time for yourself to be a kid, okay? Go call your friends or play some video games."

"You're actually telling me to play video games? Can't pass this up. You wanna play with me, Bells?"

When she didn't hear an answer, Lainey bent down to kiss Bella on the head. "Bella?" The little girl was staring towards where Darren had stormed out.

"Mommy? Dawwen mad at me?" The pout on her face was enough to shatter even the coldest hearts.

Lainey kneeled. "No, bug, he's not mad at you. You know how you feel sad in here?" Lainey pressed a hand over Bella's heart, and the young girl nodded, pouting even more. "Darren feels that, too. It's not you, my sweet girl. He's hurting."

Bella thought about that for a moment, putting her hand over Lainey's. "He misses Momma, too?"

"Yes. We all do."

Bella nodded. "I draw him a pitcher of Momma. C'mon, Wexie, you help me, pease?

"Of course." Lexie smiled at Lainey and took Bella's hand.

As they walked off, Lainey couldn't help but think of how much Bella was like Eve. Bella was pushing past her inner turmoil to help someone she loved. Eve would be so proud.

"I guess I'm on my own," Kevin shrugged. "Want me to text you when the pizza is here?"

Lainey thought about declining but didn't want Kevin to worry any more than he already was. "Yes, please. Enjoy your downtime."

Lainey quickly made her way to the backyard to find Darren. She heard a sharp whistle and turned towards it. James pointed in a direction, and Lainey found Darren sitting in the pavilion. She nodded politely at James.

"I don't want to talk," Darren grumbled when Lainey sat beside him.

"Fine. I do, so listen. You are not the only one hurting in this house. That little girl lost her daddy and has no idea why her momma isn't here. Bella can't comprehend any of this, but she knows you and Kevin are still here with her." Lainey took Darren's hand. "I'm not asking you not to feel what you're feeling, Darren. But I *am* asking you not to take it out on the rest of us. I'm doing the best I can to just keep going here. I can't... *can't* take any more. Please, sweetie. Please help me keep this home and the people in it together for when Eve gets home."

She knew she was asking a lot of a child, but Lainey believed Darren needed to be included as much as Kevin was. If he felt useful, perhaps he wouldn't have the energy to feel sad. It wasn't working for Lainey, but that was different.

"Sorry, Mom," Darren sniffled. "I'll do better."

"Thank you. Now, will you go inside and tell Bella you're not mad at her?"

"S-she thinks I'm mad at her?"

"Mmhmm. She's in there right now drawing you a picture of Eve so you won't miss her so much."

Tears cascaded down Darren's cheeks. "Momma Eve *has* to come home, Mom. B-Bella needs her." He wiped his tears away with his sleeve. "I'm gonna go sit with her, 'kay?"

Lainey nodded. She held on tight when Darren hugged her. It was brief but something they both needed. Darren ran into the house, calling out for Bella. Lainey quickly retreated to her bedroom before she lost it right there in the pavilion—in front of James and whoever else was out there watching. Lainey closed and locked the door, then laid on Eve's side of the bed, deeply breathing in Eve's scent.

*"I* will *get you out, my love. This family needs you."*

Lainey drifted off, dreaming of the first time Eve kissed her. She remembered every moment of their times together, but the first time Eve's tongue touched Lainey's lips was seared in Lainey's heart. The desire that filled Lainey's body when Eve licked her lips from bottom to top was so intense it had scared her. She had never felt passion that profound before. She could have let that fear consume her, but Eve's pull had been stronger than Lainey's fear. Lainey fell utterly, unequivocally, and irrevocably in love with Eve that night. A love that was tested, ignored, and finally given in to. There was absolutely nothing—or no one—that could make Lainey give it up again.

*"I need you."*

# Fourteen

Lainey's knee bounced with nerves as she waited for Eve. It wasn't out of the realm of possibility that Eve would refuse to see her. It had happened before. So, when Eve walked through the door, Lainey released the breath she had been holding. She waited for Eve to sit down before picking up the receiver.

"Hi, my love."

Eve's eyes fluttered closed. She lay awake the night before, fearing that Lainey wouldn't visit her. It wasn't until she walked in and saw Lainey's beautiful face that the fear dissipated.

"Hi, baby." Eve studied Lainey's appearance. Light makeup didn't hide the exhaustion. "You haven't been sleeping."

Lainey raised a brow. "Neither have you," she observed. "Are they treating you okay?"

Eve chuckled. "Are you going to ask that every time you come to visit me?"

"Yes," Lainey answered seriously.

Eve's smile faded. Lainey was having a difficult time with this, and Eve didn't need to make it worse by being flippant about Lainey's concerns. "I'm sorry, baby. Though I thought the bodyguard you hired would have reported back to you." She winked at Lainey to show she wasn't upset with being looked after.

Lainey frowned slightly. "If you know about her, that means something happened."

"Nothing more than someone trying to mark their territory. That is until Jefa stepped in." Eve leaned forward, a curious twinkle in her eye. "How do you know anyone who goes by the nickname Jefa?"

Lainey finally smiled. "I know people who know people."

"Hmm. James?"

"Maybe," Lainey answered vaguely. "I'm told she's excellent at thwarting unwanted advances."

"*Thwarting unwanted advances*," Eve repeated. "God, I miss you so much."

"I miss you, too, love."

"And just to ease your mind, I don't think I have to worry about the inmates."

There was something about how Eve said those words that caused the hair on the back of Lainey's neck to stand up. She narrowed her eyes but saw Eve shake her head slightly, eyes flicking to the camera.

"I'm *done* with this conversation, okay? Is it alright to be *done*? I want to talk about the kids now, please?"

Lainey moved off the subject and spoke to Eve about their children without hesitation. Despite worrying about making Eve feel worse, she didn't leave anything out. If the roles were reversed, Lainey wouldn't have wanted Eve to sugarcoat anything.

Eve lowered her head as she listened. What she wouldn't give to hold each of her kids in her arms and tell them it would all be okay. Eve wanted to be tucking Bella in and reading her a story using dreadful voices. She wanted to be playing video games with Kevin and listening to him laugh when he won. Eve would even rather be helping Darren with his math homework than sitting in this hellhole for a crime she didn't commit.

And Lainey. Eve would sell what was left of her soul to be in Lainey's arms again. To feel Lainey's lips on hers. To feel Lainey's body... It took effort, but Eve stopped that line of thinking. As much as she wanted it all, wishing for it would only make it harder to survive however long she was stuck here.

"Goddamn it, Lainey, I should be there for my daughter." Eve felt like screaming, but she managed to keep her tone low. "What am I going to do if she hates me?"

"She could never hate you, my love. Bella is fervently waiting for you to come home."

"What if she sees the news and hears what happened to Adam? What if she believes..."

"Eve, honey, trust me to take care of Bella."

Eve's eyes widened. "I do! I didn't mean to imply you weren't."

"No, I know. What I'm saying is, if Bella happens to hear something, I will talk to her. Just like you always do. With honesty. As young as she is, I think she knows you well enough to know you'd never hurt her like that."

"I don't know how to thank you for everything you're doing, baby. And for not leaving me."

Lainey shook her head. "Please don't thank me, Eve. You make it seem like I feel like I *have* to do this. Bella is my daughter, and you are my wife, love. There's nothing I wouldn't do for either of you."

Eve touched the partition in front of her. "I hate this."

"You and me both, my love. Have you spoken to Reghan?"

Eve nodded. "House arrest was denied."

One more piece of hope was torn away from Lainey. "Because of the withdrawals?" It was a question Lainey already knew the answer to. The more Lainey thought about what was happening, the angrier she became. "I will talk to Reghan and see if there are any other avenues to pursue."

"I don't think there are, Lainey. I'm mainly concerned about Bella staying with you if things don't go our way. What does Reghan say about her future with you?"

"First, I'm not allowing anyone to keep you away from me again."

"Lainey..."

"No, Eve. It has been three days! I know I'm not a miracle worker like you but give me some damn time! I said I would get you out of here, and I will."

Eve was speechless. It wasn't often Lainey snapped at her—even more rare since they've been married. *It's the stress*, Eve thought as she tried not to take Lainey's assumptions personally.

"Baby, I'm sorry," Eve said quietly. "It isn't you I don't have faith in. It's the system. My cellmate, Milly, is seventy-two. Her husband abused her, and she killed him. While I don't condone what she did, I don't believe she deserves to die in this place. She went from one hell to another. No one cared that she was abused, baby. And the people doing this to me don't care that I'm innocent. The difference is I have you helping me. But anything can happen, and I'm terrified of not being there for you or the kids."

Lainey's frustration dissipated. She wasn't angry with Eve. She was angry at the situation. "I —" she shook her head. "I didn't mean to snap at you. We weren't prepared for this, Eve."

"How could we be? We thought this was all behind us. Now, Katherine is visiting me, and Charlie's integrity is being questioned."

"*Your* integrity is being... wait. Katherine was here? Why?"

Eve took a breath. She wished she could smell Lainey's sweet scent to cleanse her of the stench of this place. "She was wired," Eve explained. "Someone who knew that she embezzled money found her and told the authorities, Lainey. They offered her immunity if she helped them."

"By coming here and trying to get you to say something incriminating?" Lainey's relief from frustration was short-lived. "What the fuck is going on, Eve?"

Eve knew when Lainey started using words she usually reserved for their private times—with incredibly different definitions—the stress was next level.

"I don't know, baby. There's one thing I *do* know, though. You'll stop at nothing to figure this out." Eve leaned forward, holding Lainey's eyes with hers. "But you don't have to do it alone. I've made that mistake before, Lainey. Please don't be like me."

---

"THOUGHT I'D FIND you in here."

Eve was lying on the bottom bunk and turned her face away from her visitor. Her time with Lainey left Eve with conflicting feelings. She had tried giving Lainey permission not to come to visit every day. As much as she needed to see Lainey's face Eve didn't want to be insensitive to Lainey's needs. Of course, that didn't go over well.

*"You promised you wouldn't push me away again, Eve."*

*"I'm not pushing you away, baby. I'm giving you options. You're taking care of everything. I just want you to take care of yourself, too. I'm trying not to be selfish."*

*"Be selfish,"* Lainey said softly. *"It reminds me that you long to be with me as much as I long for you."*

Oh, Eve longed for Lainey. That longing made it that much harder to walk away after their visit. It also made it harder to hold onto hope, and it was nearly impossible to stay strong. When Lainey was gone, Eve felt another panic attack coming on. If anyone saw that—or the tears that Eve couldn't stop—Eve would have more problems on her hands. Even with Jefa looking after her.

"I want to be alone," Eve muttered.

"Yeah, Mami, I get that. Pero, it's not a good idea. Especially in here." Jefa leaned on the small desk. "Unless Milly is with you, of course. But on your own, you're like, what they say? A barrel of... something."

"Fish," Eve supplied. She wiped her tears and sat up. "Who are you afraid will get me in here, Jefa?"

Jefa glanced out the door. "Someone I can't protect you from, Eve." She cleared her throat and pushed away from the desk. "Besides, guarding you against others isn't my only job."

"Oh?"

"Mrs. Sumptor has given me strict instructions to save you from yourself. So, come with me, yeah?"

Eve sighed. She had no desire, no motivation to get up to do anything. But since this was Lainey's wish—or order—Eve got up. "Fine. Where are we going?"

"Somewhere to cheer you up a little." Jefa looked back to make sure Eve was following her. "I hear you like to draw and shit."

Eve's eyebrow quirked. "Something like that, yes."

"We have a library where you can find some art stuff. It ain't the best, but it's something. And there ain't no fancy stands or that scratchy paper stuff."

Eve couldn't help but smile. "Easels and canvases."

"Yeah, that's what I said. There's a few paint by numbers things in there if you want to do that." Jefa came to a stop by a wooden door with a small, rectangular window. "Like I said, this ain't much, but maybe it'll keep you busy while you're here. And if that wife of yours has anything to say about it, you won't be here long enough to care about what you ain't got."

That's where Jefa was wrong. It took less than ten minutes for Eve to care about not being with Lainey or their children.

"Thank you for this," Eve said sincerely.

"Don't thank me, thank Mrs. Sumptor. She's, uh, a beautiful lady, by the way."

Eve looked up at Jefa in surprise. "You've met my wife?"

"Just for a minute after your time was up this mornin'. I think she wanted to make sure I knew who the boss really was. And to tell me about your thing for art."

Oh, to have been a fly on the wall for that conversation, Eve thought. It always tickled her that people thought Eve was the intimidating one. Lainey, however, was the real tiger.

Jefa held the door open for Eve. "I won't be far, so don't worry 'bout anything, yeah?"

Eve took a minute to look around. Women were in their own little worlds doing something that gave them a little bit of joy in a joyless situation. The library was stark compared to the number of people who used it. The smell of old books, even older paint, and body odor filled Eve's nostrils, causing her to breathe through her mouth. She would have left if her hands didn't itch to have a paintbrush or pencil in them. Besides, Lainey knew this would help Eve cope better, so she owed it to Lainey to stay and do what she did best.

"Yeah," Eve answered distractedly.

She spied an older woman dressed in khaki slacks and a white button-down shirt. Her badge hung from around her neck with LIBRARIAN in bold letters above her name. Tabatha Goodwin.

"Excuse me." Eve waited until the woman looked at her. "I was told you had art supplies here. How do I go about getting some?"

146

The woman took off her glasses, allowing them to dangle on the chain that secured them. "What are you looking for? Pencil? Paints?"

"May I see what you have available?"

The librarian stood there for a moment, just looking at Eve. "You're very polite," she observed finally.

"Is that a yes?"

"Of course. Follow me, please." Tabatha pulled open a couple of cabinets. "We have little in the way of paints." She grabbed a few paints in the hinged plastic pots Eve would get for Bella when she was one. The colors were bold and bright—and more than half gone. The paintbrush wasn't in any better shape. The artist within Eve wept at the plastic bristles.

"How about charcoal?" Eve asked, opting not to take the paints—or the paint by number sheet Tabatha pushed Eve's way.

"I'm sorry, but our budget doesn't allow us to spring for... charcoal. What you see here is all we have. If you prefer a pencil, we have these." Tabatha handed Eve a tiny pencil akin to one used while keeping score in mini-golf. Before Eve could ask, Tabatha passed Eve a piece of copy paper.

"Thank you." Eve was proud of her restraint. Getting upset over the lack of usable art supplies in jail got her nowhere. After all, it wasn't Tabatha's fault the supplies here were abysmal. *Make the best of what you have, Eve. Keep yourself sane until you can get back to your family.*

---

"Is he in?" Lainey didn't stop at the receptionist's desk, vaguely hearing a hurried *yes* before barging into Greyson's office. "I need you to do something for me."

Greyson stared up at Lainey. "I'll call you back," he said and hung up the phone. "What can I do for you, Lainey?"

"I'm sorry. I didn't mean to interrupt..."

"No apologies necessary. You and Eve are our first priorities." He stood. "Let's go see what Jules has."

"Before we do that, I need some information, and I would rather not pull Jules off of what she's doing if possible."

"Alright. What's up?"

Lainey sat and gestured for Greyson to follow suit. "Can you access the employees where Eve is being held?"

Greyson scratched his stubbled chin. "I can. Usually, that information is not public record for safety reasons, but I can access employee records as a security firm. What are we looking for? Or should I say who?"

"I need you to find out if there's someone who works there—maybe a CO—with a name that sounds like *done*."

Greyson tapped a few keys on the keyboard, concentrating on his monitor. "Common spellings of a surname that sounds like that would be Dunn or Dunne," Greyson muttered as he typed. "Here we go. Gregory Dunne. He's been a correctional officer for five years. This is his third year at Lynwood."

"Any complaints against him?"

Greyson looked up sharply. "What's this about, Lainey?"

"It could be nothing." Lainey sighed. Maybe she was reading into things. But she'd rather be overly cautious than ignore her gut when dealing with Eve's safety. "Something Eve said to me during our visit stuck with me. Complaints?"

A few more taps. "None are popping up here." Greyson tapped a finger on his mouse, narrowing his eyes at his monitor before looking at Lainey again. "Your instincts tell you that's wrong, don't they?"

Exhausted, Lainey rolled her head side to side, stretching the muscles as she contemplated Greyson's question. *I'm* done *with this conversation.* Eve didn't talk to Lainey that way. So were her instincts telling her there was more to Gregory Dunne? "Yes."

Greyson nodded. "Let me try something else."

Lainey tapped her fingers on her thighs as she waited. She forced herself not to get up and pace or bounce her leg. Her nervous energy was causing all kinds of havoc within her. The lack of sleep wasn't helping.

"You were right."

Lainey's twitching stopped immediately. "What?"

"There are multiple complaints on this guy, which is why he's been moved multiple times in his five years of being a CO."

Lainey got up and walked around Greyson's desk to look at his computer. There was a list of complaints by various inmates against Dunne. "Why would they hire him at a *women's* prison? Why the hell is he still free while my wife sits in jail for a crime she didn't commit?!"

"None of these charges are on his official record. They've been dismissed."

"Why? How?"

Greyson sat back, a look of disgust gracing his handsome face. "There could be any number of reasons. No one will believe an inmate over an officer. They were paid off."

"Or no one cared," Lainey said. Quiet fury ran through her veins. If Dunne laid one finger on Eve, Lainey would see that the man spent the rest of his castrated life in prison.

"What would you like to do with this information?"

Lainey's hands clenched into fists. "Sit on it for now," she ordered. As much as it pained her, she couldn't risk Dunne finding out they were looking into him. Not while Eve was still vulnerable to him. "Once Eve is released, we go after him."

Greyson saved the info to his desktop. "The women will have to come forward, Lainey. Or we'll have to find someone they haven't strong-armed into dropping their case."

Lainey sighed heavily. "We'll cross that bridge when we get there. Right now, I want to see if Jules has anything new."

"You got it." Greyson led Lainey to the communications room, but it was empty when they walked in.

"Is she at lunch?"

Greyson shook his head as he pushed the intercom next to the door. "She's been practically living in here since we caught this case. Shari?"

"Yes, Mr. Steele?"

"Do you know where Jules is?"

"She rushed out of here about an hour ago, sir."

"Did she say where she was going?"

"No, sir."

"Maybe she needed a break to unwind a little," Lainey suggested. It didn't make her happy, but she could understand being overwhelmed.

"Jules's idea of unwinding is sitting in that seat clacking away at that computer." He took out his cell phone and dialed a number. "Voice-mail," Greyson muttered. "Jules, it's me. What's your 20?"

"You know I'm not ex-military, right?" Jules slugged Greyson on the arm as she passed him. "Hey, Mrs.—um, Lainey."

"Hello, Jules." Lainey watched the young woman closely. There was a look of accomplishment on her face that gave Lainey hope.

"Before you think I'm slacking, I left for a reason. The big guy here knows I rarely go out into the cruel world if I don't have to."

"You deserve a break, Jules," Lainey assured her.

"Do you take a break?" Jules asked as she settled into her seat. "I didn't think so," she continued when Lainey didn't answer. "Big G, do you remember when Mrs. Steele was abducted?"

"Vaguely," Greyson answered dryly about the worst time of his life.

"You became all paranoid about it happening again. And then, Dr. and Mrs. Vale had that issue with the bitch."

Greyson cleared his throat.

"Sorry." Jules rolled her eyes. "But it's a true statement."

"Do you have a point to this walk down memory lane?" Greyson grumbled.

"Of course. I remembered what that paranoia caused you to do." Jules held up a VHS tape and a DVD. "You hardwired a surveillance system in the vacant building behind the flower shop."

Greyson pushed away from the wall he was leaning on. "Shit. I forgot about that. But, wait. One is pointed at Blaise's door and the other at Ellie's Diner. The gallery falls out of view. How is that helpful?"

Lainey's head swiveled back and forth as she listened carefully to the conversation. She wasn't quite sure what was going on, but more video sounded good. Especially if it hadn't been doctored.

"Eve has to drive past the flower shop. I can use these ancient things," Jules held up the tape and DVD, "to compare timelines to the evidentiary vid."

"You really are a genius." Lainey's pulse quickened. If Jules could establish that Eve was nowhere near Adam at the time of the shooting, that could be all the prosecution needed to drop the charges.

Jules blushed slightly. "I mean, I am, but this is pretty basic stuff. I'm having trouble finding the coder, though."

"Do we need a name to prove the video is fake? Do *you* need a name?"

Jules frowned. "Well, no, I don't think so. But don't you want to know who's doing this to you?"

"My first priority is getting Eve home. Once that is accomplished, we will go after the person responsible at full force. I'll do whatever I need to do to see them punished." Lainey bit her bottom lip as thoughts swirled around in her head. *What would Eve do?* "Jules, if you can get me irrefutable proof that Eve didn't do this in the next twenty-four hours and she comes home, I will give you one million dollars."

Jules nearly choked, and Greyson remained quiet, but Lainey could see the surprise on his face.

"Uh, I—" Jules looked at Greyson, who merely shrugged. A million bucks would be a trip for Jules. She could pay off bills or buy a car that she'd never use. Invest it. Jules mentally rolled her eyes. She knew she wouldn't invest it. And truth be told, a million bucks wouldn't give her what Jules really wanted. So, she made a counteroffer. "Keep your money. I get you proof in the next twenty-four, and you give me a job in research and development at Sumptor, Inc."

"Wait, what?"

Jules glanced at Greyson, who was now frowning. "Don't worry, Big G. I'll always be around to help you when you need me. But there's no growth here. I mean, what we do is awesome, and I want to keep doing it. I just want more, you know? And I think Sumptor, Inc. is the perfect place for me to grow."

Lainey remained quiet for a moment, measuring Jules's sincerity. A job at Sumptor, Inc. was highly coveted and competitive. Eve never relied heavily on formal education because she knew firsthand that life experience was a great tool. But to even be considered for a position, you had to be invited by Eve herself. Or go through the internship open only to the girls of Sumptor House. Lainey believed Eve wouldn't mind her making an executive decision in this case. She held out her hand.

"Deal."

They shook on it, and Jules shooed them away so she could get to work. Lainey followed Greyson out. He had been reticent throughout the entire exchange. Lainey wondered if he was pissed that she practically stole Jules right from under him.

"I'm sorry, Greyson. I really didn't mean to poach your employee like that."

Greyson waved away the apology. "Don't worry about it. I always knew Jules would leave sooner or later. She's young and ambitious and wants to develop software that negates having to do some things that aren't quite legal. At least that's what I understood when she was trying to explain what she was doing once."

Lainey hummed thoughtfully. "You trust her?"

How did Eve do this? When your enemy is faceless, you see that enemy in every face you encounter. Did Jules do this to get a position at Sumptor, Inc.? She had the expertise, but did she have the ruthlessness to do this? Especially knowing Lainey would find out the truth come hell or high water. Why chance it instead of just asking for a chance at the company?

"I think I know what you're thinking," Greyson said softly. "I trust Jules implicitly. But I promise you, if something happens, and that trust is broken, I won't hold you back from doing what you need to do."

Lainey nodded. "Thank you." She touched him lightly on the arm before glancing at the closed door Jules was behind. "For everything."

"You're exhausted, Lainey. Why don't you let me drive you home?"

"I appreciate the offer, but I use the drive time to think. And to breathe. Call me if Jules gets anything?"

"Of course."

Lainey left, leaving her faith in Jules. With any luck, Eve would be home soon.

# Fifteen

*L*ainey pulled into the driveway and shut off the engine. A few reporters still camped out in front of the gate, but not as many as before. She wondered if that was James's doing or if the interest had died down without anyone giving interviews. Either way, Lainey was grateful for the slight reprieve. It was, however, Sunday. And it looked as though the ladies still thought girls' night was a good idea. Lainey knew they meant well, but she didn't know if she had it in her to be social. Even with the women who had been nothing but supportive.

She closed her eyes, breathed in deeply, and counted to ten before letting it out slowly. Perhaps since Ellie insisted on being here, they could have a yoga session. Bella would enjoy that. Once she felt emotionally stable enough, Lainey slipped out of the car and headed to the front door.

"Lainey?"

Lainey's hand paused on the doorknob. She turned slowly to see the man standing beside James. "Charlie." Her first instinct was to go to him and embrace him. If he were here for any other reason, she would have. But now... "Are you wearing a wire?"

"What?"

"It seems Howell is pulling people from Eve's past and coercing them to wear wires. What did they promise you?"

"Lainey, I'm not wearing a wire. I wouldn't do that to Eve. Or you."

Lainey narrowed her eyes. She didn't know who she could trust, and that was wreaking havoc on her mental well-being. She stepped back when Charlie stepped forward.

"Lainey, please."

"Are you here on the job, Charlie?"

"Yes. I'll always be here if you and Eve need me."

Lainey heard the pain in Charlie's voice. She also hears the pain in Eve's at each visit. "We shouldn't need you. Either of you," she said, glancing at James. "And until this is over, I can't worry about your feelings. I don't want to believe you would hurt us, Charlie, but I need to be sure after Katherine. Right now, though, I need to go inside and be with my family." She paused, wanting to apologize for her attitude. Instead, she continued inside without another word.

"Don't take it personally, Harris. She's under a lot of stress."

"Yeah. What did she mean about Katherine?"

James lifted a shoulder. "Don't know. Why don't you take some time to find out? If Katherine is a threat, we need to know."

Charlie nodded. "I'm not wearing a wire," he reiterated to the man that was now his boss.

"I know. Make sure it stays that way. You betray Eve or Lainey, and you'll deal with me personally. Got me?"

---

"I'M HOME!" Lainey tossed her keys on the small table next to the door. The house was oddly quiet. With the cars out front, she expected to walk into chaos. "Hello?"

"Mommy!"

Bella ran from the kitchen, straight into Lainey's arms. Lainey didn't miss the glance towards the door or the extra-long embrace.

"Hi, my sweet girl." Lainey allowed Bella to stay right where she was until Bella was ready to let go. When she did, Lainey kissed the tip of Bella's nose. "I see a lot of cars out there, but no one in here. Is everyone playing hide and seek, and you're it?"

Bella giggled. "No, Mommy. We in the kitchen. Auntie Ellie making tookies!"

"Ooo! What kind?"

Bella's face scrunched up in concentration. "Nick doobles."

Lainey bit her lips, holding in a laugh. "Nick doobles, huh? Are you sure they're not called snickerdoodles?"

Bella frowned and tilted her head. One little eyebrow lifted just like her momma. "Dat's what I said!"

"Of course, it is. I'm sorry I misunderstood."

"Momma come home today?"

Lainey shook her head. "Not yet, bug."

"How many more sweeps?"

"I don't know, sweet girl, but I *do* know she's working really hard to get home very soon. Okay? Can we be strong and wait for her?"

Bella's little head lowered, and her bottom lip trembled. But she nodded. "We strong, Mommy." She looked up, tears shining in her eyes. "We save some nick doobles for Momma?"

"Absolutely. Nick doobles are Momma's favorite. We better go in there and get some before Darren and Kevin eat them all, huh?"

"Auntie Ellie made a lot!" Bella smiled. She held her hand out to Lainey, and they walked hand-in-hand to the kitchen.

And that's where everyone was congregated. Ellie was smacking Hunter's hand away from a fresh out of the oven batch of cookies. Mo was stuffing cookies into her mouth while Patty shook her head and handed her a glass of milk. Cass was feeding Rebecca a morsel, making even that look sensual. Kevin was tossing pieces of cookies in the air while Darren jumped around to catch them. And Blaise was complaining that cookies were *not* red velvet cake. It was all so ordinary and so... them. Lainey burst into laughter.

All heads turned to her. Mouths full of cookies dropped open with confusion. It only made Lainey laugh harder. She didn't blame them for looking at her like she was crazy. It was entirely possible that she was losing what was left of her sanity. Bella didn't care, though. She was laughing right along with Lainey. She probably didn't know what was so funny, but the girl was going all out with the giggles. Of course, that made Lainey laugh even more. By this time, the others had joined in.

The guffaws got louder when Lainey sank to the floor, holding her stomach. The cramping made it feel like she hadn't laughed in so long. God, time without Eve stood painfully still. Nothing felt right anymore. Colors were less vibrant, food tasted bland. On a typical day, Lainey would have walked into the house and immediately caught the aroma of Ellie's cookies. But nothing had been normal the past couple of days. All she wanted—all she *needed*—was Eve's scent. Eve's touch. Even that was ripped away from them by a piece of plastic that felt like an ocean between them. Someone was trying to drive a wedge between them, and Lainey was terrified it would work.

How would she function without Eve in her life? For years Lainey was merely going through the motions. She loved her children dearly. There was never any question about that. But being with Jack, Lainey had lost her will to be the woman she knew she was inside. Then she met Eve, and Lainey's entire world was brought to life like a blooming flower. She couldn't go back to being lonely and miserable.

She felt so cheated. Her life with Eve had just begun. They had finally found their true happiness, and someone had to come and attempt to fuck it all up. Lainey wasn't naïve enough to think Eve would survive being locked up without coming out as a different person. A reverted person. Lainey had already seen Eve's uncaring, cruel side directed toward her. If that happened again... The laughter turned into wracking sobs.

Rebecca sobered quickly when she realized Lainey was no longer in control of her emotions. "Kevin."

Kevin nodded. "Hey, Darren and Bells, let's go, um, play some video games!"

Darren got the hint and jumped up with enthusiasm. "Yeah! C'mon, Bells! Wanna play some *Animal Crossing*?" He grabbed Bella's hand and pulled her along with him.

Rebecca then eyed her wife. "Cassidy."

"Yep. Hunt? Mo? Let's . . ." Cass gave up making an excuse and merely gestured for her friends to follow her. She lifted her phone in Rebecca's direction and received a nod in return. With permission granted, Cass sent a text to Aunt Wills as she left the kitchen with Mo on her heels.

Hunter lowered her head to Ellie's ear. "Should I stay?"

Being a doctor had its advantages when tense situations arose. But when that situation involved a friend who was breaking down because of something they didn't deserve, it became a disadvantage. Hunter knew all too well what it was like to watch the woman you loved suffer at the hands of others. She was intimately familiar with the all-consuming ache and fear of the possibility of losing the love of your life forever. Because of that, Hunter was incapable of leaving her emotions out of this, and her heart broke for Lainey.

Ellie shook her head. "Patty is here," she whispered. She knew her wife well enough to know what was going on in her head and heart. Hopefully, being with the kids—including Cass and Mo—would help ease that lingering pain. "I'll call you if we need you, okay?"

Hunter nodded and kissed Ellie on the cheek. Before she left, Hunter laid a calming hand on Lainey's head, wishing she could take all the pain away.

Once they were alone, Rebecca, Ellie, Blaise, and Patty all sat down on the floor, surrounding Lainey in a cocoon of solidarity. They said nothing, simply allowing Lainey the time she needed to expel the intense emotions she was feeling. None could say they weren't expecting this. Something had to give with everything that was happening in such a short period. And all of them had someone they loved as much as Lainey loved Eve. Some had even experienced life-altering hurdles with those loved ones. So, they offered Lainey strength and understanding. And a safe place to let go of all the pain she had been holding inside.

"I'm sorry," Lainey hiccupped.

"No apologies necessary, child. You get all that out. We got you." Patty rubbed Lainey's arm, surreptitiously checking her pulse simultaneously.

"Patty's right, sweets. What's happening is unjust and just plain shitty." Blaise reached above her and grabbed a bottle of wine she had just opened. She handed it to Lainey as Ellie wiped tears from Lainey's face with a tea towel. "Take you a long swig of that."

Lainey smiled woefully, accepting the bottle. She managed to swallow down a generous gulp past the lump in her throat. If her life wasn't falling apart, Lainey would have appreciated the smoothness of the wine. Blaise never failed to bring the finest. She leaned into Rebecca, who had her arm wrapped around her.

"We moved here to get away from the dreadfulness of Eve's past. This was supposed to be our forever home."

"It still is, babe. You and Eve are going to get through this."

Lainey hoped Rebecca was right. Each second without Eve made it harder to keep seeing the light at the end of the tunnel. "I feel guilty being able to come home to this place while Eve is... there. I lie awake at night, wondering what she's thinking. Is she okay?" *Does she feel like she's back in that tiny room in Paris?* "She's locked up in a cell, and here I am, in this enormous house with my freedom."

"You're exactly where Eve would want you to be, sweetie. Taking care of your home and children until she gets back." Ellie pushed a strand of hair off Lainey's tear-stained face and handed her the towel. "Don't minimize your role in this, Lainey. If I know Eve—maybe Rebecca can tell me if I'm right—she's holding on because of you. She knows she doesn't have to worry about anything out here because *you* are here."

Rebecca took the bottle from Lainey and held it up. "No truer words!" She saluted her friends and took a drink. She passed the bottle over to Patty.

"Hear, hear!" Patty tipped the bottle in salute, then took a drink before handing it to Ellie.

"To Lainey and to getting Eve home soon." Ellie raised the bottle—sending up a silent prayer that Eve really did come home soon—and took a drink.

Blaise accepted the bottle of wine from Ellie. "*Kia ora!*"

Lainey's eyebrows furrowed. "Pardon?"

Ellie chuckled lightly. "You know things are serious when Blaise starts speaking in her native tongue. Now, let's get you cleaned up and bring the kids back in. Otherwise, we will have to eat all these cookies by ourselves."

EVE SILENTLY FOLLOWED Dunne back to visitation. After what happened with Katherine, she was wary of what was behind that door. But there was no way she was missing a visit from Lainey if she decided to come back. And since Dunne was a grade-A asshole, Eve had no idea what—or who—she was walking into. Lainey had assured her that she had told their friends of Eve's request not to have visitors. Knowing how the close-knit group was, Eve wouldn't hold her breath that they would listen.

Dunne unlocked the door and ushered Eve to the middle cubicle. Eve sighed and stood there for a full fifteen seconds before sitting down. Even then, she didn't pick up the receiver until her visitor gestured to it.

"I have to admit," Eve began once the receiver was to her ear. "I expected Rebecca to be the one to defy my wishes. Not you."

Willamena smiled warmly. "As rebellious as that woman is, one thing Rebecca respects the most is a person's desires. Though, I would expect a good lashing once this is over."

Eve bit the inside of her cheek. Eve knew the woman was deliberately making a Mistress joke about her niece by the sparkle in Aunt Wills's eye.

"I'll keep that in mind."

Silence.

"How are you, Eve?"

"Are you here for a session, Dr. Woodrow? Did you forget your notebook?"

Willamena let Eve's attitude slide. The woman was under a great deal of pressure. And if Willamena knew Eve as well as she thought she did, there was a lot that Eve wasn't processing.

"That was a question from a friend, Eve."

"As my friend, you should be with Lainey. I'm fine." Willamena merely stared at Eve until the normally unflappable woman fidgeted. She leaned in and lowered her voice. "It's a nightmare, but it's nothing I haven't been through before. But I have something now that I didn't have back then to keep me going. I have a family. I will hold on as long as I can for them. Willamena, I saw something in Lainey's eyes earlier. Such a determination that it fed my hope. If I have that, I won't regress to the person I was before. I owe that much to Lainey and our children. Anything less would be unfair."

"It's unfair to you to not allow yourself to feel the way you need to, Eve. But I understand that may be difficult in your current situation." Willamena glanced behind Eve, noting the guard watching them intently. "Promise me something? Promise that you *and* Lainey will come talk to me once this is over. I'm asking not only as your doctor but as family. Not even the great Eve Sumptor can come out of a situation like this unscathed. And if you let it fester," Willamena tapped on the partition that separated them. "It will be like you brought this damn thing home with you."

Eve let that sink in, then nodded. "Fine. I will talk to Lainey about it later."

"Time, Sumptor!"

Eve's nostrils flared with frustration. It had been many years since Eve took orders from anyone. She was looking forward to getting back to that life.

"I have to go." Eve hesitated. "Thank you for visiting, Willamena."

Willamena smiled. "I knew you wouldn't mind. I'm always a phone call away, Eve. Remember that."

Eve nodded and hung up the receiver. Willamena waited until Eve disappeared behind the door before standing. She took a moment to compose herself. It had been more difficult than she thought seeing Eve so young and vulnerable. But Willamena had no doubt Eve would bounce back from this once it was over. *Please let it be over soon.*

Willamena stopped at the desk to get her belongings back on the way out. "Thank you." She smiled kindly at the officer as she switched on her phone. As soon as it booted up, multiple messages came through. **Lainey. Breakdown.** "Damn." Wills grabbed her keys and rushed out.

---

As Eve walked back to her cell, she replayed her conversation with Dr. Woodrow in her head. *"Promise that you* and *Lainey will come talk to me..."* Eve was so worried about falling back into her past self she didn't stop to think about what this was doing to Lainey. Of course, Eve saw the fatigue. But it was what Eve couldn't see that bothered her the most. Would they be able to move past this bump in their road? Would they ever be the same as they were, or would there always be a shadow hanging over them? *All brilliant questions to discuss with Lainey and Dr. Woodrow,* Eve expected.

Milly was sitting at the small desk when Eve walked in. The older woman was thumbing through the papers Eve put there before her unexpected visitor. It was a good thing Eve liked her cellmate. Normally, she wouldn't tolerate such an invasion of privacy. *Nothing is normal anymore.*

"I thought you'd be at dinner," Eve said lightly, hoping not to startle the old woman too much.

"I was." Milly handed Eve a napkin stuffed with two dinner rolls. "Ya missed it, again, so ya get these. No arguments. Ya gotta eat."

Eve couldn't imagine anyone telling Milly no. At least, not anymore. After what the woman had been through, she earned enough respect for Eve to do as she was told. She bit into one of the rolls and immediately wished she had water to wash down the dry, yeasty bun. What she wouldn't give for *anything* cooked by Ellie right about now.

"You do these?" Milly asked as Eve chewed. Eve nodded, and a pensive look graced Milly's weathered face. "You're an actual artist."

"Thank you," Eve muttered around another dry, bland bite of bread.

"That what you do out there?"

Eve shrugged. "Kind of. I sell other people's art. I own an art gallery." She was purposefully being vague. Milly had been great to her from day one. That didn't mean Eve blindly trusted her. In fact, there was only one person in the entire world that Eve put her blind trust in.

"An art gallery? Ain't that some fancy shit." Milly shuffled the papers again, then turned one around for Eve to see. "This your wife?"

Eve's smile was instantaneous. "Yes. And our children."

Milly studied the picture. "They're beautiful. You're lucky to have them."

If Eve was being honest, luck had a lot to do with it. There were many times when Lainey could have walked away. Many times when she should have. But Lainey stuck with Eve through everything. Even being faced with the possibility that Eve was a murderer. The roll slipped from Eve's hand. Reality was starting to set in. If Eve was convicted, she couldn't ask Lainey to stay faithful to her. Sure, Bella would be in Lainey's care, but who would care for her? The mere idea of Lainey falling in love with someone else shattered Eve's heart. And her resolve to stay strong in front of others. Unbidden sobs wracked her body.

Milly was by Eve's side in an instant. Close proximity helped. She patted Eve on the shoulder as a grandmother would while gently nudging her to lay down.

"Milly's here. I want you to close your eyes and sleep. Dream of being home with that family of yours." She lifted Eve's feet and tucked them under the covers. "I keep tellin' ya you need to keep your strength up. If you don't do it for yourself, do it for your family. I can feel in my old bones that you'll be back with them soon."

Eve fell into a fitful sleep out of sheer exhaustion. With just an ounce more of that "luck," Lainey would meet Eve in her dreams.

# Sixteen

*L*ainey woke with a start. "I'm late!"

Ellie looked up from her phone. "Lainey?"

Lainey blinked, confused about where she was. She looked around, trying to ground herself. Obviously, she had fallen asleep, but for how long? Ellie and the ladies were still there, so maybe it was just a few minutes. Lainey rubbed her eyes. She hadn't been this disoriented since being sleep-deprived when Darren was born.

"I—I need to get ready for my visit with Eve."

Rebecca gestured for Ellie to stay seated and went to Lainey herself. "Babe, it's just after eleven. *PM.*" She ran her hand over Lainey's hair, noticing the sweat that beaded on Lainey's forehead. "You've only been asleep for a couple of hours. Why don't you go take a hot shower? Maybe it'll make you feel a little better."

"Two hours," Lainey repeated softly. "Where is Bella? The boys?"

Rebecca nodded to the blanket fort. "Asleep."

"You're still here." It was an unnecessary statement, but it made sense to Lainey to say it at the moment.

"We are."

Lainey looked around again. Ellie, Blaise, Aunt Wills—when did she get here?—and Patty were lounging comfortably on pillows that littered the floor. They were in sweats or pajamas. Surely Lainey would have noticed that sort of attire before. "Where is everyone else?"

"Cassidy, Hunter, and Mo went home. They didn't want to overwhelm you with too many guests for too long. We," Rebecca tilted her head, "decided to stay. Lexie is staying with her boyfriend tonight but was kind enough to let us borrow some of her clothes to get comfortable."

"Lexie has a boyfriend?" Lainey shook her head. Had she been so preoccupied with her own life and work that she neglected to know more about the woman who taught and watched her kids? What else didn't she know about Lexie? Was there more to Lexie's apparent loyalty? God, this situation was causing Lainey to question everything she thought she knew. "You didn't have to stay."

"As if we would leave," Blaise scoffed.

"You have lives of your own," Lainey argued. "People you love."

"Who are all safe and sound at home," Ellie soothed. "They understand that until Eve is home, too, we will be here with you when you need us. And you needed that nap, so we stayed with the kids while Lexie went out."

"What we're trying to tell you, child, is you're not alone." Patty grabbed a cracker from the snack plate Ellie put together and laid back on the fluffiest pillow she'd ever felt.

Lainey truly appreciated the sentiment. But there would always be something missing in her heart and life when she was away from Eve. "I love you all. I hope you know that. And I'm grateful for everything you're doing for us. But no matter how many people I'm surrounded by, without Eve, I'm always alone."

---

LAINEY STOOD in the enormous walk-in shower allowing the multiple jets to wash away the rest of the fog that lingered in her mind. She tried —unsuccessfully—not to think of the conditions Eve had to shower in. Eve never liked crowds or attention. Lainey always found that ironic, given Eve's profession and notoriety. But now, Eve was unwillingly made to do everything that caused her pain. The cramped, locked room.

164

The mob of people. Being forced to be away from her family. Being completely out of control. Lainey knew Eve. This was torture for her. A slow and painful death of her soul. Lainey's stomach dipped, and she had to sit on the bench to catch her breath. *Stay strong, my love.*

She turned the shower off and stepped out, shivering as the cold air hit her wet skin. It struck her then how much her body missed Eve's touch. Lainey attributed the nerves and restlessness to stress. But it was also related to the fact that she hadn't had physical contact with her wife. Not just the lovemaking, but simply touching. Seeing Eve and not being able to touch her was pure misery. There was a connection between them, a need to hold hands or put their arms around each other, that they were denied. Lainey had the privilege of wearing Eve's robe or a piece of her clothing to feel that connection. Eve had nothing. Lainey feared that would interfere with Eve's spirit as much as being locked away did.

"So, you work harder at getting her out," Lainey told her reflection in the mirror. "Stop standing here feeling sorry for yourself and get to work."

She chose a pair of Eve's sweats, a matching sweatshirt, and a pair of Eve's favorite fluffy socks. To the outside world, Lainey looked ready to curl up by the fire and read a good book. But as Eve's scent surrounded her, this was Lainey's armor. *This* made her strong. She drew in the aroma with a deep breath and held it as long as possible. With her head held high and a new sense of purpose, Lainey walked back out to her friends. She pointed to the kitchen, knowing the ladies would follow her without question.

"I've had my breakdown and shower," Lainey began as she sat at the head of the table. "Now, it's time to figure out who the fuck is doing this to us."

Blaise grinned. "I like this Lainey. Welcome to the badass bitch club." She leaned in and whispered. "By the way, Ellie is the president of that club, too."

Lainey chuckled when Ellie joyfully flipped Blaise off. The levity felt good and odd at the same time. Either way, she was pleased that Blaise and the others didn't pretend around her. The more normalcy she had, the better it was.

Rebecca raised a brow and tapped a pink nail on the table. "Are you two done?"

"It sounds like Mistress is ready to get down to business." Lainey winked at Rebecca, silently thanking her for getting them back on track. She reached behind her and grabbed a pad of paper and pen off the counter. She poised herself to write, but nothing was coming to her. "I don't know where to start."

"We start with who in the hell wants to hurt Eve," Patty suggested.

Lainey sighed. "I don't know. If this had happened two or three years ago, I could give you an entire list of people who wanted to cause Eve harm. But they're gone now." She pinched the bridge of her nose. "We have to think beyond Eve's past. What would someone's motive be?"

"What do we know for a fact?" Ellie asked.

"Well, we know the video and texts are fake." Lainey hesitated. Then she wrote her first name on the list.

Blaise craned her head to read what was written. "Really? Jules?"

"Blaise, please forgive me. I know she works with your husband, and he vouches for her. And honestly, I don't want to write any names on this list because that means I know them. I don't want to think someone close to us is capable of doing this. But Jules asked for a job at Sumptor, Inc., and right now, that's motive to me."

"Wait, she's in the middle of working the case, and she asks for a job?"

Lainey could see Blaise's fiery side start to ignite. She put a dash next to Jules's name and wrote: Possible motive is a job. "Technically, I started it. I told her that I'd give her a million dollars if she could find me proof in the next twenty-four hours. She opted for a job instead."

"So, we think she would put Eve in this situation so she could be the hero? She finds the proof to get Eve released, then gets a cush job?"

Ellie looked up at Rebecca. "Cush? Jessie says that word. Are you learning lingo from your wife?"

"Well, she does owe me after what I do for her."

"Focus, ladies. There's something I don't understand if it is Jules. Why take the money?" Lainey absently doodled money signs in the margin of the paper.

Blaise's head snapped up. She was preoccupied with going over her knowledge of Jules in her head. "What money?" As Lainey explained about the accounts, Blaise stood up to pace. "That makes no sense. If Jules took the money, she could jet off to anywhere in the world and do whatever she wanted—or nothing—for the rest of her life. Why stay?"

"Exactly. There's something else. When I met Jules, she seemed a bit... awestruck."

"That's because she admires you, Lainey," Blaise told her. "She read that article on you and Eve and the gallery. I swear she kept that thing on her desk for a month. I thought she was going to frame it."

Lainey smiled. She remembered doing that article. Eve had made sure Lainey was the main feature. When Lainey asked why Eve said it was time Lainey and her talent were front page news and not reduced to a sentence referring to her as "Eve Sumptor's wife." That lack of ego was one of the things Lainey loved so much about Eve.

"Eve is certainly someone to strive to be like," Lainey said with pride.

"She is," Blaise agreed. "But for Jules, it was you."

Lainey's nose wrinkled in confusion. "Me? Why me?"

"Why not you?" It was the first time Aunt Wills spoke since Lainey woke up and noticed she was here. Lainey assumed she was doing what Dr. Woodrow did best. Listening. "There's everything to admire, Lainey. You focus on the trials and tribulations Eve has survived, but don't think of your own. You were in an abusive relationship for years. Even if it wasn't physically abusive, sometimes the internal scars take longer to heal. And you still managed to raise two young, respectful men. You're just as strong and admirable as Eve."

Lainey let that sink in. It was easier for her to take compliments from Eve. She could chalk it up to being head over heels in love. But anyone else and Lainey had a more challenging time believing it. Her psych books would tell her that doubt came from years of being with Jack, who saw her as nothing more than his servant.

Lainey scratched Jules's name off the paper. "Okay, moving on." She chewed on the pen, hating herself for even thinking this way. "God, it hurts to write this one," she murmured. Lainey's hand shook as she wrote **Lexie**.

"Why Lexie, sweets? What would be her motive?"

"Because I'm paranoid?" Lainey blew out a breath as she sifted through her scrambled thoughts. "Her motive could be the money. We pay her very well for being here for the kids. She has a place to stay. But I didn't know she had a boyfriend. What if he forced her to betray us?" Lainey drummed the pen on the pad. "This is driving me crazy. I'm questioning Lexie's loyalty because *she* never questioned the validity of what's happening. What am I doing?"

She scratched Lexie's name off.

Ellie laid a hand over Lainey's as she kept scribbling. "Hey, we're talking it through. There are no accusations, just inquiries."

"Do you suspect any of us?" Rebecca asked carefully.

"What? No, of course not. None of you have anything to gain from this. Plus, you all rallied so hard for me and Eve to get together. I can't see you tearing us apart now." Lainey looked Rebecca in the eye. "I know you're a dominatrix, but I don't think you're a sadist."

"You're right. I'm not." Satisfied with Lainey's answer, Rebecca continued. "Let's move on to the next person." Rebecca didn't believe that Jules or Lexie was behind this in her heart of hearts. This felt more personal than a job or money. "We're *sure* it's no one from Eve's past?"

Lainey wrote **Katherine** on the paper. "Katherine is an ex-employee of Eve's who embezzled money from the company. I can't see her being smart enough to pull this off."

"Maybe she hired an accomplice," Blaise said. "If she's already stolen money from Eve before, that could be her reason."

Lainey laid her head back, wincing when it hit the wood of the chair back a little too hard. "It doesn't make sense. Eve literally saved her life. Tony was minutes away from having Katherine killed before Eve intercepted her. Eve gave her a new life in a new city. Yet, Katherine pays her back by wearing a wire while visiting her at the jail."

"Ungrateful bitch," Blaise muttered.

"Perhaps." Lainey shook her head. "If Katherine was telling the truth, someone found her and offered immunity for the embezzlement. But the thing is, Eve never went to the authorities about Katherine. The authorities wouldn't know about that unless...."

"Unless?" Ellie prompted.

"Eve kept records of everything. She has files and recordings of Katherine and Meredith working with Tony to steal money from Sumptor, Inc. She would have used it against them if need be, but... Tony got to Meredith, and Eve couldn't handle another death because of her father's unhealthy obsession with her. So, she chose to give Katherine a new life. Deep down, I don't think Katherine did this. She's selfish enough to wear a wire to help herself, but she's not a mastermind."

"Okay, so Katherine is more of a minion," Blaise suggested. "Who else do we have from that time?"

Lainey's brows furrowed. "Charlie. He was the detective from when Eve was being framed the first time."

"Jesus," Rebecca murmured under her breath. "The woman can't catch a break, can she?"

"I remember Charlie," Aunt Wills spoke up. "He turned on his partner who was creating evidence against Eve, correct?"

"Yes. His fellow officers didn't like that, and he felt his only option was to leave the force. Charlie now works for James, Eve's go-to security guy."

"Maybe he resents Eve for losing his career over her?" Ellie had met Charlie briefly. His involvement didn't ring true even as she said it. Her gut told her Charlie only wanted peace for Eve.

"You don't believe that any more than I do, do you?" Lainey asked. "Not Charlie. Not James. That brings us back to square one."

"Why not James?" Blaise shrugged when Lainey looked at her questioningly. "We're talking through everyone, but you completely skip over why James couldn't do this. He's Eve's security which means he has the knowledge to get sensitive material. He was also there when Tony was alive, yes?"

Lainey nodded. "He was Tony's henchman from before Eve was even born. I skipped over him because of that. His loyalty is to Eve. Before that, his loyalty was to Marie, Eve's mother. Tony lost James's allegiance when James fell in love with Marie."

"Child, if this wasn't so terrible for you and Eve, I'd think it would make a good movie." Patty scooted away from the table. "Mind if I boil some water for tea?"

"If you boil enough for everyone, help yourself," Lainey winked.

"You got it. Now, continue with James's story."

"Not much more to say. He helped Marie take money from Tony so she could get away from him and start a new life. Then she got pregnant..."

"Wait, James isn't?"

"No. Though I wish he was when I think about it. Maybe then he would have left with Marie, and she would still be alive. And Eve wouldn't have gone through everything she did."

Ellie put her hand on Lainey's arm and rubbed gently. "It's a cruel world, sweets. We do our best with the hand we're dealt. Eve is strong—stronger with you by her side. As much as we may want to change the past, it made us who we are."

Lainey patted Ellie's hand, giving it a little squeeze. It was amazing how different her life was now. Jack was never too keen on Lainey having her own life back in New York. That meant friends were few and far between. None ever lasted, and none were deep enough to be emotionally connected. Then she met Eve. And, through Eve, she met some of the best friends a woman could ever have. Lainey was eternally grateful they were there helping her through this trying time.

Patty set cups in front of everyone, steaming with hot water and a tea bag. "I chose a calming green tea. I hope that's okay with everyone." They all nodded, murmuring their thank yous, except Rebecca. "You want something else, child?"

"Hmm? Oh, no. I'm sorry, Patty, this is perfect. Thank you."

"What are you thinking about?" Lainey fiddled with the string attached to the tea bag. When Rebecca was pensive, the cogs were turning in that brilliant mind.

"Something I don't want to think about," Rebecca confessed. "But I can't shake the thought."

"Someone to put on the list?" Lainey pushed the pad and paper towards Rebecca. "At this point, I'll take any ideas if it gets us closer to proving Eve's innocence."

Rebecca sighed. "Even if I wrote down Adam's name?"

"Adam?" The surprise was swift, catching Lainey off guard. "I don't understand. You think he... killed himself?" A chill washed over Lainey, causing her to get goosebumps. She wrapped her arms around herself, rubbing her arms for warmth or comfort. Maybe both. Lainey had objections and reasons why that couldn't be true. *It can't be true.*

"I see you working it out in your head," Rebecca said softly. "Let's talk it out like we did the others. Give me reasons you think it can't be."

"B-because he wouldn't do that to Bella."

Was that it? Was that *all* she had for the *can't be* side? Lainey frantically looked around the table for help, landing on Aunt Wills, who bit her lip.

"Dr. Woodrow, please tell me Adam couldn't hurt his daughter like that."

Aunt Wills immediately went into psychiatrist mode. She knew Lainey trusted her instincts no matter what name Willamena was called, but this topic needed a professional opinion. "Unfortunately, I can't. From what I understand, Adam had been distant from young Bella for some time now. It's entirely possible that if he were planning this, he did that to cut off his emotions."

"But why?"

Rebecca nodded at her aunt, taking the reins. "You know I helped Eve establish Adam's architectural firm, right?" Lainey nodded. "Well, even after Eve sold him her share of the company, I retained access to the finances. Lainey, he was a terrible proprietor. If I'm being honest, I wouldn't be surprised if we found Adam had a vice—perhaps gambling. That's the only thing that makes sense as to why his firm was hemorrhaging more money than the expenses suggested."

"You're saying he killed himself because he was in debt?" Lainey asked incredulously. "If he needed money, he could have asked Eve. Adam is Bella's father. She would have helped."

"I don't know, babe. I'm literally throwing out ideas here. Take this scenario. Let's say he came here in a last-ditch effort to win Eve back. She gives him a big fat no in the form of a knee to the nuts. He certainly can't ask for money after that and humiliate himself further. His backup plan is to punish Eve for leaving him. And you for taking her away."

Lainey's belly burned and twisted. She wished to hell what Rebecca was saying didn't make sense. "He... he's not tech-savvy enough to pull this off. And if you're right about his financial situation, he couldn't afford to hire anyone this skilled."

"Unless," Blaise piped up, "he promised that person access to the accounts and everything in them."

Lainey sat back in her seat with such force the two front legs left the floor. Could it be true? Could Adam have orchestrated this all because he was broke and jealous? Could he be that cruel to his daughter? She looked to Willamena and Ellie. Both women had an incredible sixth sense on the topic of human beings.

"What do you think?"

Ellie glanced at Willamena, who nodded. Then she pulled the notepad over and wrote Adam's name.

"Shit." Lainey took the pen back and wrote **DEBT, JEALOUSY, HATRED, DESPAIR**. Then she circled Adam's name. He was the only name that checked all the boxes. But who did he hire? And with him gone, would they ever know the whole truth? Of course, this was all speculation that required verification, but it was a step. Part of Lainey—the part that loved Bella and Eve—wanted nothing more than for this theory to be debunked. The other part... Lainey didn't want to think about that part.

"If he did this to Bella," she began, her voice rough with emotion. "Eve is going to be pissed. God, if this is true, Adam turned into Tony."

How was she going to break this to Eve? Of course, they could be completely missing the mark, and telling Eve wouldn't be necessary. She blew out a frustrated, weary breath. Who was Lainey trying to kid? Herself? She knew damn well she would tell Eve everything, despite the outcome. Again, Lainey was back to how she would drop this bomb without collateral damage. Just as she was about to have a minor panic attack, her phone buzzed.

With sweaty palms, Lainey took out her phone and read the notification. It was after midnight, which meant it couldn't be Eve. But that didn't mean it couldn't be about Eve.

"Is everything okay?" Ellie worried about the deepened frown on Lainey's face.

"Um, yes? I don't know. James says Jules is here." Lainey typed a quick response for James to let her pass, then looked up. "This has to be good news, right? Blaise? She wouldn't come here this late just to tell me she has nothing, would she?"

Blaise shook her head. "No, I don't think so. But she is pretty impatient when she has news—good or bad."

They all got up and rushed to the door. Lainey opened it before Jules could ring the bell and wake the kids.

"Hey... everyone." Jules's eyebrows raised. She hadn't realized she would be presenting to an audience.

"Do you have something?" Lainey asked impatiently. It took a split second for her to remember her manners. "I'm sorry. We can go inside to the kitchen. Do you want something to drink or eat?"

"Mrs. Sumptor," Jules stopped Lainey before she could retreat back into the house. "I don't need anything. I didn't want to wait to tell you that I found it. The proof you need."

"What?" The ringing in Lainey's ears drowned out most of what Jules was saying, but she was sure she heard that right. *Proof you need.* She felt herself being led to one of the chairs on the porch. "T-they can't dispute it?"

"No, ma'am, they can't. I have the originals here," Jules patted her messenger bag. "You need to give these to Mrs. Sumptor's lawyer. Now, I didn't find out who did it yet...."

"Can you tell me what you did find?"

"Oh, yeah. Um, I made a copy of my report with the videos included. May I?" Jules nodded towards the seat next to Lainey and sat down when Lainey scooted over. "Big G, uh, Mr. Steele and Mr. Drake have a copy of the report, and this one is yours. I'll spare you all the details because you can read them when you want. But basically, the cameras that Mr. Steele set up across the alley that point at Knight in Bloom...."

"I'm sorry, what cameras?" Blaise asked.

"Uh." Jules looked up at Blaise. "He didn't tell you? I guess, like, when you got back from your ordeal, he, um, put extra security around. But, like, old-school VHS that can't be hacked. There's feed from the flower shop and Mrs. Vale's diner."

"My diner?"

Jules winced. "Yeah."

"Ladies!" Lainey inhaled deeply, hoping it would help calm her erratic heartbeat. "I'm sorry, I just need to hear how I'm going to get Eve out of jail."

Blaise and Ellie apologized and told Jules to continue as they stood back with the others. The group watched Lainey closely as Jules gave her the news.

Jules opened her iPad and brought up the file she wanted. "I have the footage used for evidence on the left here, see?" She made sure Lainey had a clear view of the screen. "On the right top is the view from Knight in Bloom. The bottom right is the view from Ellie's Diner. I'm going to play the one that shows Mrs. Sumptor, um...."

"Go ahead," Lainey ordered, her voice raw with emotion. She forced herself to keep her eyes on the video as it played. This time she was searching for anything that indicated it was a fake.

"There!" Jules announced loudly just as the gun went off on the screen.

Lainey jumped from Jules's enthusiasm as much as the loud pop. But nothing had looked different from the first time Lainey watched the video, and she frowned.

"I didn't see anything."

"Check out the timestamp. Keep that in mind, okay?" Jules zoomed in on the video feed that focused on the flower shop. "Now watch."

The video showed Eve driving out of the alley. The recording wasn't as crisp as the other, but Lainey could clearly see Eve's face. Her demeanor was calm, yet Lainey could tell by the slight flare in Eve's nostrils that she was unhappy. Still, how did seeing Eve flee the scene exonerate her from the crime? *Check out the time stamp.*

"It's the same," Lainey said with a small gasp. "The time is the same."

"Exactly!" Jules grinned excitedly. "That's not it, though. Look here." She played the vid from the camera focused on the diner. "Do you see them?"

Lainey squinted, leaning closer to the screen. "Someone else is there!"

"Yep! If we go back a little further, you'll see this person following Mr. Riley into the alley."

Blaise stepped up and bent to get a closer look. "You can't see their face. And Eve is in a blind spot in this perspective."

"True. However, after seeing these vids, I knew what I was looking for. I peeled every layer of that digital video like it was an onion with a prize in the middle. And there was!" Jules brought up another screen. "This is the original."

The group moved closer, giving Lainey strength as they watched the video intensely. The figure—dressed head to toe in black with a hood and a mask—walked up to Adam after Eve left. A gun raised, and a muted pop sounded. Again, the timestamp read the same time Eve was seen driving away. Then the figure kneeled beside Adam's body.

"What are they doing?" Lainey angled her head. "Are they saying something?"

"I've tried to isolate the sound, but I couldn't hear anything. If I figure out who hacked this shit to create the damning vid, I think we'll know who that is." Jules went back to the recording that showed the figure following Adam. "The dumpster they're standing next to is six feet tall. I stopped by there to measure just to make sure. Anyway, that makes our killer here approximately five foot seven or eight by my calculations."

"Why didn't Eve react to the gunshot?" Ellie asked.

"Oh, well..." Jules returned to the undoctored video. "See here?" She pointed to the gun. "I thought something on the barrel of the gun looked off. Mr. Drake confirmed my suspicions when he told me there was a silencer on the gun. I think they amped up the sound when they made the changes."

"I have to call Reghan." Lainey stared at the screen as though if she looked away, it would all disappear.

Jules reached into her bag again and pulled out a lockbox. "This is the original VHS and CD from Mr. Steele's security system. I also included a digital copy on a flash drive and the original video from the gallery's system. The report has all the information your lawyer might need. Except who did it. I think I'm close, though."

Lainey took Jules's hand. "What you've done is incredible, and I'll never be able to thank you enough. You've certainly earned your spot at Sumptor, Inc."

"Oh, uh." Jules blushed. "Yeah, um, I'm not going to hold you to that. Or the million bucks. I just used that as motivation. I was getting frustrated with not breaking this code. Turns out, you gave me the focus I needed to get past that and give you what *you* needed. Now, I can work on swatting this bug." She grinned. "Oh, and it was the right thing to do."

Lainey smiled. "A deal is a deal. Once this all calms down, come to Sumptor, Inc. and get your credentials. We could use someone like you on our team." She patted Jules's hand and stood up. "I'm going to call Reghan and see what she can do to get this evidence seen as soon as possible." Lainey took the lockbox from Jules and hurried inside.

"She truly appreciates everything, Jules," Rebecca assured. "Don't take it personally that she didn't say goodbye."

"Oh, no big. Totally get it. Like, you all will make sure she's okay, right?"

"Of course. We got this," Ellie answered. "Are you okay to get home?"

"Yeah. I'm hopped up on Red Bull. I have at least another hour and a half before I crash." Jules handed Blaise a folder. "Mrs. Sumptor forgot this. It's my report. Could you maybe tell Big G that I'll be a little late tomorrow? I need fresh eyes if I'm going to get this ass clown. G'night!"

"Jules," Blaise called out. "Excellent job."

# Seventeen

*E*ve followed the guard down a hall she was unfamiliar with. She had been summoned, told that her lawyer was there to see her. But this wasn't the way to visitation and the hairs on the back of Eve's neck stood up. Her hands were clammy, and Eve found herself continuously wiping them on her pants as they made the trek. How bad was the information Reghan had if she requested a private meeting?

"Here," the guard said, pushing open a door and ushering Eve in.

The first thing that hit Eve was the scent and the intense electricity in the air that Eve only felt when she was in the same space, breathing the same air as her wife.

"*Lainey.*"

Lainey ran to Eve and threw her arms around her. It felt like an oasis in an arid desert being in Eve's embrace again. Feeling those arms squeezing her tight would be a memory she would call upon when she needed reminding of how much she had—and how much she could have lost.

"We did it, love," Lainey murmured against Eve's neck.

"I don't understand." Eve was reluctant to give up her hold, so she merely looked over at Reghan while keeping Lainey close to her. "I'm free?"

"Not yet," Reghan said apologetically. She hated tainting this beau-

177

tiful reunion with reality. But there were a few hoops they had to jump through before Eve could officially be considered free. "However, we have a date with the judge in," she checked her watch, "thirty minutes. I'll present what we've found, and then it's up to his honor."

"What did you find?"

"Ask your wife," Reghan smiled. "She is the one who did all the heavy lifting."

Eve looked at her wife, who was firmly adhered to her side. "You'll tell me everything?" she asked quietly.

"Of course. Right now, you have to get dressed. I brought you some clothes and a few things to freshen up. I know Reghan is trying to rein in our expectations. But unless something is *terribly* wrong, I'm taking you home today."

*Terribly wrong.* That was Lainey's way of saying *corrupt.* The way this case was going, Eve couldn't discredit that possibility. She nodded and kissed Lainey on the forehead. She wanted more. Needed more. But Eve wanted at least three hours in her own bathroom, scrubbing every inch of her body from head to toe before offering herself to Lainey.

"Am I supposed to change in here?"

"There's a bathroom through that door," Reghan pointed. "Twenty-seven minutes."

Lainey started to follow Eve but was stopped at the door. "You don't want me to help."

It wasn't a question, and Eve knew Lainey understood. But she answered anyway. "I do." She drew Lainey to her, whispering close to her ear. *"I know you love me no matter what I wear or look like. I just... I need to feel more like me."*

Lainey smiled and caressed Eve's cheek before handing over the garment bag. "Everything you need is in there."

Eve shook her head, bringing Lainey's hand up to her lips. She kissed the back of Lainey's hand. "Everything I need is right here."

Lainey's eyes fluttered closed, and she gently pushed the bag into Eve's arms, nudging her towards the bathroom. "Twenty-three minutes, my love. Reghan will be with you the whole time. I'll see you at the courthouse."

"You're not riding with me?"

"I can't. But I wanted desperately to see you, so Reghan arranged for me to bring you the outfit. Soon, Eve. No one will tell us what we can and can't do very soon. I love you."

"I love you, too, Lainey. I'll see you there."

---

**ARE you sure you don't want us there?**

Lainey smiled at Ellie's text. Of course, the support would be wonderful, but Lainey didn't think Eve was ready for everyone to see her. Or perhaps Eve was the one not ready to see everyone else. There was also no guarantee that things would go their way. So the easiest thing was to accept that support from afar.

**I love you for offering. I'll call as soon as I can with more info.**

Lainey turned her phone off and slipped it into her pocket. The courtroom was fairly empty for a Monday morning. Quiet murmurs filled the air while they prepared for the proceedings. Lainey's leg bounced anxiously as she waited for Eve to arrive. She wanted this to be over, but she knew this was still the beginning. If they didn't find out who was doing this to them, what was to say it couldn't happen again?

The click of a door caught Lainey's attention, and she looked over just as Reghan walked into the courtroom with Eve following her. Lainey had chosen a simple black blazer for Eve, paired with a crisp white shirt and black slacks. The black shoes were low-heeled and elegant yet unassuming. It was a subdued departure from Eve's typical power suit, but it worked perfectly for this situation. Eve looked professional yet approachable. And tragically beautiful to Lainey. It was the weariness in Eve's eyes that broke Lainey's heart.

Eve's eyes met Lainey's. She winked in hopes it would bring Lainey a bit of peace during this process. She received a small smile in return and felt some peace herself. As she sat down, Eve glanced over at the prosecution. Howell didn't look happy, and Cross sat quietly, tapping the pads of her fingertips on the table. Questions mounted in Eve's brain, but she remained silent while Reghan readied herself for the hearing. Her trust in Lainey allowed Eve to sit back and not ask those multiplying questions.

"All rise!"

Eve stood along with everyone else. *Here we go,* she thought. In these next moments—however long this was going to take—Eve would find out her fate.

"Be seated." Judge Patrick opened a file in front of him. "I understand we're here because new evidence was uncovered?"

Reghan stood again. "Yes, your honor. First, on behalf of my client, we would like to thank you for agreeing to this emergency hearing."

Judge Patrick nodded. "I take it you've looked over the Information the prosecution sent over?"

"We have, your honor. We've —"

"Your honor," Howell interrupted. "We haven't received notice of any of the findings from the defense. I request a continuance until we've gone over everything."

"Relax, Mr. Howell. In all fairness, you indicted Ms. Brannigan's client without handing over Information to her beforehand. We'll be hearing their findings at the same time. Let's see where it takes us, shall we? Continue, Ms. Brannigan."

"Thank you, your honor. If it's alright with you, your honor, we would like to play some video for you." Reghan gestured to the multimedia equipment she had her assistants set up. Including a VCR.

"Your honor!"

Judge Patrick held up his hand to cut off Howell's rebuttal. He nodded for Reghan to continue.

"Thank you. We received what they labeled as surveillance video taken from my client's place of business. Upon thorough review from not one but multiple experts, we've deemed this video as tampered with."

"Objection, your honor! The video was obtained lawfully by the police on the scene and maintained a chain of custody until presented to the D.A.'s office."

"I'm sorry, your honor," Reghan interjected. "But we have reason to believe that is not true. If you could give me five minutes, I will show you what our experts have found."

Judge Patrick looked at Howell. "Objection overruled. Ms. Brannigan, you have a short leash. Let's not dawdle."

Without hesitation or complications, Reghan played the video evidence for the court. Jules's impeccable notes helped show every discrepancy between the original video and the tampered one. Reghan then introduced the VHS and CD surveillance from the system Greyson set up, which included the actual—yet still unidentified—assailant.

It was the first time Eve had seen the video. As hard as she tried, she couldn't drag her gaze away from the images on the large monitor. She saw Adam walking towards her. They exchanged words, Adam grabbed her, and Eve retaliated by kneeing him. Then Eve watched as the figure on the screen—supposedly her—took out a gun, aimed, and shot the father of her daughter. The voices around her dulled as she watched him fall to the ground. Eve didn't realize that she had audibly gasped at the sight, and she barely registered the touch of a hand on her shoulder.

The visuals changed when Reghan played the different versions. Yet, Eve watched as Adam fell to the ground in each rendition. The only thing that changed was the shooter. The Eve on the screen turned into a masked figure. Someone who had followed Adam to the alley. Someone Eve never saw as she drove away, leaving Adam behind. The slight squeeze on her shoulder brought Eve back to the present. She remembered now why she was sitting in this seat and who was there for her. She snuck a look behind her, catching Lainey's compassionate eyes. With a small smile, Eve touched Lainey's hand. If she could, she would crawl into Lainey's arms and cry until she had no more tears for everything that was happening.

"Again, your honor, I have multiple experts willing to testify against the video's authenticity the prosecution entered into evidence."

"Experts that were paid off, no doubt," Howell argued.

"Objection, your honor. Mr. Howell has made other allegations of that nature about my client without a shred of evidence."

"Sustained. Keep the commentary to yourself, Mr. Howell. Unless you would like to tell me how a video you maintain never broke the chain of custody was tampered with."

"I—I don't believe it was, your honor. If we could recess, that would allow the state's experts to examine these findings."

Eve's pinpoint attention was once again focused on the proceedings. There was something in the D.A.'s voice that wasn't sitting right with her. There was a disdain that went further than a typical prosecutor vs. defendant. For the life of her, Eve couldn't figure out why he had it out for her.

"Your honor, I believe the D.A. is stalling. The experts I have are respectable professionals that the prosecution has used before."

"Why on earth would I stall?" Howell asked Reghan directly.

"Because you know I'm about to expose you."

Howell scoffed, but Eve saw the flash of fear in his eyes.

"Your Honor, the theatrics of the defense are a waste of everyone's time. Especially yours. You have better things to do than listen to Ms. Brannigan's slandering excuses. The state is asking for a week to gather our own uncompromised experts."

Judge Patrick's eyebrows raised. "A week?" He chuckled. "Your pandering won't help you here, Mr. Howell. You're asking for a week to do what the defense has done in two days."

"With all due respect, Your Honor, we can't be certain what the defense claims is true."

Judge Patrick picked up the notes in front of him. "These findings are signed off by no less than three experts that have been in my courtroom before. And, as Ms. Brannigan pointed out, you have utilized them, Mr. Howell. Are you telling me you've called on experts you don't trust?"

"N-no, Your Honor. But..."

The judge held up his hand, cutting Howell off. "Ms. Brannigan, please explain what you meant by exposing Mr. Howell. And I warn you, I will not tolerate false accusations in this courtroom. If this is nothing more than grandstanding, I will hold you in contempt for wasting my time, as Mr. Howell put it. Understood?"

"Yes, Your Honor." Reghan opened a blue folder and took a stack of papers out. "You'll find defense exhibits two through five."

"Objection, Your Honor. Again, we did not receive any of this so-called evidence."

"Actually, Your Honor, ADA Cross has a copy of everything," Reghan countered. The shit was about to hit the fan at the prosecution's table, but Reghan knew Sloan was strong enough to stand her ground. "May I continue?"

"Overruled, Mr. Howell," Judge Patrick confirmed, nodding at Reghan. "What exactly am I looking at, Ms. Brannigan?"

Eve watched, intrigued, as Howell leaned over and whispered angrily to ADA Cross, who looked for the papers in her briefcase. It was almost comical how slow she was thumbing through the files. Was she doing that on purpose? Was she giving Reghan a chance to make her claims before Howell could step in?

"This, Your Honor, is evidence that Mr. Howell received a large donation to his campaign on the same day he indicted my client."

Howell's head whipped around. "Objection!" he screeched. "Donations are not illegal, and nothing about my campaign has anything to do with this case!"

"It does when that donation is accompanied by a certain video portraying my client as a murderer."

Howell sputtered wildly as Lainey's heartbeat pounded in her ears. Did she hear that right? If what Reghan said was true, that meant the D.A. was corrupt. But who was the donation from? She glanced at Eve. Lainey had seen that intense look before. She knew Eve was skimming through memories of her past, trying to determine how Peter Howell was connected to her. And why he was so intent on ruining her life.

Judge Patrick sat up in his chair. The air in the courtroom changed dramatically. "Is this true, Mr. Howell?"

"I don't know what Ms. Brannigan thinks she found, but if that video showed up simultaneously, it's merely a coincidence. I do not control when the police hand over evidence to me."

"A coincidence? You had a copy of that video before the police were called to the scene, Mr. Howell." Reghan clicked a button on the remote she still held. "Defense exhibit six through ten, Your Honor. This is footage from the security cameras at Knight in Bloom, Ellie's Diner, Sumptor Gallery, LA, and security cameras set up by Drake and Associates—a premier security firm. It shows police coming to the scene at a quarter to five in the morning. This timing is significant for a few reasons. Number one, there were no 911 calls reported. How did they know to be here? Second, an employee at Ellie's diner comes in at five. By that time—only fifteen minutes after the officers arrived at the scene —Mr. Riley's body had been removed. And third, at no time did the officers engage with the early employee. Nor did they ask for footage from any surveillance equipment that was clearly visible from the alley."

"That is very compelling, Ms. Brannigan." Again, the judge held up his hand to cut off Howell's objection. "Where does Mr. Howell fit in this scenario?"

"Keeping the time of the police presence in mind, Your Honor, if you turn to page three, you'll notice that the donation hit D.A. Howell's account an hour before. Page four will show you a timestamp of Mr. Howell's email that included a large attachment. That attachment, Your Honor, was the altered video. In light of this new information, the defense asks that the court drop all charges against my client."

"Your Honor, this is a farfetched narrative to cast doubt on my ability to prosecute this case. In fact, it's almost laughable if it weren't so desperate."

"Defense exhibit eleven, Your Honor. We've obtained records including messages from an anonymous source who promised more money and a high-profile 'slam dunk' case. Mr. Howell was all but guaranteed another term for District Attorney."

"Your Honor!"

"That's enough, Mr. Howell. One more word out of you, and I'll hold you in contempt." Judge Patrick read through the evidence carefully. "This is a serious accusation, Ms. Brannigan."

"So is murder, Your Honor. Yet there was no proper investigation. The prosecution relied on that fake video. We learned that D.A. Howell ordered authorities to arrest my client immediately during our own investigation. And, without sharing their evidence until it was too late, the D.A. sent tainted evidence to you without taking a moment to verify the authenticity of what was sent to him."

"And these are affidavits from detectives, private investigators, and witnesses?"

"Yes, Your Honor."

"And the authenticity of the emails and messages from the D.A.'s campaign have been verified?"

"Yes, Your Honor."

"Obviously, this is a matter that requires more attention, but we have already wasted enough of Mrs. Sumptor's time. Will the defendant please stand?"

Eve obliged and stood, smoothing her slacks as she did.

"Taking this additional evidence into consideration, I am dismissing the case against Mrs. Sumptor. With prejudice."

"Your Honor, you can't be serious...."

"Mr. Howell, you are in enough trouble as it is. My ruling stands. Mrs. Sumptor, it is within your right to press charges against the D.A. and anyone else who put you through this. That includes this court."

"I appreciate your candor, Your Honor. As long as District Attorney Howell is investigated and prosecuted, I have no interest in being weighed down in litigation. I just want to go home and be with my family."

Judge Patrick nodded. "Very well, Mrs. Sumptor. You are free to go." He banged his gavel. "Counselors, I want you *all* in my chambers in fifteen minutes." Judge Patrick glared at Howell. "Do not be late, Mr. Howell, or I will issue a warrant for your arrest." He stood and left the courtroom.

As soon as Eve turned around, Lainey was there, tears in her eyes and a tremulous smile. Lainey held her arms open to Eve, and instead of wasting time going to the opening in the partition, Eve swung her legs over to get to Lainey. Eve buried her face in the crook of Lainey's neck, willing herself not to lose it here in the courtroom.

Reghan's eyes teared up, and she cleared her throat. "I hate to interrupt, but I'm sure you want to get home to your kids."

"I have to go back to the prison," Eve said, still holding onto Lainey.

Lainey's head snapped up. "What? Why?"

"My wedding ring is there, baby. I need it back."

Reghan motioned for someone to join them. "We picked up your things earlier, Eve." She took the bag from her assistant, thanking her quietly, and handed it over. "Make sure everything is in there."

Eve was already digging through the bag. She took out the watch Lainey gave her and her phone and put them in her pocket. After a moment of anxiety, she found her ring at the bottom corner of the bag. The relief that flowed through her was intense. Eve dropped the bag, not caring about anything else that was in there, and handed the ring to Lainey.

"Will you put it back on me?"

Lainey heard the quiver in Eve's voice and saw the slight tremble in her hand as she took the ring. "Always," she whispered as she slipped the ring on Eve's finger.

Reghan backed away to give them privacy, but stopped when she felt a hand on her arm.

"Was she involved in putting Eve away?" Lainey asked, nodding toward ADA Cross.

"No."

"Did she give you the information about Howell?" Reghan remained silent, and Lainey nodded. "Forgive her."

"Excuse me?"

"Forgive her," Lainey repeated. "She was only doing her job. And when it came down to it, she chose to do the right thing."

"How?" Reghan shook her head. "I'm not confirming anything, but if Sloan—ADA Cross—gave me anything, I'm sure it was to further her own career."

Eve had been listening quietly to the conversation. She never questioned Lainey's ability to see more than people thought they were showing. Hell, even Eve hadn't known about Reghan and ADA Cross. But if that woman had a hand in getting her back to her family, Eve owed her more than she could ever pay.

"Hypothetically, if someone were to turn against their boss, that would put a target on their back, not a medal around their neck. Perhaps you should take Lainey's advice."

Reghan frowned. She couldn't think about all of this now. She had a case to build against Peter Howell. And there was still work to do for Eve and Lainey. Even though Eve was released and the charges dropped, that didn't change the fact that the actual killer was still out there. And the Sumptors were still in danger.

"I'll, um, be over later with papers for you to sign, and we can go over the next steps. Right now, I have to get to the judge's chambers, and you need to get home. Stacy will take you out the back way where your car will be waiting."

"Thank you, Reghan." Lainey stepped up and hugged the lawyer. "I should have never doubted you."

Reghan shrugged. "And I should have never suggested you convince Eve to take a plea deal. I underestimated you, Lainey. That'll never happen again. Go. Take your wife home. I'm sure the kids are excited to see her."

As Reghan walked away, she passed by Sloan.

"They're a lovely couple. Seeing them together makes you want to believe in love."

Reghan looked over, observing the sadness in Sloan's eyes. *Forgive her.* "Walk with me to chambers?"

Sloan nodded, taking one more glance at Eve and Lainey. She didn't need to hear what they were saying. The love was so mighty between them that Sloan felt its warmth wash over her. A sad smile touched her lips as she fell in step with Reghan.

Lainey smoothed the lapels of Eve's jacket for no other reason than to touch her. This was real. She was taking Eve home. Later, Lainey would be able to comprehend everything that happened in court. How Reghan was prepared with much more than just evidence that the video was tampered with. But for now, all Lainey wanted was to help Eve forget about this hell.

"Ready to go home, my love?"

Eve breathed in deeply through her nose. She closed her eyes as Lainey's scent filled her nostrils. Gone were the stenches of stale air and despair. She wasn't done with the prison yet. But for now, it was time to move on.

"I'm ready."

# Eighteen

$\mathcal{E}$ve peered out the window as Lainey drove them home. Blurred buildings and cars passed by without regard. Being in the passenger seat gave her mind too much time to wander. She couldn't help feeling worthless. Or maybe the correct word was unworthy. In the business world, Eve Sumptor was a powerhouse. Her presence generated healthy doses of fear and respect. What would that world look like now? Would her credibility take a hit because of this? Did she care? Perhaps Eve Sumptor was done with being a target. What was it doing to her family? Could Lainey keep loving someone who constantly put her in the crosshairs? Would Kevin and Darren want Eve in their lives for that same reason? And Bella. Eve's stomach rolled.

"Pull over, please."

Lainey immediately turned on her blinker and slowed down. She pulled over to the shoulder and before she could stop, Eve was out of the car. Lainey threw the car in park and hopped out just in time to see Eve heaving on the side of the road. This was a side of Eve Lainey had never seen before. It wasn't the sickness that worried her. It was Eve's demeanor. With everything Eve had been through in her life, this was the most defeated Lainey had ever seen her.

She had been stealing glances at a very pensive Eve since they left the courthouse, hesitant to speak. Mostly because she wasn't sure what to

189

say. It had been a long time since she felt a disconnection with Eve. Of course, Lainey had expected Eve to be upset or triggered by being locked up. What she hadn't expected—and didn't understand—was the feeling that Eve was pulling away from her. Surely it was just the effects of all the horrible things happening in such a short amount of time. So, she would give Eve the space, time, and love she needed and they would get over this hurdle. They had to.

"Are you okay?" Lainey gently stroked Eve's back as she remained bent over, panting. Even with Eve's hands firmly on her knees, Lainey noticed the shaking.

"Does she hate me?" Eve managed, her throat raw from getting sick. After nearly four days of not eating much, it surprised her she had anything in her stomach to expel.

Lainey knew exactly who Eve was asking about. There were four people in Eve's life that could bring out such breathtaking, soul-shaking emotions in a once stoic woman. Their daughter was one of them.

"Do you know what Bella does every time I come home?"

Eve looked up at Lainey and shook her head.

"She stares at the door, waiting for you to walk through it with me. I see her hope. And the disappointment when you're not there. If she's not sleeping in our bed waiting for you, she's out in the living room sleeping in the blanket fort Darren and Kevin made. She doesn't hate you, my love. She misses you. She's so confused about what's going on, but one thing she knows for sure is she needs her momma. We all need you."

Eve scoffed but said nothing. Why would anyone need someone who brings so much drama to their lives? But Eve knew if she voiced that fear to Lainey now, they would have to have a conversation Eve wasn't ready to have.

Lainey, however, had no problem reading the fear on Eve's face. "Do you want me to call Dr. Woodrow?"

"No!" Eve closed her eyes and took a breath. "I'm sorry, but no. I don't want to talk to anyone but you and the kids tonight. Is that okay?"

"Of course it is, love. I've already talked to the ladies, and they know they should give us—you—some time. But you know they won't stay away for long."

The ghost of a smile touched Eve's lips. "I wouldn't dare think otherwise." She touched Lainey's arm lightly. "This hit me harder than I thought, baby. I just need a...minute."

"Take all the time you need, love. I'm not going anywhere."

*Maybe you should*, Eve thought sadly. It wasn't what she wanted, but if being with her put Lainey or the kids in jeopardy, was it worth being selfish? *Stop, Eve. You're feeling sorry for yourself.* She could feel herself closing off but vowed not to do that to Lainey again.

"I think being home with you and our kids will help." Eve straightened her jacket, dusting off invisible lint. "Ready?"

Lainey ducked her head into the car and brought out some mouthwash she kept in the console. Eve laughed when Lainey handed it over to her. She opened the travel-sized bottle and drained the entire contents into her mouth. After swishing it around, she unceremoniously spat it out. Oh, if her rivals could see her now, spitting unladylike on the side of the road. But it didn't faze Lainey. She merely took the empty bottle from Eve and handed her a piece of minty gum.

"Can I get in the car now that my breath is minty fresh?" Eve teased.

"I suppose." Lainey rested her palm on Eve's cheek. She stroked her thumb across Eve's smooth skin and watched as Eve closed her eyes as she leaned into the touch. "We'll get through this, my love. We've been through worse."

"I almost prefer being shot over being stuck in a tiny box," Eve confessed. She shook off the dirty feeling that thought gave her and kissed Lainey on the forehead. "But you're right. We will get through this."

---

EVE LOOKED around as Lainey pulled up to the gates and pressed the remote. "The press is gone."

"Hmm. I guess they had a juicier story to feed on," Lainey said nonchalantly as she drove through the gates toward the house.

"Did you... Baby, did you leak something about the D.A.?"

Lainey's hand flew to her chest in feigned indignation. "I would never. I only told a friend."

"Do I want to know who this friend is?"

Lainey shrugged. "Fine. I told all our friends. I didn't know it was confidential information. My bad."

Eve bit her lip. "God, I love you."

"It's a good thing you do."

Eve glanced around again once they were inside the property. "James and Charlie?"

Lainey shrugged again. "Skulking around out of sight, I'm sure. Most likely avoiding me."

Eve frowned. "Why would they avoid you?"

"Because with what happened with Katherine, I don't trust anyone, and I *may* have made that clear. Especially to anyone who was questioned by the authorities when they got here."

Eve's eyebrows shot up. "You suspect Charlie?"

Lainey came to a stop and cut the engine. "I suspect everyone until we find out who's behind this."

"Even our friends?" Eve asked carefully.

"I had a moment that I wasn't proud of, and I forbid you to tell them, but no. None of them have a motive to do this."

"But Charlie does?" Eve held up her hand to stop Lainey's obvious angry rebuttal. "That wasn't a criticism, baby. I'm just trying to catch up here."

Lainey relaxed. She hadn't imagined she'd have to defend her actions or thoughts to Eve. Now that she understood where Eve was coming from, Lainey could answer rationally.

"They ousted him from the police force because he helped you. I know he's found a place with James, but I can't rule anything out. If it turns out he has nothing to do with this, I will apologize. Until then, I stand by my decision to suspect anyone who might feel slighted by you or us."

"That's a long list," Eve murmured apologetically.

"Actually, it's not, love. You've wronged no one. In fact, you've done more than your share of good. If anyone feels slighted by you, that's their own issue, not yours. I know you've been compensating for things you feel were your fault, but none of this belongs on your conscience."

Eve cleared her throat, swallowing the lump of emotion that was building up. She had never had someone believe in her the way Lainey did. Not since her mother died. Eve wondered if it would ever feel normal or warranted.

Lainey took Eve's hand, lacing their fingers together. "Are you done stalling now?"

Eve blinked at her wife. "What?"

"Honey, your baby girl is right behind that door up there and we're still sitting in the car. You're stalling."

Eve blew out a breath. Yes, she was stalling. The mighty Eve Sumptor was scared. She needed time to analyze her feelings, but certainly couldn't do that now. She had responsibilities. And she had a little girl who needed her. "Do they know I'm coming home?"

Lainey shook her head. "No. I didn't want to get their hopes up just in case..."

"Just in case corruption won?" Eve finished. She squeezed Lainey's hand. "Is Lexie here?" As much as she liked Lexie, Eve wasn't ready to face anyone but her family. While she knew she did nothing wrong, public opinion was harder to convince. Despite Lainey's assurances that their friends were on her side, Eve still felt the sting of embarrassment.

"No, she's spending the night with her boyfriend to give us time alone."

Eve raised a brow. "Boyfriend? When..." She held up a hand and shook her head. "No more stalling. Let's go see our kids."

---

PER EVE'S REQUEST, Lainey walked into the house first. She heard Bella's little voice asking Darren if her colors were right. They must be drawing together again. It was one of Lainey's favorite things to watch. Darren had become quite the teacher to his little sister.

"Hello?" Lainey called out, knowing Eve was staying out of sight. She had wanted to gauge Bella's temperament herself. Lainey understood that side of Eve. While Eve always respected Lainey's advice and her assessments of situations, Eve always needed to see things for herself. It was a byproduct of the way she grew up. Eve's mother lied about everything being fine. Madam Bussiere lied about giving Eve a safe place to live. Lainey knew in her heart it was less about Eve's trust in her and more about Eve's mistrust in herself. She'd been wrong too many times to break the habit of self-doubt.

"Mommy!" Bella tossed her crayon aside and ran toward Lainey.

"I'm glad you're home," Kevin began as he sauntered into the room. "This kid is like a bottomless p..." His words trailed off when he saw who walked in behind Lainey. Kevin's eyes tracked to his mom, then to Bella, who had yet to see Eve. Not wanting to spoil the moment between Eve and Bella, Kevin stayed back, draping his arm over Darren's shoulder when his brother came up next to him.

As she always did, Bella looked past Lainey to see if her momma was coming home. This time, instead of disappointment clouding her blue eyes, they grew wide with excitement. And perhaps a bit of disbelief.

"Momma?"

That one quiet word was both a question and an oath full of hope.

"Hi, bug."

"Momma!!"

Bella sprinted toward Eve and flung herself into Eve's waiting arms. Sobs were broken up by sniffles and hiccups, and little arms held on to Eve's neck as though if she let go, Eve would go away again.

"It's okay, baby girl. Momma's here," Eve murmured in Bella's ear. Her heart swelled and broke at the same time. She had done the one thing she swore to herself she would never do. Eve hurt her little girl. Of course, she didn't do it on purpose... And it was at that moment Eve understood why her own mother told her everything was okay so many times. Eve would have done anything in her power to have kept this pain away from Bella.

"You stay home wif me, Momma?"

"Yes, bug, I'm staying home with you." Eve stood up, bringing Bella with her. The little girl's arms were wrapped around Eve's neck so tight it was a wonder Eve could breathe. But she didn't complain. Bella needed comfort, and Eve was more than happy to give it to her. "With you and Mommy and your brothers."

Eve's eyes brimmed with tears as she held her free arm out to Darren, who immediately came to her and burrowed himself into her embrace. He didn't say a word, just held on, and Eve felt everything he wanted to say in his silence. Her eyes then tracked to Kevin, and she smiled when he joined in the group hug.

"Welcome home, Mom." Kevin failed to keep the emotion out of his voice. Eve coming home meant his mom could breathe again. Darren could laugh again. And Bella could finally mourn her father the way she needed to.

"Thank you," she whispered in his ear. "For everything."

"Always."

Lainey could see Eve becoming overwhelmed with emotions. While Eve was getting better at allowing those emotions to flow without stifling them, this was bound to be too much. Hell, it was almost too much for Lainey. She blamed lack of sleep, stress, and poor nutrition for the insufficient capacity to steady herself.

Lainey wiped tears from her cheeks and cleared her throat. "You, um, were mentioning something about a bottomless pit when we came in."

"Right. Aunt Ellie had a ton of food sent over and this one," Kevin ruffled Bella's hair, getting a small giggle from the little girl, "keeps sneaking into the kitchen to pick at everything."

Eve chuckled. "Is that true, bug?"

Bella shrugged. "I hungy."

"You're always hungry." Eve tickled Bella's tummy. "Kevin is right. This little belly is a bottomless pit. I guess we should get in there and eat before it's all gone."

Bella squirmed until Eve set her down. She took off toward the kitchen before stopping abruptly and running back to Eve. "You comin', Momma?"

"Right behind you, baby girl."

Bella hesitated as though she were gauging whether her momma was telling the truth. "'Kay. Huwwy or I eat your feetas."

"My fajitas! Don't you dare! I just need two minutes with your mommy, okay? You leave my fajitas alone."

Bella sniggered. "I eat your cheeeeeese!" she teased as she ran after Kevin.

As soon as the children were out of the room the smile fell from Eve's face. "She didn't mention Adam at all."

"She hasn't since I told her what happened," Lainey disclosed.

Eve brought her attention to her wife. "Should we be worried?"

"I think once everything settles down and you can talk to her properly about what has happened, we'll have a better understanding of where she is."

Eve nodded. "Promise to be there with me when I talk to her?"

"Of course." Lainey's phone chimed, and she pulled it out of her pocket to check the incoming text. "Reghan will be here within the hour with whatever papers you need to sign. She said she wanted to get it over with as soon as possible so we could have the rest of the night worry-free."

"It won't be worry-free until we find out who did this to us."

*To us.* For some reason, that simple statement gave Lainey comfort. Maybe it was because Eve recognized she wasn't the only one suffering. That they were in this together.

"Tonight it will be," Lainey insisted. "Tonight we focus on our kids and you being home. Tomorrow we'll sort out the rest."

Eve smiled. Bold Lainey never ceased to amaze Eve. For the past two years Eve had watched Lainey become more secure with herself. And with her power as a Sumptor. Eve still didn't know how Lainey pulled off getting her released in such a short amount of time. But she was certainly looking forward to hearing the story.

"You're right, as usual. We better get in there or Bella will make good on her promise to eat all the cheese."

"Are you sure you don't want to take a shower and rest first?"

Eve longed to shower the past four days off her body and mind, but that could wait. "And risk missing Ellie's famous fajitas? No way. Baby? I'm fine, okay? I promise."

Lainey searched Eve's eyes for any sign of deception. There was fatigue, but also a genuine need to be close to those who loved her. Besides, now that she didn't have to worry about how Eve was doing, Lainey was famished.

"Let's go eat before those rugrats leave us nothing but bell peppers."

"You don't like bell peppers."

"Exactly!"

"Here, Momma!" Bella held out her hands revealing something wrapped haphazardly in a napkin.

They had just finished devouring the meal Ellie had lovingly sent over for them. A quick look in the fridge and Eve could see they wouldn't have to cook or order in for an entire week. *An entire week of not leaving the house*, Eve thought. It sounded like heaven to her. Hell, if she didn't have to leave the house ever again, that would be fine with her. For now, they all sat there with full bellies and smiles on their faces. They didn't talk about the problems they were going through. Instead, the kids treated Eve as though she had just come home from a business trip instead of jail.

"Whatcha got there, bug?"

"I made you tookies! Nick doobles!"

"Wow! You made these for me?" Eve glanced up at Lainey who mouthed "*Ellie.*"

"Yep! Mommy says dere your fabrite, so I make dem."

Eve slid off the chair to her knees so she could be at Bella's level. "Your mommy is right. I love them. And I love you, bug. So very much. Thank you."

Bella's grin was proud. "I wuv you, Momma. You eat one?"

Eve unwrapped the napkin and caught a whiff of cinnamon goodness. She loved Ellie's cookies, but she also just ate a lion's share of fajitas. One look at Bella's hopeful face, though, had Eve picking up a cookie and taking a big bite.

"Mmm! That is yummy, bug. You really made these just for me?" Bella nodded vigorously. "Well, there's only two things that could make these cookies even better."

"What, Momma?" Bella kept eyeing the cookies in Eve's hand.

Eve could practically see Bella licking her chops. *Bottomless pit.* "One, a big glass of milk. And two, if you, Mommy, and your brothers had one, too!"

Bella's eyes lit up. "'Kay! I get the milk!"

"Whoa there, Bells!" Kevin scrambled to get up when Bella opened the fridge and tried to get the gallon of milk out all by herself. "Let me help you. Darren, wanna get some glasses?"

"You're so bossy," Darren grumbled playfully. He gathered the used plates as he got up and winked at his moms.

"What's wrong? Can't reach them, squirt?" Kevin teased. "Need a stool?"

"Need a bag for your ugly face?" Darren shot back, kicking Kevin in the shin as he passed by.

"Kids," Lainey chided. "Let's not earn punishments tonight, okay?" She dipped her napkin in her waterglass and wiped dust off Eve's knee as she sat back in her chair. "I need to mop. You're only sharing because you're stuffed, aren't you?" Lainey looked up from her task and saw Eve smirking at her. "What?"

"You are such a mother."

Lainey crumpled up her napkin and threw it at Eve. "Next time I'll let you walk around with stains on your knees like Blaise does after a visit from Greyson during girls' night."

That threat tickled Eve's funny bone, and she laughed heartily for the first time since Friday morning. "I love you so much." She leaned over and kissed Lainey softly.

"I love you, too."

"'Scuse me." Bella pushed her way between her moms and set a big glass of milk on the table. "No kiss, mommy. It's tookie time!"

Lainey chuckled. "Bring on the nick doobles!"

# Nineteen

$\mathcal{E}$ve stood under the hot spray of water, her eyes closed, as it cascaded over her body that was raw from scrubbing the past four days off. The shower was larger than the cell she had been in the past few days, yet Eve struggled not to feel caged in. Dinner with her family was incredible. Hearing them laugh and joke around was music to Eve's ears. Especially after hearing women fighting all hours of the day or COs barking instructions. So why was she having such a hard time ridding her mind of the bad thoughts?

When Reghan stopped by earlier with papers for Eve to sign, Eve's mood deteriorated considerably. The couple of hours of pure bliss with her family coaxed Eve into a false sense of being back in an uncomplicated life. She forgot about Milly and Jefa. She didn't think about Dunne once. Nor did she dwell on the basic necessities that weren't so basic in jail. You had the meals, showers, and bathrooms. But privacy didn't come with the package.

The worst part was Eve forgot about Adam. Bella was eating, laughing, and showing Eve some drawings she and Darren had done recently. It was all... normal. So normal that Adam's death ceased to exist in her mind. Until now. Reghan left, the boys cleaned up the blanket fort, Lainey had a few calls to make before shutting down for the night, and

Bella followed Eve around, scared to take her eyes off her. And the reasons for all of these things were a direct result of someone targeting Eve. Again.

She sat heavily on the bench in the shower, her heartrate racing. The more she tried catching her breath, the harder it was to breathe. Would she have to look over her shoulder for the rest of her life? Would Lainey? Tears merged with the water splashing on Eve's face. What if Eve no longer had the ability to keep her family safe? What if she couldn't get back to being Eve Sumptor?

———

"HEY, BUG. WHAT ARE YOU DOING?"

Bella looked up at Lainey. "Waiting for Momma. She's been in dere so long, Mommy. She okay?"

Lainey looked at the bathroom door Bella was leaning up against before sitting down next to her. Once they were finished with dinner and not expecting anyone to come over, Eve announced she was taking a shower and getting ready for a peaceful night in. That was over thirty minutes ago.

"Your Momma is fine, sweetie. She just needs a little time to herself."

"She pway wif wubber duckies, too?"

Lainey bit her lip. Bella loved spending more than an hour in the bathtub playing with her toys. Her rubber duckies all had names with complete backstories that entertained Lainey and Eve to no end.

"Maybe." Or Eve had a horrible few days and needed to get the stench of jail off, Lainey thought sadly. "Why don't you go brush your teeth and put your jammies on?"

Bella glanced back at the bathroom door. "Momma no leave?"

"No, sweetie, she's not going anywhere. I promise. I will stay here while you get ready for bed. Deal?" Lainey held out her hand.

Again, Bella thought about it for a moment, scrunching up her nose in concentration. After careful consideration, she shook Lainey's hand. "Deal, Mommy. I be right back." She got up and—since Bella had two speeds, sloth slow and lightning fast—she ran to the door. She stopped with her hand on the doorknob. "I sweep wif you and Momma?"

"Yes, bug, you can sleep in here tonight."

A smile bloomed on Bella's face, but Lainey caught the sadness in her eyes. The excitement of having her momma back made Bella forget why she was away in the first place. Lainey could imagine it was all coming back to her now that things had quieted down. She was hopeful —and perhaps a bit nervous—that Eve and Bella would be able to have the conversation they needed to have tonight.

Lainey stood up once Bella closed the door behind her. She hated feeling uneasy when it came to going to Eve. Normally, she would have no problem letting herself into the bathroom while Eve was in the shower. It was something they both did. Often. She took a deep breath and turned the knob, hoping Eve wouldn't be angry with her for caring. What she walked into would live in her soul for the rest of her life.

Eve sat naked on the floor of the shower, knees hugged close to her chest. Her head was down as quiet sobs caused her shoulders to shake. The sight rocked Lainey to her core. She didn't think, she merely reacted to the woman she loved more than life itself and walked into the shower fully dressed. Kneeling next to Eve, Lainey opened her arms and held on tight when Eve slumped into them.

"Lainey."

"I'm here, my love. I'm right here."

---

"Do you want me to ask Bella to sleep in her own bed tonight?" Lainey shivered as she peeled her wet clothes off.

"No, she needs me. And I think I need her, too." Eve wrapped a fluffy, warm robe around her wife's shoulders. "Is that okay?"

"Of course it is." A soft kiss on the lips accompanied a towel for her wet hair. "Thank you."

"Thank *you*," Eve returned. "I'm sorry. I didn't expect to break down like that."

Lainey scrubbed her hair to get most of the water out before tossing the towel into the hamper. She pulled Eve to her, caressing her cheek softly.

"You never have to apologize to me, Eve. I'm your wife, your best friend, your lover... your confidant. There will never be a time when I won't be there for you."

Eve kissed Lainey's palm. "You've seen me at my worst and you still love me. You'll never know how much that means to me."

"Oh, I don't know," Lainey smiled. "If it's anything close to how much your love means to me, I have an idea."

Eve lowered her head, her lips close enough to Lainey's to feel her warm breath.

**Knock, knock, knock.**

"Momma? Mommy! You in dere?"

Eve touched her forehead to Lainey's and chuckled. "Raincheck?"

Lainey tapped the tip of Eve's nose. "Anytime, my love."

---

"ARE YOU COMFORTABLE, BUG?"

Eve peered over Bella's head and mouthed *I'm sorry* to Lainey. Of course, Lainey being Lainey, she shrugged good-naturedly as she pulled the comforter up to their daughter's chin. The little girl insisted on sleeping right in the middle of the big bed. Which meant right between Eve and Lainey.

"Yes, Momma." Bella wiggled her toes and moved her feet side to side like windshield wipers. "Momma?"

"Yeah?"

"You hewp the peece find who hurt daddy?"

Eve's eyes darted to Lainey. They hadn't had the opportunity to discuss in detail what Lainey had told Bella about where Eve was. Obviously, she took liberties with the truth. But Eve imagined it was as close to the truth as Lainey believed Bella could handle at the moment.

"Um." Lainey sucked in her lips.

"Kind of, bug," Eve answered, playing along for the moment. "We know who *didn't* hurt him." *At least not physically.*

"You mad at him, too, Momma?"

*Yes.* "Is that how you feel, Bella? Mad?"

Bella shrugged her shoulders. "Don' know. Why he go be wif gwan-momma? Mommy say he wuved me, but he weft."

Wow. Lainey definitely pulled out all the stops with attempting to ease Bella's pain. Just another reason Eve loved the woman so much. She sat up and turned to Bella, crossing her legs in a lotus position.

"Come here, bug."

Bella scrambled out of the covers she'd just been tucked in and sat in Eve's lap.

"Do you want to talk to your momma alone, sweetie?" Lainey offered.

Bella shook her head, her bottom lip trembling in a little pout.

"That's right, Mommy. We want you to stay, don't we?" Eve winked at Lainey before turning her attention back to her daughter. "First, I want you to know that you are allowed to feel any way you need or want to feel. I think you've been angry at your daddy for a while now, haven't you?"

Bella nodded and sniffled.

"And you feel bad for being mad at him for leaving?"

Another nod.

"I'm mad, too, baby girl."

"You are, Momma?"

"Mmhmm. I'm mad that he hurt you when he was here. I'm mad that he hurt your mommy. I'm mad that he... hurt me. But we can be mad and still be sad and miss him, right?" The "miss him" part was purely for Bella's benefit. Eve still hadn't mustered up the emotions she thought she should have for Adam.

She watched Bella's eyes move rapidly. She was thinking about everything Eve had told her. Comprehending it. It continued to surprise Eve just how intelligent the little girl—who was missing two teeth and had trouble with her Ls and Rs—was.

"Yes, Momma."

"Good." Eve breathed in deeply. "I'm sorry *I* hurt you, bug. I hope you know I never would have left without talking to you first if I had a choice. And I never would have stayed away from you or your brothers or your mommy for that long if it was within my power not to." *Please tell me you know that.*

Bella twisted in Eve's lap, getting up on her knees. She took Eve's face in her little hands. "I know, Momma. Mommy tol' me you wanned

203

to teww me." She paused, her brows drawing in with contemplation. "I not mad at you, Momma. I wuv you."

Those nine words lifted an enormous burden off Eve's heart. She hugged Bella to her, willing herself not to burst into tears again. Good lord, when did Eve Sumptor become such a blubbering mess?

"I love you, baby girl."

Eve's eyes met a tearful Lainey's. Oh, that loving smile healed her heart just as much as the reprieve her daughter had just handed her.

"Momma, smooshin' me!"

"Yeah? Well, I'm going to smoosh you some more!" Eve blew a raspberry on Bella's neck and the little girl broke into a fit of hysterics.

"Mommy! Hewp me!" Bella managed between bursts of laughter.

Lainey hopped off the bed and ran to the other side. When she climbed up again, Eve's back was to her. "Should we get Momma?"

"Wait, what?!"

"Yeah, Mommy! Git hew!"

Bella tickled Eve's neck while Lainey went straight for those sensitive spots on Eve's sides. She tried moving away, but she was sandwiched between two very tenacious ladies that were determined to *git hew*.

"Hey! Two against one isn't fair!" The three of them fell to the bed, laughter filling the air. "Uncle!" Eve surrendered finally as she attempted to catch her breath. The tears in her eyes now were a far cry from the ones she had not even an hour before.

Bella and Lainey ceased their tickle assault, high-fiving each other in victory. After days of fearing she wouldn't have this again, this light-hearted, playful time with Eve and Bella restored Lainey's hope. And it restored her resolve to find the bastard who sought to destroy them.

---

"Do you think she'll be okay?" Eve asked quietly.

An extremely tired Bella had crawled back to her place in the middle of the bed over two hours ago. Lainey opted to stay on Eve's side, not ready to relinquish the warmth from Eve's body. Enjoying the closeness, Lainey propped herself up on one elbow, allowing Eve to rest against her chest as she held her. Both were exhausted, but having trouble falling asleep for similar, yet very different reasons.

Lainey feathered a finger up and down Eve's arm in a relaxing motion. "Yes. Now that you're back, we'll all be okay."

"You know, I'm not used to being a 'little spoon,'" Eve said instead of acknowledging Lainey's response.

Of course, Lainey noticed Eve skim over what she said, but wouldn't push. If she did, Eve could shut down even more. Besides, she was curious about Eve's admission. Surely there had been times with...

"Not even with Adam," Eve said softly, reading Lainey's mind when the light touches stopped. "I was never comfortable with it."

Lainey bit back the disappointment as she readied herself to move. The last thing Lainey wanted to do was make Eve uncomfortable. "Would you like me to go back to my side?"

"No, baby." Eve reached back and pulled Lainey's arm tighter around her. "I think I never felt comfortable because full trust wasn't there with him. It isn't like that with you." Eve's body relaxed considerably when Lainey kissed her shoulder. "Besides, I kind of like being your little spoon. I feel... safe."

Lainey hooked Eve's chin with her fingers and tilted her head back enough to kiss her.

"Momma!"

Startled by Bella's outburst, Eve immediately turned to her daughter to console her.

"I'm right here, bug."

Bella's wild eyes searched for Lainey on her side of the bed. "Mommy!"

Lainey jumped off the bed and ran around to the other side. Once she was in Bella's eyesight, she smiled warmly to ease her fears.

"Right here, sweetie." She crawled into bed and scooted closer. "Everything is okay. We're here with you."

Bella looked at both her moms before relaxing back into the pillows.

"'Kay," she mumbled and drifted back to sleep.

"Has she been doing this a lot?" Eve stared down at her little girl, pain from guilt touching her heart.

"Yes," Lainey answered truthfully. There was no reason to lie to Eve. Not only would she have known, but lying was something they swore they wouldn't do to each other. No matter how painful the truth was. "She'll wake up every couple of hours searching frantically for you. I don't know what she's dreaming about, she won't tell me. But we'd talk for a little while and then she'd go back to sleep."

Tears that Eve was tiring of formed in her eyes. Her baby girl didn't deserve this pain.

"This isn't your fault, Eve."

"Isn't it?" Eve kept her eyes averted from the intense gaze she knew Lainey was giving her.

"No. It wasn't back then, and it isn't now."

"Lainey, someone out there is trying to destroy me and they're hurting my family in the process!"

"And what if I'm the target?" Lainey asked suddenly. "Did you ever think of that? Because I do. I've thought of every goddamned scenario I could imagine. What if it's me they want to destroy by taking you away from me? Surely I'm not cunning enough to get you out of jail. And I'm certainly not independent enough to live without your money."

"Lainey..."

"I'm not done," Lainey interrupted. "I'm not Bella's legal parent, so with you and Adam out of the picture, I lose her. You gave me the only job I've ever had, but without you I wouldn't have anything, right? So tell me, Eve. Let's say that scenario turns out to be true, and it was me someone is trying to destroy. Would you blame me?"

"No, of course not."

"Then why do you blame yourself?" Lainey took Eve's hand that was resting on Bella's tummy. "I'm not weak, Eve. I can handle just about anything that is thrown at me. Except you pulling away from me. We're in this together. For better or worse."

Eve linked her fingers with Lainey's. "What did I do to deserve you?"

"You love me," Lainey answered simply. "You encourage me to be the woman I was always meant to be. And if I falter, you're there to pick me up. Because of that—and many other things that may not be appropriate in front of our daughter even though she's sleeping—I'm forever yours."

Eve smiled. "Forever, baby.

# Twenty

"Hey. Come on in." Lainey accepted kisses on the cheek and gifts of food and liquor as her friends filed through the door. They were the first guests to stop by since Eve came home nearly a week before. Even Lexie stayed away, giving Eve and Lainey the alone time they needed with the kids.

Unfortunately, that also meant no alone time for each other. Their days were filled with work—with Lainey taking the helm there until Eve was ready. Afternoons brought back the routine of homework, snacks, and naps. At night, the five of them would spend quality time at the dinner table, in the living room playing games, or in the theater room watching movies. It all would have been lovely and normal if Eve didn't spend the time *not* occupied by their children keeping to herself. But Lainey vowed to give Eve the space she needed, and that's what she would do. Even if it hurt.

"Are you sure she's up for this?" Rebecca asked, jumping slightly when Cassidy swatted her ass as she passed by.

"Yo, Lainey!" Cass winked and made a beeline for the kids and video games.

"Yo, Cass," Lainey laughed, then turned back to Rebecca. "She said she was, but, honestly, I don't know." She nodded toward the patio.

"She's been out there for the past hour. I should tell her everyone is here."

Rebecca laid a hand on Lainey's arm. "Ellie and Hunter brought enough food for a small army. Why don't you go help them, and I'll go get Eve."

"You didn't bring a whip, did you?"

Rebecca grinned. "What kind of person do you take me for? Of *course*, I brought a whip. A legendary Mistress never leaves home without one."

Lainey shook her head, an amused smile gracing her tired features. When all this was over, Lainey was taking her family on a long vacation somewhere, *anywhere,* where they could lie in a hammock and do absolutely nothing for an entire month.

"That's my niece," Aunt Wills quipped. "But it's true. There's one in the car."

They shared a laugh and a hug.

"It's good to see you, Aunt Wills."

"I was hoping to see you sooner."

"Oh?" Lainey glanced outside to make sure everyone had made it inside. "I thought everyone was coming tonight," she said, shutting the door and automatically locking it. Even with the gate and James, Lainey still felt uneasy. The person doing this—and their reason—was still out there. Hidden behind codes and technical jargon Lainey didn't understand.

"Dani and Claire thought you two needed more 'grown-up' time," Willamena explained.

"Yet, Patty brought Mo," Lainey joked. She knew Eve still intimidated the young couple, but was hoping they had reached a turning point during the multiple gatherings for different occasions. "And Jessie? Greyson?"

Jessie, Ellie and Hunter's daughter, had recently moved back to LA after a rough stint at medical school. Ellie and Hunter welcomed her back with open arms and were letting Jessie choose her path. Ellie knew all too well what it was like to have someone make decisions for you.

"Jessie is out with her girlfriend." Willamena paused and let that sink in.

"Girlfriend? God, I feel so out of the loop."

"For good reason. Come on, let's go help Ellie set up. And by help, I mean watch her do it because the kitchen is that woman's element and we shouldn't interfere."

Willamena slipped her arm through Lainey's and guided her to the kitchen. Lainey glanced over her shoulder, hoping Eve was okay and Rebecca wasn't being too hard on her. Willamena tugged on Lainey's arm to bring her attention away from the back patio.

"Don't worry about Eve, sweetie. Rebecca may not always be gentle, but she's honest. Perhaps that's something Eve needs."

Lainey knew Aunt Wills was right. She would never complain about the extra work brought on by Eve's inner retreat. But it left little time to get to the root of why they were in this position without requesting everyone else put their lives on hold to help. She stopped in her tracks.

"That's where Greyson is, isn't it? Working instead of being here with his family?"

"He's exactly where he wants and needs to be, Lainey. You and Eve *both* need to remember that you're not alone anymore."

The weight of responsibility that rested on Lainey's shoulders eased somewhat. She wouldn't pretend that this wouldn't be easier with Eve fully there by her side. But, until Eve was ready, Lainey would carry her.

---

"YOU LOOK LIKE YOUR MOTHER."

Eve peeked out from the hood of her sweatshirt and saw James resting his hip on the railing.

"Except she didn't run away from her problems like a petulant child."

James lifted a shoulder, the pain of Marie's death still lingering in his heart. "Maybe she should have. It could have saved her life and she would be standing here with you now." He pushed away from the rail and walked toward Eve, sitting on the edge of the lounge chair next to hers. "But you have someone standing with you, Eve. Someone who lifts you up, not beats you down. Someone to help protect you."

"It's not Lainey's job to protect me."

"Bullshit!"

Both Eve and James turned toward the outburst and saw Rebecca standing there with her hands on her hips. And a furious look on her face.

James stood abruptly. "I should..." He jerked a thumb over his shoulder and hurried away. It didn't matter he was twice the size of Rebecca. A woman with that kind of fire in her eyes was no one he wanted to tussle with.

"Hello, Rebecca." Eve instantly knew she had made a mistake being so flippant with Rebecca when the petite—yet scary—woman stalked to her.

"Don't you 'Hello, Rebecca' me. Not after what you just said about Lainey."

"All I said was it wasn't her job to protect me. And I stand by that," Eve said defiantly.

"And I stand by my earlier assessment. Bullshit. Why do you treat her like a weakling?"

Eve stood so fast it made her head spin. But so did Rebecca's accusation. "I don't think Lainey is weak!"

"Really? That's not what I see or hear from you." Rebecca pointed at the house behind her. "You have a *remarkable* woman in there who has bent over backwards making sure the life you built—that you're building together—didn't crumble around you and the kids."

"I know that, Rebecca," Eve said, her voice ice cold.

"Don't use that tone with me." Rebecca stepped closer to Eve. "I don't scare easily, Eve Sumptor. I've stared death in the eye and lived to tell the tale. If you think you can make me go away by trying to intimidate me, you don't know me very well."

"I wasn't..."

"Save it. This isn't about me. Or you. This is about giving Lainey the respect she deserves. I get it, Eve. Life has been shit for you. Then that woman came into your life and made it worth it. I have that with Cassidy. The difference is, I've learned to let Cassidy in while you're still pretending you're alone in your grief."

Eve's nostrils flared with anger. "That's not fair."

"You're right, it's not. For Lainey."

"Enough, Rebecca, please." Eve slumped back down onto her chair and buried her head in her hands. Was Rebecca right? Was she treating Lainey as though she were weak? That certainly wasn't what Eve thought. She just hadn't wanted to be a burden on Lainey. But there was more. What Eve had been feeling was... fear.

Rebecca read the raw emotion on Eve's face. Perhaps she had been too harsh on the woman after everything she had just experienced. But brutal truth was the fastest way to snap someone out of their self-pity.

"Fine. But, Eve, I need you to listen and never forget what I'm about to say, okay?"

Eve nodded, swallowing the lump in her throat.

"Lainey stepped up because she had to. She fought for you because she needed to. But that woman—that incredible woman—loves you because she *wants* to." Rebecca laid a gentle hand on Eve's shoulder. "Whatever's trapping fear inside you, talk to her, Eve. After everything I've seen, Lainey can handle anything that comes at her. Except losing you."

Eve closed her eyes briefly before opening them again to stare out at the ocean. She never wanted Lainey to think Eve was pulling away from her. She just needed to get a handle on why this all hurt so much. She had been through worse, hadn't she? After everything that went wrong in Eve's life, what was it about this time that shook her to her core? *Except losing you.* Rebecca's words rang in Eve's ears. Was that the answer she had been searching for?

"Could you ask Blaise to come out here, please?"

Rebecca's eyebrows shot up. "You think Blaise would be on your side?" she scoffed. "We're all a little scared of getting on Lainey's bad side, so don't count on it."

Eve's lips twitched. Mistress was afraid of Lainey? Oh, *that* was fantastic. Her wife was officially a badass. Not that Lainey hadn't shown that side of herself to Eve in other...situations. "I don't want Blaise to take my side, Rebecca. I think it's time I stop pretending I'm alone in all this, and I need Blaise's help to do that."

"Oh." Rebecca frowned. "What can Blaise do that I can't?"

Eve looked up at her friend. "You want kids running around your house cockblocking you?"

"Blaise!" Rebecca called out. "It's a good thing you came to your senses," she said in a softer tone.

"Yeah? What would you have done if I didn't?"

Rebecca tilted her head and gave Eve an evil grin. "I would have taught Lainey how to use a whip. And *not* for pleasure."

Blaise walked out on the deck before a stunned Eve could respond. "You bellowed?"

"Mmhmm." Rebecca patted Blaise on the shoulder as she brushed past her. "Good luck."

Blaise watched Rebecca walk away, then turned to Eve. "Why exactly do I need luck?"

Eve narrowed her eyes. "What happened to your accent?"

Blaise shrugged nonchalantly. "I've been in the States long enough to adopt a new accent. Nothing to get all excited about."

"Are you doing this to fit in more with Americans or to have something in common with all the lesbians surrounding you?"

It was a fair question. But it was a question Blaise didn't know the answer to. So, she did what Blaise Steele did best. She deflected. "That's the first time I've heard you put a label on yourself. So, you're a lesbian?"

Eve smiled, knowing exactly what Blaise was doing. "What I am is a woman who can't imagine being with anyone other than Lainey. Ever."

"Ah. You're a Lainey-bian."

Eve snorted with laughter. "This is why we all love you just the way you are, Blaise. Don't change to fit in somewhere where you're already welcomed with open arms."

"Sound advice, Eve. Do you practice what you preach?"

Eve lifted her hood from her head, standing again to face Blaise head on. She allowed her eyes to turn glacial, adopting a look that brought many a foe to their knees. But Blaise wasn't a foe. She was a friend. A friend who merely raised a brow as she stood her ground.

Finally, Eve grinned. "I'm trying. Which is why I wanted to talk to you. How would you feel about watching the kids for tonight?" Eve paused. "And maybe until the afternoon tomorrow?"

Blaise tapped her chin with a fingertip. "Ezra loves playing with Bella, and vice versa, so they're good. The boys have a great time playing video games with Greyson, and vice versa, so *they're* good. As long as there are no kids sleeping in my bed between me and my husband, I'm good. You got yourself a kid-sitter." She looked Eve up and down. "You may want to give me a call in the afternoon to let me know if you can still walk after the marathon sex you're planning."

Eve laughed as she hugged Blaise to her. "Don't ever change, Blaise."

---

"Hey, bug. Can I talk to you for a minute?" Eve kneeled on the floor, a supportive Lainey next to her. Of course, she had run the plan by Lainey before initiating conversations with Darren and Kevin. Now it was Bella's turn.

"'Kay, Momma."

Bella stood in front of Eve, her lip trembling with what Eve could only guess were nerves. *She thinks I'm leaving again.*

"How would you like to spend the night with Auntie Blaise?" Eve hoped her voice conveyed excitement. But with Bella's narrowed, suspicious eyes, that hope quickly deflated.

"You go away again, Momma?"

There it was. Eve's confirmation that Bella was scared her momma would leave her again. That fear was something Eve could understand all too well.

"No, my sweet girl. Momma isn't going anywhere. Mommy and I need to... talk. All that talking will probably bore you, so we thought you'd have more fun at Auntie Blaise's."

Bella looked completely unconvinced as she continued to stare at Eve with doubt. So, Eve tried a different tactic.

"Kevin and Darren will be there with you. And Ezra. You love playing with Ezra, don't you?"

Bella pursed her lips. That old soul shining through blue eyes. Suddenly, Bella took her gaze off her momma and looked at Blaise. "Auntie Bwaise, can I pway in the sandbox wif Ezwa?"

"Absolutely." The *sandbox* was a small greenhouse where Blaise kept her sandy loam for her plants and flowers. It was one of Ezra's favorite places to play when Blaise was out cultivating her garden. "But you have to bring your dirt clothes, remember?"

"I 'member," Bella reassured her. She looked up at Lainey. "You no let Momma go away again?"

Lainey kneeled beside Bella, taking her little hands in hers. "I won't. I promise, bug."

Bella's eyes traveled from Lainey to Eve and a few times as though she was making sure she could trust what they were saying. Eve had a fleeting thought that she should have had this conversation with Bella in private, with only Lainey in the room with them. Alas, friends who were watching the exchange with interest surrounded them.

"Auntie Bwaise? Can we make a bwanket fort?"

Blaise's eyebrows furrowed. "Well, that's a silly question! How on earth can we have an indoor s'mores party without a blanket fort?"

Bella's eyes lit up, but was still reluctant to agree with leaving for the night. After another silent moment of contemplation, Bella nodded her head once. "'Kay. I go pack my diwt cwose." She ran off only to stop abruptly and ran back to Eve, holding Eve's face in her hands. "You be here when I back." It wasn't a question, but a demand.

"I will be," Eve vowed.

"I wuv you, Momma." Bella hugged Eve with all the strength her little four-year-old arms could muster. She backed away, then turned to Lainey, hugging her. "I wuv you, Mommy." With that, she ran toward her bedroom shouting *diwt cwose* the entire way.

Kevin chuckled at his little sister. "I don't know why she likes playing in that stuff. It stinks."

"That's because it's mixed with compost." Blaise waited a beat. "And manure."

Lainey's head snapped up. "You let my daughter play in shit?"

"Uh, I'm going to go help Bella pack. Darren? Wanna get your bag ready?"

"Right behind ya!" The two ran off, leaving Blaise to fend for herself. They didn't worry too much. Blaise had a way of getting herself into and out of trouble a lot.

Blaise laughed. "Technically, *I* play in shit, too. Ezra and Bella are excellent helpers. She's going to have a green thumb, you just watch."

"Just make sure you clean that thumb appropriately before she eats anything. Eww, and don't let her eat the dirt!"

Blaise saluted at Lainey with a cheeky wink. "I got this. I haven't lost a kid to composted manure yet."

Eve fought to keep her composure. Nerves for letting Bella go and laughter at Lainey's response were battling each other quite ferociously. The others weren't so conflicted. They laughed uproariously.

"Okay, well. Now that is all settled, Hunter and I are going to take off so you two can... *talk*." Ellie kissed Lainey on the cheek. "There's plenty of food in the kitchen to help you keep up your strength," she whispered close to Lainey's ear, winking at Eve.

"Yes, I believe Cassidy and I will go, too." Rebecca leaned close to Lainey. "I left you a gift." She nodded at a small bag on the table by the door. "Use it if you have to. Or want to during your... *talk*."

Lainey blushed, playfully pushing Rebecca away. "Anyone else want to comment on Eve and I talking?"

Mo stepped up with a sly grin. One look at Eve's stony glare and raised eyebrow, Mo's grin faded. "Um, have a nice night," she muttered as she shuffled off through the door. Hunter and Cass threw their arms around Mo's shoulder, comforting her by telling her they were sure Mo's joke would have been funny.

"Kids," Willamena scoffed flippantly, hooking her arm with Patty's. "What do you say we ditch these youngins and go get us a drink?"

"Make it three and you got yourself a deal, sugar!"

"Hey! Why do the two of you get three drinks and I get three kids?" Blaise whined as Patty and Aunt Wills sashayed out the door. She glared at Eve and Lainey. "You *so* owe me."

"We really do," Eve agreed sincerely.

Blaise smiled and brought them both into a fierce hug. "I'm happy to do this." She heard the kids coming back and decided one more tease was in store. "Remember, we have access to a couple of wheelchairs if you need them by tomorrow afternoon."

"Fuck you, Blaise."

Blaise laughed. "Save that for your wife, Eve. Oh look! Here are the children!"

Bella and the boys gave their moms hugs and kisses. The goodbyes lingered, as all of them harbored the same separation anxiety.

"Come, come, children." Blaise ushered them to the door. "Come, come, ladies," she quietly threw back at the couple, winking saucily. "Toodles!"

Eve and Lainey stood there in silence for a full minute after Blaise shut the door.

"Should I tell them to come back?" Lainey asked finally.

"No." Eve turned to Lainey, wrapping her arms around Lainey's waist. "We need this."

Lainey's body tingled, being so close to Eve. "So we're not going to talk?"

"Oh, we're going to talk. I have things I need to say to you. Then we're going to let our naked bodies do all the talking."

# Twenty-One

"Do you want some chamomile tea?" Lainey asked softly.

Eve smiled. Tea was Lainey's go-to when she wanted to help "soothe the troubled soul." Lainey had made Eve tea the night Eve purged her soul of her past. She was hoping this conversation would be much easier. Still, it made Lainey feel better not sitting idly around waiting for whatever shoe to be dropped.

"I'd love some, thank you."

"Okay. Settle down on the couch and I'll bring it out to you."

"I can help."

Lainey led Eve to the couch, nudging her gently until she sat down. "I'm perfectly capable of getting tea, my love. Besides, I think I need a moment to prepare myself for this conversation."

Eve cocked her head to one side, looking up at Lainey curiously. "What do you think I'm going to say?"

"I don't know. But you've been silent for days about what happened. And that was *after* I found you in the shower crying, your skin red and raw. So, let me have a few moments to myself while I get the tea and then you can lay everything on me."

Eve opened her mouth to assure Lainey that nothing had physically happened to her in jail, but Lainey had already hurried off. Eve pushed up the sleeves of her hoodie, slipped off her shoes, and tucked her legs up under her as she settled in on the couch. As soon as Lainey came back, Eve would put her mind at ease.

---

LAINEY STARED at the patterns of the backsplash as she waited for the water in the teakettle to boil. She tried settling the thunderous beating of her heart by convincing herself that if something terrible had happened to Eve in jail, she would know. Wouldn't she? Yes, Eve had been drawn inward, quiet and standoffish. But surely that was the product of the unbelievable things that had transpired in such a short amount of time and not because she was...

God, Lainey didn't even want to think that vile thought. Yet, her mind wandered to that night a few years ago when Eve told Lainey about her horrific past. She knew it was impossible to feel the pain Eve felt all those years ago, but it still hurt. Lainey hoped Eve would never feel that pain again. Yet, she couldn't help but wonder if that's another reason she and Eve hadn't been intimate since Eve's return. The loud whistle of the teapot jarred Lainey out of those morose thoughts. She went through the motion of filling mugs with the steaming water, allowing the tea bags to steep thoroughly.

After taking a deep, cleansing breath, Lainey picked up the mugs and headed back to Eve. No matter what was said tonight, Lainey would remain by Eve's side and carry any burden she could for Eve.

---

"HERE YOU GO." Lainey handed a mug to Eve. "Be careful, it's hot." She placed her own on the coffee table and sat down next to Eve, mirroring her position.

"Thank you, baby." Eve carefully tested the tea, burning her top lip as she did. "The first thing I need you to know," Eve began as she set her mug next to Lainey's. "Is that nothing happened to me in there."

The relief nearly came out of Lainey in an audible whoosh. "Dunne?"

Eve's eyebrow lifted. "You understood my message." She should have known Lainey would. "He enjoyed handing out his threats about how *close* we would be if I were to be convicted, but that's all."

Lainey nodded. "I'm still having Greyson open a file on him. He shouldn't be allowed anywhere near a women's prison."

Eve grinned. "I would expect nothing less from you, baby." She leaned over and tweaked Lainey's nose. "As for the other inmates, I'm sure your *hired hand* would have told you if anything happened." She was especially curious about Lainey's reaction to that. Eve knew Lainey was resourceful, but to know someone in prison? That seemed very... un-Lainey like.

"Hmm. I suppose she would have." Lainey breathed in again, the weight of panic lessening with each new heartbeat. She offered no other explanation, even though she could see the curiosity and anticipation on Eve's face.

Eve draped her arm on the back of the couch, her fingertips brushing Lainey's shoulder. Her wife's coyness was always intriguing. "How exactly do you know Jefa?"

"What? You think you're the only one who has friends in questionable places?"

Eve snickered. "Questionable places, hmm?" Lainey lifted the shoulder Eve was stroking with her fingers. "Did James help you out there?"

"Actually, it was Reghan. She has a list of people who could be helpful now and again. I needed help." Lainey picked up her tea. It was cool enough now for her to take a large sip. One hurdle down. Now comes the next one. "Do you want to talk about your breakdown in the shower?"

*And that was the end of that conversation*, Eve thought. She had learned over the years that when Lainey needed swift resolutions to the issues swirling in her head, she wouldn't tolerate much banter.

"Should we break out the record player and brandy?"

Again, Lainey's mind drifted to the night Eve first talked about her past. They sat in Eve's living room drinking wine and perusing Eve's vinyl collection. When Lainey coaxed Eve into talking, brandy replaced the wine. Liquid courage. Did Eve need that now?

"I can unlock the liquor cabinet if you need it," Lainey said quietly.

"No, baby. *You* give me courage these days." Eve shifted her body until their knees touched. "I've been trying to figure out why this affected me so much. After everything I've been through—*we've* been through—why did this hurt more than anything before?"

"He used to be your husband, honey. It's only natural..."

"That's not it," Eve interrupted gently. She inhaled deeply, closing her eyes briefly to gather her thoughts. Hopefully Lainey wouldn't find her despicable for what she was about to reveal. "I... Lainey, I don't feel much of anything regarding Adam. I thought the grief would come once the shock wore off, but it hasn't. I'm... angry with him. For showing up here, for all the agony he caused. For how he hurt Bella. But the sadness isn't there."

Lainey took Eve's hand, holding it firmly in hers. That was quite a confession coming from Eve. One Lainey understood all too well. "I know how you feel. Adam and I were once friends. I should feel *something* about his death, but..." She brought Eve's hand up to her lips, brushing a light kiss over the knuckles. "Maybe we're just too angry to be sad? Don't get me wrong, my heart aches for Bella's loss. And yours. He was her father and someone you once loved. I find I can only mourn for the two of you."

Eve's brows furrowed. "I never loved him. Not in the way he wanted me to. No matter how hard I tried, it was never there."

Eve recalled constantly keeping Adam at arm's length. When they were dating, she had withheld most of the things she readily shared with Lainey. From the beginning, Eve wanted to cook for Lainey, have her stay the night... love her. Hell, she even poured her guts out to Lainey mere months after they'd met. All the things it took years for Eve to do with Adam. Then there were the things she *never* shared with Adam. Bank accounts, deeds, businesses. She readily put Lainey's name on everything the moment Lainey agreed to it. That blatantly conveyed Eve's true feelings.

If anyone understood the absence of love for someone, it was Lainey. Hadn't she tried for years to feel that all-consuming love for Jack? "No one should have to *try* to feel love, Eve. You taught me that."

"I don't have to with you," Eve confessed. "From the day I met you, it felt like I stepped off a cliff into an abyss. And I just keep falling."

Lainey thought about that statement. It was a familiar feeling inside Lainey, though hearing it said out loud was quite jarring.

"That's both beautiful and scary," she said finally.

Eve smiled. "It is. There's nothing more beautiful than finding someone who continues to light your soul every day. And nothing scarier than giving your complete self to that someone."

"Unless that someone knows what they're holding in their hands, my love." Again, Lainey kissed Eve's knuckles, then intertwined their fingers together.

Eve squeezed Lainey's fingers, holding on to them like a lifeline. "It's been hard accepting you as my protector, Lainey. Not because you're not capable. I trust you with my life. But the last time someone tried to protect me, she was murdered."

Lainey knew Eve spoke of her mother. "Oh, honey, that was different."

"How?"

"Because you're not a helpless little girl who can't defend yourself or those around you anymore. You're strong. And you have someone standing beside you, fighting with you now. I think that only strengthens us more. Together, we can conquer anything. That's what has been keeping me going. I knew this day would come, and we'd work through this as a team again."

Eve wished she felt as confident as Lainey made her out to be. "I felt pretty helpless in jail."

"Well, I didn't say one of us wouldn't have to step forward a bit more every once in a while. But the other is always right there watching our back."

Eve studied Lainey's elegant features. The dark circles that had formed since this all began were fading. Her green eyes were becoming vibrant again and everything clicked into place. "I know why this hit me so hard," Eve announced suddenly. "It has nothing to do with my past and *everything* to do with my present and future. There was a very real possibility that I could have lost you and my family. I feared losing half of my soul, Lainey."

"So did I. And when you came home and became distant, I thought I'd lost you anyway."

Eve lowered her eyes. "I'm sorry. I ran through the gambit of nega-tivity. 'Am I good enough for you? Is she better off without me constantly bringing this to her life?' And the big question was, am I strong enough to live without you? The answer is no. I think I'm still getting used to needing someone so much that it hurts to breathe when you're not with me."

Lainey blinked. Eve's raw confession was full of unrestrained emotion. "What the hell did Rebecca say to you?" Lainey teased. What-ever it was, she owed Rebecca... whatever the hell Rebecca wanted.

Eve chuckled. "She threatened to teach you how to use a whip—not for pleasure—if I didn't get my head out of my ass."

Lainey's eyebrows shot up as she peeked over her shoulder at the gift Rebecca left. "Do you think that's what that is?"

Eve craned her head and squinted her eyes. "Hmm. Wanna open it and see?" she asked with a sexy wink. "Though, I feel I've gotten said head out of said ass. Perhaps we could try... pleasure?"

Lainey's smile faltered. Oh, how she wanted to try many things with her wife. But there was always something in the back of her mind that caused her to hesitate.

Eve caught the look and took Lainey's hand. "Will my past always inhibit you from giving me every desire you have inside of you?"

"I—" Lainey, poised to deny Eve's question, blew out a breath. "The last thing I ever want to do is hurt you, my love. What if something I want triggers the pain of your past?"

Eve silently considered her answer, allowing her feelings to guide her. "This week has taught me a great deal about myself and how I feel when I'm with you. And without you," she added with a slight shudder. "I don't want my past standing between us. I don't want fear being a part of the equation when we're together. Not for you, or me."

She stood, kissing Lainey's hand before letting go. She walked over to get the gift Rebecca left them, feeling Lainey's eyes on her the entire time. While she knew Lainey didn't care what she was wearing, Eve wished she had chosen something more appealing than lounge pants and a sweatshirt.

Lainey, however, admired the way Eve's clothes draped over her body. The loose pants hung on every curve. The sweatshirt was large, but still managed to exhibit the delicate swell of Eve's breasts. Lainey realized it didn't matter what Eve wore—or didn't wear. The effect on Lainey's libido was still the same. She snapped out of her fantasies when Eve dangled the gift bag in front of her.

"You want to open this now?"

Eve tilted her head. "Did you need to talk more? I think I've said what I needed to say. Now it's time to back my words up with action."

Lainey bit her lip, suppressing a smile. *Action* with Eve always spoke louder than any uttered words. She took the bag from Eve and waited for Eve to join her again on the couch.

"Ready?" Lainey asked. Eve nodded and Lainey carefully opened the bag. She didn't know why she acted as though something would jump out at her like a freakin' snake in a can. Her breath caught in her throat when she peered inside.

Eve hooked a finger on the edge of the bag, pulling it toward her to look inside. One perfectly arched eyebrow raised.

"She wasn't kidding." Eve reached in and pulled out a pink flog. Her fingertips traced the buttery smooth leather. *Only the best from Mistress,* Eve mused with amusement.

"It's soft," Lainey muttered as her fingers trailed after Eve's. "It's hard to imagine something so soft causing pain." She looked up into Eve's eyes. "I don't want to cause you pain, Eve, but if I could bring you pleasure with this... New beginnings?"

A beautiful, beaming smile blossomed on Eve's face. "New beginnings."

# Twenty-Two

*L*ainey set the gift bag aside, moving their teacups so she could sit on the coffee table in front of Eve. Her new beginning didn't involve their new toy... yet. No, Lainey had something else in mind.

"Do you remember our first kiss?"

The memory sent a delicious chill down Eve's spine. "Of course I do. I remember everything about that night, baby."

"*I* remember how terrified and confused I was. You were trying to comfort me that night, but when your breasts touched mine as we hugged..." Lainey closed her eyes briefly, inhaling deeply through her nose. "I know you felt the way my body trembled. I know you felt the heat of my excitement. My body and heart battled with my brain the entire time. Then you did something to me that ignited my soul like never before."

"Keep talking, baby." Lainey's recollection of that night was igniting more than Eve's soul. God, she remembered that night like it was yesterday. Lainey was right. The tremors, the heat. Both singed Eve's senses. But it was the push and pull between desire and duty to someone else that had Eve restraining her instincts. "Tell me what I did so I can do it again."

Lainey leaned in. "Not this time, my love. New beginnings, right?

That means I get to replay that night without the fear or confusion. *I get to do to you what you did for me.*"

Eve didn't know what she was expecting, but when Lainey's tongue snaked out and licked her lips from bottom to top, Eve's heart stopped for a split second before it practically thundered out of her chest. Her hands curled into fists at her sides as she fought the urge to grab Lainey and fuck her senseless. Then she whimpered when Lainey pulled away.

"Don't stop, Lainey."

Lainey stood, feathering a fingertip across Eve's cheek. "Never, Eve."

She took Eve's hand and pulled her up, holding on tight as she guided them to the bedroom.

"Wait."

Lainey backtracked to pick up their gift from Rebecca. Who knew when the thing would come in handy?

---

"LAINEY?" Eve came out of the bathroom in the white silk nightshirt Lainey had given her to change into. "If I recall correctly, *you* were wearing this."

Lainey stopped pacing, her breath catching in her throat. *Incredible.* She willed herself to stay calm on the outside, even as her racing heart was anything but.

"Yes." Lainey waited until Eve was standing in front of her, then switched their positions so that Eve's back was to the bed. "You laid it next to me when I was too afraid to change out of my clothes. It smelled of you. The pillow smelled of you. God, your scent surrounded me. My body ached for your touch. It hurt more not to be with you than it did to lose myself in you with the risk of losing everything else. It drove me insane."

"It drove you to me," Eve corrected. She reached out to Lainey, happily aware that she had changed, too. But Lainey shook her head.

"I wanted to touch you, but I couldn't make my hands work." Lainey admitted and began unbuttoning her own shirt. "I watched you get naked for me. Each button you undid was the undoing of my resistance to being with you. When I saw your body for the first time," Lainey slipped off her shirt, having rid herself of any other barriers between her and her wife in anticipation of this moment. "I don't know how to describe the craving that coursed through *my* body."

Eve's eyes traveled down to Lainey's naked breasts. The dark, taut nipples begging to be sucked. But she would let Lainey lead. *Let,* Eve thought with mirth. *Like you have—or want—a choice.*

"I'm pretty sure I know exactly how you felt." Eve's voice was thick with arousal. Her mouth salivated at the thought of tasting Lainey's skin.

Lainey hummed a sound of pleasure as Eve's eyes drank her in as though she were an oasis in the middle of an arid desert. If she wasn't careful, everything she was trying to accomplish here would go up in a cloud of sex-filled smoke. *Tempting...*

Steadying her hands, Lainey pushed the thin, clingy shirt off Eve's shoulders. *God, had it been that revealing when I had worn it,* she wondered as her fingertips trailed over Eve's sun-kissed skin, starting at the heightened pulse at Eve's throat and moving slowly down.

She lingered at Eve's breasts, rolling the pad of her thumbs over hard nipples. Lainey knew Eve's moan was a mixture of pleasure and pain when she pinched the tender peaks between her fingers.

"You're so beautiful," Lainey murmured, letting her fingernails graze down to Eve's toned belly.

Eve's skin prickled with goosebumps when Lainey lingered at her bellybutton. God, had she ever been *this* turned on before? Obviously, being with Lainey always brought out the best in Eve. But when Lainey was in control and unrestrained, it ignited a fire within Eve like nothing she'd ever felt before. And right now, Lainey was the most fearless she'd ever been.

"I've been called beautiful before, but I've never felt the true meaning of the word until you looked at me," Eve confessed softly.

Lainey looked up into Eve's eyes and saw the truth of those words staring back at her. "I wish we had known each other before." Lainey wondered how much sorrow they both could have avoided had they met years ago. Before Jack and Adam.

Eve shook her head. "We weren't ready for each other then." She took Lainey's hand and moved it down to rest between her thighs, where she was hot and wet. "I'm ready for you now."

Feeling how drenched Eve was, Lainey's knees buckled. If she didn't do something bold to stay in charge, Eve would undoubtedly take over. And while Lainey was certainly a fan of being dominated by Eve, she wasn't ready to give up the reins just yet. She carefully coated her fingers with Eve's essence and brought them to her lips. Without losing eye contact, Lainey painted her lips and licked them just to get a taste of what was to come. She threaded her fingers in Eve's silky blonde hair and pulled her closer. *"If you want to stop, just tell me,"* she whispered, her mouth a breath away from Eve's.

Eve's pulse surged. Lainey's assertiveness was intoxicating and sexy as fuck. The familiarity of their first time together created an electricity between them that felt... different. It was achingly divine having their roles reversed.

*"Don't stop,"* Eve told her.

Lainey closed the distance between them, kissing Eve passionately. Her tongue slipped between Eve's lips, sharing the mouthwatering elixir that was pure Eve.

Much to Eve's delight, Lainey wasted no time following the actions of that night a few years ago. The cool sheets were a sharp contrast against her heated body as Lainey nudged her onto the bed and lay down next to her.

Lainey gazed into Eve's gray eyes, taking just a moment to appreciate the differences that bridged the gap between then and now. Gone was the fear that nearly kept them apart. Now, when they kissed, there was a mixture of belonging, excitement, and pure love that created an extraordinary unbreakable bond. Tongues danced together like well-seasoned partners, each knowing the movements of the other, giving and taking in perfect balance.

As they kissed, Lainey's hands roamed freely over Eve's body—the way Eve did to her that first time. God, she remembered how alive her body had felt that night. Every touch, every kiss, every flick of Eve's tongue brought new sensations that Lainey felt in the depths of her soul. Of course the fear and guilt had been inevitable. There was so much stacked against them then. But thinking about it now, Lainey knew that at the core of her fear was the possibility of never feeling that way with Eve again.

Tonight was about concentrating on giving Eve the same incredible sensations she had given Lainey. She wanted to show Eve what it was like for her their first time making love. Only this time, there would be no fear. No dread. No wondering what tomorrow would bring. Nothing could tear them apart. Nothing.

Keeping on track, Lainey distinctly recalled the hot trail Eve's lips and tongue left as they traveled down her body. It would be the same trail Lainey would take tonight to get to her desired destination. She feathered soft kisses over Eve's collarbone, slipping her tongue out to sample a taste here and there. When she got to the swell of Eve's breast, she stopped her journey long enough for Eve to groan in protest. Then she did what neither of them expected. She sucked—hard—on Eve's sensitive skin.

Eve lifted her head, a smile playing at her lips. "Are you branding me, Lainey Sumptor?"

Lainey's eyes found Eve's, but she didn't stop sucking. Green eyes sparkled with mischief as she flicked her tongue over the skin she had suckled into her mouth. When she was satisfied that her efforts would leave a suitable mark, Lainey let go with a distinct pop.

"All mine," she said as she admired her handiwork.

"I could have told you that, you little vampire minx." Eve angled her head to see the dark purple mark that proudly stood out from the lighter skin of her breast. "Nice work."

"Thank you. You may get more in other places," Lainey winked. "For now, all you need to do is lay back and let me please you."

Eve's nostrils flared with passion. Oh, yeah. Bold Lainey had Eve on the verge of coming before even being touched. Lainey owned her. Mind, body, and soul. She could brand Eve, whip her, *fuck* her any time, any way, and Eve would be on her knees begging for more.

"*Take me*," Eve breathed. Her head fell back on the bed, eyes squeezing shut as Lainey's teeth nipped her skin and her tongue teased her belly button.

Lainey felt the words course through her. Every inch of her body ached to be touched by Eve. She wondered if this was how Eve felt their first time. Had she yearned to be touched? Had she craved the staggering release of passion that had been building between them since the moment they met?

Eve's scent filled Lainey's senses as she neared her desired target. That scent. Oh, that was Lainey's favorite aroma. And her favorite thing to taste, she thought as she lowered her head, her warm breath hovering over Eve's glistening sex. She looked up at Eve, who was watching her intently.

"I'm more confident than you think," Lainey said unashamedly. "I know every inch of your body and how to make it vibrate with pleasure." She then lowered her head and tasted Eve.

"Fuck!" Eve's body arched off the bed, her hands gripping the sheets tightly as Lainey's actions echoed her words. Lainey flicked her tongue over her clit long enough to get her to the brink of orgasm, just to pull away right before Eve went over the edge. But Lainey didn't allow Eve to lose sight of that edge for long.

She sank her tongue into Eve's saturated pussy, stimulating her from the inside by rolling it around the delicate sides. She felt the tension creep back into Eve, and each time Eve reached that peak, Lainey backed off. She was edging her wife. And when Eve brought her knees up too, hugging them to her chest, Lainey knew Eve loved every fucking minute of it. The position granted Lainey all the access she needed to drive Eve crazy with want, all while delaying the relief of an orgasm.

She lapped at Eve's wetness, felt the tightening, and pulled back once again. It was a dangerous game she was playing. Mostly because paybacks were blissful torture. But wasn't that part of the allure? In their sexual discovery together, Eve and Lainey had learned each other's turn-ons and -offs. And delaying orgasms was a turn-on for them both, whether they were giving or receiving. A win-win, Lainey thought as she slid her tongue lower to the delicate area Eve truly enjoyed when she was feeling particularly primal.

Lainey rimming her sent Eve's need for relief clamoring to be sated. She grabbed Lainey's head, fisting her hand in her hair. No more teasing. She needed to come. And she needed to touch Lainey, to be inside her, to fuck her as senseless as Eve felt right now.

"Fuck me, baby! Fuck my pussy with your tongue until I come in your mouth."

Lainey moaned against Eve. She loved it when Eve got this way. The hornier she became, the dirtier Eve talked. Hearing those words while tasting Eve's pussy was enough to have Lainey grinding her own sex against the bed just to find a bit of relief. She also knew that when Eve started demanding, she had reached her limit. There would be no more putting off what they both needed.

Lainey hugged one arm around the front of Eve's thigh. She spread Eve's lips and coated her fingers with Eve's arousal, then massaged Eve's clit with her lubed fingers while simultaneously fucking her with her tongue. Lainey used her other hand to stroke that sensitive area just below her tongue, and there was no stopping the powerful climax that ripped through Eve.

"Fuck!" The word was drawn out with the length of the orgasm. Eve's legs came crashing down as her body arched up, desperate to get more from Lainey. Her pussy contracted, grabbing on to Lainey's tongue, holding on until it was good and ready to let go. Her hand was still tangled in Lainey's hair and she somehow stayed mindful enough not to pull it out by the roots as she repeatedly fell over that edge Lainey had held back.

Lainey took one more euphoric sip of the gift Eve gave her before crawling up Eve's body. "Inside me. Now."

Eve immediately obeyed. She thrust three fingers inside Lainey, knowing she was ready for it. She rested her palm against Lainey's clit as Lainey bucked her hips, urging Eve to go deeper. Harder.

It wasn't enough. Lainey needed more. "Four!" She spread her legs wider as Eve slipped another finger inside her. She reared up, her head falling back in ecstasy, writhing furiously against Eve.

"Come, baby! Fucking give it to me!"

"Eve! Fuck! Don't stop! Don't ever stop!"

The orgasm exploded from deep inside Lainey. As many times as they had made love, had sex, fucked... this was something different. Their new beginning opened something up inside Lainey that she never knew she had. It was in that moment Lainey knew she had just given her entire soul to Eve. Until death did them part.

EVE, clad in the treasured white sleep shirt, sat on top of the sheets, legs crossed, and watched Lainey sleeping peacefully. The steam from her coffee filtered uninterrupted from the mug she held close to her chest. A hint of a smile touched her lips as she replayed every second of the incredible night she just shared with Lainey in her mind. They spent hours exploring this unbridled side of Lainey. There were no hesitations, no worries about dredging up feelings from Eve's past. Just pure, uninhibited, lustful fucking. Maybe tonight they'd even try the whip, Eve thought with a wicked grin.

She should feel exhausted after the sexual acrobatics, but Eve had never felt more invigorated or inspired. She had closed herself off for most of her life, afraid she wasn't worthy of love. Then she met Lainey. That meeting didn't change the core of who Eve was—she didn't think that was ever Lainey's intention—but it changed the perspective she had on the world around her. From the moment they met, Lainey saw beyond Eve's facade, straight into her soul. With Lainey, Eve could allow herself to be the Eve she was before her world fell apart. Or perhaps the Eve she would have become had her mother lived and showed her what the meaning of a real family was. She knew that meaning now because of Lainey and their children.

Eve Sumptor. Artist. Wife. Mother. Who would have thought that was possible after so many hopeless years?

"Do I smell coffee?"

Eve blinked, her attention coming back to Lainey. Even with the mussed hair and sleepy eyes, Lainey was the loveliest person Eve had ever laid eyes on. Her smile brightened when those eyes tracked to her, and she held out her cup to Lainey.

Lainey sat up, sucking in a breath when the delightful soreness welcomed her as she moved. *Worth it.* The sheet fell to her waist when she reached out to take the mug from Eve, but she didn't care. She needed the coffee too much to lift some of the haze from her brain.

"How long have you been awake?"

Eve's eyes were fixed on Lainey's breasts, mesmerized by the gentle rise and fall with each breath Lainey took.

"Eve?"

"Hmm?" Eve tore her eyes away. "I'm sorry, what?"

Lainey smirked. "I asked how long you've been awake."

"Oh, um, long enough to make some coffee, call Blaise, and watch you sleep for a bit."

Lainey coughed, nearly spitting out the coffee she had just taken a sip of. "You called Blaise?"

"Yes."

"This early?" Lainey leaned over, placing the cup of coffee on the nightstand. "Love, we do not wake the redheaded beast before double digits. The ramifications…"

Lainey's breasts bounced with every excitable gesture she made as she warned Eve of… something. Eve had lost focus somewhere between Lainey flashing her ass at Eve when she leaned over and the hypnotizing sway of boobs. Unable to keep her hands to herself any longer, Eve tackled Lainey.

"Oof!"

"I'm sorry, baby, but I didn't hear a word you said because…" she glanced down between them. "Tits."

Lainey snorted with laughter. "I'm trying to decide how many vine-yards I need to buy Blaise to atone for you waking her up, and you have a problem with my tits?"

"Oh, baby, the only problem with your tits was they weren't in my mouth or my hands… or pressed against mine. We're all good now." Eve grinned down at Lainey. God, how she loved this woman. "Hi."

Lainey touched Eve's cheek. "Hello, my love. If you plan on ravaging me again, will you at least be gentle?" she teased.

"I think we have different ideas of who ravaged whom, baby." She kissed Lainey sweetly, tasting the coffee on her tongue. "Seriously, are you okay?"

Lainey beamed. "I'm fantastic. I mean, if you're not sore the next day, are you really doing it right?"

Eve laughed. This was a nice feeling. Of course their troubles weren't over yet, but right here, right now, belonged to Eve and Lainey. "We *rocked* it last night."

"Yeah, we did." Lainey accepted another kiss that Eve abruptly ended just as Lainey was getting her hands involved. She opened her eyes and saw a slight frown marring Eve's beautiful face. "What is it, love?"

Eve shook her head. "You know, with everything I said to you last night, I didn't say THE one thing I should have started with. Thank you."

Lainey's brow furrowed. "For?"

"God, Lainey, for so many things. For standing by me, not believing what your eyes saw, fighting for me. For taking care of the kids while you took on everything else. For being there for Bella when she needed you the most. When she needed me." Eve kissed the tip of Lainey's nose. "For not giving up on me when I was being an idiot. I was *here*, and you *still* took care of everything while I wallowed in self-pity."

"Honey, after what happened to you..."

"Happened to us," Eve corrected.

"You needed time to reclaim yourself."

"Reclaim. I like that." Eve sat up, bringing Lainey with her. She covered Lainey's naked body with the sheet so she could keep her concentration. "But I think you helped me *renew* myself last night. The reason I called Blaise this morning—and risked the wrath—was to ask her if she could watch the kids a little longer."

"Oh? Ready for round two?"

"Two?" Eve laughed. "I thought we were on at least round fourteen!"

"Hmm. Maybe fifteen," Lainey winked.

Eve revealing how she felt renewed intrigued Lainey. It mirrored how this ordeal had changed—or renewed—Lainey. Eve had always been the strong one. The one in control. And Lainey was content with that. But when Lainey was unexpectedly thrust into that role, she had a choice to make. Cower like she did with Jack. Or step into that role and own it. At first, she told herself she had to keep it together for the children. For Eve. But last night, she recognized she had stepped up for herself, too.

"While I *do* want to go another fifteen rounds with you, baby, I thought maybe we could sit down and talk about our next steps. I want to hear your theories. All of them." Eve took Lainey's hand in hers. "I know you have people working on this, and I trust who you trust. But my real faith is in you. I need you to get me up to speed. And when I go back to the office tomorrow to face the interns that I was supposed to mentor, I would like you to be there."

"Do you think you'll need me?" Lainey worried that Eve's confidence had taken a hit with this mess. When she didn't feel worthy—in this case, of being someone those impressionable girls looked up to—Eve shut down. It would be a tragedy for both the interns and Eve if the program failed this year because of something completely out of Eve's control.

Eve saw the concern in her wife's eyes. It was a legitimate unease with their background. But Eve shook her head. "I always need you, baby, but this is more of a want. You know them. You've worked with them. I want to see you interact with them. I think it'll help me understand what I've missed so far. Besides, you're the role model they need around them, too."

The corner of Lainey's mouth curved up. Eve was opening up without fidgeting, or even getting a twitch in her eye. That's what Lainey called progress. "I have to say, I am *really* loving this *renewed* you."

"Yeah? Well, *I* really love dominant you. Please tell me that will happen more often. Like, *every* night."

"I don't know, love," Lainey grinned. Oh, she thoroughly enjoyed last night, and will definitely revisit the world of dominating Eve. But... "I think I would miss you being in control too much."

"Maybe we can compromise... ma'am." Eve unbuttoned her shirt, letting it fall off her shoulders. "A little give, a little take."

Lainey dropped the sheet that covered her and laid down with her head at the foot of the bed. "Sounds like a good plan." She tugged Eve's thigh. "Come and give me what I want while you take what you need."

Lainey spread her legs as Eve straddled her face. She moaned against Eve's pussy when Eve sucked Lainey's clit into her mouth. Give and take was an exceptional plan.

# Twenty-Three

Eve placed a new cup of coffee in front of Lainey and kissed her on top of the head. They were getting a late start, but the lingering taste of Lainey on her lips made the delay justifiable.

"Thank you," Lainey murmured, taking a sip. Normally she would go for tea this time of the morning, but she needed the extra oomph of caffeine. *Still worth it*. Part of her wished they had just stayed in the bedroom until the kids came home. The more practical part knew they needed to deal with the elephant in the room.

"What's that?" Eve asked, nodding her head toward the notebook Lainey was tapping her fingernails on.

Lainey took a deep breath and pushed it over to Eve. Hopefully this wouldn't destroy the progress they had made with each other.

Eve's brows furrowed as her eyes scanned the list of names and... motives. Then she got to the last name that was circled. She looked up at Lainey. "Adam?"

"You wanted *all* the theories," Lainey reminded her.

"He wouldn't do that to his daughter." Even though she spoke the words, doubt crept into Eve's mind.

"Honey, you know better than anyone else what a father is capable of."

"Adam wasn't Tony."

The anger on Eve's face scared Lainey. Had she done the right thing by sharing this with Eve? They had promised to be truthful with each other. Even when that truth hurt. But maybe suggesting Adam was behind this was a mistake. There was no turning back now. The best thing for Lainey to do was go all in and explain the thought process behind the idea.

"He was broke, Eve. Greyson did some digging and found he owed two million dollars just to get his firm back in the black." Lainey sighed. "And he was obsessed with you and getting you back. Desperate people do desperate things."

"Like killing himself?" Eve asked incredulously. "And framing me for it?"

Lainey had to get Eve to see the logic in the accusation. Hell, *she* hadn't wanted to believe Adam could do this either. Not to Bella or Eve. But the more she learned about Adam, the less doubt she had.

"Eve, this theory isn't me being a jealous wife. I struggled to write his name down. But the more Greyson and Cade found out, the more I couldn't ignore the possibility."

"Tell me." Eve wanted to know everything. And nothing. But she meant it when she said she trusted who Lainey trusted. And Lainey wouldn't put her through this turmoil without cause.

Lainey brought out her phone and opened it, scrolling to the file Greyson had sent her. Handing the phone to Eve, Lainey began reciting the damaging information that was in the file.

"Adam was in over his head. Rebecca noticed that his company was hemorrhaging money, which made little sense to me. He was talented, and his work with Sumptor Gallery opened the door to so many opportunities. Why was he sinking?"

"He was always more about the design and not the business," Eve remembered.

"I thought that, too. But both you and Rebecca vetted the people employed at the firm. The two most brilliant business minds I know. You would have made sure someone there knew how to run the company."

Eve had to admit that was true—and gratifying coming from Lainey. When Adam came to her with his dream to have his own architect firm, Eve was supportive, but skeptical. Skill wasn't enough to sustain a business. It took a certain type of person to create, build, and maintain a successful empire. Adam wasn't that type. That's why Eve and Rebecca installed someone in the company that could... help Adam stay afloat. Apparently, that didn't work.

"Keep going," Eve urged sharply.

Lainey tried not to take Eve's curt demeanor personally. This was a lot to take in. She leaned over and scrolled further down. "He borrowed money from different banks, but didn't put that money back into the business. And when the loans came due, he defaulted or tried borrowing from someone else to pay back what he already owed."

*Fuck.* That was Tony's MO. "I offered him money to terminate his parental rights. I would have paid double what he owed to give you the opportunity to be Bella's legal parent. Why didn't he take it if he was drowning this much?"

Lainey watched as the realization of familiarity dawned on Eve. Even Lainey felt as though she was reiterating the story James told her about Tony. "Well, that's where his obsession with you comes in." Something else Adam shared with Tony. "The theory is, he came here hoping to get you back. You gave him a very definitive no, and that's when..."

"That's when he went to Plan B." Eve sat back in her chair. It was on the tip of her tongue to ask Lainey why she was just hearing about this now. But Eve already knew the answer. She wasn't ready, and Lainey understood that. "Okay, help me comprehend why he would... kill himself."

Lainey wished she understood it herself. "Maybe he felt there was no other way out of the mess he made for himself." She paused for a beat. "Why didn't he go after me, Eve? You are what he wanted and I was standing in his way. Why didn't he kill me?"

Eve drew in a sharp breath. Hearing those words was like a sharp, twisting stab in the heart. "Because he knew I would tear him apart with my bare hands if he hurt you." She grabbed Lainey's hand. "Never say that again, please. You're my heart, baby. The thought of losing you," Eve shuddered, unable to finish contemplating that idea.

"I'm sorry, my love. You wanted to understand why he took such drastic measures and I don't know the answer because I can't fathom leaving you or our children. He may not have had you any longer, but Bella is still here. Even giving up his parental rights, he must've known we would let him see her. *I* would have wanted him to have a relationship with Bella as long as it wasn't hurting her."

"Desperate measures," Eve repeated softly and shook her head. "I shouldn't have married him. I shouldn't have led him on, thinking I was in love with him when I wasn't."

"This isn't your fault, Eve. He was a grown man. And while I'd go bat shit crazy if I lost you, I'd own it. Why blame you? Why *frame* you? Again, I ask, why not me if he wanted to hurt you?"

Eve got stuck on Lainey saying *bat shit crazy* for a moment before thinking of an answer. She tried to think like a dejected ex who lost their love to someone else.

"Because maybe you were right," Eve said finally. "What you said before about the possibility of someone targeting you. I know this is pure speculation, but if this theory is right and Adam is behind this, he would've done it to hurt *you*, not me. To take me and the money away so that you're left with nothing. Just like he was."

When Lainey said that to Eve, she had hoped it was a ridiculous idea. But it rang too true. Adam would have expected her to fall apart. Even being an unproven motive, what pissed her off the most was the assumption that she needed the money as much as she needed Eve. Obviously they had no way of knowing what was really going through Adam's mind, but considering his attitude of late, it was as plausible as any other speculation.

Eve squeezed Lainey's hand. She knew all too well what it was like to be a target. She hated that Lainey now had to feel that. One thing that helped Eve was figuring out who was trying to destroy her.

"How do we prove this?" she asked Lainey, hoping to get her mind going in another direction.

Lainey looked at Eve. "By finding who he hired to help him."

"Hired. That's why they took our money." God, Eve hated that it all made sense. "I know you trust Jules. But is she in over her head? Do we need to find..."

"No. We stick with Jules. At this point, it's personal for her. That's why I think she'll stop at nothing to find the answers. Besides, it'll be a good test of her skills since I hired her at Sumptor, Inc."

Eve's eyebrows raised, and her mouth stretched into a smile. She reached over, grabbed Lainey, and pulled her onto her lap. "I love that you didn't ask if that was okay. It means you now see Sumptor, Inc. as yours, too. Your newfound confidence is such a turn on."

Lainey grinned. "So, you like Lainey 2.0?"

"I *love* Lainey. Every single version of her." Eve brought Lainey's head down for a passionate kiss.

"Hmm." Good lord, that was an incredible kiss. But... "You're not using sex as a way of ignoring your feelings about all this, are you?"

"No, ma'am. I'm trying not to fall down the rabbit hole that always seems to be open for me. What we have is a bunch of hypotheses that don't even add up to circumstantial evidence." Eve paused. "Be sure to tell Reghan I said that. She'll be proud." She smiled when Lainey laughed. This is how their lives should be. Not constantly hunting someone who is hunting them. "Maybe we should hand this off to the police and let them deal with it?"

Lainey raised a brow. "The same police who arrested you without even investigating? No, we do this ourselves with the people we trust."

"Okay, baby. You're the boss." Eve smirked at all the ways Lainey could boss her around. "Speaking of boss. Tell me, how did Greyson take it when you poached his employee?"

Lainey tsked with feigned indignation. "I did not poach anyone. What I did was unite Sumptor, Inc. and Drake and Associates. Think of it as a mutually beneficial merger."

Eve gripped Lainey's ass and jerked her closer. "I would like a mutually beneficial merger with you." As much as she wanted to forget everything except Lainey, Eve had one more question before she could... merge with Lainey. Again. "Are we sure about Adam?"

"This was personal, my love. I just can't think of anyone else."

"So, we're eighty-five percent sure."

Lainey lifted a shoulder. "Ninety-three. And a half." She jumped when Eve pinched her ass.

"If it's personal, what about Jack? He's definitely not a fan of mine. Or yours, if we're honest."

Lainey snorted with laughter. "Jack lives in upstate New York. He goes to work at precisely eight o'clock. Comes home at precisely five twenty-three. He has twenty-two thousand, four hundred and sixty-three dollars and seventy-two cents in the bank. He's married and has a new baby boy named," she paused for dramatic effect. "Jack Jr."

"Wow." Eve let all that very *precise* information sink in. It was obvious Lainey had everyone investigated. Very thoroughly. "How does that make you feel?"

"What?"

"The wife and baby."

Lainey's eyes sparkled with amusement. Surely Eve wasn't worried Lainey was jealous of Jack's new life. "Extremely grateful that it's not me," Lainey answered honestly. "I don't know if you know this, but *I* have a wife, too."

"Oh, you do?"

"Mmhmm. She's beautiful, brilliant, incredibly sexy." Lainey put her mouth close to Eve's ear. "And she fucks me like I've never been fucked before."

Eve buried her face in Lainey's neck and growled. Her fingers gripped at the shorts Lainey had on. "Take these off," she demanded.

Lainey stood. She hooked her fingertip under Eve's chin, lifting until Eve's eyes were on hers. "Take them off yourself."

Eve sucked in a breath. Lainey was going to be the death of her, and she would go out with a smile on her face. She slipped off the chair to her knees in front of Lainey. Her pulse raced with anticipation as she curled her fingers into the waistband of Lainey's shorts and lowered them. She looked up to see Lainey watching her. Her green eyes darkened with arousal.

Lainey lovingly brushed Eve's hair back. "*Taste me,*" Lainey whispered, her voice hoarse and needy.

Eve obeyed, sinking her tongue between the lips of Lainey's sex. She snaked her hands up Lainey's legs and cupped her ass, massaging and tugging at the same time. She wanted to be deeper, so she lifted one of Lainey's legs, draping it over her shoulder.

Lainey leaned back on the table to keep her balance. She released a low, throaty sigh of pure ecstasy when Eve sucked Lainey's clit into her mouth. "*Amazing*."

*Amazing, indeed.* Eve hummed against Lainey's clit and thrust two fingers inside her just as she felt Lainey's body tremble. She curled her fingers, hitting that one spot that drove Lainey crazy.

"Yes, Eve!" Each thrust of Lainey's hips drew Eve deeper inside her. "Make me come!" Her leg fell from Eve's shoulder, muscles tightening as the orgasm swept over her. She gripped the edge of the table, nails digging into the wood. "Eve!"

Eve was relentless. Mercilessly feasting until she was sated. Her own shorts were rubbing against her swollen clit, bringing her to the brink of climax. When Lainey's pussy tightened around her fingers and Lainey screamed her name, Eve came hard. She panted against Lainey's clit, unable to move for at least a full minute.

"Are you okay, my love?" *Am I?* Lainey's entire body shook from the intense sensations pulsing through her.

"Mmhmm. I think so. You?"

"I'm still assessing the situation."

Were her eyes closed, or had she gone temporarily blind? Lainey opened one eye, happy to know she still had her vision.

"I think so," Lainey said at last. "Can you get up?"

"No, I think I'll stay here for a bit. Care to join me?"

Lainey laughed. "Honey, if I get down there, we won't be able to get up. I'd rather not have our kids walk in on us when I have no bottoms on and your face and fingers smell like my pussy."

"Christ, woman! Are you trying to drive me insane?!"

Lainey peered down at Eve and winked. "Is it working?"

Eve checked her watch. They had two hours and fifteen minutes until the kids came home. Just enough time to show Lainey just how well it was working.

# Twenty-Four

"*Y*ou pwomise?"

Eve smiled at her daughter through the iPad. "I promise, bug." Lainey walked in just then and Eve pivoted the tablet around to show Bella. "Look, there's your mommy. She'll tell you."

"Hi, Mommy!"

"Hi, sweet girl. What am I supposed to tell you?"

"You bwing Momma home wif you!"

"Oh!" Lainey glanced at Eve. The poor woman was battling such guilt for Bella's insecurities. "Yes, bug, I will bring Momma home. Four o'clock, just like we talked about."

Bella turned away from FaceTime and asked Lexie how much longer it was until four o'clock. Lexie showed Bella on a clock and Bella groaned.

"Why so wong?" Bella whined.

Eve turned the tablet back to her as Lainey joined her behind her desk. She had to find her balance between being cognizant of Bella's feelings and not getting exasperated with her constant anxiety. None of this was her fault. It was a lot to go through for Eve. She couldn't imagine what it was like for a four-year-old.

"Bug, you will not even miss us. You're going to draw, eat snacks,

247

take a nap, and before you know it, Mommy and I will be home. Can you be a big girl for Momma and trust me?"

Bella sighed heavily. "'Kay, Momma. Can we have hot dogs fow dinner?" She turned away again for a second, then looked back at Eve. "And macwoni cheese?"

Lainey leaned over to get into the picture. "Darren! Get back to your classes."

"Yes, Mom!" Darren yelled back, giggling.

"We'll discuss dinner when we get home," Lainey answered Bella. "Right now, Momma and I need to get to work, okay?"

"'Kay, Mommy. I wuv you. I wuv you, too, Momma!"

"We love you, bug. See you soon!" Eve clicked off FaceTime and blew out a breath. "That was the fourth call today, and it's only ten."

"It's your first day back to work since everything happened, honey. She's just nervous." Lainey circled behind Eve's chair and kneaded her shoulders. "Give it a little time. Soon she'll be wanting us to leave her alone."

"Ugh, let's not think that far ahead," she grumbled. "Besides, maybe we'll get lucky and she'll turn out like Kevin, who only wants us to leave him alone sometimes."

"Maybe," Lainey chuckled. "Are you ready for the interns?"

Eve pushed herself up from her chair and turned to Lainey. "As ready as I'll ever be," she smiled. "Thank you for being here with me."

"There's nowhere else I'd rather be, my love."

They gravitated toward each other, lips aching to touch. Just as they were a breath away, there was a sharp knock at the door, right before it opened.

"Oh, excuse me for interrupting," Dorothea smirked. It wasn't the first time she had walked in on the two women hanging onto each other like lifelines. She was sure it wouldn't be the last.

"It's okay." Lainey soothed Eve's annoyance by rubbing circles on the back of her hand with her thumbs. "We were just talking."

"Right." Dorothea looked at Eve. "The interns are ready for you, Mrs. Sumptor."

"Thank you."

"Will you be joining her, Lainey?"

"Hang on! *Still*?! After everything, it's still Mrs. for me and Lainey for her?" Eve glared and pointed at both of them. "I will get to the bottom of this conspiracy."

"Of course you will, dear." Lainey patted Eve's chest and gave her a quick peck on the lips. "Yes, Dorothea, I'll be joining. Let's go."

---

EVE HELD the door of the conference room open for Lainey, smiling when Lainey winked at her. She indulged in watching Lainey's ass—discreetly, of course—as she guided her to the conference table.

"Take a seat," she ordered her interns, pulling out Lainey's chair for her at the head of the table. Once Lainey was situated, Eve went to the opposite end and took her seat. One Lainey had been keeping warm for her.

"I know this internship has been unconventional, to say the least. My first order of business today is to thank you for sticking it out."

Eve made eye contact with each young woman in the room. There was still an air of admiration, but it had to have waned slightly with the scandal. Even being absolved of any wrongdoing, Eve couldn't ignore that her reputation was tarnished. This would all be a distant memory soon, but for now, she would have to work that much harder to regain the respect she once had. Maybe this really could be about renewing herself. This time around, she would do things right.

"Lainey has caught me up to speed on how you all have been handling your work here. However, today I will spend time with each of you one on one to see for myself how you're faring here at Sumptor, Inc. We started this internship intending to give young women an advanced opportunity in the ever-changing, competitive world of business. Unfortunately, I have been absent. Until now. We'll get past this glitch, and..."

"*Problème*," Emilie scoffed under her breath.

"Excuse me?" Eve wasn't used to being interrupted. Especially not while she was at the head of the table in a conference room. But these weren't board members. These were young women who had been thrust into a situation they weren't prepared for. At least, that's what Eve told herself to keep her cool.

Emilie shrugged casually. "You call it a glitch. I call it a lesson in being a rich *américaine*. In our world, the poor world, we get punished for murder." She laughed, slugging the arm of the girl next to her. "Yes?"

"Stand up."

Everyone, including Eve, looked at Lainey, who snapped the order.

"Stand up, Emilie," Lainey demanded again, her tone cold. Emilie stood, the look on her face a picture of apprehension. "Pick up your things." She waited until Emilie complied. "Now walk out that door. You're no longer a participant in this internship."

Eve's eyebrows raised, but she said nothing. Not even when Emilie looked to her for help. This was Lainey's show just as much as it was Eve's. Whatever decision Lainey made, Eve would back her.

"You can't be serious," Emilie exclaimed.

"I'm very serious. You knew the rules. I told you if you disrespected Eve, you are gone. Did you think just because she's back, I wouldn't follow through? Don't look at her for help," Lainey said when Emilie turned to Eve again. "You have a choice. You can walk out that door voluntarily, or I will have security escort you out. Either way, you're no longer deserving of that badge."

"But I am the best here! You fire me, you will get no one better!"

"One thing you need to learn about life, Emilie, is there's always someone better ready to take your place. You need to make yourself indispensable by being more than just your skill. You failed to do that." Lainey pressed a button on the intercom in front of her.

Dorothea opened the door and ushered Jules in. Lainey smiled at Jules and gestured toward Emilie's seat.

"*Qui Êtes-vous?*"

"This," Lainey began before Eve or Jules could, "is your replacement. Have a seat, Jules. The one next to Eve is unoccupied." Emilie looked at her with wide eyes, but Lainey showed no mercy. Emilie had pushed the limits one too many times for Lainey to ignore. "Across from you is your partner, Giselle. We'll do proper introductions with everyone else once we've concluded business here."

Jules squeezed past a flabbergasted Emilie and nodded at Giselle.

When she had received the call from Lainey this morning, she was reluctant to come in. Mostly because she was eyeball deep in her search for the hacker fucking up the Sumptors' lives. But a gig at Sumptor, Inc. was impossible to pass up. Lainey had explained she would start with the interns for a week to determine where her abilities would fit best within the company. That was fine with Jules. Her endgame was to be the head of the research and development department at some point, and she would prove herself worthy of that position.

"You can't do this!" Emilie looked from Lainey to Eve and back again. "I worked hard to get here. What did *she* do?"

"Jules also worked hard to get here. And her disposition fits what we're looking for here at Sumptor, Inc."

"You will regret this," Emilie said in French.

"*Je doute que ça soit vrai,*" Lainey responded.

Eve's eyes widened. This was a new development. Hello, Lainey 2.0! Why was hearing French coming from Lainey's lips so fucking sexy? Not to mention the unadulterated authority in Lainey's voice and body language. "Lainey has spoken, Emilie," Eve said when Emilie continued to stare in disbelief.

Emilie whirled around and stomped out of the room, muttering expletives in French the entire time.

"Well, what would Sumptor, Inc. be without the theatrics?" Eve quipped. "If anyone else feels this internship isn't for them or that Lainey and I do not meet your standards of suitable leaders, please feel free to follow Emilie." She waited a beat, giving the interns a chance to make their move. When no one did, Eve nodded. "Very well. This is the first and last time I will address this issue. I was falsely accused of a crime. If you're following the story in the news, you know that evidence was faked to frame me for reasons not yet known. I admit my reputation has taken a hit, but I am still the boss and will not tolerate being condemned at my own company. You had your opportunity to leave on your terms. If you force us to dismiss you, there will be no second chances. Is that understood?"

*Yes, ma'ams* filled the room without hesitation, and Eve felt a burden lift from her shoulders. Perhaps this was a sign that her name still held esteem under the layer of tarnish.

"Okay, that's it for now," Lainey announced. She stood, indicating for the others to do the same. "Go back to your departments. Eve will be around soon."

The interns silently filed out, and Lainey took a steadying breath when she and Eve were left alone. Had she overstepped in firing Emilie? This differed from hiring Jules. For one, Eve sat at the head of the table. She had come here to reestablish herself as the boss, but Lainey had interfered.

"I'm sorry, my love. I shouldn't have…"

Eve snaked a hand around the back of Lainey's neck and yanked her to her with passion. Their mouths crashed together in a fiery kiss. Eve's free hand unbuttoned and unzipped her pants enough to give Lainey access. She grabbed Lainey's hand and pushed it past the waistband.

"Before you apologize," Eve breathed against Lainey's lips. "Feel what watching you take control did to me."

Lainey's body vibrated with need when her fingers came into contact with Eve's saturated pussy. "*Eve.*"

Eve caressed Lainey's cheek. "I love you, baby. I never want you to be sorry for being you. Or for defending me." She kissed Lainey softly on the lips. "Now, as much as I want you to keep touching me like that, we have work to do. Raincheck?"

Lainey slipped her hand out of Eve's pants and licked her finger clean. "You started it," she reminded Eve when she whimpered. She pressed the same finger she had just tasted to Eve's mouth. "But I'll finish it."

With that promise, Lainey sashayed away, leaving a stunned Eve staring after her. A smile slowly spread across Eve's face. If there was a silver lining in all this mess, Lainey finding her inner strength was certainly it.

---

"JULES?"

Jules shot up from her chair. "Um, hi, Eve. I mean, Mrs. Sumptor."

Eve smiled. "Please. You're the only one who will call me Eve." She leaned in and dropped her voice. "There's a conspiracy going on around here to drive me crazy. Don't let them rope you in."

Jules frowned, then saw the spark of mischief in Eve's eyes and laughed. "Got it. It's, uh, nice to finally meet you. I wish the circumstances of me being hired here were better."

"Oh, I think the circumstances were just right." Eve held out her hand to Jules. When Jules took it, Eve held on for a long moment. "Thank you. I should have sought you out before this to tell you that. Thank you for everything you've done to help Lainey. To help me."

Jules blushed. "Yeah, I mean, y-you're welcome. Anytime. But, like, I'm not done yet. I'm just sorry it's taking me so long to figure this shit, uh, stuff out. I will, though. I swear."

"Lainey believes in you. That means I do, too. However, neither of us wants you to burn yourself out. If you need help or another set of eyes, come to me. You can have your pick of someone to work with."

"I appreciate that." Jules had examined the setup here at Sumptor, Inc. and nearly had an orgasm. "This equipment is, like, way superior to Drake's. He totally needs an upgrade. Maybe I could use it?"

"It's all yours. You focus on that, and I'll pair Giselle up with someone else. When you're done, we'll see about a spot in R&D."

"But, I thought Lainey, uh, Mrs. Sumptor, wanted me to intern for the week?"

Eve nodded. "I'm sure she'll agree to us counting this toward your time. I don't want the others to know what you're working on, though. Think you can do it on the down low?"

"Yeah, not a problem. I can keep up appearances while doing a bit of side work."

"Great. I'll formally introduce you to Giselle and the others. If you find that any of them could be helpful to you, come talk to me. We'll determine if they're trustworthy enough to be involved in something this personal."

"Got it." Jules felt a surge of pride. Eve and Lainey—two of her heroines—trusted her. She would do what she could to maintain that trust. First, she'd have to endure the one thing she hated most. Meeting new people. A necessary evil for a chance of a lifetime.

# Twenty-Five

*L*ainey stirred awake, stretching the kinks out of her sore body. The sound of family filled the air and the aroma of bacon filled her nose. She reached out, feeling nothing but cool sheets where Eve was supposed to be.

"What time is it?" she asked... well... herself since she was alone in the room.

"Nine fifteen."

Lainey yelped at the sound of Eve's voice close to her ear. "What the... I just... you weren't..."

Eve dangled a cup of coffee in front of Lainey's confused eyes. "Need this to finish a sentence?" she teased, earning a glare from her lover. "How can you possibly be grumpy after last night? Was I not thorough enough? Did I not make your body quiver uncontrollably? Should I..."

Lainey slapped a hand over Eve's mouth. "Stop trying to arouse me before I'm fully awake, my love."

"Trying?" Eve's words were muffled behind Lainey's hand. She kissed Lainey's palm before removing it from her face. "Damn, I must be losing my touch. You should be a puddle by now."

"Believe me, you're not losing anything. But there are at least three things preventing us from taking this further right now. One, the kids are up, I can hear them. Two, I smell bacon. And three, my coffee is getting cold."

Eve laughed. "You win, baby. For now." She gave Lainey her coffee and stood back from the bed to get a gaze at her lovely wife.

Unfortunately, Lainey wasn't in her usual sleeping attire. Which was no attire at all. With Bella still crawling into bed with them, alone time —and naked time—was scarce. Oh, they managed to eke some time out here and there. Like in the shower last night. A far cry from the last time they were in the shower together. This time, being on their knees meant someone was getting a taste of what they craved the most. But Eve craved... more.

"We should take a vacation," Eve said suddenly.

The cup froze at Lainey's lips, and she looked over the rim at Eve. "Pardon?"

"A vacation. We deserve that, don't we? We could rent an entire island just for ourselves. We'll go snorkeling, lay in hammocks, and soak up the sun. Decompress."

Lainey tilted her head and set her coffee to the side. "Are you okay?" Eve had just gotten back in the swing of things at work. Now she wanted to take a vacation?

"Baby, does something have to be wrong for us to take a vacation?"

"No, of course not. The timing is just... off. The internship program is still going, the kids are still taking classes, nothing has been solved yet."

Eve sighed. "I know." She sat next to Lainey on the bed just to feel her closeness. She wasn't trying to run away from her problems. She was just ready for problems to stop chasing her. "Wishful thinking, I guess."

"Eve, if you need to get away, we will. It doesn't matter what's happening around us. Your happiness means more than anything else." It hadn't escaped Lainey that Eve had painted nothing since she got home. A part of her worried Eve had slipped back into the depression that stole her creativity before.

"I know what you're thinking," Eve said quietly. "It's not that." Her easel sat untouched since before the police showed up at their door. But this was different. There was no creative block. She had plenty of ideas, but the desire wasn't fully there yet. Eve was sure once her mind settled, there wouldn't be an issue getting back to her art.

"Then what is it?"

Eve took Lainey's hand in hers. "Do you know how alive you've made me feel? Not just these past few days, but since we met. The world tried—again—to close in on our little bubble, threatening to pop it."

"And escaping to a private island where no one can find us sounds like paradise?" Lainey guessed. Eve nodded. "We'd miss the kids."

Eve erupted in laughter. "I love you so much, Lainey," she managed.

"Oh. You wanted to take the kids?" Lainey grinned cheekily. She loved it when Eve laughed like this. That magical sound that started deep in her belly. It reflected the happiness in their lives. Even now, when a threat still lurked in the shadows, it didn't take away what they felt between them. In fact, going through this together had brought them closer. "I kinda thought you wanted to just walk around the island naked and make love wherever we pleased."

Eve stopped laughing abruptly. "Interesting," she said thoughtfully. "Adjoining islands? Kevin is totally old enough to babysit. Or Lexie could go, but she has to stay on the kids' island."

Lainey snickered, bumping Eve's shoulder with hers. "Want to discuss a vacation with the kids?"

"Yeah, I think so. Maybe it'll be good for all of us. When the time is right, of course." She kissed Lainey on the cheek. "Also, I think we should talk to Dr. Woodrow. As a family. I don't want any of us bottling up emotions that can hurt us later."

Eve Sumptor, volunteering to go to therapy. Lainey almost thought she was still sleeping and having a wonderful dream. But she felt the heat of Eve's body next to hers and knew she was awake and this was all real.

Lainey nodded. "Anytime you want, my love. I have one important question."

"Hit me," Eve responded, feeling lighter and ready to take on the world.

"Do you think they left us any bacon?"

Eve shook with laughter and stood up. "Not a chance." She held her hand out to Lainey. "Want to go check?"

Just as Lainey opened her mouth to answer, a loud, persistent knock on the front door caused them both to freeze.

"No."

The fear in Lainey's voice broke Eve's heart. She felt that fear, too. What if they had come back to take her away again? Did Eve have it in her to leave her family again? To be locked up in hell again?

"I'll get it," she said dully. She turned to walk away, but was stopped by a trembling hand on her arm.

"No!" Lainey reached frantically for her phone to see who was at the door.

She didn't know what she was going to do if it was the police. Hide Eve? *If I have to,* she answered the silent question in her head. She fumbled with her phone, finally getting the app she needed open. The relief that it wasn't a threat to her family left her weak and emotional.

"It's Jessie."

Eve blew out the breath she had been holding. "Jessie? As in Ellie's Jessie?"

"Do you know another Jessie?" Lainey asked with a raised brow. "Come on. If Kevin hasn't answered the door yet, he's feeling the same thing we did. Let's not let that linger."

Lainey grabbed her robe, throwing it on and tying the sash around her waist. She'll be glad when this dark threat against her family was drug out into the light. And punished.

"Mom?" Kevin stood by, his arms draped around his siblings, his tawny eyebrows furrowed with concern.

"It's Jessie, sweetie. Everything is okay." She peered out the peephole and saw Jessie fidgeting and pacing. Every few steps, Jessie would stop, knock, then pace again. "She's talking to herself," Lainey whispered to Eve, who was peeking over her shoulder.

Eve turned to the kids, smiling reassuringly. "Why don't you guys go back to the kitchen and finish breakfast? Mommy and I are going to talk to Jessie for a minute, okay?" Jessie seemed upset, and while she liked the girl, Eve didn't think it was fair to expose her own kids to someone else's drama. She rubbed Lainey's back when the kids took off.

Lainey pulled open the door, immediately worried by Jessie's demeanor. "Jessie?"

Jessie spun around. "Oh!" Her hand flew to her chest, resting over her heart.

"What's wrong, sweetie? Is it Ellie? Hunter?"

"No, no! T-they're fine. Good. They're good."

Eve frowned. Something was definitely going on with this kid. Jessie was normally a calm soul. Being raised by someone like Ellie Vale had been a good influence on her. But this Jessie was... scared.

"Come in." Eve stepped back, trying not to be as intimidating as people thought she was. Her concern grew when Jessie hesitated crossing the threshold. Eve glanced at Lainey, who looked just as confused as Eve was. "Are you sure everything is okay?"

Jessie jumped at Eve's voice. "Huh? No. Yes. I don't know. I—promise me you won't tell my moms I'm here, please."

"We can promise to listen and do what's best for you, sweets," Lainey said, using Ellie's nickname for Jessie in an attempt to put her at ease. She touched Jessie's arm, snatching her hand back when Jessie jumped again. Lainey exchanged another look with Eve.

Eve shook her head and shrugged. She guided Jessie to the couch, gently coaxing her to sit down. The white plush sofa was custom made for maximum comfort, but Jessie Vale was so rigid even Eve was feeling uncomfortable. She sat in the chair across from Jessie while Lainey tentatively sat next to her.

"Jess, what's going on? Are you in trouble?"

Jessie bowed her head. "I don't know." Her eyes lifted, tears forming in those familiar hazel eyes. "I swear to you, Mrs. Sumptor, I didn't know."

Eve's skin prickled. If Jessie was calling her Mrs. Sumptor, Eve had a sinking feeling she wasn't going to like anything else Jessie had to say. "Didn't know about what?" Eve's tone earned a frown from Lainey.

"Jessie," Lainey said softly. "We can't help you if you don't tell us what's going on. Whatever it is, trust us to listen."

A tear rolled down Jessie's cheek. "It's all my fault."

"Maybe we should start at the beginning," Lainey suggested. "Do you want something to drink?"

"No, thank you." Jessie drew in a deep breath. What the hell did her mom say about that yoga breathing? Breathe in through the nose and let out all the bad energy through the mouth. She'd probably hyperventilate before that happened. "Did mom tell you why I came back home?"

Lainey recalled Ellie saying something about Jessie being over-whelmed at Harvard and wanting to change directions in her studies.

"She gave us the Reader's Digest version," Lainey answered.

"Huh?"

Lainey rolled her eyes. *Kids*. "She summarized, telling us you just weren't happy with the path you chose and wanted to come home to start over," she clarified.

Jessie nodded. Her mom was pretty good at being discreet about Jessie's private life. Especially since Jessie was still trying to figure out what the hell she wanted. After what she just learned, that was going to be even more difficult now.

"Yeah, okay. Well, that's half true. I also... met someone when I was at Harvard. I was homesick, overwhelmed, and lonely. When this person came into my life, they said everything I needed to hear. I fell pretty hard."

"In love?" Eve asked, still wondering what this had to do with her and why Jessie was nervous and feeling guilty.

Jessie shrugged. "I don't know if it was love or just the attention. But we had so much in common, you know? I'd never felt so connected with someone before. We would talk for hours and I'd come away from those conversations feeling validated and seen. When she told me she was moving to LA, I thought it was a sign. I kept trying to find reasons to come home, and now I had one. I'd finally get to meet her. We met online," she explained when Lainey looked at her questioningly. "It's much easier to pretend you're not making a mistake when you're not standing face to face with it. It turns out she wasn't anything like the person she was online."

Lainey's patience was wearing thin, and she knew Eve's was, too. She adored Jessie, and if it had been any other time, Lainey would have loved listening to this story and offering advice. But right now, her nerves were shot. She hadn't finished her coffee, and she was pretty sure breakfast was gone. Playing a guessing game as to what Jessie felt responsible for wasn't on Lainey's agenda today. Nor was hearing about Jessie's failed love life. It made her feel wretched to think like that, but she had too much going on to worry about that.

"I'm sorry, Jessie, but what does this have to do with Eve? What was your fault?"

Jessie's mouth was dry, and she wished she had accepted Lainey's offer for a drink. "I told her about you," Jessie answered, looking directly at Eve. "She loves art and I thought I would get points for name dropping and telling her I knew the owner of, like, the most famous galleries in the world. But she told me she didn't know who you were. That she had to google you. I believed her." Jessie reached into her back pocket and brought out her phone. "Then I found some sort of diary about you. I swear I didn't know she would do this. It's like she's obsessed."

Eve held her hand up, cutting off Jessie's anxious chatter. "Who is *she*?" The doorbell rang in three rapid successions, followed by a banging before Eve could get her answer. "Stay," she ordered Jessie.

"*You* stay," Lainey said, pointing at Eve to sit back down. She'd be damned if she let anyone take Eve away now that they were making progress. She made her way to the door, took a deep breath, and opened it.

"I know who it is!" Jules pushed her way inside, too excited to be mindful of what she just did. "I freakin' know... oh." She stopped abruptly when she saw Jessie. "Um, sorry, I..."

"Join us, Jules," Eve demanded. Her capacity to tolerate any more delays was quickly dwindling. "Jessie was just telling us she thinks *she* knows who is doing this to us." A wave of calm drifted over Eve when Lainey sat on the arm of the chair. "Someone please give me information I can use."

*At least she was polite*, Lainey thought as she laid a hand on Eve's shoulder. She couldn't blame her for being annoyed. Hell, Lainey had hit her limit at the word diary. It bubbled over when she heard "obsessed." If people didn't stop trying to take her wife away from her, things would get really ugly, really fast.

Jules looked at Jessie, suddenly confused. "You? How? Were you working on this, too?"

Jessie shook her head. "No, I..."

"Girls!" Lainey snapped. Both jumped, looking at Lainey. "Names. Please. I don't care which one of you goes first, but do it quickly."

Eve swiped a hand over her mouth to keep the smile at bay. This was a fucking serious situation. But hearing Lainey use her *mother* tone to get results—which always worked—tickled Eve.

Jessie brought up the photos she took of the diary she found at her girlfriend's apartment and handed her phone over. "Her name is Giselle."

Eve froze. "Giselle? Giselle Cadieux? Our *intern*?" She shook her head. Giselle was quiet and respectful. She excelled in her work. Work that helped many underprivileged people. "That can't be right," Eve uttered weakly as she read through entry after entry of the dossier Jessie took photos of.

"Unfortunately, it is," Jules said apologetically. She plopped a folder on the table and slapped it open. "I was using your superior system last night to see if I could dig deeper into your..." she glanced at Jessie. "Situation."

"You may speak freely in front of Jessie. She's family," Lainey assured. She wanted Jessie to know this wasn't her fault. Eve might feel differently at the moment, but she would see the truth once the shock wore off.

"Right, yeah." Jules flipped to a printout of code that meant nothing to anyone in the room but her. "Anyway, I noticed that someone attempted to upload spyware to your company's system. But, like, your firewall there is total boss, so they never got past the first security block. I deleted it," she confirmed. "And I dug deeper to see if it was connected to all the other shit going on. That's when I found the same hacker name."

She shoved the printout over to the Sumptor women. Jules knew it was gibberish to most people, but she circled the name she wanted them to focus on.

"Here's the code from the video," Jules said, pushing that paper to them, too. "Do you see the same alias? But the weird shit is, this wasn't coming from some remote location. I don't think they could get in without being on the actual system. I tried. So they had to be there. I searched for who was logged in at the same time the spyware was uploaded. It was Giselle."

Eve shook her head. "This doesn't make any sense." She looked up at Lainey. "We vetted her. There was nothing in the report that suggested any of this. How did we miss it?"

"I don't know, my love." Lainey was just as shocked and confused as Eve was. Their process was thorough and tough. Blemishes on the girls' records weren't an automatic dismissal, but they were investigated to see if those blemishes were a threat to Sumptor, Inc. and the company's mission. Giselle Cadieux's record was impeccable.

"Uh, you may have missed it because Giselle isn't her real name." Three sets of eyes snapped up at Jules in complete surprise. *Freaky.* She flipped through the sheets in her folder. "Yeah, uh, I asked the big guys—Cade and Greyson—to come in and do what they do best because something just felt off to me. They grabbed some fingerprints and DNA from a coffee cup 'Giselle' had used earlier in the day. When they ran it, they came up with the name," she checked her notes. "Jacqueline La Pierre."

Eve sat back heavily. "*That's impossible.*"

Lainey watched as the blood drained from Eve's face. Obviously that name meant something to her, but it didn't sound familiar to Lainey. "Do you know her, Eve?"

Eve stood, taking Lainey's hand. "Stay here," she told Jessie and Jules as she pulled Lainey out of the room with her. "Jacqueline La Pierre," she said when they were alone. "That's the name of Laurence's daughter."

"Oh my god." Lainey's entire body trembled with rage hearing the name of the man that brutalized Eve when she was just a teenager. "I don't understand. You saw her when you... visited him a few years ago. She was just a child. Are we sure this is the same girl?"

Eve exhaled heavily. "I don't know. But hearing that name..."

Lainey wrapped her arms around Eve's waist, resting her head on Eve's shoulder. She held on, offering her solidarity as Eve took a moment to ground herself again. "I'm here, my love. Take what you need, then let's go back in there. We need to end this."

And that was the difference between then and now. She no longer had to be alone, digging deep to find the strength to survive one more hurdle in her life. She could allow herself to believe that it was her burden alone, but Lainey wouldn't agree. *For better or worse.*

"I love you, Lainey," Eve murmured against Lainey's silky hair. "I think you know this would have sent me into a tailspin before. But you're here now. Your unflinching love and support makes this just another speed bump we will maneuver together."

The honesty and emotion behind Eve's words, so freely given, touched Lainey. They had come a long way since that first day they met at Sumptor, Inc. They may have taken the long way, but that didn't matter now. Their love was timeless.

"I love you, too, Eve." She pulled back slightly. "How much do you want them to know?"

"Only the basics unless it's otherwise necessary."

Lainey nodded. "You take the lead. I would, however, suggest that we get the kids to go for ice cream or something that will keep them occupied for a couple of hours."

"I don't want them out there alone, baby. Not until this is truly over."

"James can take them." Lainey felt Eve's body shake with silent laughter. "That's funny?"

"It is if you imagine that mountain of a man with a tiny Bella sitting on his shoulders, dripping ice cream on his bald head."

"Oh god." Lainey buried her face in Eve's neck, trying desperately to hold back the laughter. On the one hand, this was no laughing matter. But on the other, she was grateful that this would not break them. They wouldn't allow it to. "Come on. You get the kids, I'll get the mountain."

# Twenty-Six

"*B*ug, come here and sit with me for a minute, please."

"'Kay, Momma."

Bella trotted over and climbed up into Eve's lap. Jessie and Jules sat quietly on the couch, waiting. Jessie waited to learn her fate. Jules waited to reveal everything she'd learned. Lainey stood next to James, who towered over her. James had the strength to break every bone in a man's body. But when Lainey asked him to watch Bella and the boys for a couple of hours, she saw fear in his eyes for the first time since she met him. He had claimed not to be good with kids. Lainey didn't buy it. She had seen his compassion. She had faith he'd be just fine. Wrapped around the little girl's finger, but fine.

"Mommy and I need to talk to Jessie and Jules for a little while, okay? Grown up talk."

Bella looked over at the two on the couch and frowned. "Jessie gwon up?"

That caused Jessie's mouth to twitch. *Fair.*

"Well, she's older than you, isn't she?" Eve tickled Bella's tummy. "Anyway, we thought you and your brothers could go get ice cream with James. Would you like that?" Eve did her best to pretend nothing was wrong around Bella. If the little girl sensed anything amiss, Eve would never get Bella to leave her side.

"I just ate bwekfast, Momma!"

Eve's eyes widened. "Are you telling me you're... full?"

Bella's little brows furrowed. "No." She paused, tapping her chin with her finger. "I get a toy?"

"You want to go shopping?" Eve glanced up at James, who blanched at the thought. "I think that's a fine idea. What's the rule for getting toys?"

"One fow me, two fow kids who can't buy dem!"

"Exactly. So? Are you okay with going out for a bit?"

"Kevin and Dawwen go wif me?"

"Yep."

Bella looked up at James, nearly toppling over before she got to the bald head. "You wan' a toy, James?"

Eve bit her lip, holding in her laughter. "Yeah, James. Would you like a toy? It's on me."

"'Member the wules, James!"

"One for me, two for those who can't buy them," James recited. "C'mon, Tiny Eve, let's get this show on the road." James held his trunk of an arm out and Bella jumped on it like a monkey.

"*Tiny Eve*," Lainey smirked. "If that isn't true..." She received a playful slap on the thigh from "Big Eve."

"Bye, Momma! Bye, Mommy! Bye, gwon ups!" Bella waved frantically. "Wet's go, James!"

Jules stared at a retreating James, with Bella perched on his shoulders. "That dude's arm is the size of my waist." She shook her head.

"Yes," Eve agreed. "Our kids are safe with James. Now, let's talk about this Jacqueline La Pierre," she said, ready to get down to business. "I once knew someone with that name. But Giselle can't be that girl. She's too old. Jacqueline would be..."

"Sixteen," Jules supplied.

"What!" Jessie jumped up from the couch. "She said she was twenty-three!" She paced, muttering about being sick. Jessie was barely nineteen herself, but she never would have talked to Giselle—or whatever her name is—if she knew she was that young.

"She's right." Lainey went to Jessie, wrapping her arms around the distressed girl. "We do extensive background checks on our interns.

Nothing in Giselle's files raised any red flags. If she's not Giselle, then who is?"

"Oh, she is." Jules, again, flipped through pages in her file. "Once I knew *who* the hacker was, I could trace everything she's done under that handle. She's freakin' good at what she does, but sloppy." Jules handed Eve a report. "It looks like she's been planning this for at least three years."

"Since her father died," Eve said quietly.

"Whatever the reason," Jules continued. She was curious about what was really going on here, but wasn't stupid enough to ask. "It was a very elaborate plan. She watched you, kept notes on you. She created Giselle when you opened your first school for girls to get closer to you. I think she had planned to dismantle it from the inside."

Eve clenched her teeth. The girls she helped with the schools did nothing to deserve Jacqueline's wrath. But Eve would not blame herself either. Karma came for Laurence, not Eve.

"Why didn't she?"

Jules lifted a shoulder, giving Eve an apologetic look. "I don't think it was enough for her. Closing a school would hurt the girls, but not you. You'd just open another one up. So, she started studying those closest to you. Adam, Mrs. Giles," she paused. "Lainey."

"Trying to find a way in," Lainey assumed. "She found it with Adam, didn't she?"

Jules cleared her throat. They said Jessie was family, but how much did they really want her to know? She would leave that explanation for later. "He was one way. She had a lot on him. According to her notes, she was going to use his financial problems to reel him in. Well, that and his obsession with you that he didn't bother to hide. The internship was the other. I think she had tried hacking Sumptor, Inc. before with no luck. But the internship gave her direct access to Eve and everything she held dear."

Jules bent and picked up another page. Taking a breath, she turned to Jessie, handing her the paper.

Tentatively, Jessie took it. "What is this?"

"She sought you out."

A tear slid down Jessie's face as she read everything *Giselle* knew about her. Everything they had talked about, everything *Giselle* told her, was a lie. "Why me?"

"You were close to her age, and..."

"And you knew me," Eve finished. "She used you to get to me. I'm sorry, Jessie."

"But I don't understand. If she could do all this, what did she need me for?"

Jules raised her hand. "I can answer that. She needed a failsafe. The Sumptors are unpredictable when it comes to choosing their interns. If she didn't get in..."

"She'd ask me to put in a word for her." Jessie grabbed Lainey's hand. "And I would have. I'm so sorry."

"Jessie, she manipulated you. None of this is your fault."

Lainey glanced at Eve for support, but Eve just stared at the report Jules gave her. If Lainey had to guess, she wasn't seeing anything in front of her. No, Eve was staring at her past. *Time to wrap this up and get Eve back to the present.* Lainey plucked the paper from Eve's grip, and took the paper from Jessie, placing them both back in the folder they came out of.

"Eve and I will read through this report in depth," Lainey said, ushering the girls to the door. "If we have questions, I'll let you know. Jessie, talk to Ellie. Let her be there for you." Jessie nodded sadly. "Jules, thank you. You've gone above and beyond. You're a perfect candidate for a permanent residence at Sumptor, Inc."

Jules waited for Jessie to pass by her, then leaned in to speak to Lainey quietly. "There's more. Neither of you are going to like it, but it's all there. I'll, uh, be around, so text me if you need to."

"Thank you, again. Be careful going home." Lainey shut the door softly behind them, and sent a quick text to Ellie telling her Jessie was okay, but could use her mom right now. She smiled when she heard Jules ask Jessie if she wanted to go for a coffee...or 'something' as she stuck her phone back in her pocket. But that smile fell from her face as she took a moment to gather her thoughts and emotions before going back to Eve.

"Eve? Honey, are you okay?"

Eve frowned. "She blames me for the death of her parents. But it wasn't my fault."

While Lainey agreed wholeheartedly, she recognized the need for Eve to work it out—all of it—for herself. She watched how the emotions flickered in Eve's eyes, the twitch of her eyebrows, and the quiver of her lips as she visited her past again. Hopefully, for the last time.

"Laurence killed his wife because she threatened to expose him for what he did to me. Something I never wanted or asked for." Eve tilted her head. "Billy killed Laurence over his unreciprocated love for me."

"I think you mispronounced obsession," Lainey muttered.

The corner of Eve's mouth curved. "Obsession," she conceded. "But I had done nothing to lead Billy on. I never once told him I loved him. That whole fiasco was karma coming back around. Not me." Eve looked up at Lainey, who was sitting on the coffee table in front of her. Apparently, that is a good place to be when emotions were involved, Eve thought with a dash of amusement. "She's misguided, Lainey."

"Nope."

"Pardon?"

"You're about to tell me how she needs leniency. How she's just a kid, and this isn't her fault."

"You know who her father is, baby. She never had a chance."

"I know who *your* father is, my love," Lainey countered. "You never killed anyone."

That was true enough, Eve accepted. Though... "I've put things in motion knowing full well the outcome, Lainey."

Lainey blew out a frustrated breath. "That was different, Eve. I'm not the biggest Adam fan, but he didn't deserve to die. What those men did... you just gave karma a head start."

Eve sighed. She couldn't very well argue with Lainey. She was right. But still...

"No, Eve."

Eve narrowed her eyes. "I'm not sure I like you knowing what I'm thinking all the time."

Lainey slid off the coffee table to situate herself between Eve's thighs. "You love it." She reached up and cupped Eve's cheek. "I can't give this girl a pass. I'm sorry. She took you away from me. She hurt our

family. The only way she can learn from this is to deal with the consequences, not leniency."

Eve admitted defeat. She wouldn't defy Lainey's wishes to have
Jacqueline prosecuted. "Such a waste of talent."

Lainey nodded. "She could have done so much good. Like you. I'm
so proud of you for not taking the blame for this, my love. And I love
how generous you are willing to be with her after all she has done. But
she is not your responsibility. She's a reminder of your past, and it's time
for us to live for now. And our future."

Eve turned her head and kissed Lainey's palm before taking her
hand and holding it to her chest. "You're right, baby. I owe her nothing.
I'm tired of running from my past. It's time to put an end to this."

Lainey's eyes closed briefly, grateful that Eve agreed with her. She
was ready to spend the rest of her life with Eve. Happily. But before they
could do that, they needed to know everything. How did Adam figure
into all of this? How accurate were their theories? She reached behind
her and picked up the report.

"Are you ready?"

Eve pulled Lainey up and onto her lap. "We have to know, right?"
With her arm wrapped around Lainey's hip, she squeezed lightly.
"Open it."

Lainey did as Eve asked. She skipped the pages they had already seen.
"I really hope Jessie tells Ellie what's going on," she said as she got to a
page that was unfamiliar and began reading. "She doesn't need to go
through this... oh my god."

Eve was immediately alert. Whatever Lainey just read sent a shiver so
strong down her body, Eve felt it. "What is it?"

Lainey's hands shook as she turned the folder toward Eve.

The color drained from Eve's face. She looked up at Lainey, whose
confusion mirrored hers. The pain in Lainey's eyes set Eve into action.

"We have some calls to make. Call Greyson, baby. If she figures out
we're on to her, she'll disappear." *It's what I would do.*

"Okay." Lainey was still trying to wrap her head around what she
just read. She knew Eve was giving her an unnecessary task, as Greyson
and Cade would no doubt be surveilling Jacqueline already. But Lainey
was thankful for the distraction. "What are you going to do?"

"I'm going to call Reghan. She's going to need all this information to start the ball rolling on everything that needs to be done."

"I want to be there. When the realization of the consequences for all this hits, I will be there. I want them to know if they fuck with the Sumptors, there will be hell to pay."

"And you'll be there to collect?" Eve asked with a proud smile.

"Abso-fucking-lutely." Lainey patted Eve's ass. "Get dressed, my love. We have a world to reconquer. Ours."

# Twenty-Seven

*L*ainey watched as the girl she knew as Giselle walked into the small room. Gone was the sweet, timid young woman. The scowling Jacqueline in front of her, dressed in a white jump-suit with an inmate number emblazoned in bold black on the chest, was hard. Just sixteen-years-old and already hating the world. Or just the Sumptors, Lainey thought bitterly.

"She couldn't face me herself?" Jacqueline snarled as she glared at Lainey.

Lainey raised a brow. She sat at a small white table, a sharp contrast to her charcoal suit. She clasped her hands in front of her, discreetly digging her nails into her palm. The slight pain helped Lainey stay calm as she faced the young woman. *Child,* she reminded herself again as her stare challenged a defiant Jacqueline.

"Don't worry, she will be here. But first, you deal with me. Sit down."

Jacqueline scoffed. "I don't have to..."

"Sit. Down." Lainey didn't recognize the brusque detachment in her voice. But it worked as Jacqueline sat down with a thud. "Poor, misguided soul."

Jacqueline frowned. "What?"

"That's what Eve said about you. She wanted to be lenient with you.

But you tried to take her away from me. From her children. You hurt my family. For that, I cannot forgive you."

Surprisingly, that hurt Lainey to say. Even after everything this girl had done, a part of Lainey wanted to do as Eve requested. *Why?* Because... "You have a great deal in common with Eve," she said quietly.

"I'm *nothing* like her! She killed my parents!"

Lainey shook her head. "You are blind to the true nature of who your father was. Perhaps when you get out of here and can use a computer again, you will look Laurence up." She leaned in closer. "Dig deep, Jacqueline. Go into that dark web you're partial to and find out who he truly is. Then maybe you'll understand why I had to do this."

"You don't understand why *I* had to do this!" Jacqueline cried. "I'm not the bad guy here. *She* is! She had to pay. She doesn't deserve to be free, doing whatever she wants in this world!"

"The bad guy?"

It wasn't new, having someone see the complete opposite of who Eve was. She was a private, mysterious woman. People loved writing their own stories about such figures. Especially if they were as wealthy and beautiful as Eve. But Lainey couldn't fathom how anyone could believe *this* story. She narrowed her eyes, studying Jacqueline, trying to determine if she genuinely accepted what she was saying as the truth. It was obvious she did. This was Jacqueline's own version of the past... and Eve. For Lainey, that made Jacqueline too dangerous for compassion.

Seeing the belligerence on Jacqueline's face caused Lainey to doubt anything she had to say would get through to the young woman. All she could do was speak the truth and... hope.

"The girls' home you wanted to destroy? Eve built that for young women in need of a safe place to live and learn how to conquer the world. *Their* world. Sumptor, Inc., the company you longed to dismantle from the inside? Eve created that business to lead the industry in philanthropic revenue, innovation, and environmental awareness. Her galleries cater to the unknown artists around the globe, giving them an outlet to release their creativity. *That's* what you were trying to deprive this world of. And she did all of that despite the monster her father was. She's not the evil villain you portray her to be, Jacqueline. My wife is a loving mother, an incredible artist, and a brilliant woman.

You could have learned from her. You could have done so much good in this world. Like Eve."

Jacqueline merely stared blankly at Lainey. Not one emotion could be read in those harsh brown eyes. Lainey shook her head, confidence in her decision to have Jacqueline prosecuted growing. She stood, her fingertips resting on the table.

"I truly hope you spend your time here wisely, Jacqueline. And know that if I ever have to go through this again, if you try to hurt my family again, this..." Lainey gestured around her. "Will seem like a country club compared to where you end up next."

She straightened, squaring her shoulders and tugging the creases out of her suit jacket. With one last look at the girl who tried to tear her world apart, Lainey turned on her heel and walked away. Her heart jumped into her throat when she saw Eve standing silently in the shadows. Had she been there the entire time? The shimmer of love shining in Eve's eyes told Lainey all she needed to know.

Eve reached out and squeezed Lainey's hand in passing. She had stepped into the room shortly after the guard escorted Jacqueline in, only intending to stay for a minute to gauge the situation. But then Lainey started talking, and her confidence and authority mesmerized Eve. Of course she had always known how Lainey felt about her. Her wife was an open book. If Lainey didn't say the words, she showed her. But to hear the way Lainey defended her today touched Eve's heart more than ever. Hell, she was on the verge of thanking Jacqueline for this unwarranted stunt. It somehow managed to do something Eve hadn't thought was possible. It brought her and Lainey closer.

"Are you here to condemn me, too?"

Eve watched Jacqueline for a full thirty seconds, never saying a word, just one perfectly arched eyebrow displaying any type of reaction.

"No," she said finally. "I believe Lainey covered it."

"You won't be happy until you've gotten rid of my whole family, will you?" Jacqueline sneered.

Eve closed her eyes briefly and took a breath. "Jacqueline, I never met your mother. But your father..." She swallowed the lump of emotion in her throat. Was it cruel to want to reveal Laurence's true nature to his daughter? Perhaps it was a blessing. A way to pull Jacqueline out of this life of vengeance that was sure to bury her. "I met your father when I was about your age."

She glanced around the room, spying the surveillance cameras. Decision made, Eve leaned close to Jacqueline and whispered in her ear. After a few excruciating moments, Eve stepped back.

"That's not true!" Jacqueline yelled, tears brimming in her eyes.

"You have no idea how I wish it weren't," Eve responded softly. "I'm sorry you lost your family, Jacqueline. But I will no longer carry the guilt of your father's sins."

Eve turned to leave, her steps faltering when Jacqueline begged Eve not to leave her there. She looked back to see Jacqueline crying. "I can't carry your guilt, either. You have the potential to do extraordinary things, Jacqueline. Take this time to reflect on what I've told you and how you want to spend the rest of your life."

Lainey was waiting for Eve when she came out of the room and immediately opened her arms. "Are you okay?" she asked as Eve burrowed herself in Lainey's embrace.

"Yes."

Lainey was pretty confident Eve would have told her if she wasn't okay. But she had also seen the tears in Jacqueline's eyes and the sadness in Eve's. Watching through the small glass window in the door, Lainey obviously couldn't hear what Eve whispered to the young woman, but whatever it was, it caused an outburst from Jacqueline.

"Are you reconsidering agreeing with me about taking this route?"

"Because of her crocodile tears?" Eve asked with a mirthless laugh. "No, baby. You were definitely right. I told her what Laurence did to me. And to her mother. She doesn't believe me yet. But I think time here with nothing to do but live with her mistakes will open her eyes."

"You told her?" It surprised Lainey that Eve was so willing to disclose that to Jacqueline.

"She needed to know. She's in here because she's defending the honor of a man who had no honor." Eve recalled the dead eyes behind the manufactured tears. "The crying was a good touch, but she needs to work on the emotion if she wants people to believe her."

Lainey smacked Eve's tummy lightly with the back of her hand. "Do *not* give her pointers. She's in enough trouble as it is."

Eve smiled at her wife. "Yes, ma'am."

Lainey raised an eyebrow, her lips quirking into a saucy grin. "I quite enjoy hearing you call me ma'am. You should do that more often. In a different setting, of course."

"Of course." Yep. Lainey 2.0 was well on her way to sending Eve to an early—yet incredibly satisfied—grave. "Are you ready for our trip?"

Lainey snickered. Eve was changing the subject to keep herself from making a scene here at the detention center. *So, let's change venues.* Lainey tucked her arm around Eve's and walked toward the door. "I am. The kids and Lexie are on the plane waiting for us. Passports are in my bag. We filled suitcases with bathing suits and practically nothing else. We're all set."

Eve squinted when they walked out of the dull, drab building into the intense sun. She slipped her sunglasses on as she opened the car door for Lainey.

"Are we doing the right thing?" she asked as Lainey climbed into the Porsche and fastened her seatbelt.

Instinctively, Lainey knew Eve wasn't asking about Jacqueline but their trip. They had spent most of the week going back and forth about what to do with the information they had learned. Jacqueline was the easy part. There was still time for her to better herself. Both Lainey and Eve agreed Jacqueline could do that best in a detention center that offered classes and therapy.

They still had other things to sort out before putting this mess behind them. However, doing that the way Eve preferred meant being away from home for a few days, and there was no way Princess Bella would allow that. So, Lainey and Eve decided they would take that family vacation Eve wanted after all. A little fun in the sun with the kids was just what they needed. They just had to make one important stop first.

Lainey reached up and cupped Eve's soft cheek. "Yes, my love. We're doing the right thing."

---

"ARE YOU NERVOUS?"

Lainey looked up, taking the glass of water Eve offered her. "Thank you. I think I'm getting used to flying, my love. Though I may have had a different answer if we were alone. Only because I love the way you distract me."

Eve chuckled as she slipped into the seat next to Lainey. "I can say you weren't feeling well and we can go into the bedroom so I can distract you with my mouth." She wiggled her eyebrows suggestively.

Lainey laughed, the water she was sipping dribbling down her chin. "Tempting. Very tempting."

Eve grabbed a napkin and dabbed Lainey's face, biting her cheek to keep from cracking up. "Ahem. Well, if you change your mind, let me know. But what I meant was, are you nervous about what we have to do?"

Lainey's brows knitted in contemplation as she tried to determine exactly how she felt. Was she nervous? She shook her head. "Not nervous. I'm angry and I'm trying not to be."

"Why?"

"Why am I angry?"

Eve took Lainey's hand. "No, I understand that part. Why are you trying *not* to be?"

Lainey laced their fingers together and looked over at her family. "Because of them," she said, nodding her head at their children. "To them, this is just a vacation. A getaway from the sadness and stress that has been surrounding us for the past few weeks." She focused on Bella. She still had nightmares, waking up and crying out for her momma. "I want this trip to be the end of her anxiety."

Eve gazed at Lainey long enough to cause her wife to blush.

"Why are you looking at me like that?"

"Because I've never met anyone like you," Eve answered softly. She feathered her fingers across Lainey's cheek. "Sometimes I can't believe you're with me. That you love me."

Lainey leaned over and brushed Eve's lips with hers. "*I love you more than you'll ever know,*" she whispered.

A meek cough interrupted their intimate moment and Eve looked over to see Lexie standing there in front of them.

"I'm so sorry to interrupt."

"It's okay, Lexie." Lainey patted Eve's thigh to quell her annoyance at being disturbed. "Is something wrong?"

"Oh! No." Lexie jerked a thumb over her shoulder. "They're engrossed in that video game, so I thought I'd come over and thank you for inviting me and Sean on this trip."

Eve and Lainey finally met Lexie's boyfriend, Sean, just two days before leaving for the trip. Fortunately, they liked him enough to allow him to tag along as a favor to Lexie. After a thorough background check, of course.

"You're welcome. We appreciate you agreeing to join us and being there for the kids," Eve said amicably.

"I know you had your doubts about me." Lexie held up a hand before Lainey could explain. "It's okay. I totally understand. Your family comes first, and everyone falls under suspicion. I never resented that."

Eve narrowed her eyes. In her experience, no one enjoyed being a suspect. She certainly didn't. "You're taking that awfully well."

Lexie shrugged. "I have nothing to hide. You probably checked Sean out before allowing him to come with us, too. You do what you have to do to keep your family safe." She glanced back. "You didn't find any red flags, did you?" she asked in a hushed voice, grinning.

"You seem to have a good one," Lainey smiled. It was difficult for her to trust the information they received in the background check. Knowing Jacqueline faked everything they discovered in hers made Lainey wary. But Jules did the review herself, and Lainey trusted her. "Is it serious?"

"Serious is a... serious word. This will be a good test for us." Again, she glanced behind her to watch Sean with the kids. "We'll see how he handles Bella at her, let's say, finest." She turned back to Eve and Lainey, a sweet smile gracing her face.

Eve chuckled. "That's quite the test. If he survives that, marry him."

"Hmm." A crinkle formed between Lexie's eyebrows. "When did you both know it was love?"

"The moment we met." They answered together, looking lovingly at each other.

"There were a lot of obstacles for us, Lexie. We wasted a lot of time being afraid of things that seem so silly now. But you're young. Focus on being happy. Whatever that looks like for you," Lainey advised. And because she didn't want to get sucked into painful memories of life without Eve, she changed the subject. She had no doubt Lexie would come to them in a more private setting if she needed to talk more about her relationship. "Do you have the itinerary for you and the kids?"

"Yes, ma'am," Lexie answered, taking the change in stride. "The boys have agreed to help me keep Miss Bella occupied until you and Eve can join us."

Lainey nodded. "Good. Our business should only take a couple of hours, but we don't want to create undue anxiety for her. Charlie went a day early to make sure everything was secure where you'll be. If you have any concerns, let him know. James will be with us, so please ensure his number is programmed on your phone. We don't anticipate any problems, but...."

"But we're Sumptors," Eve finished with a smirk. "Always better safe than sorry."

"Gotcha!" Lexie saluted. "Please don't worry about us. I promise to keep the kids safe and entertained. Now, I'm going to let you get back to whatever it was I interrupted." Lexie glanced toward the luxurious bedroom concealed by a glossy white door. "I'll be over there with the kids if you two need to take a... nap."

Lexie tossed them a cheeky wink, ducking when Eve threw a wadded up napkin at her.

"She's getting awfully comfortable," Eve teased loud enough for Lexie to hear. Then Eve slid her glance over to Lainey. "Tired?" she grinned.

"So tempting," Lainey muttered. She pulled a book and sketchpad out of her bag. The sketchpad she handed over to Eve with a pack of drawing pencils. "Occupy yourself, please."

"I was trying to!" Eve laughed enthusiastically when Lainey flipped her off. "Promises, promises."

# Twenty-Eight

$\mathcal{E}$ve and Lainey stared up at the luxury estate in front of them. The electric blue roof stood out against the painted white concrete and cloudless crystal blue sky. The sprawling property was bold, almost intrusive on the conflictingly serene landscape of colorful flora under a canopy of trees indicative of the area. The croak of a distant toucan drifted by, riding the refreshing breeze that kissed the warm air surrounding them.

"How much did the bank say?" Lainey asked, counting at least three separate rooftop sitting areas.

"Four point six."

"Reasonable for this amount of property, I suppose."

The mood since landing and leaving the children had been somber. Even the tropical setting and hot sun beating down on them couldn't chase away the dread. Lainey kept telling herself that all they needed to do was get through this part and they would be done with this whole ordeal. *Just get it done.*

"Hmm. Are you ready?" Eve dangled the keys in front of Lainey. Part of her was ready for this. It was the final piece of the puzzle to the events that turned their life upside down so quickly. The other part was hoping against hope that all of this was just a huge mistake.

"Let's do this. We have snorkeling to get to."

Lainey marched up the driveway, glimpsing James in her peripheral. His presence gave her courage a boost. Until she heard it. That voice she thought she'd never hear again. She looked at Eve.

"Yeah, I hear it," Eve groused as she changed her course, a tight grip on Lainey's hand. The deck where the sounds came from was two flights up stone steps lined with white railings. If she wasn't sick to her stomach, she would find this place intriguing. Not quite her style, but Lainey could fix that.

They reached the top of the stairs and stopped in their tracks. The enormous deck surrounded a massive pool, but had only two lounge chairs. A man and a woman scantily clad in barely there bathing suits occupied both. In one hand, they held tropical drinks. Their other hands groped and teased each other.

Eve narrowed her eyes behind her sunglasses as she studied what she could see of the woman. Even from the back, there was something eerily familiar about her. She then turned her attention to the man. Her stomach turned, and there was an anger inside her she'd never felt before. Lainey's presence was the only thing keeping her rage confined. She took a deep breath and counted to ten in her head, feeling the warmth of Lainey's hand at the small of her back. How Lainey managed to keep her cool was beyond Eve, but she welcomed the strength Lainey gave her to do what she came here to do.

"Hello, Adam."

The glass shattered as Adam dropped his drink—and his companion's tit—and stumbled, trying to get up.

"E-Eve! Wha... How... I..." Adam glanced at the woman he was with before frantically looking around. "W-what are you doing here?"

Eve heard Lainey scoff beside her, but her wife remained otherwise quiet. She was allowing Eve to set the tone of this confrontation. "What are you doing *alive*?"

The woman on the lounge chair sat up at that. "Adam, who is this?"

Eve and Lainey looked at each other. Sunglasses couldn't hide the disbelief etched on their faces.

"*Wish Eve*," Lainey whispered low enough that only Eve could hear her. She felt bad about saying it. Lainey had no quarrel with her unless this woman had something to do with this whole mess. But it was true.

282

Adam had found himself a knockoff Eve Sumptor. The woman's boobs were bigger (of course), her hair was blonder, her voice high-pitched instead of Eve's sultry timbre, but there was no mistaking the intent on Adam's part.

Eve pressed her lips together, holding in a laugh. There was absolutely nothing funny about finding out Adam had faked his own death —and blamed her for it. Hell, she had been fighting this anger within her since she and Lainey had read the report. She knew Lainey was fighting it as well. Perhaps even more so. But it was the little moments like this, when Lainey let her unfiltered words go, that granted Eve room to breathe.

"It's no one," Adam answered curtly. "Go into the house, Ava. I'll take care of this."

*Ava*? Another look passed between Eve and Lainey, both knowing what the other was thinking. Eve took a step forward.

"Now, now, Adam. Let the woman stay." Eve turned her attention to *Wish Eve*. "Ava was it?" The woman nodded, bringing her hand up to grasp onto Adam's arm. The ire inside Eve kicked up another notch. "Your... husband?" Eve paused, giving Ava time to clarify.

"Fiancé."

"Ahh, congratulations. Nice ring," Eve said, nodding toward the rock that adorned the woman's left ring finger. The platinum ring had a cushion-cut diamond center stone, framed by micropavé diamonds, set on a micropavé band. She knew very well how many diamonds were on the ring and how much it cost. And she knew because it used to sit on her finger.

Eve toyed with her wedding ring. The ring Lainey had given her wasn't as garish. It was a simple band of diamonds that Lainey chose solely to reflect the effortlessness and brilliance of their love. It was the perfect symbol of... them.

"Thank you. It was Adam's grandmother's."

Eve lifted a brow, slanting a look at Adam. "Was it? Fascinating. How long have you two been together?"

"Ava, please," Adam interrupted, not allowing Ava to answer the question. He grabbed Ava's hand, covering the ring. "Just go inside while I take care of this."

Again, Eve took a step forward, lifting her sunglasses to the top of her head. She squinted against the sun, but wanted Adam to know she *saw* him and everything he did. Oh, how she longed to lash out at Adam. To make him feel a fraction of the pain he put Bella through. But physically hitting him wouldn't do the trick. No, Eve needed to hit him where it counted. His ego.

"How rude of me," Eve began, blocking the direct path to the home. "Allow me to introduce myself."

"Eve, don't. Please."

God, the fear in Adam's voice did wonders to lift Eve's mood. She kept her eyes on him for a moment before turning back to Ava.

"I'm Eve Sumptor." She glanced back, winking at Lainey who hadn't moved from her spot since walking up those stairs. "This is my wife, Lainey Sumptor."

"Sumptor?" Ava's brows furrowed. "Are you relatives of Adam?" She looked at Adam, then at Eve again. "You have the same last name."

Eve snorted. "Oh no. No, no." She glared at Adam. "No." He would *never* be a Sumptor. The fucking audacity of this man. "I'm..."

"Eve, I'm begging you. I know what I did hurt you, but I had no choice. Don't ruin this for me."

*The fucking audacity*, she thought again. Adam's words caused the venom in her veins to reach a boiling point. Did he really think she would spare him and his fucking ego after what he did? Not only to her, but to his daughter. To Lainey. To Kevin and Darren. Fuck him.

"I'm Adam's ex-wife," Eve revealed, her tone ice cold. She stared at Adam as she lay his lies bare to roast in the hot sun of Belize. "He's not a Sumptor. His name is Adam Riley. And the last I heard, he was dead. Murdered. By me, apparently."

Ava spun toward Adam. "What the hell is she talking about?"

Eve turned her back on the couple as Adam tried to stutter his way through a useless explanation. She heard the crack of a slap before Ava stomped away. That slap was nothing compared to what Adam deserved. Eve held Lainey's gaze, drowning herself in the comfort of the love that shone through.

"You took my daughter away from me. You couldn't just let me have this?"

Something inside of Eve snapped, and she whirled around, rushing toward Adam.

"No!" She poked him hard in the chest, pushing him back as she forcefully invaded his personal space. The way he invaded hers. "*You* don't get to play the fucking victim here! *You,*" poke, "faked your fucking death! *You,*" poke, "took *yourself* away from Bella! *YOU,*" poke, "hurt her! Then you fucking devastated her when you took *me* away from her! Don't you fucking dare blame me for this! Whatever the fuck you thought you were going to get out of this, it's fucking over, Adam! I hope to hell you love your final resting place, because if I *ever* fucking see you or hear you have stepped foot in the States again, so help me God, I will put *every* ounce of my power, *every* cent of my money—*MY* money —into making you pay for what you did! I will put you in a tiny, putrid cell like you did to me! You *knew* my past, and yet you still did this to me because you couldn't stand that I never loved you the way I love Lainey! *She* is the best of us! *She* is what Bella deserves. But your fucking ego wouldn't let you just walk away! No, you turned into the man I hated the most in this world!"

Eve raised her fist, ready to strike. Her entire body visibly shook as she struggled not to act on her overwhelming need to watch Adam bleed.

"The man I used to care about *is* dead. You're pathetic, Adam."

She turned and walked away before she did something she would regret. Not for Adam's sake, but for Lainey's. They certainly didn't come here just for Eve to get thrown in jail again for homicide.

Eve's outburst stunned Lainey. She had never seen Eve yell or lose control. A rage had replaced Eve's normally calm demeanor. That serene look Eve had just given Lainey was gone. This Eve was red-faced and breathing hard, as though the simple act of inhaling was painful. In Lainey's experience with Eve, never once had she erupted so violently as she did just now. Nor had Eve ever raised a hand out of anger. The realization of that caused Lainey to hate the man who brought Eve to that point.

She took her sunglasses off, letting her love and compassion be fully visual. As Lainey held her hand out to Eve, she hoped her wife could see that love through the red haze she knew was still there. How could it not be? Eve had just released years of pent-up anger and sorrow in a matter of a few intense moments. Lainey's goal now was to not let it take Eve down a torturous path. She blew out the breath she had been holding when Eve took her outstretched hand.

"This is all your fault," Adam snarled at Lainey. "I should have killed *you*."

Lainey gripped Eve's hand, stopping her from tearing Adam apart with her bare hands. It was one threat Lainey knew Eve would go through with if something happened to her. She pulled Eve close, kissing her gently on the lips, lingering longer for the benefit of their audience, and then calmly approached Adam.

"Yes, you probably should have. But you did what everyone in my life, except Eve, has always done. You underestimated me. You underestimated my love for Eve and my family. In case you're thinking of doing that again, let me warn you, Adam." Lainey stepped even closer, both of them closing in on the edge of the pool. "If you come near my family, if you try to contact *my* daughter, if you try to contact Eve or make her look over her shoulder ever again, if you become a threat to my family again, *I* will kill you. And the best part about it? You're already dead. *No one* will miss you." She stepped back, jaw clenching with anger. Being in Adam's presence—someone she once called a friend—disgusted her. The faster they finished up here, the faster they could get back to their kids. "Now, get off our property."

Adam's expression was a mixture of anger, defeat, and confusion. "T-this is my house. I bought it."

Eve scoffed, sliding up behind Lainey and wrapping her arm around Lainey's waist. "You couldn't even do that right. How much of mine and Lainey's money did you keep for yourself, Adam? A few million? Enough to buy three of these houses. But what do *you* do? You put down the bare minimum and default on the second payment. The bank was more than happy to hand over the deed to someone who can pay. That's me and Lainey. The *Sumptors*."

"Where am I supposed to go?!"

"It's none of our concern where you go, Adam. You just can't stay here." Lainey said coolly. Oh, her hands itched to just reach out and push him into the pool he was dangerously close to. But it would prolong their time here waiting for him to get out and leave.

"I need time to get my things."

"Did you buy those things with *my* money?" Eve clicked her tongue and shook her head. "I'm afraid you're stuck with what you have on. And that's only because I don't want you taking off those speedos." Eve shivered with exaggeration. "The ironic thing is, I would have given you money. All you had to do was let Lainey adopt Bella. And Lainey, being the amazing person she is, would have wanted you to stay in Bella's life. But you chose this path. Now you have to live with the consequences."

"I'll take your deal." The defeat in Adam was almost palatable. "Ten million and visitation. I won't contest Lainey adopting Bella."

Eve barked out a mirthless laugh. "Are you fucking kidding me? After everything you did, you think I'm going to give you *anything*? The last time you *talked* to Bella, you scared her into thinking I would send her away if she did something I didn't like. How could you do that to your daughter? God, Adam. Go fuck yourself! Now get off our fucking property!"

Adam took a threatening step toward them.

"Adam!" James's booming voice stopped everyone. His dominating presence was there from seemingly out of nowhere. "I believe these ladies told you to get the fuck out of here." His large hand wrapped around Adam's throat. "I should kill you right here for what you put these women through. Mrs. Sumptor said it best. No one will miss you, you fucking bastard."

"James," Lainey said delicately. Adam's face was turning red and his toes were the only things touching the ground as James held on tight. "Let him go."

"Just a simple twist and I can snap his neck, Mrs. Sumptor."

Lainey laid a soft hand on James's boulder of an arm. "James, that would be too easy for him. Let him go with his speedos and nothing else. He lost, James."

James growled in Adam's face. "Count yourself lucky that *Mrs.* Sumptor is a lot nicer than I am. And pays me."

"Wait." Eve stepped up beside Lainey, glaring at Adam. "Loosen your grip, but keep him there," she ordered. "I want to know something. Did you know who she was?"

Adam's hand wrapped around James's wrist, but he stopped struggling. It would only make things worse. "Who?" he squeaked out.

"Don't fuck with me, Adam. Did you know she was Laurence's daughter?"

Adam's eyes grew wide, and he squirmed uncomfortably. "That's not true. I would never..."

"Never what?" Lainey interjected hotly. "Hurt Eve like that? Do you think we would believe that after what you did? You take her away from her family, lock her up. Why wouldn't we think you sought Laurence's daughter out to cut even deeper?"

"I wouldn't! I love Eve!"

"Bullshit! You never loved Eve. Not the way she deserved to be loved. Not the way *I* love her. You loved the idea of Eve Sumptor. The beautiful woman on your arm, the notoriety, the money," Lainey paused for a split second. "The incredible sex. But when it came to knowing and loving her for who she is, you didn't fucking care."

"You don't know what the fuck you're talking about! You *stole* her from me..."

"There it is. You see Eve as a possession. Something to own, to make *you* look better. What is her favorite color, Adam? Her favorite food? What does Eve love to do when the world around her is quiet? Hmm? Can you tell me anything about the woman you claim to love?"

Adam opened and closed his mouth like a fish, but nothing came out. "I didn't know she was his daughter," he said dejectedly. "I don't even remember how we met, but I was having money problems and she was there offering to help."

Jules had said Jacqueline had been watching Adam, taking notes. It wasn't hard to ascertain that she sought him out when the time was right. With his hatred for Lainey and obsession with Eve, he was an easy target to manipulate. Still... "Who's idea was it to frame me?" Eve asked coldly.

Adam couldn't look at either of them. "I wanted Lainey to suffer the way I did when I lost you. I mentioned that to the woman, and she told me what she could do."

"Girl, Adam." Eve didn't know why she was torturing herself by listening to this. She could have just let James... escort Adam off the property. But she had needed answers first. "Jacqueline La Pierre, who you know as Giselle, is a sixteen-year-old girl with a delusional idea of who her father was." She tilted her head. "Somehow I don't think it would've changed anything if you had known."

As that rang true deep within her, Eve pulled Lainey close. She nodded at James who finally released his grip. Adam gasped in air as James's hand dropped from his throat.

James bent slightly, getting in Adam's face. "The only reason you're not dead or fucked up is because of these two women. Go. Get the fuck out of here, or I'll quit working for the Sumptors and fucking kill you right now."

Adam, pale and scared, looked pleadingly at Eve. "Please let me just get some of my things."

Eve shook her head. "No. Do you know what the police did when they came to my house? They took me, Adam. No warning, no chance to explain to Bella what was happening. They took me away from my family with nothing but the clothes on my back. The difference is, *you* had a choice. You've always had a choice. You just keep making the wrong one."

---

LAINEY AND EVE stood there in silence for a full five minutes after James escorted Adam off the property with just the tiny bathing suit covering his lying ass.

"That just happened." Lainey blinked, taking a deep breath through the nose and letting it out slowly through her mouth. *Inhale the good. Hold. Exhale the bad. Thank you, Ellie.*

"Yep." *That just happened,* Eve thought. Her ex-husband, the man she had a child with, the man who framed her for murder, was out there walking around Belize in what equated to his skivvies, broke and bested. She should feel good about that, shouldn't she? Part of her did. But her heart bled for her daughter.

Lainey moved in front of Eve, taking her hands. "Are you okay?"

289

Eve squeezed Lainey's fingers. "Yeah, baby." She sighed. "I wanted James to kill him. That's a hard thing to admit about the father of my child."

"Eve, he stopped being a father to Bella the minute he put his self-ishness ahead of her happiness."

Eve smiled and brought Lainey's hand up to her lips. She kissed Lainey's soft knuckles one at a time. "Thank you for reminding me of that."

If Lainey had to remind Eve what a prick Adam was every day, she would. But she worried about Bella and how this would affect her.

"What are you going to tell her?"

Eve cocked her head as she studied Lainey's beautiful face. "I don't know. What are *we* going to tell her? Official or not, you're her mother, too. This is a decision we should make together."

Lainey's heart filled with joy at that. What a welcome feeling after this battle with Adam. They may have come out victorious, but it had been emotionally draining. Thinking of finally becoming Bella's legal parent certainly gave Lainey's morale a boost.

"I think she's too young to understand all of this. Hell, I'm in my forties and I don't understand a goddamn thing Adam was thinking."

Eve chuckled. "Then it's settled. We don't tell her. Let Adam stay dead."

"And if she asks questions when she gets older? What if she sees stories about why you really went away?"

Eve's brows furrowed. What a fucking rollercoaster day it had been so far. And now she dreaded the future when that scenario could happen. The day Bella finds out her daddy tried to take everything away from her.

"Then we tell her the truth and hope to hell she understands we only wanted to protect her."

Lainey nodded. "I can get behind that."

"Good," Eve winked. "Now, do you want to go inside and see what we just bought?"

Lainey blew out a breath. What she wanted to do was go back to their kids and start their vacation. But... *four point six million.* "Let's do it."

They made their way, hand in hand, inside the vast house. It was certainly big and imposing. Space wasn't a concern at all. But the furnishings had to go. Wicker did nothing to make this place feel like a home. In fact, everything was too small for the room, causing it to be more intimidating than welcoming.

"This is... interesting."

Lainey chuckled. "It's hideous. Adam may have been good at architecture, but interior design is not his strong suit."

"Hmm. Do you want to keep it?"

"For us?"

Eve shrugged. "We could use it as a vacation home, I guess."

"Hell, no." Lainey looked at the space with a critical eye. In her mind, she could see the transformation from hideous to luxurious. From uninviting to embracing. From nondescript to inspiring. They would get rid of everything currently in Lainey's eyesight—and the things she couldn't see. Adam's things. If she knocked out the wall in front of them and put in an expansive wall of glass, the view would be breathtaking. The place was close enough to the water that the panoramic scene would be exquisite. "I think it would make a great private resort. Maybe a nice honeymoon spot for Vanessa and Emma?"

Eve smiled at her wife, who was always thinking of others. "I'm pretty sure they already have their honeymoon planned. But I'm confident you'll make it irresistible to anyone who wants to get away from reality for a while. Or we could sell it."

Lainey gave the space one last look. "I have a feeling this place was grand before. I'd like to make it that way again and open it up during the tourist season. Would that be okay?"

Eve wrapped her arm around Lainey, squeezing lightly. "Of course. But not for us?"

"We don't need it, my love. We have an island." Lainey hid her smirk as she waited for that information to sink in.

"Okay, well... what? We have a what?" Eve turned Lainey to her. "Say that again."

"We have an island." Lainey shrugged nonchalantly. It was a big deal, buying an island. Even for the Sumptors. But when Lainey was looking for a safe place for the kids to stay while she and Eve took care of business, she had come across a small island for sale a few miles off the coast. Maybe she should have talked to Eve about it before, but Lainey had wanted to surprise her wife. The way Eve had surprised her many times before.

She thought of the Jade statue of Buddha that she still kept by her bedside. Eve had bid for that ridiculously expensive pot belly thing without Lainey's knowledge at their first auction together. All because Lainey had expressed interest in it, even playfully bidding on it herself. Of course, she never had a real chance to win it with the bidding starting at $10,000. But as much of an adrenaline rush as it was to bid, it quickly escalated to $60,000 and Lainey laughably felt defeated.

Little had Lainey known at the time that Eve won it solely as a gift for her. This island—while slightly more pricey—was something Lainey bought solely as a gift for Eve. *"We could rent an entire island just for ourselves. We'll go snorkeling, lay in hammocks, and soak up the sun. Decompress."* Eve deserved a place to do just that. They just wouldn't be renting.

"You... bought an island?"

"Yes. It had been on the market for a while, so I got a good price for it. I wanted a place where you..."

Lainey never got the chance to finish her sentence as Eve crushed her mouth to Lainey's in a fiery kiss. The emotion in that kiss scorched Lainey's soul. Was it possible to feel gratitude, belonging, happiness, and peace in a kiss that curled your toes? *Yes*, Lainey thought. *Yes, it was.*

*"I love you, Lainey,"* Eve whispered against Lainey's lips. "I wish I could explain how happy you make me."

"You just did, my love." Lainey kissed Eve again, touching her cheeks with her fingertips. She looked into Eve's gray eyes, her own shining with unshed tears. Tears that had nothing to do with sorrow. *"You just did."*

# Epilogue

"Hold on, time out." Blaise threw her hands up, crossing them like a T. She looked around to make sure there were no kids around before continuing. "You're telling us that *Adam*," she whispered the name just in case, "is fucking *alive*, living in Belize, and screwing some *Wish Eve*. Wish Eve who is his fiancée?"

Eve glanced at Lainey, then raised a brow at Blaise. "You didn't get all this info from Greyson?"

"Pfft. He doesn't tell me shit when it comes to clients. Even if they are two of my dearest friends. But enough of what my husband doesn't do for me."

The group of friends laughed. Leave it to Blaise to ask what the others wouldn't ask—but still wanted to know. They had been sitting at the kitchen table for the past fifteen minutes, trying to squeeze out information from Eve and Lainey. Delicately, of course. Until Blaise tired of pussyfooting around the issue. They already had to wait two weeks for the couple to come back from their... vacation. Then another week before they could all get together and discuss what had been another rough patch for the bunch.

But the time away had been worth it for the Sumptor family. Eve and Lainey had found their peace again while vacationing with the kids on their new island. It was everything Eve needed. Privacy, sun, family,

293

snorkeling, laying in the hammock with Lainey and just listening to the sound of their kids laughing. The days had been perfect. And the nights? Oh, the nights were mind-blowing. The new intensity they had found in their lovemaking continued to flourish with Lainey demonstrating every night that she was willing to take the lead and be vocal about what she wanted and needed from Eve. They had found their balance with each other, creating a new layer of love and happiness between them.

"Okay," Eve said finally. "Yes, Adam is alive. He is in Belize. But he's no longer *screwing* Wish Eve. When we saw her last, she had left the engagement ring..."

"*Your* ring," Cass added with disgust. *Fucking Adam.* The dude was a fucking waste of Belize air, in her opinion. What he did to Eve and Lainey—and that cute kid of theirs—was the same as abuse in Cass's eyes. And anyone who abused people they claimed to love was a fucking bitch. It made her feel marginally better that the women kicked him out in just his budgie smugglers. She snickered to herself and thanked her friend Emma for the new word. Though the image it left in her head was pretty gross.

Eve held up her left hand, thumbing her wedding ring. "*This* is my ring. The other one was..." She held Lainey's gaze. "A mistake."

"That 'mistake' brought us Bella, my love." Lainey brought Eve's hand to her lips and kissed the ring she had given her. "Anyway, Ava was lucky enough that she hadn't fully moved in with Adam. And smart enough to run the other way, knowing Adam lied about everything. Including telling her his last name was," she paused for dramatic effect. "Sumptor."

Their friends exploded with expletives of disbelief. Having had time to absorb everything they learned in Belize, Lainey and Eve sat back and allowed the pandemonium. Lainey squeezed Eve's hand, tossing a wink in her direction.

"Wait a minute," Ellie said, cutting through the noise. "Ava? *That* was Wish Eve's name?" Lainey nodded, rolling her eyes. "Could he have been any more obvious about his obsession?" What Ellie really wanted to know was if Adam had anything to do with the manipulation of her daughter. Because if he did, she and Hunter were taking a trip to

Belize… with some of Hunter's surgical gear. By the time they were done, Adam wouldn't even have his speedos. "How did he know Jacqueline?"

Eve could see the tension in Ellie's usually tranquil features. "She manipulated herself into his life like she did Jessie's," she explained. She wouldn't excuse Adam for any part he had in this, but Ellie and Hunter deserved the truth. "Jacqueline studied everyone, becoming familiar with them and their presence in my and Lainey's life. Adam said he didn't remember how they met and that's probably the only thing he said that I believed. Jacqueline was very good at situating herself into people's lives with no one questioning it." She reached over and patted Ellie's hand. "How is Jessie?"

Ellie trusted Eve enough to take her at her word. "She's struggling. But Jules has been helping her."

Lainey leaned in. "Jules? Really?" She grinned, guessing that coffee really did turn into *something*.

"Mmhmm. They're just *friends*. At least that's what Jessie keeps telling me. But they're cute together. And I'm really grateful Jules has given Jessie an outlet to talk about all this."

"Okay," Hunter raised her hand. "Being the doctor here," she glanced at Aunt Wills. "One of the doctors," she amended sheepishly. "I need to ask the obvious. How the hell did he get away with faking his death? His sister identified his body. The coroner signed off on it. Were they in on it?"

Eve shook her head. "From what Greyson and Cade tell us, his family is mourning him. Including Jill. It was Jacqueline who impersonated Jill. As for the coroner, they bought his compliance."

"Son of a bitch. A fucking doctor," Hunter groused.

"A death doc," Mo muttered, speaking up for the first time. "I never trusted that dude."

"You didn't like him because he constantly hit on me." Patty tweaked her wife's nose playfully. But she agreed. There was always something shady about Dr. Pratt.

"Yeah, well, he knew we were together," Mo muttered with a *fucker* under her breath.

"This is all very sensational," Willamena said softly. How did these

295

women stay sane? It was a very *unprofessional* thought, but it couldn't be helped. Eve had been through so much in her life. More than most people could handle. Yet, here she was, flourishing in her relationship with Lainey.

"Sensational is a very... shrink word," Eve joked.

Rebecca watched with silent interest as Lainey placed her hand over Eve's again. A small smile formed as she caught Lainey's eye. *Interesting.*

"Well, I am a shrink," Willamena replied, making a very un-shrink face at Eve. "And, honestly, it's the only word I could think of while listening to you."

"I, for one, think the word fits." Kiara, who had been quietly sitting with Lauren, was just now getting caught up on everything that had been going on. "I swear, I go home to Germany for the first time in months and the two of you..." She shook her head and looked at Lauren. "*Da ist die Kacke aber am dampfen!*"

Lauren snickered beside her. "*Ja.*" She laughed even harder when everyone surrounding them called for a translation. "The literal translation is, 'The shit is really steaming there.' But I think the more common way of saying it here is 'the shit hit the fan'."

Blaise lifted her glass of iced tea in the air. "Hear, hear! Let's just hope the steaming shit stays over there in Belize. And may his speedos get caught on the sharp spines of a palm tree." She touched her glass to everyone who toasted with her and slammed back the iced tea as though someone spiked it with the whisky she preferred. "Now, I say we forget about all this and get to partying. My husband is out on your deck grilling with our son. Jessie, Jules, Piper, Claire, and Dani are sunbathing. Kevin, Darren, and Bella are probably trying to drown Cade. It's time for some fun, ladies!"

"Translation," Ellie said, winking at Lauren. "Blaise is ready for the booze portion of this party."

"Hear, hear!" Blaise shouted again. "You get that started," she said to Ellie. "I will go make sure my husband isn't letting Ezra lick the barbecue sauce off the tongs."

---

"YOU'VE BEEN AWFULLY QUIET," Lainey said when Rebecca walked up to her.

"Just taking everything in. How are you?"

Lainey took a moment to seriously consider her answer. "I'm better," she said finally. "Everything happened so fast, yet felt like a lifetime at the same time. Does that make sense?"

"It does." Rebecca knew that feeling all too well. The worst night of her life lasted mere minutes. But when in the throes of it, it felt as though it would never end. It had been over three months now since the police showed up at Eve and Lainey's front door. Rebecca could only imagine how long each dreadful minute felt for her friends. On the other hand... "What does she call you?"

"I'm sorry?"

Rebecca's lips curved into a knowing smile. "Don't think I didn't see the shift in the dynamic between you and Eve. You've changed, Lainey. You've evolved into someone more... dominant."

Lainey raised a brow. "Oh?" Of course *Lainey* felt the change within her. And Eve no doubt benefitted from it. But to have Rebecca notice surprised Lainey.

"Oh, indeed. Do you need more varieties of whips? I can get you the number of my supplier."

Lainey snorted with laughter. "I think we're good for now, Mistress. But I'll be sure to let you know when we're ready to expand our collection."

Rebecca threaded her arm through Lainey's. "You do that. I'll even set up your own room at the club." She glanced over at Lainey. "It'll be white."

Lainey nearly blushed at the thought. Not out of embarrassment, but anticipation. "Ma'am," she said suddenly, not even sure why.

Rebecca nodded her head in approval. "Welcome to the club."

---

"EVE?"

She knew it was coming. Eve had seen Dr. Woodrow eyeing her the entire time she and Lainey were telling the story of what happened. Yet, she still winced when Willamena cornered her before she could make it outside. Okay, corner was an over-dramatization. Willamena merely walked up to her in a friendly manner.

"Hello, Willamena."

"Oh, I get your serious voice. I always know when you're closing yourself off when you call me Willamena and not Aunt Wills. Relax, Eve."

"My apologies, *Aunt Wills*," Eve winked. "But you're going to ask me about my feelings, aren't you?"

"Maybe. But not as your doctor. As your friend. It couldn't have been easy finding out someone you once shared a life with—the father of your child—could do something so heinous."

Eve sighed. She owed a lot to Willamena. Hell, if it weren't for her, Eve would probably still be living miserably without Lainey. Dr. Woodrow was responsible for getting Eve to open up about her true feelings. She would probably even be proud of the outburst Eve had. "It wasn't. But before you can think I'm keeping it all in, I assure you, I got it all out in Belize. I yelled. I cried. I said exactly how I felt. And then I went home with my wife and we fucked our brains out. It was... cathartic."

If Willamena didn't know Eve so well, she may have been dismayed by the vulgarity of Eve's confession. But Eve hadn't said it to be shocking. Willamena had learned a long time ago that when Eve stayed quiet, that's when she should worry. The blunt honesty showed Willamena that Eve was comfortable opening up now.

"I bet that was a show." Willamena immediately reddened with humiliation. "The yelling! Not the... not you and... I'm going to go outside now. Just know that I'm always available to talk if you or the family need it."

Willamena rushed away, leaving a chuckling Eve. It wasn't often the affable expert got flustered. *Lainey's going to be sorry she missed that.*

Eve stood in the space between the living room and kitchen—alone —and closed her eyes. Part of her had been dreading coming home and having to have this conversation with their friends. It was private and humiliating. But then she remembered how they had stood behind her and Lainey, never faltering. They deserved closure just as much as Eve and Lainey did. Eyes still closed, Eve let the sounds of laughter and talking fill her soul. Home wasn't just a place. It was friends who believed in you. It was family who loved you. And it was moments like this.

It surprised her how well she was taking Adam's deceit. Perhaps there was a piece of her heart that always knew who Adam was capable of being. Or maybe it was going through this, knowing she wasn't alone. Lainey was instrumental in saving Eve's life. Both figuratively and literally. God, had it not been for her wife and kids, Eve would have given up the moment they took her away. But she had something to love and live for. And she finally understood that she didn't have to do any of it alone anymore.

"Eve?"

Lainey's soft voice brought Eve out of her reverie. She smiled widely. "Hi, baby."

"Hi, yourself. Are you okay?"

"I'm... happy." Eve let the feeling wash over her as she said the words. "I don't know if I should be feeling this happy after all the turmoil, but I do."

"Why shouldn't you?"

Eve shrugged, taking Lainey in her arms. "I'm sure if I dwelled on the answer to that for too long, I'd come up with something. But I don't want to. We won, baby. We won, and you were right beside me the entire time." She tucked a piece of hair behind Lainey's ear. "I've never known that kind of loyalty until now. And I'm grateful."

Tears threatened to fall down Lainey's cheek. "You're my soulmate, Eve. There's nowhere I'd rather be than right beside you."

Eve let those words sink in. *Soulmate.* She felt the truth of that deep down. If she thought back to the first time she met Lainey, she would see that feeling was there from the very beginning. *Something* drew her to Lainey. She could fret over the time they wasted apart. Or she could live in the here and now, in absolute bliss. Eve chose the latter, pulling Lainey in for a kiss. But the doorbell chimed before their lips could touch, causing both to groan playfully in frustration. What they didn't feel was fear. That was another sign that the nightmare was over.

"I suppose we should get that," Lainey said, reluctant to relinquish her hold on Eve.

"I suppose." Eve practically dragged Lainey with her, not ready to feel the chill of empty arms. "Are we missing someone?" she asked along the way.

"Hmm." Lainey counted their guests in her head. Ellie, Hunter, Jessie, Jules, Rebecca, Cass, Aunt Wills, Patty, Mo, Blaise, Greyson, Piper, Ezra, Cade, Claire, Dani, Kiara, Lauren... Lexie was staying with her boyfriend. James and Charlie were taking care of loose ends. Reghan said she had work to do. "I *think* everyone that could be here is here."

Eve opened the door to a beaming Reghan. "Hey! I didn't think you'd make it. Come in." She stepped aside, still managing to keep Lainey firmly in her arms.

"I didn't know if I would myself. Hello, Lainey." Reghan leaned in and kissed Lainey on the cheek before handing her an envelope. "For you, fresh off the presses, as they say."

That little area between Lainey's eyebrows—the one Eve thought was cute—creased in confusion. "What is this?" She looked up at Eve, who shrugged with an equal amount of bewilderment. So, since Eve wasn't fond of envelopes—and because it was handed to her—Lainey opened it, pulling out the contents. She read the first few lines before her vision blurred. Her hand flew to her mouth, holding in a sob.

"Baby, what is it?" Immediately alarmed, Eve held Lainey tighter before taking the papers from her. The first few words hit her just as hard as they did her wife.

"Is this real?" Lainey managed to ask a still smiling Reghan.

"Signed, sealed, and now delivered!"

"She's mine? Bella is mine?"

"All yours *and* a Sumptor," Reghan said excitedly. Out of nowhere, Reghan held up a bottle of champagne. "It is time to celebrate, Mommy!"

Eve hugged Reghan, thanking her and discreetly asking for a few moments alone with Lainey. As Reghan strode away, Eve once again took Lainey in her arms. The adoption was final. Lainey had always been Bella's mommy, but now it was legal. The cherry on top was no more Bella Riley. It was Bella Sumptor now. Their family was complete.

"She's mine, Eve." Lainey sniffled, happy beyond words. Hell, there were no words that could describe this feeling. But Lainey knew Eve heard everything Lainey wanted to say in those three words.

"Forever yours, baby. Just like the rest of us." She kissed Lainey softly, wiping the tears from her cheeks with the pads of her thumbs. "Are you ready to tell the others and celebrate?"

"I'm ready to tell the world."

LAINEY PRIED ONE EYE OPEN, shutting it quickly as the sun nearly burned her cornea. *Dramatic much*, she thought groggily as she reached for Eve. When her hand made no contact with a warm, naked body, she opened both eyes. Why the hell was it so bright?

"Eve?" She cleared her throat, smacking her lips. Her mouth felt like it was stuffed with cotton and she sounded like a habitual smoker. What in the hell happened last night?

"Good morning, sunshine!"

Lainey narrowed her eyes. Her wife was the picture of perfection against the backdrop of the clear blue skies of the morning. Seriously, why was it so bright? And why the hell did Eve look like she just stepped out of a magazine while Lainey felt like an ogre?

"Do I look like a ray of sunshine?" Again, Lainey cleared her scratchy throat. "Is there water somewhere close by that you can pour down my throat? And maybe over my head?"

Eve chuckled as she stood up from behind her easel and made her way to her wife. "You know, I didn't think you were serious when you challenged Blaise to a drinking contest."

Ah, so *that's* what happened. It was all coming back to Lainey now. Bella's tears of joy, Kevin and Darren whooping and high-fiving about their new *legal* sister. The champagne flowing. Happiness knocked down the walls of constraint, and festive chaos ensued. The celebrations carried on into the wee hours, long after the kids went to bed. Lainey was feeling so exhilarated, she playfully challenged Blaise to a drink off. What the fuck had she been thinking? Blaise Knight Steele could drink the burliest man under the table and barely get a buzz.

"If she's not feeling this horrible this morning, I'm going to rethink this friendship."

"I'm sure she's suffering just as much, baby." Eve hid her grin as she handed Lainey a glass of water. She was almost certain it was true. Greyson had carried Blaise out to the car after the showdown while Cade followed with a passed out Ezra. The others hadn't lasted as long, slowly filing out, while both Lainey and Blaise were too determined to win to say more than a quick *love you, bye.*

"Sure," Lainey muttered, guzzling her water. "What time is it? And why are you up and cheery at this dreadful hour?" She hadn't even waited for Eve's answer before determining it didn't matter what time it was. It was dreadful.

Eve chewed her cheek, trying to keep a straight face. Hungover Lainey was cute. But she would never say that out loud *to* hungover Lainey. "It's after ten, baby. Lexie is here with the kids if you want to sleep in a little longer. Or I could run a cold shower for you and get you some carbs for when you're out."

She handed Lainey two aspirin and refilled her glass from the pitcher she had prepared when she got up earlier that morning. Lainey wasn't a big drinker, so Eve wanted to help relieve the aftereffects as much as she could. The room would be darker had inspiration not hit her as she waited for Lainey to wake up.

"A shower sounds good." Lainey knocked back the aspirin, draining the glass of water without a breath. "You didn't drink, did you?"

"Oh, I had a little. Do yourself—and me—a favor, baby. Never challenge Blaise to a drink off again, okay? I believe she's part fish. I *know* she's competitive." Eve kissed Lainey's temple. "And I don't enjoy seeing you in pain."

"Don't worry, I learn from my mistakes." Lainey squinted up at Eve. "Shower and bagel?"

"On it." Eve helped Lainey up and led her to the bathroom. "Cold?"

"Ugh." Lainey peeled off the t-shirt she apparently passed out in, oblivious to Eve staring at her tits. "Might as well. Want to get in with me?" Lainey wiggled her eyebrows suggestively. Or at least she thought she did. When Eve laughed, she wasn't so sure what her face was doing.

"A cold shower is not favorable if I want to devour your body, baby.

Our teeth will be chattering and that's a little dangerous," Eve winked. She turned on the cold water, stepping back quickly as the water sprayed out of multiple shower heads. "Ready?"

Lainey slanted a look at her wife. "First a hangover, then you get me all hot with your talk of devouring my body. Now you want to shove me in a cold shower. When I'm feeling better, I'm going to punish you for this."

A sexy grin spread across Eve's face. "Promise?"

Lainey laughed and swatted at Eve's ass. "Get out of here, you fiend, and bring me some food."

"Yes, ma'am."

---

LAINEY STEPPED out of the bathroom, rubbing a towel over her wet hair. The aroma of food hit her nostrils and though her stomach felt a bit queasy, she realized she was famished.

"Feel better?" Eve called out from her painting nook.

"A little." Lainey wrapped the fluffy robe around her tighter, fighting off the chill of the cold shower. "Thank you for bringing me food, my love." She picked up half a bagel and a strip of bacon.

*My love*, Eve thought with a smile. *She really must be feeling better.* "My pleasure, baby. Do you want to go back to bed? I could close the privacy shades and finish this later."

Lainey padded over to Eve. "No, I'm okay. I think. Besides, I don't want to interrupt your creativity by making you stop. What are you working on?" She peered around the easel, knowing Eve would stop her if she wasn't ready to reveal her work yet. When she saw the painting, her breath caught in her throat, barely escaping in a gasp.

"Do you like it?"

"It's..." Lainey inhaled, trying desperately to hold in her emotions. "Stunningly perfect, Eve."

Eve beamed up at her wife as she studied her painting. "I've never had a family portrait before. With the adoption going through, I thought this was the perfect time to paint one."

Lainey stared at the painting of the five of them. Their little family.

Kevin and Darren stood behind Eve and Lainey while Bella sat on Lainey's lap. Eve's one hand covered Darren and Kevin's on her shoulder, while the other held on to Lainey's and Bella's. No one was looking back at the person viewing the painting. Their eyes remained within the family. Lainey smiled at her sons as they smiled back. And Eve looked adoringly at Bella. Bella's eyes were full of love as they gazed back at her momma. It was so familiar to Lainey. *The perfect time.*

"I have something for you," Lainey said softly.

Eve watched with interest as Lainey walked away, disappearing into their closet. After a brief moment, Lainey reemerged with a wrapped gift.

"What is this?" Eve took the gift from Lainey when she held it out to her.

"Open it."

"Baby, you already bought me an island. What more could you possibly...?" Eve's question faded into stunned silence when she uncovered the elegant frame. She wept, her tears falling on the glass of the frame, as she focused on the drawn picture it protected. "*Momma,*" she whispered reverently.

"She drew it, my love." Lainey failed miserably at holding back her own tears. "James gave it to me and asked me to give it to you when the time was right."

She looked back at the portrait Eve was painting of their family. The time was right. Eve had opened her heart fully. Unafraid of the future, unburdened of the past. The truth of that shined through each of the faces she painted of those she loved.

"She would be so proud of you, my love." Lainey's voice was raw with emotion as she watched the tears flow freely down Eve's cheeks. "She loved you so much." Lainey reached out, lifting Eve's chin with her fingertip. "Look at your painting, Eve. You got your talent from your mother. And your capacity for love. That look in her eyes is the same one you have for Bella. She may be gone, but she's right here."

Eve closed her eyes when Lainey placed her hand over her heart. She would remember this moment for the rest of her life. The moment her past lost its ability to hurt her. The moment her future stood before her.

The moment love outshined the darkness she thought she'd always have. The moment Lainey, the love of her life, gave Eve her mother back.

"I love you, Lainey. I'm forever yours."

***Things do not simply end. They merely become the beginning of new memories.***

# Acknowledgments

This is it! The conclusion of the Eve and Lainey saga. A story that began twenty years ago. Can you believe that? I saw Diane Lane in Unfaithful, and so Lainey Stanton was born. Yes, Lainey was my first character. In fact, Eve wasn't Eve at the beginning. She was Jules (a WHOLE different Jules than the one in this). Something About Eve was supposed to be a comedy. Obviously, that didn't happen. These two women have been through quite a lot. After this book, it's time to let them be happy. But don't worry. Eve and Lainey will still be around with the LA Lovers group. And in short stories. I could never leave Eve and Lainey behind for good. But you made it to the end of this book. Now you can imagine them happy, healthy, and so much in love.

### *THANK YOUS:*

Writing can be a very solitary thing (unless you're co-writing). But to get what you've written ready for the public, it takes a village! My village is small but mighty.

Momma – You will always be the first one I thank. In everything. You are the one who fueled my love for the written word. You were the one who always told me I could do anything I wanted in life. And even when I wrote things you didn't "agree" with, you were the one who read and encouraged me to continue. I love you. I miss you.

Daisy – You're forever standing with me and supporting me in everything I do. You even support my weird' obsessions.' I can't thank you enough for all you do. I would never be able to do what I do without you.

Melissa – When I had doubts about finishing this book, you kept telling me I could do it! You let me discuss everything I wanted to accomplish with this book and listened enthusiastically. That enthusiasm helped me keep going. Thank you.

Karen – You continuously treat my characters like they're real. You were ready to throw down against the 'villains' and praise the heroines. I always appreciate your feedback. I'm doing something right if you get upset with someone in the book. Thank you.

Ami – My Lainey-bian! Thank you for beta reading for me and letting me know everything I did for Lainey met your approval. I appreciated your notes (especially when Lainey did something you particularly liked). Thank you.

Janice – As always, I appreciate you beta reading for me. Your attention to detail always helps me when I'm completely engrossed in writing but not the grammar. Thank you.

Shell – Your first time beta reading for me! Your notes were constructive, and your enthusiasm was palatable. Thank you.

Monna Herring – I appreciate you proofing Fighting for Eve with such detail and quickness! I learned quite a bit! Thank you.

Nicole Fletcher – Thank you for the amazing artwork!! You've captured the essence of Lainey and Eve perfectly.

My Patrons – First and foremost, thank you to Ellie Kay and Sharon, two of my Patrons, who gave me the name of one of my "villains." To my VIP Patrons: Alice Allen, Cindy Thomas, Ariel Sumler, Melissa Tereze, and Nellie Canham, I appreciate your continued support of me and my craft. To my All-access and Official Patrons, I thank you all for your support by being a Patron. You are all part of my village to get a polished book out. You all help me a lot by contributing to my Patreon.

My readers – Eve and Lainey are the couple I get the most correspondence about. Eve is undoubtedly very popular for how confident, successful, beautiful, generous, and talented she is. But Lainey is the one most of you identify with. I genuinely hope you all love the way Lainey has grown into her own confidence in this book. This growth happens when you've found your place within yourself. You all have been there for me and with me throughout this journey. I've had moments when I didn't think I would write again. And moments where I thought what I did write was never good enough. The words of encouragement and excitement from you all allowed me to listen to my heart and not my head. I'll be forever thankful for your continued respect and support. Could I write without you? Probably. Would it be as satisfying? Absolutely not. Thank you from the bottom of my heart. Just one more chapter...

# About the author

Jourdyn Kelly lives in Houston, Texas, with a beautiful zoo of pets ranging from furry to aquatic. Jourdyn attributes her passion for writing and sharing stories to the love of the written word she inherited from her mother, who always surrounded them in books. After losing her mother from Alzheimer's complications, Jourdyn started her own company, Jaded Angels, as a tribute to her and the strong women who have inspired Jourdyn throughout her life. A portion of the proceeds goes to alz.org in her mother's memory. Jourdyn collects Grogu merchandise with startling avarice, paints 3D printed models as a hobby, is a Dim Sum fanatic who loves going to the movies, and of course, penning her novels.

*Cameo characters can be found in the LA Lovers books.*

# Connect with Jourdyn Kelly

My Website
(http://www.jourdynkelly.com/)

Patreon
(https://www.patreon.com/JourdynKelly)

Twitter
(https://twitter.com/JourdynK)

Goodreads
(http://www.goodreads.com/author/show/2980644.Jourdyn_Kelly)

Facebook
(https://www.facebook.com/AuthorJourdynKelly)

Secret Society on Facebook
(https://www.facebook.com/groups/JoKels/)

Instagram
(https://www.instagram.com/jourdynk/)

Amazon Author's Page
(http://www.amazon.com/-/e/B005O24HK8)

Made in the USA
Columbia, SC
07 August 2023

f516f773-ec54-462f-9066-0f0e7aaa5d39R07